Blood-red Sweat

Blood-red Sweat

Abhimanyu Unnuth

PRABHAT PRAKASHAN

Published by
PRABHAT PRAKASHAN PVT. LTD.
4/19 Asaf Ali Road,
New Delhi-110 002 (INDIA)
e-mail: prabhatbooks@gmail.com

ISBN978-93-90900-72-5
BLOOD-RED SWEAT
by Shri Abhimanyu Unnuth

Translated by
Rashi Rohatgi

Edition
First, 2023

Paperback Price
₹ 500.00 (Rupees Five Hundred only)

Printed at
R-Tech Offset Printers, Delhi

**Dedicated to the future
of our family,
my grandson
Aryan Eklavya Unnuth**

Preface

Little did Mauritius, at the dawn of modern times, look like a costly tourist paradise that it turned out to be today (and yet, this current image raises scepticism). It was the kingdom of the rich white landowners where the latter, so as to maintain their extravagant lifestyle and absolute power, had established a system in all ways comparable to that of slavery. As it was, the landowners were the direct heirs to the colonisers of the 18th century who, at the time of the abolition of human trafficking and the proclamation of the principle of equality between all human beings by the 1789 Revolution, had rebelled against the Republic and expelled the government emissaries who had come to free the slaves. In 1802, these same people had managed to wrest from Bonaparte, First Consul, the shameful decree that re-established slavery in French colonies, after bloodily crushing revolts, especially that of Toussaint Louverture in Haiti.

In the middle of the so-called industrial century, during the 1860s, the situation remained unchanged in Mauritius. Almost all arable land was in the hands of a white minority that ruled ruthlessly over half a million Indian and Creole[1] workers. The abolition of slavery by the British government in 1830 had resulted in particularly inhuman mass imports of labourers from India. To fuel this machine-since the plantation system became, as from 1860, when Mauritius entered the sugar market monopoly,

1. In Mauritius, the term 'Creole' refers to a person of African origin. (T.N.)

a model of both modernity and barbarism-more and more hands were required. The early small artisanal sugar refineries metamorphosed into huge estates, thanks to latest big profit-oriented manufacturing methods but indifferent to the misery endured by massively abused, humiliated and underpaid labour.

Allured by local recruiting agents, men and women from rural zones of the centre of India and of Bengal would commit over false promises: on the other side of the oceans, there was a wonderful island with abundant food and water, where they would be able to work in Edenic gardens and become rich in a couple of years. It was the war and famine era, when the convulsions of the Cipayes' upheaval and the pitiless repression of the British army put India to fire and the sword, as civilians would jump on the roads to escape poverty and death.

Every month, during these terrible years, ships would leave Calcutta, Madras, Bombay, with their loads of coolies – the indentured or the 'engaged' labourers – going to work in the West Indies, in Fiji, in South Africa, in Mauritius. Muritch Desh, where they would lead a better life, as promised to them. The journey would take place in appalling conditions, with hundreds of men and women locked up in hulls, deprived of beds or hygiene, dying of starvation and thirst, desperate. Many of them would never reach their destination. Hardly had the survivors been disembarked when they would be literally sold off to rich white owners, be filed and photographed (as it was one of the earliest uses of photography) by the latter, be then given a registration number on a tin plate and taken to their place of torture by them. Of course, all landowners were not monsters. After 1860, Mauritius was no more the penal colony that it had most probably been during the times of the East India Company and of the Code Noir introduced by Colbert in order to suppress slave insurrections. The British, who would always abide by the law, had established bureaucratic mechanisms and sanitary controls to temper the owners' greed.

Moreover, eminent people within the white population, such as the landowner Adolphe de Plevitz, or the Creole lawyer Napoléon Savy, would raise their voice against injustice. But the plantation system itself was inherently wrong, while promoting abuse.

When he took over from the African slave, the Indian labourer was not a full-fledged human being. He was a mere tool, at the hands of the landowner and of his watchdog, the sadly famous sirdar, who had unlimited power over him, except that to kill him, as one of the big bosses puts it in Unnuth's novel. He was posted to one specific plantation from which he could not move away, subject to being declared a vagabond and chased away like an animal by the owners' militia. He was deprived of the right to civil marriage, to property, to practise his language and religion or to teach them to his children, and he could not organise meetings. On the owner's estate, daily corporal punishments would sometimes attain unimaginable cruelty. Under any pretext, the owner could get the coolie arrested and whipped, coat his wounds with salt, tie him naked to cacti or hand him over, covered with sugar, to ant bites. In spite of improvements, many of these conditions were maintained till modern times. According to a survey conducted by the Mauritius Royal Commission, between 1867 and 1872, fifty Indian workers died of splenic rupture caused by caning. By an 1867 ordinance, Governor Barkly, pressured by landowners, stipulated that any man found far from his workplace without his 'pass' would be considered a vagabond and liable to imprisonment for up to three months. Those who protested would be sentenced to the 'stocks', or security quarters, some of which were iron cages, one-metre-fifty-centimetre long by one-metre high, where the prisoner would languish for weeks in his own excrements.

With the exception of the early standardised tortures, rapes and murders, one of the most barbarous institutions of the plantation system was the double cut principle, officially in force between 1839 and 1909, whereby a worker's one-day absence would be punished by two-day work without pay, even though his absence might be due to illness or work injury. If he had worked only ten days in a month because of an illness or an accident, an Indian labourer earning ten shillings a month (for twenty-six working days by ten hours) would thus be inflicted with a twelve-shilling fine and condemned to work without pay for twenty-two more days.

Due to lack of hygiene, epidemics and frequent accidents, a large number of labourers would work most of the time without earning any salary. Those who tried to protest against the current state of affairs were considered seditious and dangerous, and were thrown into prison. During the year 1869, thirty thousand eight hundred and twenty-four coolies (i.e. 20% of the Indian population in Mauritius) were sent to jail, most of them for having rebelled against bad treatment by the landowners. In 1878, more than twenty thousand 'vagabonds' were reported to have escaped from the infernal plantation system. In 1907, six years after Gandhi's visit, the number of prisoners was reduced to 1492 and represented only 3% of the population of Indian workers.

This is the cruel world, hidden for so long from Europe under the guise of the languid Creole society and beneath the 'vieille France' banner of the landowners' mansions, that *Blood-red Sweat*, Abhimanyu Unnuth's great novel, unveils to us. As highlighted by the author himself through some sort of epigraph, it is not a historical novel but the celebration of characters who are 'brave and devoted to the land that eventually crushes them between the millstones of history'.

By inviting us to follow Kundan, Kissan, Phoolvani or the young Pushpa in their long fight against evil represented and perpetuated by the plantation system for a better society, Unnuth takes us on a real epic. His characters are not abstract. They are made out of flesh and feelings, they experience doubt, fear, anger, desire. They are themselves victims of treachery, dishonour, they are often desperate, sometimes cowards or unjust with their own family. In this barbaric world, they have no security apart from memory, religion that connects them to their ancestors, and the pride of their origins. Unnuth depicts the great forces that are India's genius, very ancient knowledge, the sense of tolerance and the labourers' mysterious ties to the land shaped with their hands and watered from their sweat. Everything around them is a reminder of their contribution to the prosperity of the sugar estates. The fields surrounding them, the roads built by them, even the rock piles scattered over the island, that Mauritians call 'Creole walls' and that my aunt Alice, who knew about the abuses of the landowners' era, had renamed as the 'sugarcane martyr monuments'.

The heroes of Unnuth's novel belong to this island as much as it belongs to them because they arrived in circumstances of considerable hardship to plant the 'arrow of Ram'. Many of them were born here and know that they will also die here. It is their prison as well as their only future. Their revolt against the landowners is not a class struggle nor a social upheaval. It is a slow and tough revolution made across generations, and born out of men's anger as much as from women's strength and love.

There is a mythical grandeur in this novel, in its duration, interspersed with hymns and proverbs, with long dialogues as in an Indian opera. Horror continually leads to laughter, inhumanity to the banality of everyday life. It presents moments of delicate happiness when Kissan dreams by the river while listening to birds, or when he makes love to the beautiful Satya, laying on the wet land in the sugarcane field. At other times, anger shines on the axe blade as on the sugarcane cutters' machetes in Mexico or the West Indies, and blood flows on this land, blends into sap and mixes with sugar. Because, as stated by the mad Tamby to Madan, Kissan's son, there are two varieties of sugar, one that is very soft and light, reserved for the rich whites on the estates, another that is intense and bitter with the coolies' blood and sweat.

Throughout this slow-paced novel, flows ancient Indian music, full of fabulous episodes from the Ramayana. The flow of the river, the thick forest surrounding the villages, the undulating movements of the sugarcane crops in the large fields and the eerie peak of Pieter Both where fugitives find a haven, are Kundan's, Kissan's, Santou's and Madan's genius guardians, participating in their struggle and guiding them. Since Mauritius, thanks to these legends, is no more a cruel and desperate jail. It is also the place where the mental Ganges flows secretly and the antique Goddess Mother of Bihar reigns.

Abhimanyu Unnuth's beautiful novel is indeed neither a historical nor a polemical narrative, although the truth it unveils is among those that nobody would discard. It is a hymn, profound music, deeply rooted in humanity's most distant past, giving a new meaning to the Mauritian reality.

—J.M.G. Le Clézio
Translated from French by
Sachita Samboo

PART-I

PART-I

1

India, 1st millennium B.C., the port of Tamraparni.

The two monks came from Kalinga, known today as Orissa. In the stories of their predecessors who'd tried their luck outside India, they'd heard of Java, Cambodia and Asia Minor; at Tamraparni, they'd crossed paths with many monks in search of these lands and in exploring new horizons. But they also dreamt of something else: their desire was to be the first to tread on one of what were rumoured to be numerous islands dotting the vast Indian Ocean. They took advantage of their stay in Tamraparni to build a solid boat, choosing the wood themselves, and then they set off.

They sailed past the coasts of nearer isles, one after another, but soon they came to the vast, full sea, where they could spot no one and nothing else. The ocean lay before them, passive and gigantic. After a few days, their gourds were empty. The last peepal stem had been dried out for its oil. They lacked water, and ironically their eyes met the waves, salty and bitter far as the eyes could see.

One of the monks turned to the other and murmured, "Courage. We must persevere. There is well-being of all mankind to consider."

The other moved his lips slightly, but no sound came out.

The first monk closed his eyes and began to recite: "I take refuge in the Buddha..."

The boat went on its way, sliding smoothly through the water.

The sky darkened. At the height of the afternoon, it was as dark as dusk. The two monks, silent, threw one another apprehensive glances. On the distant horizon, where a few minutes earlier the sky had mixed with sea in the same deep blue, a reddish glow appeared. In an instant, the swell formed – the waves breaking over the bow, swooping down on the deck. The rudder began to scull and the two monks ran to the sails. They set the boat as fast as it could go.

The boat swung with each gust of wind. The swells broke through the surface and rose in a terrible roar, spraying everything with their milk. The monks were terrified. A great storm! A tempest! The roar of the waves, of the stormy sea... above them, the fiery red light now kindled the whole sky.

"A cyclone!" said one of the monks, whose voice trembled.

"It's awesome," responded the other in a voice just as weak.

The two men knew storms, had met others in their travels, but this was beyond what they had experienced. So thick was the air, they couldn't see a metre in front of them.

Their hearts pounded. As the boat keeled more and more treacherously, the monks saw their end approaching. The winds that had whipped their faces seemed to be slapping them now, propping them up. They stood pressed against one another, holding hands and facing the elements.

The storm was at its height. The heavy rain fell in a liquid curtain, flooding the boat. The ocean had reached an angry boil. Suddenly, lightning tore through the darkness and the monks screwed up their eyes to make out anything at all.

They saw monstrous waves approaching them at full speed. From top to bottom, the sky and the sea had indeed become one – an amazing spectacle of spark and cinder, of streams released into the air by the suffocating heat, and, on the monks' faces, sweat mixed with sea-water.

Little by little, calm returned. The waves became less menacing. The sea was rough, but the storm was receding. The hurricane appeared to abate. The boat, however, had filled with water and threatened to sink.

There was thunder as the swell turned into thousands of tiny blades and the water became so hot that it was smoking. A muffled roar then rose through the waves, more disturbing than the crackling lightning. The two monks, frightened, wondered which volcano was erupting when, like a mountain, a piece of land rose before their eyes from the depths.

A strong wave took the boat, then, lifting it into the air before plunging it into the sea, swallowed the boat's passengers. The two small monks perished, fragile and claimed by the water.

The confused historical accounts say that the first sailors to land on the island were from the south of India. They were lost and for a time, the islands remained uninhabited. There must have been a reason why they did not linger.

Time passed. During the first century AC, Arabs en route to India saw the coast of the island, but they soon decided, too, that it was pointless to settle there. Others approached and left just as quickly.

With the arrival of the Portuguese, the pages of history became more legible. The Portuguese met no serious difficulty on the island; they gave up because, at the time, India interested them more.

Then came the age of French and British rivalry for the conquest of India. The island of which we speak played a strategic role – from here the French led their offensive against the British based in Madras, and it was during the reign of the French that Indians first trod the soil of the island. When the British realised the importance of its location, they attacked the French with the help of Indian troops to become its master after all.

At that time, a veritable flood of immigrants began to arrive in Mauritius. Alas! History only retains a little of those early days. The pages that tell the story are dusty, some are burnt, but those that remain are written in an ink that no flame can alter. They carry within the sweat and blood of the Indian workers... and those pages which fire has destroyed end up as ash in the fields, fertilising the Mauritian soil. The island's fields, on which have been spilled sweat and tears, bear the true memory of this tormented history, this struggle of men for their freedom. My story will try to tell the tale of this crushed past of a remote and beautiful island.

2

He was lying on the grass, short of breath and the sound of his breath pierced the silence. Around his head spun a thousand stars, buzzing in contrast to the immobile constellations that lit the sky. Kundan took a deep breath, trying to see through the darkness, but he could discern nothing. It was better to wait until the night ended. As his hands groped in the grass, he felt, in the warmth that emanated from the earth, an echo of his own body heat. 'I am alive,' he murmured.

He tried to move his feet, and found he could. He leaned on his palms and rose slowly. Once up, though, he realised that his legs would barely support him. He touched his right foot to gauge the extent of his injury. The wound on his foot had opened when he'd fallen from the wall. His fingers found the blood that flowed from the wound; a blood he did not see in the black night, but he imagined it was bright red. The wound was deep and the slightest pressure of his fingers caused excruciating pain.

He lifted his eyes towards the stars and resolved to get up, even in the dark. He had not gotten far enough yet and had to take advantage of the dark as much as possible. Only distance could counteract the fear that gripped his stomach – and only a distance that opened on to the infinite horizon. But the road was long. Kundan took a step, then a second. The third asked of him more energy than he could easily give, and then the fourth even more. Fatigue overwhelmed him. Resolutely, he rushed on, using all his inner stores to silence the pain. His wound was bleeding and slowed his pace, his right foot barely touching the ground, but still he advanced. His body grew heavier at each step, as if it bore on its shoulders all the burdens of history – history that is so often forgotten by individuals but nevertheless rests on each one. It had never burdened him so heavily.

The wan smile on his lips disappeared, but, that night, was there any reason to smile? He worried about his right foot; would he lose it? He would be forced to go forward on his knees, he thought, and this made him smile again. That smile faded as soon as it came.

The bush scratched his hands. He made his way through the

gaps and continued his journey with all the determination he could muster.

He was in such a bad way that the buzzing of insects and the chirping of crickets seemed to come from his leg. Sometimes, he lost his bearings; sometimes, he ventured forward. The slightest sound of bird or animal made him jump. His heart, its beats throwing his chest into upheaval, made him jump. Fatigue clung to his legs, reminding him of the days he'd been a soldier. But even then, he had never lost his breath. By now he was sweating like an ox.

Soon his feet refused to move, and he stopped. He was alone in the lugubrious night. 'I can't be found here, lying on the ground. They will bind me hand and foot. No, no,' he thought. He left. He could not create enough distance between himself and the prison to forget the spectre of the large building, with its shadows that fell on his back, covering his whole body.

He could see every corner of that hell. The place where he had spent so many years loomed very near. If he should die, it must be far from here, or those days would torment him eternally. In the time that remained to him, Kundan wanted to be free and to forget the horrors and cruelties he'd suffered.

His feet fell heavily. If only he could glimpse the light of a lamp, a lantern, to lead and nourish his hopes. But let the devil despair! He recovered and continued his journey, his leg sluggish. It seemed to him that his bones were disintegrating. Fear crept ever in his heart, his strength diminishing against his will. The fear of a return to the confines of the prison was more terrible than all the tortures he'd had to endure there.

In leaving India, he had left his village and country only to understand that he had been told a profound lie. During the boat trip, he realised that there was nowhere in the world better than his native land, despite his penury and misfortune there. Today, the situation was just the opposite. Once free, he understood how the atmosphere of the prison had been so horrible, and for so long. Nothing in the world would induce him to return there. He stumbled against a large stone and sat down for a moment. Even living in the jungle seemed possible. It was probably one of the only parts of this country that wasn't populated by animals. Here, he could live freely near rivers and springs. At times, in the darkness, he saw forms that reminded him of the prison guards, and then he grew faint as threatening black faces came out of the shadows.

In prison, the newcomers brought the latest news from the outside. They were people of his native village, sometimes. They had the same customs, the same language. Recently, he'd met a prisoner reciting the *Hanuman Chalisa.* Kundan mentally relived his life in the Bihari village and thought of Goddess Kali. He could still hear the words of his compatriot, "We want to build a temple to Mother Kali in the village, but the white men of the establishment have not permitted it. Go, tell them that one day everyone quits this earth; the king governing, the queen adorning, the *panditjis* reading the *Vedas.* Who are they, these people, to come and interfere in our customs and our religion? They have not yet suffered the wrath of Kali, but they lose nothing by waiting, those miserable ones."

Lately, that which he had heard from the lips of new prisoners had piqued his interest, and he wanted to see with his own eyes, if he had to go crawling, one of those villages in which labourers had retained, by their own efforts, a sense of their native Bihar.

Kundan heard a voice like one from his village. It was not loud and he forced himself to go more quickly towards it. Through the darkness, he soon saw the flickering of a lamp, but as soon as he saw it, it disappeared into the foliage. Another light appeared, and then others, weak and distant. Despite his leg, he quickened his pace and felt his energy grow tenfold, as if approaching the threshold of his own home. Quickly, he entered the village, and suddenly stopped, indecisive. Dawn was near. The night that was so damned would end, and the darkness did protect him from onlookers. A shiver of fear overtook him.

What time was it? The first light of dawn dimly appeared on the horizon, but one could still count on three or four hours before sunrise. A murmur arose nearby; a river, no doubt. Kundan abruptly changed course and, instead of going further into the village, he went to the river around which the trees still had their branches full; shreds of night guards. He sat on a stone and thought. Ideally, he would meet an inhabitant of the village, to be aware of what he could expect. He did not want to be discovered in the process of watching. Even at a safe distance from the prison, he exercised the prudence of a condemned man.

Several hours would go by before he would see anyone. The time seemed to drag even before he could expect anyone to be out. He sat, and thought. The memories of those he had left behind – were they not also his own?

The freshness that rose from the river seemed suddenly to penetrate his body. By what miracle had he escaped? Was it possible that he was really free? Kundan waited for the day to break. His mental images of the prison were of a world with limits, where one's aspirations were restricted daily, but which had become his whole universe. Kundan remembered the solidarity amongst the prisoners, but also the lashes and the kicks. He was breathless. Tenuous visions haunted him. He returned in thought to the infirmary where he had been transferred, and where he could contemplate the cane fields through the window.

3

From his bunk in the prison infirmary, Kundan looked out onto the lush green. It had not been a long time, but the plantations had wholly changed the landscape. Kundan wanted to reach out and touch it. Two years in prison had felt like two centuries... the prisoners, when they were in good humour, had christened it 'grandmother's house'.

Kundan had been stifled, if not actually in chains, in his infirmary cell. They had thrown a reed mat on a bunk of wood that served as a bed. The thin layer of mat did nothing to diminish the discomfort of the board. And the living conditions of the infirmary closely resembled those in the prison.

The prison infirmary comprised a dozen bunks; it was situated in the back of the prison. A few days earlier, a large stone had dropped on Kundan's foot while he'd been assigned to build a wall. The wound was serious enough to be looked into. The infirmary to which he'd been brought projected no less of a feeling of locked-in-ness than the prison. A guard sat in the middle of the hall and another stood permanently near the door. If you wanted to go out and do your business, a guard came with you. It had been ten days in the infirmary for Kundan. But how many days had passed since his arrest? He had stopped writing the dates on the walls since the wall had become fully covered, and since then he felt that he could have covered it again at least ten times.

The wound wouldn't heal, and he'd been consumed with a nagging pain. The first three days, he had shared his bed with another patient. This sharing of beds was not uncommon. During those first hours, his partner had kidney failure. Kundan had been given a black ointment for his foot; it had no effect on the wound.

Through his window, he contemplated the young, still tender shoots of cane leaves. Beyond the plantations, there was a village whose memory filled his heart with sadness. It was located behind the Pieter Both mountain. There, you could find his countrymen, an army of Indians from the homeland. He was not related to them by blood, but he felt as close to them as they to him, and he had been well liked by his superiors.

One day, after ten years in the armed forces, he joined the hundreds of Indian soldiers who had set sail for Mauritius in order to seize the island. They were assured that, once the battle against the French was won, the English would provide the combatants with land on the island. The officers in the pay of the English would tell anyone who would listen that they would give this gift in exchange for their courage and bravery in battle. Kundan heard the soldiers repeat that soon the land would belong to them. The old man Gautam had summed it up: "It was as if we wanted to cry, and suddenly dust came into our eye, giving us a reason."

Hopes of escaping the degrading conditions of colonisation gave rise to still greater hopes. All the other passengers had left the boat with eyes wet with tears; they were still sad about leaving their loved ones. Kundan did not cry. For what? He had not had a family for a long time – they had died of hunger long ago. Still, as he cast his eyes across this new world, he regretted that his parents were not there to see him move away to better horizons, and this somewhat tarnished his joy.

Someone approached him, handing him a bowl of soup. Kundan reluctantly took the iron container so as not to offend. He observed the Malagasy servant, a big, beefy woman. Kundan, too, wanted to reject slavery. 'I could be brave enough to rebel,' he thought. He had often thought of what would happen if the Indians, en masse, decided to stop working in the fields. The plantation owners would be trapped. But that would never happen. The mentality of his fellow Biharis did not lend itself to insubordination.

Indeed, why would they refuse to work in the fields, these men who had always lived by their labour? But... why not at least speak out against the atrocities inflicted by their masters? More than once, Kundan had heard new prisoners complain about the Indians' living conditions. Oh, he knew what kept them from speaking out. The Biharis were subjects by nature; they accepted their fate with grace, already happy that they were lucky enough to survive.

Of all the residents of the infirmary, Mangru was Kundan's only friend. They knew one another from his first day in prison. Their bunks had been face to face. By mistake, Mangru had dropped a bowl of water a guard had given him, and it broke on the tiled floor. The guard fell upon poor Mangru and began to kick him; the violence of the blows ramming him into the wall. The other prisoners looked on in silence, and no one had the audacity to rescue their comrade. In defiance of the whip, Kundan came forward, took Mangru's head in his hands and laid it on his lap. His friend had lost consciousness.

Kundan felt an anger rise up in him that was inextinguishable, that had never since left him in peace. That day he had to remember not to jump on the guards' throats and wrest their guns from their hands. But he'd controlled himself, gnashing his teeth to contain his fury, driving back his rage. This anger, this wax melting in the hollow of a cup, varied according to his mood swings, sometimes hot and then sometimes solidifying gradually, as calm returned. Seeing the weapons had awakened his reflexes as a soldier; he knew how to use guns better than the guards and would show them as much one day. If the opportunity presented itself... this immaturity made him smile. 'Even my reasoning is trapped between two walls – here I have the sense of a five-year old child.'

The soup of the day consisted of dirty water in which rice had been thrown. There was no doubt that it was deliberately over-salted; two days earlier, the patients had complained that the salt was missing. Today it was inedible... Kundan took advantage of a moment of inattention on the part of the guard to throw the bowl's contents out of the window.

The guard who stood in the middle of the room did not understand Bhojpuri, so the prisoners could speak freely.

"Has the doctor been through today?" asked Mangru.

"It's been three days since he came," whispered Jagessur, who lay next to him.

"It takes someone dying to get him to show up. I just lay here thinking about the happy days I spent in my village, eating dried fruit and drinking sugar water." A poor, bitter smile twisted Mangru's mouth.

On the bunks nearby, two patients were lying on their backs, side by side. Nearest the wall was Jaglall, a man who twice had tried to escape in vain.

"Whether the doctor comes or not, it won't change much," he pointed out. "The days he comes are the same as the ones without him."

Two prisoners had died since the beginning of the week. Four had been admitted to the hospital with high fever. The first two days they slept on the floor, on hemp bags, and received no care. Kundan rose to give up his berth for them, but the head nurse forbade him, pushing him back on his bunk. His wound re-opened and began to bleed. The pain was terrible and he could not sleep, lying awake at night. He could be heard humming:

O dear sleep, have you gone to play
with a bat and ball, to play gulidanda*?*

In the hospital, they could wait for months for something to happen. One morning, two patients were sent back to the prison, wrists chained. The next day, Mangru was to be sent back. When the nurse told Mangru the news, he laughed. Not with joy, of course, but with the irony of the situation and the cruel absurdity of fate. His forehead was cut up and he suffered from dysentery at nights from the unbearable pain. Sometimes he would cry like a child with a stomach-ache.

On that day, the pain was somewhat calmer, but his hands were trembling with idleness. At the hospital, they gave the prisoners woven mats, but to be given work required his well-being. Mangru had never had any health problems before – not a scratch. He had never stopped working, not even for a day. Since he had come to the hospital, three weeks had passed without work and he found he could not deal with the inertia. He slept little and in his dreams, he saw himself crushing stones by the roadside. Mangru had a reputation as a great worker, able to crush more stones than anyone, even under the blazing sun. Large drops of sweat would trickle down his back, but he'd pay them no attention. He'd be so absorbed by the physical effort that he would have done the same to his own family.

Here, lying on his bunk, he could not lose himself in labour. Phoolvanti's visage haunted him relentlessly and his daughter's face, too, appeared as a haunting vision. Where was his daughter now? Seven years had passed since his arrest. Pushpa had been ten-years old then. Now she was old enough to take a husband... Mangru's blood ran cold at the mere thought. And his wife, Phoolvanti? How had she survived?

Mangru sometimes asked such questions of Kundan, and his friend invariably responded with words of comfort. But Mangru knew that the encouragement was meaningless. He confided in his friend what he could not tell the guard or the nurse: what really caused him pain.

Breakfast was brought in late. The semolina was three-days old and Mangru's lips pressed together in a grimace of disgust. Since he had fallen ill, he had not been able to swallow, but the puree gave him terrible cramps and in fact increased his pain. Mangru shared his plate with his neighbour. Kundan, compassionately, called the nurse, using the few Kreol words he knew.

"Don't you see that this man is unable to eat the porridge? It hurts his stomach and he cannot sleep then at night. Can't you find something else for him?"

The nurse frowned, fixed a menacing stare at Kundan and then laughed, "Tomorrow your boyfriend will return to the big house, where he can eat sweets all day; don't worry."

"The doctor forbade him to eat porridge," added Bissessur, armed with his courage.

The nurse responded in a contemptuous voice, "Of course, he did. He cares so much for your health that he even recommended you only eat Basmati rice. So, stop asking questions."

Then all became silent. Finally, the coarse voice of Jagessur arose: "So when are the medicines coming around?"

"When you finish eating!" cried the nurse.

"My brothers," said Bissessur in a low voice, "let's not be so passive that the dogs will lick our face."

Distribution of medicine was before or after meals, depending on the day. Sometimes there was no distribution at all. On those days, the medicine was the same for all: a white liquid poured into half a coconut, which circulated amongst the sick. A few days later, the prisoner with long hair was dead. The nurse said, "It is because he refused to drink the potion."

"Those torturers have killed a Brahmin. They will pay for it," growled Mangru under his breath.

That evening, Jaglall told them, in a low voice, about his attempts to escape. The first time, he'd tripped on the barbed wire; the second, a scared friend had betrayed him. Since then, he'd declared escape impossible. His bunkmate reminded him that some detainees had made their escape, and to that Jaglall could find no answer.

Kundan listened to this conversation very carefully. He already knew the story of Santu's escape; after three days in prison, the young man had landed a single blow to a white guard with a stick of bamboo and gone over the wall. He returned home to learn that his wife had committed suicide after being raped. Santu then returned to prison... Kundan was preoccupied with thoughts of this young man, although Jaglall's tales were not encouraging. He kept going over the mistakes that each man had made, and it was only late at night, after the others were already dreaming, that he was able to fall asleep.

Kundan was not as old as the other inmates, but he had spent the most time in prison. The day he had been captured, most of his companions had not even set foot on the island. At the end of the campaign against the French, Kundan would have returned to India with his comrades had he not been arrested along the river. This was more than twenty years ago now, maybe twenty-five. Mangru had always been curious about Kundan's story, but Kundan evaded his questions. "Another time," he would say, turning away.

When Mangru left the infirmary to go back to his cell, Kundan felt bereft. He regretted not having confided in him. In his mind's eye, he saw his arrest on the riverbank. He'd lain under raffia, his hands behind his head, the fresh wind blowing from the heights and the sweat dry on his skin, cold air filling his lungs... suddenly, a noise attracted his attention and drew him from his reverie. He sat up and looked around for the source of what he'd heard. The vision he saw left him frozen with amazement, trembling. His eyes grew round, staring at the beautiful spectacle. He had a moment to contemplate the scene and he absorbed it completely. Then he was hit in the back and was face to face with the ground. The kicks came down on him with the frequency of raindrops. A Frenchman with a bat, wearing a pith helmet, held a rock to throw at Kundan. Kundan, with the agility of a well-trained soldier, recovered his spirits, leaped to the side and fought back. The Frenchman fell to the ground, his head striking, on the way down, the same rock he'd set aside for Kundan.

Kundan was sentenced to life in prison for looking at a white woman who was bathing naked in the river, and for killing her husband. He appealed, but his request was rejected and he was only shut up in an even darker cell. Such was the story he regretted never telling Mangru. Once he was out of the infirmary and back in the prison, he would tell his story.

Many years ago, when he had just arrived here, bound hand and foot, all the detainees were Creole slaves. He soon learned that on the other side of the wall dividing the penitentiary in two were four Indians. Kundan met two in the following days. They had come to Mauritius before the conquest by the English. One was a trader, the other an engineer. Both were jailed for inciting the workers to revolt against the major planters. The charge seemed noble to Kundan. He would have preferred to be imprisoned under that charge than as a murderer.

At the time, the prison had not been large. The walls on the right side weren't ready and there were more than two hundred prisoners inside the enclosure. None of them white; all were poor Creoles, permanently in shackles. Kundan was afraid of their huge stature, especially when they were divided into small groups to break stones. Over time he got used to it, and even learned a bit of Kreol; in exchange, he taught them bits of Hindi. He became one of them the day he came forward to take the lashes that Gabriel would have received instead.

For as long as they were in prison, the Creoles considered Kundan to be a brother. "Workers are all brothers," Gabriel said.

"If only it could be true," Kundan murmured.

4

The guards may have had the opportunity to fraternise; their victims, never. The Creole prisoners gradually left the prison, except for two lifers, who died inside. And when they departed, other prisoners took their place: mostly Indians, from various provinces but all called Malabars. At first, Kundan did not pay much attention to the new prisoners, but he realised that these men were from the same country as he was, and this news filled him with joy. He laughed and wept. Every two or three days of detention, there were new arrivals; their number increasing significantly. And they all told the same story...

All had come to 'Mareech', as they called it, to find gold. But they had hardly set foot on the island when they were tied up, given identifying tags on their necks, and sent to the fields. They were to do all the work and never eat their fill. Blows from the masters' bamboo rods rained down on their backs. Some found themselves locked up for refusing to work like beasts of burden, some for asking to go home to India, and others for complaining of unfair treatment; still others were there after not appearing in the fields for two days when they were ill. All ended up in jail. There were also those who had been rash enough to take off the tag or stand up to the foreman. One committed suicide the same day he arrived in prison; he had refused to send his wife in to the boss, who wanted to claim her for the night.

In the prison infirmary, there were four windows, but they were too narrow to fit through. Unless there was a breeze, the patient nearest the door had to hold his nose because of the guard's body odour. Some said it was because the guards never bathed, but then, the sick had nothing with which to wash, either; neither water nor soap. Kundan would do a lot to be able to wash his face.

Sweat clung to his skin in a sticky jelly. The bucket latrines' faucets contained so little water they could barely wash their hands. The same stagnant water would lie in the sink for days. Small white insects swam in the liquid. But if it rained, that liquid would splash over the floor. Everyone hustled to get to the bathroom, then. If the rain came to the sink, it meant it was also coming through the palmed roof of the infirmary, through a groove immediately above their bunks.

The cassava they were fed was not cooked enough. Cassava, if properly prepared, is better than corn mush. But here, the cook did not let it cook long enough, as much out of malice as of laziness. The meals were generally inedible. One day, the cook forgot to cook it entirely. Kundan took one bite and tried to spit it out. But the gnawing hunger forced it down his throat. 'An ox that falls into the sand does everything to protect its eyes.'

The night before, his foot had hurt more than usual. The patient who had been brought in to take Mangru's place was laid on the ground. He cried all night and his cries made Kundan suffer almost as much as his injury. The wound on the man's thigh had a yellowish tint that indicated a deep infection. They needed to operate, but it had been a week now since he'd been promised the operation 'tomorrow'. During the last visit, the doctor hadn't even taken the trouble to examine the wound. "I'll wait until his leg is ready," said the doctor as he left.

When he woke up the next morning, despite the pain that tore through him at every step, Kundan went to the wounded man. He had finally got a bed, and he lay unconscious. The abscess on his leg had burst, releasing blood and pus in vast quantities. At the sight of blood, the other patients expressed their concern, but the doctor had not made a visit the next day and the nurse had simply wrapped a dirty old rag around his thigh, without even cleaning the wound. The man was still unconscious. The next day, the doctor said that the man was completely healed and could return to prison. The injured man, regaining consciousness, was aghast. He cried, screamed. Deaf to his entreaties, the nurse chained him by his wrists and delivered him to the guard on duty. The man turned, so that he could hop to the door on one leg, imploring the aid of his comrades. Some were vocally compassionate. Others, helpless, could only share his misfortune in silence. What could they have said that would not have immediately attracted insults and blows?

And such incidents occurred every day. Every man knew that he would leave the infirmary in conditions somewhat similar, before being cured. You had to be half dead for them to agree to keep you here. The doctor had the power; he decided that you were ready to return to prison, and his decisions were completely arbitrary.

Through the window, Kundan watched a pair of martins skipping along in the bare branches of a margosa tree. These birds, more than anything, reminded him of his native village. At first, he had been surprised to find them on the island; then he had been told that fifty pairs had been imported from India. Ironic. They too had come here to work... martins fed on the locusts that ate the crops. 'The men of my country toil in the fields and you, little martin, you watch the grain,' thought Kundan. When he had lived in India, he could not stand the sight of those birds. Here in prison, they spelled comfort, and Kundan had taken a liking to them. He spent hours watching them hop from branch to branch. He was accustomed, when he went to break rocks, to bring in his palm a few crumbs of stale bread or a handful of beans to throw for the martins on his way. He heard stories in their singing: those of the rivers of his village, women drawing water, lush green, but there were stories of drought as well. Kundan had a heavy heart, full of emotion, at the memory of those distant days. He would have loved for one of the birds to land on his shoulder, but it never happened, because martins were free birds, and wild, and they cherished their independence.

Kundan showed the nurse his foot in the hope that she would give him an ointment. In vain. Kundan complained again, and another nurse approached him with a kind of amphora in hand. She poured a few drops of blue liquid on his wound and left. His entire foot was seized with a painful cramp. His wound was burning as if she'd poured acid inside. Later, Kundan realised how harmful she had been: the wound was reopened. Jaglall tried to reassure him, "The medicine only hurts until it has its full effect. Be patient until tonight, and you'll see, it will get better."

After the afternoon had passed and evening came, Kundan grimacing with pain, Jaglall asked, his voice full of compassion, "Is it unbearable?"

Kundan tried to smile so his friend would not worry, just as he tried to refrain from crying all night, stifling his complaints against the wood of the bunk. He did not close his eyes for a second. From time to time, the cry of another prisoner pierced the silence and Kundan felt less alone. The suffering of others gave him the courage to bear his own.

"We have received the order to put you back in the main prison."

Kundan was not surprised to hear this the next afternoon. He had felt something brewing. The guard entered the room, shackled his wrists, and led him towards the exit. The patients he passed looked at him, and on every face he could read the same helpless pity. They all said, "See you in the big house."

When he came through to the prison, the sound of a prisoner singing resonated between the high walls,

'In the fields of Monsieur Bernard, gold on our hands full of earth, flower chains...'

Kundan recognised that voice: it belonged to that fool who'd tried to pull his chains off with his teeth. Some said that in India he had been a very active revolutionary against colonisation. The British had captured him and sent him here, to this remote island.

5

Kundan felt as though he was returning home; he felt, despite the pain in his foot, a certain joy to be back in his usual environment. The walls, the poles, the iron and barbed wire, all of that was in place, almost reassuring. The guards, the staff, his fellow inmates, he found them all just as they had been. The sound of chains, the rattle of locks, the cries of the jailers, the noise rang in his ears like so many familiar bells. He regretted only not finding himself in cell 45, the den in which he had spent years, and whose walls were covered with rows of stick traces over the months. It had been given to a dangerous individual, said the guard: a man accused of rebellion and so sentenced to seven years in prison. Kundan looked forward to meeting him, but his new cell was in the newest wing, while the other was at the far end of the old building. Between the two areas stood an impassable wall.

The prisoners had nicknames for all the guards; they didn't know their real names. The occupant of cell 135, before dying, had come up with a repertoire drawn from Hindu epics: one was Dushasan, another Jarasandh, the one who slept near the door Kumbhakaran. The soldier with the moustache was Kansa Mama. The small, lean guard was called Vibhishan because he seemed a bit more understanding than the others. He wore a sinister expression, but his heart was tender and all the inmates respected him. He was the only one who'd earned their trust.

Kundan saw him passing in the hallway. He called out, "Hello, Vibhishan."

The guard greeted him on the other side of the bars, "Hi. How's your foot?"

"A little better, thanks," Kundan lied.

Life in prison was far from soft and the prisoners were treated rudely, sometimes cruelly. Still, Kundan enjoyed a certain camaraderie with the guards, because of his seniority and because he had been a soldier. Vibhishan was not the only one to speak to him. The other guards, when they were in a good mood, would sometimes exchange a few words with him.

A guard passed him back a bundle containing his few belongings. While extending his hand to open it, he noticed that the shackle on his wrist was so worn out that it threatened to give way. Did he force it open? He seemed instead to wither... when he untied the bundle, a wave of memories flooded him, and he closed it to avoid showing emotion. This was all he had, the luggage he had brought with him to the prison twenty years before having been confiscated. He hadn't been away from these small things except to go to the infirmary, and to be back with them now was heartwarming. He stroked a handkerchief with flowers on it that a prisoner had given him just before his death; now Kundan lay down on his cot and slipped it between his cheek and his ear as a pillow.

The next day, Kundan benefitted from some unusual favours. He was not assigned to the group breaking stones on the edge of the road. Vibhishan had ensured that he was instead part of a group working with crops. A guard gave him an ear of corn.

"Here you are, free from heavy work for two days," said the guard.

Then he looked at Kundan's wound and said in a confident voice, "It's going to heal quickly; don't worry."

Kundan felt like a balm had been poured on his wound.

Sitting with two other prisoners, Kundan shelled corn. Facing him were two windows in the stone wall. The openings were wide, protected by bars that could not completely hide the view. In the distance stood a mountain whose silhouette was reminiscent of a young man he'd once known, surrounded by greenery. On the left, he saw the calm ocean, a gorgeous blue over which flew bands of birds. It was like another world, a vision of paradise.

The church bells rang and Kundan thought about the young man. He could still hear his words, "Kundan, a hundred times I've been ordered to take off my pendant of Hanuman and I've always refused. It's led me to receive countless lashes; last time, I was taken to the church, suspended on a bell rope, and made to act as the chime. They forced me to kneel and pray to their God, the one they see as the real God. Here is my crime, comrade; being humiliated as a Hindu.'

Whenever he heard the bells, Kundan's heart sank. He felt sadness, though not a tear moistened his eyes. He had cried too much; the flow of his tears was forever dried. With laughter full of bitterness and irony, smiles of consternation, and a dark grin, Kundan went on shelling corn, a loathsome but mundane task that didn't distract him from sad thoughts.

That evening, when he was in line for bread, Kundan came across Mangru. His friend looked spent; he had been breaking rocks all day in the sun. His brown face and his tired eyes betrayed him, and he could hardly stand. His legs shook and it looked like he had been sick for months.

"How's your stomach?"

"I have the impression that I will not make it this time."

"Don't say such things-"

"Just let it be. Take this, please," whispered Mangru as he slid a small bag in the palm of Kundan's hand.

"What is it?" But already they saw the guard Dushasan coming towards them.

Each prisoner was given a piece of bread that a kitchen assistant held out through an opening in the barbed wire. Guards verified their chains and they were sent back to their cells. As soon as Dushasan looked away, Kundan again addressed Mangru, "What is it?"

"It's for your foot."

"Where did you find it?"

"I prepared it from herbs near the stones. You apply it three times a day. My father told me how to make it. I know of other remedies, too, but nothing to use on my stomach. I don't know what ails me, otherwise I would have already treated it." Mangru paused a moment, then added, "Normally, we treat people in the hospital. Here, it's the opposite. For us traitors and dogs, it's impossible to get medicine." Dushasan came towards them again and the two friends fell silent. The grill opened, Kundan took his bread, hard as wood, and he returned to his building. Back in his cell, he opened the sachet and discovered Mangru's green ointment. He put it on his wound. The effect was immediate and beneficial. Kundan sighed deeply, then carefully closed the sachet and put it in his bundle.

His new cell, larger than the previous one, could accommodate two or three inmates. Curiously, Kundan was there alone. The light poured in through the iron gate that served as a door. No windows in the thick walls, but on the right hand wall, someone had dislodged a rock and made a convenient opening. Thus, the occupants of two adjacent cells could talk and even see each other.

The sun was not down, and it cast shadows on the cell. Vibhishan was the guard that night, and told him that the cell had previously been occupied by someone who had six months earlier been shot in the back by the guards. The man had tried to strangle a guard who whipped another inmate. Kundan detected a sense of respect in Vibhishan's voice for this courageous prisoner. But already the guard had walked away rapidly after slipping a piece of bread in Kundan's hand. Surprised, Kundan dropped the bread and had to crouch to get it. Then he saw the little square piece of paper in the corner of the floor. It was an old piece of paper, torn and folded and soggy, but he was curious. He opened it and could distinguish some words scribbled in Hindi, barely still legible. Seeing a message written in his own language hit Kundan like a punch; he felt his blood rise to his face and a great heat rise up in him. Light pierced the darkness.

6

A pale light filtered under the door without illuminating Kundan's cell. He turned the tiny morsel of paper over in his fingers again and again. He was so eager to read it, to finally know what the unknown hand had written. The message seemed difficult to read in daylight, so without light... Kundan slipped the paper between his skin and his *dhoti* and lay on his cot.

His foot hurt less. Through the hole in the wall, the voice of his neighbour in the next cell reached him, singing a *birha*.

Kundan fell asleep quickly. Though his bunk was just a few planks of margosa wood, it was more comfortable here than in the infirmary. His back muscles had long been accustomed to the hardness of the wood. He slept so deeply that night that he did not hear the alarm bell at four in the morning. It was Dushasan who pulled him out of his slumber by shaking on the iron grate of the door. Kundan rushed to the gathering; the prisoners were already in rows. The cold of the night made him shiver. It would be a bit longer before he could see the first rays of the sun, but already the light of dawn was announcing the day. Roosters sang in the distance.

Jarasandh hurled the orders. The inmates tightened ranks and formed straight lines. The guard shouted again, for silence. Everyone played their part mechanically; having repeated the gestures daily, they had become automatic.

"Prisoner 203?" Kansa Mama called out in Kreol. He repeated the number several times. The other guards roamed the columns, looking in the prisoners' eyes. Vibhishan translated into Hindi and Bhojpuri. No one answered.

Fifteen minutes passed, and then the whispers in the prisoners' ranks became more numerous. Prisoner 203 had been found dead in his cell. Kundan knew him well: it was Rooplall, a solid, well-built man; one of the sturdiest among them. How had he suddenly died? The chatter rose more vehemently. Did the guards poison him? That's what they had done to Ramdev. Yes, he could believe that. Poisoning. The day before, Rooplall had thrown his plate of rice in the cook's face. A man in line had intervened.

"And you know what happened yesterday? Rooplall slapped Jarasandh and it was the end of him. Yesterday was his turn and tomorrow it will be mine. Today, man, it's everyone's turn."

The prisoners remained grouped in the courtyard, whispers turning into uproar when they realised they were going to bury their comrade. Kundan addressed Kansa Mama, "In case you've ever wondered," he said in a firm voice, 'you don't bury a Hindu. This is contrary to our practices. We are cremated."

Silence fell like a cloak.

"Fine," said Kansa Mama in a surly tone, "We'll do what is necessary for cremation."

"Why such a hurry?" he asked. "Wait at least for the doctor." The guard yelled at him. Kundan was silent.

"The doctor won't change anything," a friend whispered in his ear.

When they were lined up to be given cassava, Kundan heard that he would no longer be granted sick leave. The prisoners were to build a road into town. Despite his injured leg, Kundan would have to work like the others. The news had no effect on him. He ate his manioc, took a good sip of water, and stood up. He was ready for the chore.

Day broke. Two columns of prisoners extended from the enclosure outside the prison door. They were chained to one another by the ankle in groups of three. They moved forward in the cold of late winter, their chains jingling at every step. The guards, uselessly, screamed at them to keep in line.

They were working east of the city, and the sun was bright. The guards gave the orders impatiently: "You, here. You, parallel." The long march awakened the pain in his foot, but Kundan set to work bravely to transport stones for the road.

The prisoners were building barriers. They were kept tied at the wrists and ankles. Sometimes, they were not even allowed a moment's rest. If one of them put his hand to his forehead to wipe off the sweat that ran down his eyes, he received a rifle butt in the back.

They had been working for five hours when the first whistle sounded. Everyone sat in the place he had stood. Hands full of earth, they were given bread and porridge for lunch. Kundan was eager to read the little paper stuck in his *dhoti,* but there was no question of it now, surrounded by guards.

Jarasandh stood in front of him. If only he could move a little, for even a minute, that would be enough to read the message. But the guard stood there, watching the world, munching his bread. The opportunity came a few moments later. Jarasandh, in the heat of the sun, withdrew abruptly to stand in the shade. Kundan checked that no one was looking and quickly pulled the paper from his *dhoti.* The text was from ink made with an herb and fruit colouring. On it he could read:

That day, I was punished and I ran along the walls, a big load of weight on my head. My sharp eyes took in the wall, the height of my cell, a detail that I remembered. I knew long ago that pirates had built tunnels in this area. This evening, I began to search my cell for traces of a tunnel. Today, I found what I wanted. I dug up two tiles under my bed and I put them back in place. Below passes the tunnel, at a depth of forty feet, which makes me think that it should lead outwards. Even if my neighbour is rather cowardly, we must at all costs leave tomorrow. Here one is not sure of anything, and anything can happen from one day to another. We do not know what to expect on the other side, and that is why I write this message. If we are lucky, we will take the paper. If not, the one who finds it will be free.

Kundan began to fold the paper and put it back. His heart beat loudly. Who could have left this message? The whistle sounded, signaling the return to work. Kundan's hands were active already, but his heart was excited, his mind was full of questions. Was it the assassin who had been shot? Kundan contained his impatience poorly. He wanted to quickly return to his cell and check under the bed. The years spent in prison had changed his life, and his time in the infirmary had given him a sense of terrible constraint. Kundan had finally persuaded himself that he had no hope of escape. Of course, at times, he allowed himself to dream of freedom, but his body never left the chains holding him prisoner. Now that he had abandoned all his illusions, he was suddenly presented with new hope. How many days longer would he live? And how would those days be? Could it be that the future provided a wider horizon? Kundan saw before his eyes rivers, valleys, lush fields. He breathed in fresh air. His horizon was already wider.

But these happy thoughts were of short duration. That evening, as he waited for Vibhishan to close the door of his cell, he saw Mangru. All the inmates had returned to their cell and they were alone in the hallway.

"My days are numbered," whispered Mangru. "But no matter... I believe that fate has allowed me to die by your side. They have allowed me to change cells and I'm coming here."

Kundan did not have time to respond when Vibhishan was at his cell. "Tomorrow afternoon, you will be presented before the director," he said. Through the opening of the grill of the neighbouring cell, he could hear Mangru enter. Kundan caught his friend's eye for a fraction of a second. Death already lived in his dark eyes.

He sat for a time on the cot, thinking of Vibhishan's message. The director? It smelled like punishment... one hundred lashes on his back in the middle of courtyard, in full sun, then a fifteen-day period of having to work the hand-mill, something of that nature. Or worse, even...

Kundan was waiting for the night. He was dying to look under the cot, but restrained himself. It was getting dark and soon the darkness would be total. The neighbour to his left had resumed his chant and Kundan could trace its melody. When it became totally dark, Kundan moved the bed and examined each slab of the floor. Suddenly, a stone came up in his hand, then another. His heart beating, his breath on hold, Kundan slid them, finally freeing them both from the floor. He had discovered the passage and tried to get an idea of its width, passing his hand through the interior of the cavity. Three feet... that would be enough.

He could hear nothing from Mangru's cell. Only the trembling voice, humming, pierced the silence. Kundan grabbed his bundle and his eyes accustomed themselves to the darkness. He wanted to see his cell, because for the first time it was a dark cave with a certain charm, an unexpected freshness. There he could almost detect a slight smell of serenity, a very low murmur of peace.

7

When sugar cane juice is heated, a sweet scent permeates the air and black smoke escapes from plant chimneys in a dense mass. Today, this large dark cloud covered the blue sky around the mill like a dirty cap.

As soon as he finished working, Kissan headed to the river in the mountains. The thick smoke did not travel that far, and the young man gazed at the shimmering surface of the water. His work seldom left him time to come and taste the freshness and peace, and he savoured the moments of calm along the river. The green trees with branches overhanging the river, the water lilies, the sparkling beads of dew: all these moved him deeply. In the ripples that formed around the rocks, the water moved in smooth arabesques. There, he escaped from the exhausting routine of his identical working days and began to dream of freedom and happiness.

The night before, he had spent several hours here at the river. He'd admired the moon's reflection, and looking up he'd been able to see the tapestry of stars that graced the night. They'd seemed so close, as the sky was clear, and Kissan would have been able to catch them if he'd held out his arm. But when he looked at the small town nearby, the starlight was lost in the heavy air and the pollution. He'd come to bathe in the river after work, and then he had gone home; he'd returned after dinner, despite the protests of his mother, who understood nothing of moonlight.

Kissan was nineteen-years old. Not even a year ago, he never ventured out alone at night. But in that year, the young man had changed, and it had surprised many, beginning with his own father, who would not have thought him capable. Not that the river was so far from home, but it was not that close either. One day, Kissan tried to calculate the number of steps that separated him from the river: twelve hundred.

The next afternoon, he was heading back out to the river when Raghusing caught up with him. "You got back at 10 o'clock last night. Your mother was concerned."

"I'll be back earlier today, Papa, before nightfall."

"What's that you have in your hand?"

"It's a change of clothes for after swimming," Kissan lied.

He set upon the winding path that led to the river and soon reached its banks. The thick trees lining the water stopped the last rays of light, and dusk was already falling, darkening the countryside. Kissan climbed a large rock, took a look around and gave a long whistle. Then he put the cotton jacket on the rock and sat on the stone. He looked around him, his feet up against the pebbles. On a large tree, a little later, dozens of birds gathered and were chirping in chorus. It was a wonderful place, peaceful and relaxing.

He was twelve-years old when his parents had left the village where he was born to come here. It was only four years later that Kissan had discovered the river. The day he started work, he'd left early in the morning, pick-axe in hand. And it was through this hollow valley that the river flowed lazily. The mountain that stood in the background was beautiful. Kissan, since that day, often asked why the village hadn't been built there.

But Kissan knew it wasn't the villagers who had decided anything. The landowners dictated everything; they could send you to live on the top of a hill, or let you sleep in the cane field. One day they decided to prohibit entrance into the village.

Kissan asked a lot of questions. He also never answered them. He could barely open his mouth when Raghusing would silence him, "When one is virtually a slave, you don't ask questions. You obey, that's all."

The young man turned to his father, "Why are we practically slaves?" he'd ask.

Kissan was quite serious; he sought answers with a gravity that Raghusing did not understand. He saw his son's questions as childishness that would pass with age. But the child did not give up and continued to harass him, despite the silence in which his father had taken refuge. Kissan was well aware, observing the people around him, that all of them had long since lost the urge for asking questions. They underwent the cruelest punishment without flinching, not daring to argue, as though speech had abandoned them.

He had worked for three years so far. He followed the path forged by his elders; hard work met with insults and blows. Yet he never opened his mouth. Why? Because no one had dared to do so before? Or simply because he, too, was as afraid of being helpless as the poor comrades he was constantly annoying with his questions. 'I'd better go and ask someone who can respond,' he said to himself sometimes.

Last week, while working in the fields, he had fallen in a ditch. For two days, he could not go to work. Only when he received his pay did he realise he'd been docked four days, not two. How could the workers work if they were sick? And why be so unfair in the double penalty? Kissan promised himself he'd ask a white man these questions, but the one time that one approached him, he could not find the words and was silent again. Why? What made him dumb, too?

The day he found his father harnessed with the cattle to the heavy cart on which they threw the cut cane, all his questions gave way to rage. Again, he restrained his fury and did not explode. He stood still and said nothing, despite his pain and shame. He shed tears, but they could not dilute the accumulated set of questions in his head, and they would not leave him in peace. His whole world rested on those responses, as necessary for his life as food; as needed as water. Kissan would have loved to accept his father, to understand all of them.

'If in the beginning he had refused to be silenced, and asked questions, we would not be here today,' he thought. He also knew that if he did not raise his voice, no one would listen. And he did not dare to speak up. The coward that had been asleep in him needed more than a few walks in the woods to disappear.

The banks of the river where he found refuge calmed the torments of his soul with their calm and beauty. He let his gaze get lost in the stream that skirted the rocks, capricious and fluid and felt the stream to be a reflection of himself. 'I am like the water, agitated, indignant; I pretend to have courage and boldness, but like the ripples that explode into thousands of drops I end up in pieces, and my courage is but empty breath.'

The man he had met the previous night embodied the courage that he lacked. When he'd found himself face to face with the man in the darkness, he'd felt a thrill of fear and anguish, but tonight he came to find him fascinated by the audacity of a man no longer very young, who yet shrank from no obstacle. They had agreed to meet after sunset. The horizon had already lost its red colour and the light faded gradually as the dark night extended to the water. The day before, Kissan had not talked to the man at the river for very long. He had to learn more tonight. It was for him he'd brought the shirt. Kissan had only two: this one and the one on his own back. He knew he would struggle to cope with only one. 'We'll see later,' he'd concluded, chasing away the unpleasant thoughts.

It was dark now. 'And if he does not show up?' Only the constant chatter of the birds and the murmur of the water penetrated the silence. 'Why hasn't he come?' The man had exchanged his uniform trousers for an old, torn *dhoti,* but he still wore his jacket; he would be easily spotted. Kissan grew quieter, and almost jumped when he heard the rustling of the brush near him. He turned around and saw, despite the darkness, his silhouette. When they were close by, the man asked, 'You are alone, right, my son?'

"Just as I promised."

"You've told no one?"

"No, no one." Kundan sat on a rock near the young man. He seemed exhausted. "Have you had anything to eat?'

"I had some papayas in the forest."

"I've brought you a shirt... it's old but it should suit you all the same. I wasn't sure of your size, but it's anyway all I have."

Kundan put on the shirt and took a deep breath, as if delivered of an oppressive burden. Kissan turned to him and grinned. He had the feeling then that time stood still, the river suspending its race and the stars themselves turning to watch the instant a man, with a large sigh, found freedom in his own existence.

8

The wound still hadn't closed; the joy Kundan had experienced on the first day, walking across the fields, free, dwindled as the leaves' sharp edges aggravated it. In the afternoon, when Kundan wiped the blood away with a corner of his *dhoti,* he heard a voice that he at first took for Vibhishan's. He listened and heard it once more, muttering insults. Kundan stood up and did not even have time to turn when the cane rod fell on his shoulder. The foreman struck him a second time on the back.

A short time later he regained consciousness, lying on a bundle of sticks. He could make out the silhouettes of the labourers. Pain twisted his flesh to the bone. He felt for more injuries with his hand, without looking, and felt his fingers in pain as well. He was so badly off that he could not even consider getting up to look at his leg. It was impossible to move his ankle... even on the night of his escape, he had not been in this much pain. It was unsustainable. Kundan groaned.

Kissan helped Kundan get up, putting an arm around his torso to support it as they walked. He took the path leading back to the village. The wind in the trees around them echoed his groans, and sometimes there, he heard Mangru's voice. It had been a long time since he had thought of Mangru. He heard Kissan's voice asking softly, "Are you in a lot of pain, Uncle?"

Kundan nodded.

When they at last arrived at the young man's home, Kundan leaned against the outer wall and asked for something to put on his wound.

"Yes, Uncle, here we can find what we need to put on it."

"You know what to put on it?"

"Salt."

"Salt? Definitely not. Horrible."

"The remedy looks like the poison: that's what we say here."

The next day, his leg was not much better, but Kundan went to the fields with everyone else, limping. For a moment, he wondered if he wouldn't have been better off still in prison... he could hear Mangru's voice again, bitter with irony: "We get to heaven and fall in a cactus thicket." By late afternoon, fever seized him and he agreed to spend the night at Kissan's rather than going home with Gautam, his host since his arrival. That night, Raghusing fashioned a plaster of fresh ginger to the wound, while Kissan pressed a copper bowl on Kundan's forehead to bring down the fever.

Kundan got into the habit of spending two or three nights a week at Kissan's. The rest of the time he lived with Gautam, and when he got the urge to spout a few verses, he would spend the night with Ratan. Those evenings reminded him of evenings in his native Bihar, lulled by the chanting in his mother tongue.

One night when Kundan was at Kissan's, he witnessed a quarrel between the son and the father. Raghusing was chiding Kissan for his insolence and lack of respect for the foreman, "If you continue like this, you're going to end up in big trouble. Searching for history, meddling in other's affairs... the devil doesn't care that the fool cares for others."

Kundan could not help but intervene, "Raghu, my brother, you have to admit they don't make it easy for us."

At that, Kissan's father exploded, "Oh, come on, Devnanan. You can let them follow your lead, but they don't understand their plight."

"The way you speak, Raghu, is nothing but cowardly". Later, Kundan was ashamed of his words. He could not blame Raghusing; he was a victim, like all the others. They looked like poor unfortunate hands trapped under a pile of stones. They could be removed, but not without injury. They looked at the situation like one looks at a bear, without flinching, but without a solution. They were too afraid of having their hands bloodied; they preferred not to move.

Often he had read in Kissan's eyes the question that troubled the young man: "How long shall we endure this injustice?" Kundan spoke to him so often that he knew by heart all the questions Kissan asked with words and with bright eyes. But he had never been able to give him any answers.

His wound still oozed. The caning incident preoccupied his thoughts, but he still didn't dare complain. Why? He'd learned quickly that it was better to be silent. Twenty days had been enough to learn that lesson. The others had learned it for the last twenty years... Although he had lived horrible days in jail, he had never thought that it could be worse outside. At least, he'd had the chance to escape from prison... the village was just another form of prison, one without walls and without guards, but one in which they lived as slaves, beaten, their lips sewn and their tongues muzzled. And walls can be jumped over and chains broken, but when the walls and the chains are not of concrete and metal, in what secret recesses of the soul can the key to freedom be found?

Kundan felt helpless, ill at ease. He was already old, and he had spent most of his life in prison. What future would he have in his remaining time: at most one or two years of being unafraid? Time to breath, to sigh, to stretch, and he would be dead. However, as short as it would be, it only made sense to live it fully, no longer encumbered. This resolution had grown stronger with age.

The previous day had been terribly long, as long as some days in prison; the kind of heavy, monotonous day that Kundan hated. In the fields, Jatan had been criticised by the boss and beaten. Kundan could still hear Rooplall's cries as he'd been beaten in prison. Kundan had wanted to help Rooplall, but he couldn't get through the bars separating their cells. Yesterday, nothing had separated him from Jatan, but he'd stood immobile, mute, stupefied by his fear of the foremen.

The gap separating him from the whites seemed insurmountable. Kundan knew that he could never cross it. Everyone here was habituated, and everyone bore the injustice. These people were like a sleeping dog brutally pelted with stones. Nobody moved at the sight of the animal running away, moaning, tail between its legs. The plight of the labourers inspired only indifference.

Kundan, new to the village, was not yet habituated. He still felt the difference between the lament of a dog and the cries of a man. He went to Jatan's home and, with his own hands, applied an ointment to his open wounds. He made him swallow a few bites of the rice brought over by the neighbours. Lying on his bed, not worrying about the sores covering his back, Jatan began to softly hum a *birha* verse whose words told the wedding of Udal. His voice was incredibly sweet, evoking an infinite sadness. However, the melancholy tune contrasted strangely with the words of a song celebrating courage and vigour, and the juxtaposition left Kundan stunned.

A roof covered the long house, divided into pieces by thin raffia partitions: this is what housing was for the labourers. Jatan, who was young and single, took the smallest section. When he spent the night in this room, Kundan invariably thought back to the prison infirmary, although there was no real resemblance. There was a resemblance, that evening, between Jatan's lean face and Mangru's. Kundan's leg injury still throbbed, but the sight of Jatan's ugly wounds made him forget his own suffering and think of that of his friend.

Kundan loved singing with Jatan late at night. But that voice so sweet was silent as dawn approached, and he could not yet hear the day. Had the fear of blows made the young man mute? Kundan saw images of burdened women and children pass between his eyes; he fell asleep and dreamed of a donkey and a horse. Upon waking, he told Jatan what he remembered, as if to capture the images: a donkey, chopped up, upon which the horse feeds.

The rice was so inedible that even the donkey did not want it. When it had been distributed earlier in the week, it had been full of bugs. Kosila, Kissan's mother, was sitting in the shade of the awning and sifting through it. Beside her, Gopal's mother, Gautam's mother and Sandhya were listing all the difficulties they had faced during the last outbreak. Everyone but Kosila had taken ill. They had been quarantined in a barrack where more than fifteen people died a day. Their corpses were piled in a cart and taken to the cemetery. Kosila'd kept faith that her husband would come back or that soon it would be her body balancing the cart on its way to the communal grave.

They both survived, however, and that was certainly the first surprise. In the eyes of her husband, Raghusing, it was like a second birth, a form of reincarnation. The next day he went to make offerings to the goddess, in secret, because worship was forbidden.

Kosila wanted to honour the mother goddess of her native village in Bihar. Kosila's family also prayed to Sunuwa, whose shadow stretched across the whole household. To calm Sunuwa, each year they prayed for his wrath to be appeased.

Gopal's mother wanted to hear the whole history. Kosila told it gracefully: "Sunuwa was an old servant in our family. We were rich then and lived comfortably. I myself was still a child when it happened, but I was told the story, too, so often, later... Sunuwa was a deaf-mute. He was entirely dedicated; he worked obediently, faithfully, zealously. During planting season, he helped my father on the fields. My father would send him home with the loaded sacks of grain. My older brother had just married and his young wife was alone at home with us, the infants. When she saw that Sunuwa was struggling to lift the large bundle of seeds, the young woman wanted to help place it on his head. In the manoecuvre, some *sindoor* powder fell on the bundle. When Sunuwa returned from the fields, my father immediately noticed the red colour. He became enraged and overwhelmed, accusing the servant, 'Have you been abusing my daughter-in-law? Explain how you have gotten *sindoor* on the bag. Immediately.'

"But Sunuwa could articulate nothing. He remained silent, and my father, more and more choleric, grabbed his pick and dealt the poor mute a blow to the head. He was dead. After that day, our fields dried up, and Sunuwa haunted my family. And I am still living in his shadow, my sister," lamented Kosila.

Sandhya laughed.

"She considers it all to be superstition," complained Kosila. "Kissan is like that, too. But they will understand what I am saying when something terrible happens."

Gopal's mother had closed her eyes and was praying. By the time Pushpa came to join them, her hands busy in mending her wrap, Gautam's mother was telling them how the ghost of an aunt who died in childbirth, was the ruin of her family. After causing the death of Gautam's brother, she continued to attack the health of her seven children, making them sick, one after another. Nothing could cure them.

Pushpa smiled and sat on the bench. Gautam's mother had no sooner finished her story than Gopal's mother began. She spoke of how her husband knew how to overcome many devils. It was enough to prostrate before the home altar and acquire power to repel them. He would seize a piece of glowing camphor and twist it in all directions, chanting, "Tell me, my lord, what would make you happy." The fiercest of devils or ghosts would instantly disappear.

Sandhya and Pushpa began to laugh. Gautam's mother shrugged her shoulders, grumbling. The two young women walked away to the small brick terrace that had been built under the banyan tree.

"You aren't ashamed of coming to visit us non-stop?" asked Sandhya, but she was smiling.

"But why? Is there some trouble?"

"Not at all, but after you've married my brother, you won't have to space out your visits."

Pushpa blushed and lost her concentration on the wrap's seams.

"Anyway,' said Sandhya, "it's not just you who has noticed him."

"Who else?"

"Satya sent Kissan a dhoti and a turban."

"She's given him presents?"

"Yup."

"But why?"

"How do you expect me to know?"

"And Kissan? What did he do?"

"Guess."

"I imagine he took them."

"No, he sent them back immediately!"

The conversation moved on to other topics and eventually, the girls got up to return to their homes. "Today, I want to have your mom apply henna to me," Sandhya said as they turned to leave.

"Ah, you're thinking about it again. As long as my mother is not too busy... ."

"It's always the same with her, some good excuse... but this time, I will not give in and will not go home until I'm decorated."

She took Pushpa's left arm and admired the designs on her hand and wrist. They were elegant and original. Phoolvanti had spent time on her daughter's skin and done an outstanding job. Sandhya wanted the same kind of adornment as her friend, but it took time and Phoolvanti was often too exhausted to perform the minute movements it required.

She was cooking when the two girls reached the house. "Hi, Mama. I'll do the cooking. Do you have time to apply henna for Sandhya?"

"I'm very busy, still, dear. Come back tomorrow, Sandhya, and I promise I'll do it."

"No, today please, Auntie," Sandhya stood her ground.

"Come on, Mama, be nice; give in."

Phoolvanti let herself be convinced and she went to wash her hands while Pushpa got the dark paste ready. "What style do you want: *shankha churi* or *kadamb?*"

"The same as Pushpa."

"*Shankha churi*, then... give me your hand."

"Which one?"

"The left."

"You'll do it slowly; right, Auntie?"

"What, are you scared before I even begin?" Phoolvanti set to work, humming the henna song.

If Phoolvanti was reluctant, it was because of her husband. She had beautiful *kadamb* designs on her own hand, including his initials, drawn by his own steady hand. It was from him that she had learned how to do it on others. Drawing in his absence made her feel sorrowful, melancholy.

Pushpa continued to stir the pot. "Did you know, Mama?" she asked.

"Know what?"

"What was said around the well this morning?"

"How would I know what was said around the well? I've been in the house."

"What about you, Sandhya, have you heard?"

"Me, neither."

"It seems that a pregnant woman from the nearby village was shot dead." Phoolvanti stopped tattooing to turn to her daughter, her eyes full of anguish.

"They forced her husband to turn the wheel at the big mill, then they hung him from a tree, half dead. The woman spat in the face of one of the whites, then they shot her."

"When did this happen, Pushpi?"

"The day before yesterday, I think."

Phoolvanti took a deep breath and returned to her design. In the sky, not a cloud came to adorn the uniform blue.

9

Raghusing contemplated the moon and the twinkling constellations in the night sky. The stars closer to the sun lost their intense lustre. The old man compared his situation to that of the stars in their veiled softness. Raghusing had lost influence in the village since the arrival of the man called Devnanan. In a few weeks, this man had taken the central place in the community and he was relegated to the margins.

Seven years ago, he had settled in the village; he knew everybody. He had seen the cane mill built, he had seen the village gradually populated until it reached its population today of one hundred and fifty souls. He had dug two wells and had been head of the village council for two years. He had also organised the ceremony in which Soma and Santu had married according to Hindu rites. This had been the first wedding, as labourers did not actually have the right to marry. But Raghusing had remembered his own wedding. He had seen no more of Kosila than the bracelets that adorned her wrists. He had seen a series of girls, a series of ornaments... his choice of bride was almost random.

At first, there were not more than fifty people in the village. Moreover, there was only one row of houses. The second was built later, when a hundred people had sought refuge here. They had fled from another property whose boss was bothering women. Some complained that the newcomers had been hunting. Raghusing pleaded their case in front of Mr Langlois. The patron agreed to hire them. In reality, he was sorely lacking in workers at the time and would even consider those who had forgotten their documents. But Raghusing's intervention was necessary, since he was considered a village head of sorts. And Raghusing had been at the root of many improvements of the villagers' quality of life. For this, he had been held in high esteem. Now, though, he felt a certain indifference towards him.

The irony was that the two men bent on admiring Devnanan were Kissan, his own son, and Gopal, the son of a man who Raghusing had felt had narrowly avoided prison.

The moon was full that evening and Gopal sat next to Devnanan on the strip between the two housing blocks. Raghusing could not sleep. Gopal was singing an endless *birha.* At times, he could hear Kissan's voice.

"Our son is out of the house at this time of night?" he growled aloud.

"Why does it bother you?" responded Kosila. "Everyone has the right to have fun."

"Of course."

"Bamboo makes flutes, and it also makes baskets."

Kundan had not only changed his name, but also grown out his beard and moustache, which gave him an air of gravitas. The day he was presented before the boss to ask for work, the Lame Man had suggested he shave. But there was no need: Kissan, who had accompanied him, pleaded his case in impeccable French. "Patron, Devnanan is a Sikh from Punjab. It is against his religion to shave his beard."

Ordinarily, the boss was not a man to make anything easy for anyone, but today he didn't make a fuss before signing Kundan on as an employee. When he asked for his papers, Kundan said that his previous employer had taken and confiscated them before chasing him off the property. That concluded the discussion.

After all those years in prison, Kundan enjoyed his freedom tremendously, except for the injustices. He soon forgot to take advantage of each and every instant. He was astonished this evening at his own vitality, but in fact jubilation had come over the entire village and he could not resist the vibrant atmosphere. They lit a fire on the porch and in the glow of the flames, he could see brilliant young eyes full of hope. Kundan sang badly, but he joined in Gopal's choruses.

The songs and dances lasted late into the night, and the Lame Man's men had to come and put a stop to the noise. The next day, Kissan was called to boss's house along with Kundan and Gopal. The Lame Man's nickname came from the way the Indians pronounced his name, Langarwa, which meant 'lame' in their native Bhojpuri. Mr Langlois, who initially almost refused to see them, told them he tolerated no such nonsensical revelry. The three friends made a resolution not to yield. And that evening, they began again. Until midnight, they sang and laughed around the fire. Today Kissan was called before the boss. The Lame Man, whose first name was Raymond, restated his ban.

"You are like savages when you amuse yourselves. I shall have none of that here."

"But Boss," replied Kissan, "we are simply using amusement to surmount our fatigue. It makes us more efficient workers."

The argument ended with Raymond calmed down a bit. That night, the festivities continued even more heartily. At last, Gopal's voice trembled with fatigue:

The canes are cut, my brother
they're pouring over my shoulder,
soaking wet; now I seek to know
who hides under the veil of my beloved...

They assisted him in the chorus, repeating the last words of each verse. Kissan tapped in rhyme and some began to dance. The fatigue of the day disappeared, the memory of the lashes of bamboo and cane were stomped out. They found themselves in a moment of collective joy. Labourers obscured their emotional misery and physical suffering for as long as the song lasted.

Then came the day when Gopal was defeated in the fields. The foreman descended upon him, kicking and striking him with bamboo. Kissan clung to himself to stop from intervening, clenching his fists, biting his lips until they bled. His heart wept. That evening on the banks of the river, he sat on the rocks, singing all the songs he knew and even those he didn't know because he was told it was the best way to overcome sadness... it seemed that, on the contrary, singing left him more and more depressed. Despite it all, he knew such a state wouldn't last and already he was thinking of the future, what he wanted, and how he would fight.

One day when the deputy boss seemed cheerful enough, Kissan began, "Say, sir, why should you abuse us? We work hard enough all the same."

The man had already changed colour, "What do you mean?"

Kissan hesitated a moment, but the questions were pressing against his mouth. He resumed in a low voice, "I wondered why you always give us a stick on the back."

"To see you as human beings."

He had other questions, but Kissan dared not ask. The boss handed him his dog on a leash. "Go, swim in the river," he ordered.

The dog has its place reserved in the river for a bath, and no one was allowed to bathe in it. That day, Kissan entered the water, and someone saw who hastened to denounce him. He expected to receive seven lashes for it. Instead, he got ten new opportunities to ask questions. That evening, Kissan composed a song, and it was so successful that within three days, it was on everyone's lips.

They were also punished for this song. The foreman walked through the centre of the field behind two white bosses to announce that anyone who dared to sing this song would be immediately returned to the village. They did not hear any more of it, but the workers continued to sing it between the walls of their homes, out of earshot of the enemy. The song said:

In the kingdom of Mr Lame
Dogs are treated better.
They only have to wag their tails
and anything goes...
In Mr Raymond's kingdom
It is men who are ready
to lick the master's boots:
the foreman, for example
behaves like a dog.

Kissan's song pleased Pushpa very much.

10

Pushpa and Kissan were talking about the last cyclone. Six months after the terrible epidemic decimated their community, another disaster befell them. It was the beginning of a new month. They all remembered the storm's approach: the red sky, the intense wind blowing harder and harder. In the dead of night, it began to rain heavily. The wind roared; lightning streaked the sky. The inhabitants of the village huddled in their houses and chanted verses of prayer to Hanuman, trembling in fear.

It was the third occasion of late that they'd been faced with such adversity. Three months before the epidemic, a comet in the sky had set off a panic. The elders thought that such a sight presaged problems in the future; the young ones were won over by the fear, and for the seven hours the comet made its passage through the sky, they all kept their doors and windows closed.

Pushpa returned to the cyclone. For on that terrible night,

her friendship with Kissan was born. The trees had swayed menacingly in the wind. The walls of the houses were pliant; the roofs flew to pieces.

Pushpa and her mother had been upset. The roof of their house had blown away and they wandered, distaught, in search of shelter. Kissan had just seen them in a lightning flash when a big branch cracked and fell from a banyan tree just above Pushpa. He sprang forward and pushed her to the side. They rolled around on the ground strewn with leaves.

The cyclone raged; the young men spent the night at Jatan's. Kissan was so afraid, his emotional nature deeply shaken by what had happened with the comet and now with the storm. Yet, he hadn't hesitated to jump to save Pushpa. A sort of supernatural valiance came over him at the sight of her.

Once the cyclone calmed down, he was one of the first to start repairing his home. Pushpa wanted to make things up to him somehow, but Kissan would not hear of thanks.

A few days after the cyclone, Kissan was spending the evening on the riverbank, trying to write down the words to a song. Pushpa came upon him, a bundle of dry cloth under her arm. She was the village laundress for the day, washing the clothes in the river and laying them on the banks to dry. She had just picked up the dried clothes.

The evening was peaceful. Through the bare branches of the trees, stripped by the blast of the storm, they could see the last rays of the sun on the mountain. To the west, the horizon had spread its colour over the sea, a colour as deep and sombre as the sea itself. Kissan knew it was the sea at low tide. He wanted to go to it, but it was not easy to get away from here. Pushpa came and sat behind him.

An idle birdsong echoed sadly in the leafless trees. The birds looked as though they were crying for their destroyed nests and broken eggs. The village's roofs had been torn, and two people had died in the hurricane. But Kissan turned from those memories to his friend and as he saw her smile, he left the plaintive song of the birds far behind.

How had the daughter of the Indian foreman, Ramjee,

got wind of their meeting on the banks of the river? However she did, the next day she came to Kissan and reproached him, overwhelming him with embarrassing questions. He lied several times, then regretted it. Why should he fear Satya's wrath?

At the end of her journey, Pushpa had found him on the banks of the river, still and pensive.

"Do you sleep here?" she asked, shaking him softly.

Kissan had truly been dreaming. He had almost fallen asleep and was startled when Pushpa's hand touched his shoulder. They laughed. Sitting on the bank, Pushpa, feet in the water, folded the leaves into the shapes of birds. The last rays of the sun bathed everything in a golden light, and nothing could be heard but the lapping of the water.

Kissan read his friend the first words of the song he had just written:

The bird flies away,
its nest destroyed.
He has gone to seek
refuge elsewhere...

Pushpa loved Kissan's songs and hummed them all the time, their familiar melodies keeping her company, so she never felt alone. Kissan rose and held his hands out to Pushpa, helping her up. They walked even further from the village and awoke some of the forest as they came. Two hares fled at their approach. Kissan thought of Gautam: if his friend had been there, they would have immediately started in pursuit.

The path skirted the edge of the woods, bordered on one side by trees and bushes, on the other by a cane field. The cane had been cut. The pair walked in silence together. There were always hundreds of things to talk about, but once they were together, they could not find the words and were silent. Pushpa started to speak at last, "Mama has been speaking of India again."

"It's useless to think about it."

"Oh... it's a comfort."

"I would say that it makes you grieve more."

"I'm missing something..."

"What's that?"

Pushpa didn't respond immediately; she waited until they had crossed the cane fields. "Mama says that the temples there were so high that when you looked to see the top of them, your hat would fall off."

"So?"

"So... how can you be so poor in a country that has the means to build such temples? Were our parents pushed out?"

"They weren't the people with the means or the power, that's all."

"You describe what it's like over here... are we oppressed all over the world?"

"Let's talk about something else, if you don't mind."

"Mama said that my grandfather had seven cows." Pushpa was silent for a long moment, then continued, "How I would love a cow of my own."

"We don't have any money, and we're always at work."

"You're right, Kissan... but if we only had a cow, I would find grass for it to eat."

"Come down from the clouds, darling." A gust of wind took the wrap off Pushpa's shoulders; she ran to catch hold of it and Kissan followed her, still holding her hand. Kissan caught it. "If the wind wants your *orni*, it'll have to try a bit harder."

Pushpa took the cloth from Kissan's hand and rewrapped herself, "I'm not daydreaming, though, Kissan, I'm serious. If we had a cow in the village..."

"You could drink milk."

"You just speak nonsense," she said, pushing Kissan's hand away.

"You're crazy, Pushpa."

"But why? Why not? The next village over has four."

"Because we live like rats. And if the rats don't have enough to eat, how will we feed a cow?"

"How long can we live in this misery?"

"See, that's an interesting question, at least. You see, my Pushpi, that we've become used to living so poorly, like an inferior class. We've become attached to it, and to change our lives, we have to change our idea of what life is."

They were both silent. The sky darkened. They had ventured far enough and it was time to turn back. Pushpa again took Kissan's hand and placed a leafbird in his palm. As they entered the village, she asked him point-blank, "Kissou, who is your dearest friend?"

"It's you."

"Really?"

"Yes."

"I'm your friend?"

"Yes, my best friend."

"Only a friend?"

"Yes, Pushpa, you're my best friend."

They separated at the entrance to the village. As they passed Jatan's house, Kissan saw small children reciting the story of Rama in low voices. The sun had set, and soon the dry clothes would hang nonchalantly in the breeze.

11

The heat was sweltering. Dust devils were flying about the dried cane fields. The labourers who cut the cane were in the furrows under a blazing sun, steaming with sweat. The breakfast bell rang. It was really only a short break and if the foreman had spit on the floor at that time of day, his saliva would not have had time to dry up before work was resumed.

Kissan retrieved his bag, made of sheets of braided reeds, suspended from a branch. A piece of barley sugar had attracted ants inside the bag. The bowl containing his meal was infested. Kissan started to pick out one or two grains of rice, but it was hard to get them unstuck from the ruined lentils. Discouraged, he dumped the bowl's contents and put the bowl back in his bag. He didn't say anything, for then one of his comrades would have gone half-fed to share with him. He joined the workers on the other side of the rocks, sitting next to Kundan, who was eating his bread under a tree. Kundan gave him a piece of bread, made from milled corn. It was sometimes accompanied by a bit of chutney. He never accepted anything from anyone, except Kissan, whose curry or chutney he sometimes shared.

Kundan asked how he was, but Kissan turned away from conversation. At the end of the day, he returned home, feverishly hungry, but nothing had yet been prepared for dinner. He raged against his mother and his sister and left for the river. He sat on a rock and lost himself in contemplating the water; the last rays of the sun played on the surface and were reflected, coppery, in small ripples.

Kissan thought back on the day. When the foreman had departed, Sonallal, thinking himself alone, had started to hum Kissan's last song:

When you sucked the juice
from the cane, Ramjee,
you did not leave me any fibre...

The foreman heard him and ordered him to be silent. Sonallal obeyed, but Gautam's father took up the next verse.

"I am warning you, if work isn't finished today, you'll hear from me," shouted the foreman.

"Sirdar..." Kissan grumbled.

"What did you say?"

"Both my grandfather and yours would return from beyond the grave to help me, but what do you see on this field today?" He said to the Indian foreman, "Get to work."

The foreman approached Gautam's father, "It's good that you have seven children, right? You have fun with your wife and you make the little pigs... but when it comes time for them to work, they aren't there anymore."

Gautam was nearby. He stood and frowned. He no longer lived with his father, after his father's marriage to Rookmeen, but he could not bear to hear him insulted in that way. Droplets of sweat rolled down his face. He stared at the foreman without blinking. At his side, Dawood whispered, "Gautam, just get back to work..."

The foreman continued to insult his father and Gautam trembled from his head to his toes, not from fear, but from an angry desire to slit the throat of that despicable man. Yet, he could not attempt the slightest movement, and though he had in his hand a small sickle, he felt completely unarmed. He raised his hand to wipe the drops of sweat that had accumulated on his brow, and the blade of his sickle sent out a bright flash when it was over his head. Dawood begged him to go back to work. Sonallal chimed in. Dawood had to ask a third time before Gautam agreed and bent down to return to work. After that everything happened fast. He had cut a cane at its base when he received a blow to the back. No sooner had he stifled a cry than other blows followed.

"But what have I done?" Gautam would have done better to remain silent. One should never complain while receiving blows; that was the rule. No sooner had he opened his mouth than he was grabbed by two foremen. The Lame Man watched from the top of the hill as they hoisted Gautam atop a pile of sticks and balanced him on the rocks. He fell as he lost consciousness, and the foremen whipped him to revive him.

They made Gautam's father take the place of the oxen harnessed to the cart. As a beast of burden, he had to pull the cart forward with the foremen inside. The foremen sang the forbidden song and every word was accompanied by ten lashes.

At the end of the day, when Kundan was taking the path back to the village, he said in a loud voice, "It's no longer impotence, at this stage."

"I, too, am ashamed," said Jatan. "We all are."

It was still warm, although the sun was almost down. The labourers felt so frustrated and miserable they dragged their feet. Their faces reflected their anxiety and despair. Their feet were heavy, and yet they tried to make haste to return home after an exhausting day. There were many who would have to be satisfied with a dinner of stale rice. Others could not eat anything because they had no leftover rice, and their new rice and lentils were overrun with vermin. Pushpa's mother, leaving her house, went to the cluster of men under the banyan tree.

"The rice is full of insects. No one can eat it. Not even a dog. We need to decide who from among us will speak to the boss."

No one responded. The moonlight shone weakly on their faces and on it she could read the same resignation, the same discouragement. Cymbals and drums lay in the corner under a canopy, but no one had the heart to make any music. Several women had come out to complain about the rice, and it was the first time they had the upper hand. It looked like a real battle. They spoke in brittle voices and employed harsh and hurtful words. They had worked during the day, too. They, too, were exhausted.

Kissan never flinched. It was the first time he'd seen his mother under the banyan tree. He'd always thought women were stoic; they all seemed to take refuge in silence. Then his thoughts took a different direction.

Kundan was also thoughtful. He thought about how to fill this growing gap between Kissan and the others. If there could be a 'movement' worthy of the name... but overcoming the resistance of the elders and containing his protege's impulses to revolt were both important. Kundan had endured much, reflected much, and demanded much. Not that he had become insensitive to the miseries of others, but he did not consider compassion and sympathy as values in themselves. They could be as hollow as the empty words of the villagers. As Kissan's grand declarations in song...

Looking like the Goddess Chandi, Pushpa stood before the group of men, a handful of rice in hand, and shouted, "Since none of you wants to do it, I'll go. I'll find the boss. You are only good to sing and dance and forget your troubles; no one cares to fill the pantry."

Some were silent, others aghast. Kissan checked the rice and the lentils, and sure enough a smell was emanating from the bags. Nobody knew what to do, so they prevaricated, and nothing was resolved when the siren sounded at the mill. Two foremen entered the village and one of them shouted in Kreol, "Work is backed up; we need fifteen men."

Kissan knew very well why work was falling behind at the mill. In it were employed forty men who had not eaten since yesterday. They hadn't had anything since no food could be prepared in the village. Kissan intervened, "How many men do you need?"

"Fifteen, didn't you understand?"

"How about you look somewhere else?"

"What are you saying?"

"No one here has eaten this evening. We are all hungry; we can't work."

"You're here to work, not to sit gaping."

"But we have already done a full day of work."

"Cretin, who do you think gives you the corn and the manioc, the rice and the lentils? Do you think they come from your mother's love?"

"Hold your tongue. We are not in the fields now."

Kundan intervened, pulling Kissan back, "We're not in a state to work, that's all."

"And why not?" countered the foreman.

"Because we haven't had anything to eat, as he just told you."

"The boss must tell us," said another foreman. "That's enough, we need fifteen men on the spot. Hurry up."

There was a silence, then Dawood was the first to get up. Kundan followed, and others after him. The fifteenth, Kissan, followed with his head down.

"How long will we endure this life as beasts of burden?' murmured Dawood to himself.

The foreman replied, without irony, "Patience heals all wounds."

"And the fruit of patience," demanded Kissan bitterly, "what does it taste like?"

The smoke from the mill was so dark that it took the shape of a silhouette against the dark sky. In the heights, it joined the dark sky and the confluence seemed like a deep lake. From the sleeping earth emanated an indefinable sadness, and the labourers on the path were as weary men in the desert. The night was so dark that one could doubt that the sun would ever again move across the sky.

12

The sun moved slowly across the sky, shuffling. It was the cutting season; the days seemed endless, and the labourers sweated under a hot sun. Even as the sun exhausted its course, it left behind it a course of exhausted men. It all just seemed endless. As for the earth, it seemed that its thirst was never quenched. It demanded a daily ration of sweat and did not stop to suck the salt from the heavy drops. Today, it was only noon...

The Lame Man had no sooner got out of his carriage than the news of his arrival went through the camp at lightning speed. A black servant carrying a large parasol, sheltering his master from the sun, followed him. The servant kept his eyes fixed on the head he had to protect, making sure that it would never be exposed to the harsh light of midday. He could not, at the same time, look at his feet, and he stumbled against the stones on the way, twisting his ankle. No matter. He kept composure without fail. Kundan and Kissan were cutting cane on the same row, at one end. Kissan paid no attention to the boss, but Kundan, like the majority of the labourers, had a feeling in the pit of his stomach. He held his guts with his bony hand.

Dawood stood nearby. The Lame Man stopped very close to him and called a foreman with a voice that shook the entire field. A Creole foreman advanced quickly through the canes and stood at attention, "Yes, sir."

"Why is this man cutting the stems so high?" The foreman quickly grabbed a rod and dealt Dawood a blow to the back, and then shouted in Kreol, "Why do you leave three inches of stem? For your old father? If you're not flexible enough to bend down to the ground, you might as well stay home pretending to be a man."

Kissan had stopped breathing. He threw his sickle to the ground and cast a furtive glance at the Lame Man. He heard Kundan whisper a few words to him, and leaned on the next pole. The Lame Man was perched on a large stone placed across the road, looking around. He took off his helmet and took a handkerchief from his pocket with which he slowly wiped his forehead. He laid eyes on Kissan, descended from his mound, and walked towards him, followed by foremen.

Kissan turned to Dawood. He was back to work, impassive, but Kundan's face was clenched, as if it were he who'd received the blows. Kissan sighed, also suffering for Dawood and his humiliation. But already the second foreman approached, and he picked up his sickle and returned to work.

The voice of the Lame Man reached them, and also the sound of bamboo raining down on the backs of the labourers. Kissan bent a little and looked at the ground as if the earth could absorb him.

"Nobody has come to bring water?" asked Kundan in a low voice.

Kissan didn't reply, but looked up the path to the village. No one in sight. This made him thirsty suddenly. He felt drops of sweat running down his cheek and grab the tip of his tongue. They tasted of salt. Then he went back to work, trying to forget the heat and thirst. The foreman had joined the boss. Kissan turned to Dawood. Canes were being cut off on both sides of the row, the view was clear, and they could easily monitor their surroundings until the tamarind tree on the edge of the field. Kissan pushed Dawood to the side.

"Sit there," he whispered.

He cut the row of canes quickly, until the stems reached the same height as those of the other labourers. He then made a sign and Dawood, without a word, took his place and went back to work. The sweat that drenched his face refreshed him a bit. In the clear sky, there were no hopes of clouds or even the slightest speck of shade.

Kundan again asked when the water would arrive. Kissan passed his tongue through his dry mouth.

"Hey, Kundan."

"Yes?"

"Yesterday night I had this dream."

"You're very lucky; I don't even dream any more."

"Do you believe that dreams have meaning?"

"How could they have? They have as much meaning as the beads of sweat running down your forehead."

"Sweat has meaning.'

"Oh? And what is it?"

"Harvest the cane stalks, the fruit of our sweat."

"Yes, my boy, but all this only benefits those who never sweat in their lives. Those people come to the field in their palanquins and leave the same way."

"We can still dream."

"Sure... but even your dreams probably belong to them, and for their profit.'

The rumour spread that the Lame Man had come back.

Everyone was silent. The boss arrived and in his booming voice threatened to reduce their salaries if the field was not cut by evening. There were sidelong glances, but then the big man got into his carriage and went away. No one dared sigh with the foremen there, within reach of them. Kissan quietly resumed the conversation, "I had a very long dream. I can't remember all the details.'

"You do not hold your tongue or do as you're told, do you? Anyway, I'm listening."

A foreman yelled in the next field. Everyone heard it. Even if they had the right to hear, there was no right to respond.

"In my dream, everyone was helpless, incapable." Kundan continued to cut the cane, looking down into the furrows. "How do you want me to tell you if you don't listen?"

"I'm listening, Kissan, I'm listening."

"You keep on cutting cane."

"I can do both at the same time. Keep going, I'm all ears."

"All the bosses were in palanquins. There was a row of guards with guns, canes, and dogs. They had their backs to the factory and the mansion, not to us. It was a picture of helplessness to the extreme."

"And then?"

"No, that's all."

"You call that a dream?"

"We didn't have anything in our hands, not picks, not shovels, not scythes. Wait... that reminds me. They were coming towards us, in close ranks. And we were retreating with empty hands."

"Your dream doesn't make any sense.'

"It was really a nightmare. I was terrified." Dawood had another strip of cane needing to be evened. Kundan got up to do it, making sure that no foreman could see him. He wiped his brow with the sleeve of his shirt and looked up the trail in the direction of the village. Still no one. He licked his dry lips and worked automatically, pruning the row. Behind his back, he heard the foreman yelling insults.

Kundan knew thirst. He had often suffered from it in prison. Once he had been left without food or drink for three days. He would have spent a fourth day without swallowing if Vibhishan hadn't thrown him a handkerchief soaked with water. Kundan had pressed it against his mouth; those few drops certainly saved his life. But even then he had not felt so thirsty. There was a real burning in his throat, accompanied by a ringing in his temple, and then a terrible anxiety, a panic that gradually took over his mind. "Why isn't there any water today?"

"Who should bring it?" asked Kissan.

"Harbassia. Where is she?"

"She should have already returned home from Raymond's house...' Their eyes were on the trail. Harbassia did not appear. Some of them secretly sucked on the cane, despite knowing that sugar juice would only aggravate their thirst. Kissan looked up in the sky, the sun flickering like a moving halo. "He drinks our sweat," he said, a bitter smile on his chapped lips. "No, it's the land that can quench us. It absorbs all we pour over it, and in exchange it gives us its best fruits. Even in these fruits, we never see colour. Why is the world so bad?"

No one stood in their path, but they lost their view as the canes swayed in the warm wind.

13

Jatan's sudden death at the mill upended the whole community. At first, everyone was stunned. Then some of those who worked in the field took the initiative to go to the funeral but were turned away by the foreman, who tirelessly repeated the order, "Let everyone remain at his post." There was no way to stop working, and the scowls of the guards finally convinced those who'd retained some hope of paying their last respects to their comrade. Only Kissan dared to violate the order, and he went on the sly across roads and laid Jatan's body atop a bundle of kindling.

Later, various hypotheses circulated regarding the cause of death. Some said he'd died of starvation, others argued that the blows he'd received the previous day had gotten the better of him, the yellow colour of his skin was suggesting something else entirely. Kissan, after taking cover in his hut, thought he saw, still, on Jatan's face all the suffering of his recent days. His irises were so depressed that they seemed like empty cups of clay. His skin was tanned by the sun, baked a hundred times. His cheeks were hollow, like a mango juiced to the last drop. A handful of rice would have sufficed... just a handful of rice. Kissan could not take his eyes off the bloodless body, an inert witness to a miserable, destroyed life. Sadness overwhelmed his heart in successive waves, hot and heavy.

Jatan was dead. A labourer who'd given the bosses his very life: this man had come from Bihar and had been, for twenty years, the faithful companion of Kissan's father, with whom he had turned over and over endless fields of the island's rocks, hoping to find gold. He who had wished to die on the banks of the Ganges, with a sip of the great river's water in his mouth, had not a drop of saliva at the moment of his death. Jatan died a slave, his number plate attached to his neck. Kissan could still but hear his voice, his cries and complaints, his pleas of human oppression.

Kissan had never felt so helpless. The grinding poverty that gripped the village made him so angry. Driven to rage, itching with revolt, he felt he would scream. Jatan had not died; his élan vital had been killed by despair, helplessness and indifference. There were hundreds like him, held under the rule of two people, who were hungry, exploited. Yet the real culprits were not the executioners but these victims, who accepted the yoke and suffered in silence.

Helplessness... Kissan hated helplessness. There were still worse conditions: fear, paralysis, all those feelings that he could read on the faces of his brothers that rendered them pale, disabled. For them, Jatan's was a death like any other. One more. Kissan, plagued by anger, went home, put his head through the old wrap that served as a curtain, and said he was not hungry. Then he went to the river.

Sitting on his boulder, he ruminated, trying to gather from his thoughts a few scraps of memories that had originally been his father's. Jatan and Raghu had left their native province of Arrah to sail for Mauritius. As they boarded the ship, white brokers hustled the watching crowd: "Come, come to the land of Mareech."

The poor, who had seen their land ruined by drought, their

families decimated by hunger, flocked to the stern and listened to the siren call.

"It's too hard to live here. You will all die like dogs if you wait until you have fed this barren land. There is no future here, no present..."

Most did not even understand what the brokers had said, but language itself impressed them and excited their curiosity. They had taken the bait. "Where is this Mareech? And what is there?"

"It's not very far. And no one is starving. The land is prosperous, fertile, and every time you lift a stone you find gold or silver. Here, you ruin your health trying to get three gains of rice; there, the riches will come to you without you having to lift a finger."

People only wanted to dream. Plans were made in the highest spirits; they would leave and start a new life, easy and happy. The ship left the port, and they scanned the horizon, eyes full of hope, believing they would spot paradise. As soon as they arrived on the island, their dreams flew off, and their big hopes turned into regrets. When they realised the fate reserved for them, they wanted to head back, immediately, in the opposite direction. But there was no way back, and they cursed the brokers who had so deceived them, so trapped them. They then bitterly reproached themselves, mortified to have acted with such haste, without thinking at all. "But, anyway, we had no choice," repeated Kissan's father.

As a young man, Kissan had never accepted the resignation of his elders. Today, however, he understood better and felt the weight of impotence weighing on his shoulders. Jatan's life had carried some form of resistance: in the greatest secrecy, for it was forbidden, Jatan had learned the Hindi alphabet and he had learned to work with numbers. Many village children had learned to read in his small house. He was known as a man of integrity, perennially honest, but the day the Lame Man came to question him, he denied it vehemently.

"I've learned that you run a school for children at your house?"

"No, sir, that's not true. You have been told stories." That was certainly the only lie of his life. It remained on his conscience until the very end. Jatan knew many passages of the *Ramayana;* he could also recite the quatrains of the *Hanuman Chalisa.* He was able to decipher some storybooks, and it was he, of the whole village, who knew best their mother tongue. He hated the submission imposed on them, and even if he could not do much to fight against the whites, he resisted in his own way, keeping alive the cultures and traditions of his people.

Kissan remembered their last discussion, ten days earlier.

"My son," Jatan told him, "take these books after my death. They are my only wealth. I brought them from India and I have saved them at my own risk and peril, because if you had found them at my home, I would not have much skin left to give. I want you to make good use of them.'

Kissan was certain Jatan had felt his end nearing and that day was somehow a test. At the time, the young man did not heed his words; until now, he did not understand their full meaning. Jatan had entrusted him with a heavy responsibility...

The old man's greatest desire was to convince the head of the plantation to cede a piece of land on which they could construct a *baithka*. Jatan had been able to talk for hours about the advantages of having such a meeting place. After Jatan's death, Kissan took over the idea of building a *baithka*, and told his friend Kundan. He imagined it could play a role, not just for meeting, but in establishing a resistance movement.

Kundan tempered his ardour and moderated his enthusiasm without discouraging him altogether, "You really think they will give us a piece of land? And then agree we have the right to do anything there: sing, read, be together at night around the fire? The only thing they know is how to give us are whippings..."

"We do not need to wait for them to give us land to build something."

"What do you mean?"

"Jatan's house is empty..."

"And you want to make it a *baithka*?"

"Why not?"

"The headman will give the house to someone else, that's all."

"We can just ask him to give it to you. After all, you don't have a home."

"Don't you think it would be better to choose a quieter place, a little further away from the village? A small room, wedged among the others: it lacks discretion."

"It doesn't matter."

"It doesn't facilitate private conversations."

"So what? It'll be just us. We have nothing to hide."

"You know, our enemies are not always where you expect. And we must sometimes be wary of our closest neighbours. After all, those who foolishly embarked on the adventure are our people, and don't forget that some of the foremen are Indian like us, too. We can't rely on others simply because they are our brothers. Remember the story of Kansa. He was Lord Krishna's uncle, but... no, believe me, there is no worse enemy than a friend who turns against you. In the *Mahabharata,* it's family members at war with one another."

"You may be right, but we must build our movement on confidence."

"You know I support you, anyway."

"It's the only thing that matters to me." Kissan was moved by the trust granted to him by a man he admired. Kundan's confidence encouraged him. He was proud to have alongside him a former soldier, brave and fearless. But when asked about the nature of the dangers he'd faced in his life, Kundan assumed an air of mystery and a smile rested on his lips.

"If life did not present us with obstacles and dangers to hone our survival instinct," he'd replied in a soft voice, 'we would find it very monotonous."

Soon, Kissan, who had taken home Jatan's library, gave readings, too. Children came to his home to hear the old stories, and gradually they began to find a common home in the house that Kundan had been given to serve as his dwelling.

The first village meeting was held at last. It followed the suicide of Gopal's mother, which shook the whole village. Despite their grief, the villagers remained cautious. They all spoke of the tragedy under the banyan tree, around the well, in the fields, but those who proposed that they all meet that evening at Kundan's to speak further were opposed by the less adventurous, who still feared trouble.

14

If the proposal had been made by anyone else, it probably would not have been met with such acceptance, but Kissan was well liked in the community, especially with Kundan's shadow hovering over him. The cane cutters gave their agreement by tapping their pruning blades together.

The time of the meeting approached and some felt themselves more frightened as it came closer. Heavy clouds darkened the sky and obscured the moon, now in its first quarter. The darkness that reigned in the streets of the village did not help dispel their fear and the participants were walking in the dark, hurrying to Kundan's house. Nobody had a light, so they did not draw the attention of the two foremen who lived near the mill.

At the stated hour, the 20 invitees were, under a light rain, in front of Kundan's door. They entered the small room lit by an oil lamp. They heard sighs of relief and relaxation.

On the other side of the street, at Kissan's, young people sang and danced, forming more or less consciously an excellent diversion. Kissan arrived last at the meeting and sat down on the mat. Kundan gave him a look and spoke, "I do not know how things were before. I was not here, and it's none of my business. But since I have arrived, this is the second time we have seen one of our own die, who otherwise would still be among us. How many will there be before we react?"

Kundan turned to Kissan, who motioned for him to continue. 'I loved Gopal's mother, just as you all did. I considered her to be a daughter. We could see that she was the mother of a great son. You know better than I how her husband was killed... and it's not easy being a young widow here. These bastards take the opportunity to take them into their homes. We know what happens at the boss's home." He was quiet. A few others around the room began to whisper, and Kundan asked for silence. "We have almost no power, but we must do what we can to protect the honour of our women and their children. It's the least we can do.'

"You're not the first to raise the issue, Devnanan," remarked Dawood's father.

"I don't doubt it. I imagine you have already addressed the matter, but nothing has yet been done."

"And nothing can be done today, Devnanan."

"Why not?" murmured Kissan.

"What are we going to do?"

"We must act together."

There was laughter; it came from the elders, especially, saying things like, "We thought like you before." The others whispered amongst themselves. They claimed Kundan even if, in fact, no one knew from where this man came.

When it was impossible for the two sides to agree, both sides abuzz, Kissan's father got up and spoke for the first time. "In previous years, Devnanan, we reached the same conclusions and made the same proposals. But there is a world of difference between rhetoric and action..."

"I'm listening."

"Nothing can be done."

"Then we should just close our eyes and let them walk over our rights and the honour of our women?"

Raghusing looked at his son, took a long drag from his pipe and answered, "What will we gain?"

Again the room erupted in murmurs. Kissan had to raise his voice to demand the attention of all present. "I agree that so far we have not been able to do anything but talk, but that is not a reason for giving up."

"Eh, good... what are you doing, you who are so smart?" asked his father brutally.

"Well, that's what we are here to decide, in fact."

"We could go to the owners and ask them to stop their little games," Raghusing mocked.

"But, father, here you speak as though it is the hardest thing in the world."

"If it's easy, then you try."

"I'm not saying it's easy, but, still, it's not impossible."

"So what are you waiting for?" his father yelled. "Why do you not go over to talk to them, if you're so strong? When will you stop bragging, you insolent little cretin? If you want to get all of us in the fields beaten, go ahead, take your dear friend Devnanan along to lecture the bosses."

"Since you've come," he continued, turning to Kundan, "you have only spread revolt in the minds of our youth. I suppose that's why they threw you out of your old village. Agitator to the core."

"The cat who cannot scratch his master attacks his mistress," came a voice from the back rows.

Raghusing raised his hand and silence returned. "We know what awaits us if we dare make any criticism."

"So we must be silent, is that it?" exploded Kissan.

"If that is what the situation requires, it is preferable."

Voices were raised, some siding with Raghusing, others with Kissan. Some lost their temper, and the debate was heated. The gap that had opened between father and son had never been so wide. Raghusing stood up, trembling in anger and spoke in a lugubrious voice, "If it amuses you to die like dogs, then you are free to do so. Do what you want, after all, but think of the consequences of your actions. We will all pay for your foolishness."

And he left the room, disappearing into the darkness of the hot night. His departure left the meeting mute and the silence was broken only by the melody of a *birha:* someone singing in the distance. Then, they all began to talk. Dawood's father asked, coughing, "What would you do?"

"We must decide tonight, right here," replied Kundan. "But how can we make a decision without the chief?"

"All the rest of us can decide," retorted Kissan. "It's a good start."

"First, we need to be treated as human beings. This is the first condition. As long as they consider us to be animals, we will not get anywhere."

"The problem is that they behave like animals," remarked Dawood's father. "To be respected by evil ones... to be respected by these people, we should behave like them."

No one interrupted this change of tone. Kissan was the first to respond, "I could, when the time comes, act like a savage beast. We must consider the means at our disposal to really improve our condition.' But before he could continue, someone interrupted.

"We should all agree."

"What do you mean?"

"We'll be effective the day all the labourers, on all the sugar plantations, mobilise."

"I think exactly the opposite," said Kundan.

And Kissan agreed with him, "If we cross our arms until all the labourers on the island are ready, we'll never act. No, you have to start somewhere. Why not here? We'll be the example around which others will rally. Little by little, they'll follow us."

Dawood's father caressed his white beard and nodded. Was he beginning to come around to this idea? "I agree we should initiate things, but how? What should we do?"

Sonallal's father had not yet opened his mouth. Now he said, in a weak voice, "There is only one way to stop them. Break the hand that strikes us."

No one could believe these words had come out of that mouth. His comrades looked at him, incredulous, with the elders more stupified than the young ones.

"No," let out Kissan. All eyes turned to him. "We are not strong enough to attempt a coup. We cannot even bend their fingers."

"So then how?"

"Gain strength."

"We barely get enough to eat."

"It'll have to do."

"You know that's impossible."

"If we fail to amass our strength when we are in thousands, if we accept our current living conditions, these people will never cease to raise their hands against us and it will be definitely the end of our freedom. Given that this country is enriched through our work, it is unacceptable to stand idly. What is needed is to act with discretion and the utmost caution. We must organise ourselves in the greatest secrecy, so that they never get wind of our meetings, our intentions. The first thing to do is to eliminate the obstacles in accessing other villages. We need to meet the other villagers, get messages to them, communicate with them, so that in time, all the labourers can bring forth the same spirit and join us in our march on the oppressor. When we are at our full strength, they dare not strike us."

Not everyone understood the meaning of this tirade, but some measured its full scope and Kissan knew he had reached them. Kundan realised this too, and was perhaps happiest of all.

15

Kissan's impatience made him sometimes irascible. Raghusing saw that his son had trouble keeping his composure, that he had become taciturn and difficult. It was useless to tell him over and over that 'man does not cook a good meal in a hurry', that 'good things come to those who wait'. How many times had he heard the same old song? Kissan knew that nothing could ever happen by itself and if they wanted something to happen, they had to go for it: build strength, train and lift themselves up. The villagers were too exhausted for such exercise.

Kissan did not stop interrogating Kundan. He wanted to know how to acquire the force that they lacked. His friend gave invariably the same answer, "It will happen gradually."

Kissan found himself with the same follow-up: "When? When?" The word was hammering at his head like a gong. He, who had wanted to rush things, to anticipate the argument, felt the inertia of things give way. Nothing could be achieved if they did not have all the forces of the region gathered. And was it even possible? To date, no one could dare say that.

For the first time, the youngest had expressed their anger, their misery, and their discontent. For the first time, the older generation became aware that this new generation, born here on this island, was ready to engage in activism. Now, the presence of Kundan stirred their revolt and Raghusing was seriously worried.

Raghusing constantly brought out one of his favourite maxims: "If milk rises too quickly, it will eventually overflow." Kissan despised these warnings and this made his father half crazy. He complained to his wife, cursing her for having given birth to such a stubborn child. With Kundan's support, Kissan thought about how to organise the resistance movement. Raghusing considered this all stupid and childish, but he did not underestimate the danger.

"Your son is going to cause trouble," he complained to his wife, "and make us lose the little food we have the opportunity to receive today. He thinks he's a leader, the little snot, but in the end, it is we who will pay the bill. What does he imagine will happen if he takes over others' problems?"

Kissan's mother was in the process of crushing fresh leaves with a pestle in the mortar, "You never stop reproaching, whatever he does."

"First he quarrelled with the foremen, now he attacks the boss. Devnanan has turned his head."

Not far away, Kissan was playing *kabaddi* with the kids. He was teaching the rules of the Indian lawn game to those who didn't know them. Two days earlier, the foreman had come to requisition these children. He intended to use them at home for shelling corn. But Kissan opposed it. "You're surely not using child labour? And without pay, no less."

Ramjee, the foreman, had gone to complain to Raghusing and all the families of the children had received a threat: "These kids may not be coming to work today, but I swear that I myself will see them one day harnessed to the cane cart."

Kissan rounded up the group in the morning and kept them occupied, determined to prevent them from leaving for Ramjee's house.

"Why the hell does this boy get into trouble when he sees the crocodile in the backwater?" Raghusing exclaimed, throwing down the stick he used to clean his teeth.

Kissan took the road to the fields, all the labourers already gone. The sun was already high in the sky and idle after its morning show. The young man was late and Pushpa was with him. She dropped Kissan's hand. "Most of the people in the village don't agree with you."

"And you, do you agree?"

"Sometimes I wonder..."

"You're telling me that sometimes you side with the old

folks?" They had reached the spot where, ordinarily, they parted. Kissan paused, looking towards the mill.

Pushpa faced him and said softly, "You did not answer my question yesterday."

"Which question?"

"People say that you're going to marry Satya."

"I have no idea who I'm going to marry."

"Don't marry Satya."

"Why? Isn't she a good person?"

"Yes, sure, but..."

"But what?"

"Fine. With her you'll enter into the circle of the powerful."

"And you don't want me to become someone important?"

"What I was trying to say is that you'd stop hanging out with us poor, and, well... I'm not sure that you'd then be able to continue to fight the battle of your dreams."

Kissan set off. He glanced at Pushpa and said, in a loud voice, "I have no intention of marrying Satya."

Pushpa turned around and ran to the village. She had just passed the well when Harbassia called out to her, "What's going on, Auntie?" responded Pushpa.

"How often you call me by the wrong name."

"Oh, what have I said wrong?"

"Help me in drawing water, please."

"Auntie, the men..."

"Ah, there's no stopping you..."

"Oh, sorry." Pushpa was less familiar with Hindi terms of address than her parents' generation, unable to remember which form of 'auntie' was the right one here.

"The men will appreciate the water you're going to bring them."

Heat shone on Pushpa's face as she hoisted the bucket to the brim. Harbassia gazed at her a moment in silence. 'Why are you looking at me like that?" cried Pushpa.

"You've become very pretty, Pushpi," she said.

Pushpa blushed more. "Let me help you raise the bucket, Aunt," she said, this time using the proper, maternal form of the word.

"Well, there's no hurry. Let's chat. Let me tell you something, Pushpa."

"Oh, I know what it'll be. It's always the same with you."

"You have no more brains than your mother."

"Take the bucket away and raise it from the well. I also want to draw water."

"If you followed my advice, you could become a lady."

"Enough of that, Auntie."

"You are very stupid. Your mother and you could have assured your future."

"Good. I'll take my leave, since you want to leave this water here."

"Just come with me once. You yourself will see the mansion and you can judge for yourself."

"Fine, later. I'm leaving now."

"Wait, help me with this water first, birdbrain." Pushpa lifted the bucket and helped Harbassia balance the burden on her head. Before setting out on the fields, Harbassia looked at Pushpa one last time and whispered, "Think about it when you get back home.'

The girl gave a sigh of relief. Usually Harbassia was much more insistent. She boasted in great detail about the benefits of living at the boss's house and the enviable existence there... and she did not spare Pushpa's chaste ears in describing the services required in return. At home, Pushpa happened to talk about all the riches, the great white house, the toilets, the jewellery, the idleness that had been described to her... and her mother had immediately given her a slap in the face. It definitely quietened any of her temptations she might have felt.

It was very hot again. On the rest of the way home, Pushpa thought went back to Harbassia's terrible proposals. She was troubled and warmth enveloped her. Kissan, he seemed still so ignorant of these things... but he seemed worth the worry. Sweating, blinking, she felt as though she was falling into his arms, soft and plaintive. She finally arrived home and threw herself on the bed, shivering in the grip of a desire that rose in her like burning waves.

16

The first time Kundan heard Pushpa's name, it was from Kissan. When he visited Jatan, he had seen this dark girl with grey eyes several times. Now that he lived in Jatan's house, he saw her pass by every morning and evening. She lived almost opposite his house, on the other side of the alley that separated the two rows of huts. In the middle of the street, halfway between their two doors, was a large banyan tree that was a kind of platform. Pushpa would often sit there grinding her grain or mending clothes, and Kundan had plenty of time to observe.

She had already entered his house in his absence, like a little householder, tidying the room, washing the dishes. Kundan did know much about her, but when she spoke of Kissan, he felt a break in her voice, a deep affection and a molten warmth. There was an innocence in her beautiful eyes that moved Kundan. Her smile was so joyful, so spontaneous, that he dreamt of a bright future in which such a smile would always be displayed.

Since he'd lived in Jatan's house, Kundan saw Pushpa very often. One night he wondered: Pushpa's house was in front of his... and if Kissan came here more and the riverbank much less than usual, surely it was to come and see him, Kundan!

The more he questioned Kissan, the more he became aware of the young man's ferocious loneliness. The embers smouldering in him would eventually ignite them all... he knew the fate of two young people in whom the same spark had burned, and he told Kissan their story. Santu had died in prison, and Radha had been crushed under the wheels of a carriage. Kundan was afraid for Kissan, and he feared his untimely death. His apprehension grew since he met Pushpa and got to know her. He trembled for both of them now.

That Sunday, at sunset, he left his home to admire the colours and found Pushpa getting some air under the banyan. He struck up a conversation.

"Your *parathas* are really good," he told her.

"My mother doesn't think so. She thinks I roll them too thick and they look like *litti*."

"Your mother is too demanding."

"You really like them?"

"Of course, I wouldn't say so if not."

"You could be trying to flatter me."

"Tell me that you'll continue to bring me *parathas*."

"While I'm here, of course I will."

"You're thinking of going away?"

"Oh, Uncle."

"Pushpa, tell me, if your father was still alive, what would you call him?"

"Well, I'd call him father, obviously."

"No, I mean... you'd call him 'father,' or speak to him formally or 'papa' more affectionately?"

"I don't know."

"What do you call your mother?"

"Mama."

"That's what I meant. See, you love me less when you address me so formally."

"And if I spoke to you like a peer?"

"Well, then I'd say you loved me a little more."

"Okay, from now on I will."

They were both silent. "Pushpa, it seems to me that your mother is not very healthy. Why does she continue to gather the fodder for the foreman's cows? It is tiresome to bend and cut the grass."

"Yes, but we need it; this allows us to have a little to eat." Kundan learned later that as a salary Pushpa's mother received two measures of rice, three packages of flour, a handful of lentils and a quart of oil per week. In exchange, she picked up enough to feed three cows and ten goats. How could they survive on so little? One day he asked Phoolvanti this question as discreetly as possible.

"We both have a bird's appetite," she replied.

One evening while returning from the fields, Kundan stopped near the well where Pushpa drew water along with other village women. It was rare that a man intruded on a circle of women, and they were a little embarrassed by the sudden intrusion. Pushpa came to him with a laugh, "Are you thirsty, Uncle Devnanan? It seems Harbassia has not brought you enough water today."

No one doubted the real reason. Kundan stopped and approached the group of women. Two guards had come and he had panicked at the sight of a chain they held that reminded him sharply of his years in prison. He learned only later from Phoolvanti that the two men regularly patrol the village, so there was nothing to fear. Kundan finally relaxed. A chuckle came from between his lips later, as he stroked his long beard and moustache; he had become almost unrecognisable... but fear was always lurking beneath his confidence. For a moment, he had felt again what it meant to be a beast, always on the alert. He knew that feeling so well; it was like a parasite lurking in his innermost parts.

Sitting under the banyan tree, the women were trying to grind corn, but in a kind of hand mill whose whirring mingled with the song they hummed. The noise of the mill awoke in him memories of prison and the melody, memories much more distant, from his native village in Bihar. His mother had sung this song and he had not forgotten the lyrics. He recited in a low voice while the women sang:

Come quickly, and bring me news of our parents
I wait, my brother, come quickly.
The village well: is it still open?
Are the fields in drought or already planted?
If your wife does not let go, my brother,
Take that beautiful necklace away from her...
Come quickly, and bring me news.

Gautam's mother shouted at her youngest one to come and take a bath. Kundan rushed and grabbed the boy. His mother grabbed his shoulders, wrap in hand, and then raised her other hand to her son. Kundan intervened, "Do not hit him." The mother shook her head in a sign of protest; she had no intention of actually hitting her son. Kundan held the little one's hand.

Then he washed his hand and feet and returned to his house, losing nothing of the song that the women hummed in unison. His thoughts flew to the past and the prison, and then farther away to the horizons of Bihar... Pushpa was suddenly before him, bowl in hand, with two pieces of candy – cut cane – in it. One for him, and one for Kissan, who was surely soon to appear.

They stole candy on the sly, as well as cane juice. If the foreman caught them eating the cane, they had to face the boss with a charge of theft. The guilty were whipped with a stick spiked with cactus thorns until they lost consciousness. Kundan had never witnessed such a scene, but he had heard stories, each more horrible than the other, and the small piece of candy suddenly seemed undigestable, a veritable stone in his stomach.

As Pushpa returned to her home, Kundan noticed that the hem of her skirt was all torn. He had been told that only one piece of fabric was given to women every year. They had to cope with it, use it for both a skirt and a blouse. For men, they used it for a *dhoti* and tunic. If he looked closer, he could see that Pushpa's skirt could not survive much more mending. It would fall to pieces.

In the bundle that he had carried with him when he escaped from prison, Kundan had a piece of cloth. It was a yellow *dhoti* that had belonged to Mangru. Memories jostled at the gates of his memory, but he drove on. It was the first time he could give anyone a gift, and he would not miss the opportunity. He entered his room, grabbed his little bundle on the shelf and pulled out Mangru's *dhoti.* He turned the cloth over several times in his hands and examined it more closely. Pushpa could figure out how to sew a skirt and a blouse from it, maybe two.

17

Phoolvanti took the *dhoti* from her daughter's hands and looked at it, perplexed. She was deeply unsettled; it seemed to her that she was floating in the middle of strange visions, as if in a dream, from one vision to another without reason or coherence. But no, it could not be a dream. Outside, someone sang and the sound touched her ears, as real as the stuff she touched in her hands.

She saw herself on the river washing the *dhoti.* On the lower edge there was a stain caused by banana sap, its white juice never fading. And with the same sticky milk, Phoolvanti had drawn on the top hem a sign: Port Happiness. This mark was still visible. It was the same *dhoti.* Phoola watched everything around her daughter and the *dhoti* without being able to make a sound. Pushpa was frightened by this sudden expression in her mother's face, by the tears in her eyes, "What's going on, Mama?"

Phoolvanti made no reply; she hastily dried her eyes but the tears formed again immediately, obstructing her sight.

Pushpa repeated her question, but when she realised her mother would not be able to respond, she threw herself into her arms and hugged her. She felt her mother's hand caressing her hair, the same hand that sometimes slapped her. Slaps and tender gestures alternated according to an arbitrary logic to which Pushpa had become accustomed. But she felt this time it was not just a simple expression of tenderness... the pressure of the hand on her hair was conveying a new feeling, more intense. Outside, the sun was playing in the branches of the margosa tree and spots of light entered through the window, playing on the wall in darkness and shadow. In Pushpa's heart, a similar *sarabande* had begun, a game of hide and seek, disturbing and oppressive. 'Mama has noticed a detail in this *dhoti* that recalled the good old days,' she told herself. 'A memory of my father, perhaps.'

Her mother wept. Not that it was the first time, but today she wept unusually hard, and Pushpa, tight against her, waited endless minutes before her mother consented to let go and talk to her. 'Where did you get this cloth, my darling?'

"From Devnanan."

A moment later, Phoolvanti stood on Kundan's doorstep and knocked at his door, "Where did you get the *dhoti,* my brother?"

"It belonged to me, but why?"

"No, that's not possible."

"But then, what do you mean?"

"Do not lie, Devnanan, tell me the truth."

"It's true."

Kundan was silent then and Pushpa pressed him further. "Speak, Uncle."

"It belonged to one of my friends."

"That's false. It belonged to my husband," cried Phoolvanti.

"To your husband?' Kundan sat, stupefied. "You're wrong, my sister, all *dhotis* look the same."

"You were in prison, is that not true?"

"No."

"Loo, I'd recognise that among a thousand *dhotis.*"

"What was your husband's name?"

"Pushpi, tell him."

"My father's name was Mangru." Kundan was defeated.

In the alley, children were making an unbearable noise. A week earlier, on seeing them play cops and robbers for the hundredth time, Kundan had gathered them around him. He'd made a stick from a branch and had taught them how to play *gulidanda* to divert their attention from the eternal lure of the good guys and the bad guys. The children were delighted to learn a new game and they played it that evening, filling the alley with their screams, dust flying around them.

Kissan was returning from the fields. He looked for a little water in the bottom of the clay pot, but there was not a drop. He'd sucked on a piece of cane on the way home and his hands were all sticky. All he wanted at the moment was to join the children in their game and forget his troubles, to find that childish innocence and that indefatigable energy.

Instead, he felt depressed, exhausted and discouraged. Gopal's father, whom he'd once asked why he was smoking *ganja,* had replied, "to help with my misfortunes." Gopal's father gathered it in the woods; he claimed he was the first to grow it on Mauritian soil. Kissan tried it once. He took a puff of the cigarettes that Gopal's father made and it had not really done the trick. Instead of making him relaxed, it turned his head and made him sick.

He could hear the grinding of grain in the houses, the women making cornmeal to replace the inedible rice. He heard his mother singing inside, and her song, which usually soothed him, suddenly made him hate everything. It reminded him of the vermin that infested the rice bags and her voice seemed to pierce his skull like a relentlessly spinning top.

It was almost dark, but Kissan didn't care. He went to the river to wash and freshen up. Why was water from the village used to operate the mill, when it was built by the river? Another aberration... or rather one of their sadistic decisions to assert their power and make light of the villagers. This allowed them, as well, to bludgeon them a bit more when the rule was not followed... Kissan felt revolt rising within him, a bitter and burning wave.

He turned around and went to Kundan's. When he got to the house, he saw Pushpa coming out of it. He felt that she trembled when she saw him.

"Uncle Devnanan has just gone to the river," said Pushpa.

"Okay. I just wanted to say..."

"What are you talking about? Just go."

"Wait! I haven't even finished my sentence."

"If it's to tell me stupid things, don't bother."

"As you wish... but don't go, please."

"I'm going."

Kissan sat on a mat of reeds. "Please stay just a minute?"

'You've changed, Kissan. You would never have used that tone before, this drought in your voice. You walked with me, you told me stories and sang me songs."

"Pushpa, you're talking about a time when I had not yet reached the age of servitude." They were both silent. On the other side of the palisade, someone was singing the *Hanuman Chalisa* softly.

18

Phoolvanti rubbed a copper bowl with a handful of ashes, then wiped it with a corner of her wrap. She stared at the shiny object, glossy with time and usage, lost in her thoughts.

She had wanted to leave India and cross the seven oceans, to try her luck in the unknown, facing a thousand obstacles, if necessary, to avoid misery and hunger. That's what she had told her mother and the old woman had hugged her goodbye. She had never recovered from the death of her husband and harboured no illusions about the future. The epidemic had decimated the population, the drought had destroyed the crops, and the land gave them nothing else as far as they could see. At the other end of the province, there were more scenes of desolation. Phoolvanti's two younger brothers had died, starved and the elder had gone to Mauritius. Many of the houses were emptied. Black ravens gathered in clusters on the roofs of the deserted huts. There was not a drop of water in the wells, the tanks had been try for a long time, and even the streams no longer flowed. The vegetation had a yellow tinge that was becoming more and more prominent.

Phoola had not eaten for three days. The village was a mere shadow of itself as almost all of the inhabitants had fled. Death hovered over the dusty ground. Her mother was waiting for the next convoy to Banaras in the hope of meeting her end there.

Phoola was a trustworthy person. A small group of about twenty people had stopped in the village that day, headed by the leader Dhanwa. The man inspired confidence: he was wearing a deep red *tika* on his forehead that commanded respect. He said to Phoolvanti's mother that which he had repeated so many times, looking at the oldest woman in the convoy: "Do it as if she was yours, madam." And she had let go of her daughter. The last object in her little bundle was this little bowl.

Phoolvanti's mother imagined her daughter would find her brother Madho in Mauritius, and they would live happily, free from want. Hadn't Dhanwa talked about this island in wonderful terms? Yes, they would be all right over there. They would find comfort and wealth.

During the journey, Phoolvanti had thought a lot about her mother. She'd also thought it was going to be good in the new country. Once she had joined her brother, they would gather as much gold as possible and then return to India. Phoolvanti was then seventeen years old, with the naivete of a little girl of eight. It was not only her: the other passengers, all three hundred, dreamed and imagined exploring the wonderful island, bucket in hand, lifting stone paths to find gold in their shovel. After a week at sea, when they could see nothing, they asked the chief, "Are we not almost to the land of Mareech?"

"Patience, my friends. We are still some days away. Believe me, you'll all do well there."

But the day passed, and the passengers felt that the boat

was not moving, that it had stopped there in the middle of the ocean. Phoolvanti, on more than one occasion, was tempted to jump overboard and try to swim. Perhaps had she known what was coming... As expected, she regretted having left her mother alone and dying, especially as the duty of a daughter is to assist her elderly parents before having her fun. It made her sad, and she began to be afraid. What would the future hold? How would she live in this unfamiliar land? What would she do?

Since the beginning of the journey, a man wearing a flowered bandana had followed her everywhere. One day when the old woman, who had taken her under her protection was on the other side of the boat, the man approached Phoola and addressed her, "Why are you so sad?"

The girl's eyes teared up. Other than him, no one had addressed her; people were indifferent.

"Not homesick, is it?" he insisted in a gentle voice.

Passengers had no seats on the boat. They travelled seated on bales on board the ship's cargo. The crew treated them rudely, sometimes more harshly than the cargo. They held their breath and remained motionless all day, anxious not to interfere. One day Phoolvanti had been accosted by a sailor who caught her at the same time as he picked up the bag on which she lay. He suddenly threw it, and her, in the corner of the hold, and the girl screamed in vain, no one to come to her rescue even though there were many witnesses.

The solder was pushed against a pile of bags, and she saw him pocket the piece of money offered to him by a clerk, leaving and leaving her alone with the smiling, spineless clerk. He approached her and spoke in a honeyed voice. Phoola trembled with fear, wanting to disappear, to sink into the coarse cloth bundles. He put his hand on her skirt, but then a hand fell on his neck. The man in the floral bandana pulled him back and violently to the ground. They fought: the man in the floral bandana stumbled and her attacker fled.

Three days later the ship docked. There were three hundred and twenty passengers, three hundred and nineteen of whom came down to earth. Phoolvanti never again saw the man who took so much care of her and saved her honour. The Indian Ocean had custody of his body, stifling his cries in its unfathomable depths.

Since then, Phoolvanti could hear in the sound of the waves smashing against the rocks a complaint. Here, the sea lamented. And it had not stopped for thirty years. In her most painful moments, Phoolvanti wondered why she had left India. The miseries of the earth were not worse there... but the circumstances had not been favourable. Her elder brother had fled the country, wanted by the British because of his political activities. He was involved in the Independence Movement and travelled from village to village, getting farmers to rally around the cause. The colonists soon had him hunted down and he was saved by his exile. In retaliation, the colonists had taken, in addition to that which they had let fall to ruin from drought, famine, and arson, anything too ruthless for Mother Nature to reduce to ash. Within months, the state of Bihar had been sent back five centuries. It was impossible to live there. The country was a field of ruins; in the village, there was nothing left, and what had been a fertile province had become a miserable desert.

Today, Phoolvanti sometimes thought it would have been better to stay in India and withstand the rigours of that life. At least she would have been at home, in familiar territory, whereas here there was only misery and loneliness. 'But why complain when the bird pecks the whole grain?' Sometimes she had access to this lucid resignation, as when she learned that seven workers had their wages withheld last month, probably for a benign fault or one they had not even committed. 'Is this the price of our cowardice?' she cried. 'We wanted to escape the land of our forefathers because it was difficult, and this is what we gained.'

When they released Gautam from the small cell in which he had been locked up, he was half dead. Phoolvanti fed him only rice water for three days, as he barely had the strength to open his mouth. Gautam had been, for fifteen days, in a cage: a box of five feet by three feet with a peephole in the ceiling. Every day, he was thrown a handful of almost raw rice. The cage had not been cleaned for fifteen years, and never aerated to remove the stench. The treatment never changed: you stayed in for two weeks without coming out. It might yield a corpse bathed in his own excrement, or a dying man crawling miserably outside, covered with mud and filth.

At the end of the third day, Phoolvanti made Gautam swallow a little water in which she had cooked lentils. He began to regain the use of his tongue, and the first words he uttered were to ask for news of his father. But he received no visits from him. After two days of extra care, Gautam could get out of bed and walk around. At the end of the day, he went to visit his father's house, in which he had not set foot for many years. His brothers and sisters gathered around, his mother took him in her arms, but his father remained unseen. They made him understand they needed a man in the house, so Gautam decided to return to live with his family. Phoolvanti wept for joy at the news.

19

The moon appeared between the clouds. It was reflected now in the girl's tearful eyes. She turned to the boy, who had picked up a few dry branches and had lit a small fire. Both watched in silence as the flames rose. The atmosphere was heavy, charged with malaise and subtext. After a while, they got up and walked off in the tree cover, dislodging a rodent hiding in the bushes who fled at their approach. The rain had left large puddles between the groves and the slack water formed a dark mirror. The girl withdrew her hand from the boy's and flicked a pebble in the water, breaking the liquid sheet in a splash. Nearby was a clearing flooded by moonlight, and fields that stretched away. The millstones were shrouded in the same light. The night gradually took procession of the hills, valleys and mountains to the horizon. But the girl and the boy were insensitive to these sublime visions, closed off into themselves. A rustle of wind murmured almost noiselessly in the night.

"Why do you walk away from me?" she asked. He did not respond. "It's because of my father, isn't it? You are afraid of him."

"I'm not afraid of anyone."

"The bonds that unite us are still fragile," she whispered,

letting herself slip into the young man's arms. They were near the sugar-processing plant. The Creoles always opened the plant, and then fifteen men of the village were assigned to it. Satya, though, had come to seek Kissan.

"You know what the boss said to my father the other day?" Kissan shook his head. "He said I was the most fascinating daughter in the village. My mother told me. And you know what I said?" Kissan shook his head again. "She could tell the boss that I had found my happiness. And my happiness is you, Kissou.' Kissan felt heat rising in him, as Satya stuck to him, pressing so close that he lost control of his senses. "Kissan, if you say nothing, I'm not going to make conversation alone."

Her hot breath was close, and Kissan could feel her breath against his mouth and he was burning and could not hide his excitement. Above their ears, the moon's large milky eye watched them. The birds fluttered in the branches, and they could hear wing beats. A few drops fell and soon there was a light rain and finally a more serious rainfall. The two young people did not move; they froze, standing against a tree. Kissan, in a gesture of protection, tightened his grip. Satya's whole body was attached to his: her head was in the hollow of his shoulder; she was all pressed up against him. The moon hid behind the clouds again and darkness came. The plant, the village, everything was lost into oblivion. Her fingers caressed his ear and forehead, her lips hot against his said, "Tell your father to come and speak to mine, Kissou." Kissan felt fingers on his face, his neck; his body was raw, screaming with desire, a thirst for caresses and embraces. He saw nothing, thought of nothing more. The beating of wings brushed past them. "Answer me, sweetheart. When will you send your father to speak to mine?'

Kissan knew that this was nonsense, that the moment would pass, and he fell back from Satya, stood inert, without foundation. "I must go."

"They have not yet finished at the plant."

"I have to be in the fields at dawn tomorrow morning."

"Well, you have plenty of time."

"And if your father gets home before you?"

"Don't worry about it." She said this with such spontaneity that Kissan was impressed. If only the boys showed this much fearlessness! Kissan needed girls of this calibre in their fight, with their energy, their spirit. He didn't like those who modestly covered their faces and sought refuge from any discussion. But for now, he would have preferred a little less heat in front of him.

It stopped raining, but the moon remained hidden. Kissan had no idea of the time. He tried to scan the horizon in search of a glimmer, or a flicker of a lamp from the village.

"Come, I will accompany you until the gloaming."

"But the roosters haven't sung yet."

"You're soaked; you'll have to change."

"You're soaked, too, much worse than me."

"I'm used to it."

"When will I see you again?"

"Do you really think it's a good idea to carry on this way?"

"I know the one thing that will render a man indifferent to rain, heat or fatigue."

"Oh? What's that?"

"You know what I'm talking about...so why not start up again right now?"

"No, we have to go."

"Are you still timid around Pushpa?"

Kissan didn't answer the question. "Come on, I'll accompany you, then."

"It seems that as Pushpa hasn't had her dinner, you have to go, is that it?"

"I have to be ready to work."

"Your mother likes her, I think."

The night retreated gradually before the dawn. They set off. "You're not afraid?" asked Kissan.

"Afraid of you?"

"No, of the night. Of silence. Of being alone at night."

"But I'm not alone.' They could smell the cane juice heater. The machines must have overheated. Kissan understood immediately that there must be some operational failure and that the compressor was being operated by hand. It was so heavy that one would sweat profusely while operating its huge arms. Sweat would stream down the crops and workers, falling into the tank and the cane juice. Kissan had a strange thought of a juice so steeped in sweat that the sugar became dirty...

The torches that lit the plant at night spread their light nearby. The two young people avoided walking on open ground and walked instead next to the great wall that surrounded the factory. Inside, they could hear the foreman's cries, fragments at least, and the labourers' hard work. Kissan could imagine what was going on on the other side of the wall, and he could only curse his weakness. He stopped. "Good. I can go to work now."

"My father should be there already... what do you want me to do?'

"You should just go home."

"Home... why not? But first I want you to tell me when we will meet again"

"... . can you do me a favour?"

"Of course... tell me."

"First promise to do what I ask."

The distance between them was diminished again; Satya approached him and he felt his breath on her lips. "I'm already so close to you. How else does one promise?"

"I want you to talk to your father."

"About our marriage?"

"No, it's something much more important."

"Frankly, I don't see."

"Ask him to be a little less hard on us."

"As far as I know, my father is indulgent."

"They lie to you."

'You mean he's cruel?'

"If you don't believe me, ask people in the village."

"I will speak to my father, but on one condition."

"Yes?"

"Our relationship..."

"Ah, our relationship."

"This isn't important to you?"

"Sure, but what do you want us to do?"

"We could make it official."

Kissan knew that he could not be innocent much longer, and he knew that it would end like this. It was the same at each of their meetings. They arrived at the same point, then they separated and no longer saw one another for several days. Invariably, they returned to one another, moved by desire and secret hopes.

Kissan wiped his face on his shirt-sleeve. "I get a feeling your mother is not lying," he said.

Satya pinched him violently and ran to her house. Kissan turned back to his. He walked without seeing anything but his feet knew the way by heart.

20

It did not take long for those who kept watch to learn that Kundan's house had transformed into a meeting place. There were Hindi lessons for children, where those who knew the *Ramayana* came to chant it, and there was singing and there were meetings. Kundan had already been warned and knew he was under surveillance. He was almost cunning. The last meeting, for example, had been held on a stormy night and the rain had discouraged the guards. Discussion that evening had been underway for two long hours, and there was growing fear and hesitation, cooling enthusiasm in general. When the issue was raised of approaching other villages, Kissan volunteered. But others thought he would be more useful here, given that he was the coordinator. Sonallal was suggested instead. Kundan explained how they could introduce their ideas to neighbouring communities.

That night, they sang until the sun dawned and the rain stopped. Everyone now agreed that Kissan's fight was just and necessary. The labourers all listened attentively, and for the first time, the goals seemed to be clear in their minds. Kissan demanded their attention one last time and cried, "One day or another, we will have to go to war against the injustice to which we are subjected. Why not today?"

His words echoed in the room, and were met with silence.

Then another voice took over. It was the voice of the guard who patrolled the main street, "Wake up: the sun has risen. Get ready to go to work. The sun has risen, wake up." The lamps were lit, piercing the pale light of dawn and the clatter of kitchen utensils could be heard.

A small bowl in hand, Sonallal went in the direction of their closest neighbours, as he would do then every morning. Today, he would go to the Antoinette plantation, where his cousin worked, breaking stones in the fields all day. It was the biggest community in the area, with nearly three hundred people. He reached the foot of the hill on which it stood, his heart beating, full of temerity and apprehension.

When Raghusing learned what had been decided at the meeting, he flew into a rage. "In my day it was much worse," he roared. "At the time, there was just one large pot for cooking rice, and we were given one ladle each. We dressed in scraps from the jute bags. Girls were violated in front of their parents. We confronted this, and now the situation has improved, but you still want to have a revolution. That's exactly what it takes to ruin everything." The old man took a breath and continued the next instant: "Cursed generation. Young idiots, incapable of patience. Your hot blood makes you courageous, ha. Ah, yes, shouting nonsense, you are. What you have is not enough for you: you want more and more. If anyone stands in your way, pity on them. If you were alive in my day, I wonder if you would support your actions now."

Kissan let him talk. He knew it was useless to argue. It was a pity that his father's resentment was not directed at something useful. His own anger – what would that serve? Or was it just as powerless? Just as aimless as before? He had chosen to revolt, but he did not know what he would find down this road.

When Sonallal's mother learned that her son had gone to the next property over, she was seized with fear and immediately went to Kissan's house for an explanation. She arrived and found Raghusing sermonising. Seeing her in tears, Kissan's mother joined the concert of reprimand.

Kissan's parents had a son and two daughters. Both of their

first two children had died in infancy, just after birth. The village women said to the young wife, "It seems you are not destined to keep your children." When Kissan was born, Sonallal's mother took a piece of silver coin that she kept tied in a corner of her wrap and placed it in the hands of Kissan's mother. Then she took the child in her arms. It was thought that he owed his life to her. She did the same for the two girls and they had always attributed their survival to her. The three children had always enjoyed a privileged relationship with her; she was another mother to them.

Kissan approached and wrapped his protective arms around her shoulders. He said, "Do not worry about Sonallal, Mama. When he returns, he will have accomplished a very important mission."

Kissan did know what everyone was saying of this tour of the neighbouring properties: it could endanger his friend's life. He could not have taken the responsibility upon himself; he understood that his absence in the village would raise suspicion. Kissan had never strayed far from the farm, while Sonallal had more often done so. Nevertheless, Kissan could not help thinking that he had let someone else do the hard part.

That evening, when he was going to the river, he came across Satya on the edge of her father's field. She was holding an ear of corn. "Do you want it grilled, Kissan?"

"No, thanks."

"Ah, I won't let you leave until you taste it." A little further from the field, Satya's mother bustled around a small fire. Satya went and grabbed a golden brown ear of corn. "It's very good,' she insisted, forcing it into Kissan's hand.

"I don't want it."

"Then go, lie naked in the river."

Kissan had already stopped thinking of her, except for what Satya had said one day. "Kissan," she had said, "I was told you were very brave.' Was she mocking him? No, that wasn't it. There was no irony in her voice. And then the other people that the phrase implied, their opinions... but what had he done that justified such a reputation?

Kissan still had Satya's ear of corn in his hand. She often gave him little gifts like this, that Kissan shared with the village children. What would he do with the corn? The smell of it tickled his nostrils, made his mouth water. It reminded him of Satya's scent, soft and warm. He did not touch it, despite the hunger tormenting his stomach. He did not swallow a mouthful. He had said so and he would keep his word.

One day, Satya took him by the hand and led him to a field away from the village. The boss had given this field to her father, the foreman Ramjee, in reward for his loyal service. Kissan felt that day he was crossing a field of thorns. Pushpa's mother cursed that field and prayed aloud for the labourers' sweat to turn to hail and destroy its harvest. But it was not like that. The foreman had had a good harvest this year, even managing to use only the labour of the plantation villagers to do his work. He'd summoned one after another, after their day's work. Kissan was the only one who had never set foot there.

Three days passed. The season was in full swing; it was sweltering heat. Kissan heard the news during a moment of pause: Sonallal had been caught.

He had been arrested as he harangued the villagers of the neighbouring plantation and encouraged them to join the movement. The foreman had sent him, feet and hands in shackles, to the Lame Man. He had been stripped, plunged in a tub of sugar cane, and tied to a tree in full sun. This was how his comrades found him, hours later, his body covered with ants. He had lost consciousness in the roasting sun. No one was allowed to approach him; the dogs stood guard and everyone feared the boss's dogs. Most of the labourers, some of whom no longer had a hand or an arm, had already had run-ins with the dogs. No one wanted to run the slightest risk of attracting the ire of those savages.

Kissan ran immediately to the Lame Man's house. "How dare you come running in like this?" cried the doorman.

"I need to see Mr Raymond."

"He is not receiving anyone."

"It's extremely urgent." Kissan insisted enough so that the guard finally relented. Finally, he was before the boss. "If you please, it's about Sonallal, sir."

"You've come to tell me what I've already done."

Kissan was instantly seized by the back and dragged from the room. He was thrown out unceremoniously.

On the way to the village, he came across Satya and sat with her for a moment. This time, Satya suggested that she could get him a job at the sugar processing plant. Kissan had refused this offer in the past and he refused again. The idea of getting something on Ramjee's recommendation, as it would have to be, was intolerable. It horrified him.

He was used to the heavy work in the fields and he would continue to endure it. When the Indians worked at the plant, they were treated like slaves. Those that worked in the mill got more respect. Only the Creoles had access to lighter work. Kissan one day dared to ask why.

"Because they are not Indians,' came the response. He took the insult at face value and its venom stung for a long time.

Though they were perfectly capable, the Indians never played any prestigious role. Whites, followed by Creoles, had total control over the distribution work in the sugar factories. The Whites were at the top of the pyramid. Then came Creoles, whether their roots lay in Madagascar or in East Africa. At the bottom of the pyramid were the Indians. They reacted to the situation fatalistically and justified it by claiming there was no 'good' or 'bad' work. All the positions on the pyramid were prestigious...

Kundan would have liked to argue that, in the future, the Indians would take the reins of the country. "We do most of the hard work around here," he used to say, 'and we'll get to the top eventually.'

Kissan took up the refrain: "We remove the stones from the field; we till the land. We sow the grain, water the plants, spread manure. We cut the cane and transport it to the mill. They monitor the plantation, extract the juice and make the sugar. They benefit and they eat. Why? Is sugar a product so great that some can get rich just by it touching their finger?"

The canes were cut and the young shoots were beginning to emerge from the ground. Kissan saw Satya from a distance. He let her approach, his eyes fixed on the necklace and earrings she wore. He knew right away where the jewellery had come from. They belonged most definitely to a woman who had just arrived, confiscated by Ramjee under the pretext that she was not allowed to wear them here. Kissan remembered the day when Roopa removed her jewellery. "Coquetry breeds laziness," the foreman had said, "and here we need hardworking people without their noses in the air."

Kissan looked at Satya advancing, smiling.

"Satya does not need to work," Ramjee had said. "She can afford to be stylish." She was very beautiful, and adorned, Kissan could not help smiling at her.

"You look ravishing today."

Satya blushed and looked down. But she approached, coming so close to him that he could smell her perfume, which seemed to borrow the fragrances of all the woods and fields. He had sat near Pushpa the day before, breathing in her woody smell, and he recalled that scent that affected him so much. Satya... 'Pushpa was very beautiful, too,' Kissan thought, while staring into Satya's eyes.

He could not resist the thrust of this girl, a sensuality that drew him like a magnet. Satya seemed slightly out of breath and this slight panic in her chest and neck made her even more desirable. "You are really beautiful today."

"Do not look at me like that. Otherwise my mother will have my head," she said, laughing.

She threw herself on him, grabbing him by the hair and fixing her eyes on his. It was already dark there under the banyan tree that sheltered them, but Satya's eyes were bright and pushy. Kissan felt waves breaking in him as he sang softly in Satya's ear:

The foreman's daughter plays with her sling, catching birds,
she paints sindoor *on the parting of her hair to find a husband.*

Satya was not angry. Much later, they found themselves lying in the grass, short of breath, silent, a catch in their throats. It was Satya who broke the silence. Her voice seemed to come from her belly, sweet and loaded with sensuality, "I told you, you could have a place at the mill if you wanted."

"You keep asking because you see how tan my body gets in the field. You find me too dark, is that it?"

"No, not at all."

"Anyway, I'm not interested."

"Work in the mill changes you."

"I don't need to change."

"The work is much easier."

"I don't like easy work."

"Why don't you go work in the boss's house?"

"Never in my life."

"But why not?"

"That's not a simple question."

"How stubborn?"

"Drop it, please. I have to go now."

Kissan got up, but Satya kept a hold of his hand. "When will you speak to my father?"

"I'm never going to speak to him."

"If you won't, at least send your father to speak to him."

"You know, your father used to say something that I hate, but that in this case seems fair enough."

"Oh?"

"It's not impatience which ripens the mango."

"I get it." It was what the labourers got when they came to Ramjee to complain about their condition. No one ever told them that the situation was not going to improve. It was contrary to the basic principles of subjugation. Year after year, the labourers were fed illusions, told to wait and not agitate to make the fruits ripen.

Back in the village, Kissan found everyone under the banyan tree. Singing and dancing had resumed. Pushpa was standing on the sidelines, under the canopy at the threshold of his house, alone in the dark.

Before going back into his house, he'd wanted to bathe and wash in the river, but he had run into Satya and then wanted her scent to accompany him for as long as possible. He carefully avoided passing in front of his house to join Pushpa. Outside on the bench, he found a bowl with a bit of water; he began to wash his feet when his sister called from inside, "Don't waste any water; I haven't done the dishes."

Kissan wiped his feet with a piece of burlap hanging outside the door. He dried his hands on the sleeves of his shirt and sat on the stone near the door. "You aren't coming to dinner?" cried his sister.

"I'll eat later, thank you."

"But I'm off to sleep..."

"Go to bed, I'll get dinner for myself." He stood for a moment to listen to the snippets of songs that reached his ears. From time to time, he hummed a few words. He looked up at the sky, whose arch was slightly veiled, with only a few bright, tiny stars. Not a breath of wind. The smoke rising from the mill was bright in the sky, obscuring the night with its thick cloud. The land retained the heat of the day and the air was still warm. He thought of Pushpa, but in his mind an image of Satya immediately popped up. What a dilemma...

Kissan finally got up and left. The joy of music suddenly seemed full of vanity. It was an illusion of more. He'd had enough of all this hypocrisy. What should he do? This impotence gnawed at him, and the brutality of life overwhelmed him. How could he go about breaking this succession of days, each more daunting than the one before?

He reached the fence that bordered the southern part of the mill. The mill was a very high building, but fragile. The wood was rotten and the rope that connected each stake could easily be pulled down. The fence had stood for a long time, but only because no one would think of trying to destroy. It was exactly the type of action that would have been a strong gesture, but no one dared attempt it. The wall stood, apparently intransgressible. A strong wind would be enough, a good draft, a zephyr, a strong gust of air.

Kissan went back, shoulders hunched under the weight of his despair. His soul was plunged in darkness, and he walked with a blind, blank stare. An idea had been circulating for some time: that they should return to India. Immigration laws had recently changed and, under certain conditions, they now had the right to return to their countries of origin. The villagers debated continuously, and, of those who were eligible, several had already decided to return. How would they go? They could not walk home...

Kissan was radically opposed to the idea. He always defended his position, encouraging young people not to leave the island where they were born and which, in some way, had become their true country. Not everyone supported his argument. "Why hold on to a land where we live in hell on a daily basis?" retorted his opponents.

It was precisely this idea that displeased Kissan. Abandonment would lead to hell itself; it was better to try and make somewhere livable. 'No one should leave this country yet, in this sorry state. What a great legacy for generations to come,' he said at the end of the next meeting.

Gradually, after much discussion, his perspective gained ground. They could no longer consider Mauritius to be a foreign land after all that sweat and blood. If the country was now flourishing, fertile, and rich, it was thanks to the arms of labourers who had contributed to its prosperity. And did it not belong to them a little? "The pride of knowing that this land is ours is worth a few difficulties,' said Kissan. 'We have suffered to make it more beautiful and now it's time to reap the fruit of our efforts."

Meanwhile, Sonallal had fled, and he had said he was taking refuge on the Pieter Both mountain. Kissan went looking for him and found him, not without difficulty. He tried to rekindle the hope in his friend's eyes, but Sonallal was traumatised.

"Look at these fields. Green stretches to the horizon! We will not let the crops wither. Hundreds of plots, thousands of people like us are working to pull life from a new land. Some have an even harder life than ours, but more than ever they are willing to see their dreams come true. Make sure that hell turns into a paradise. Do not give up the fight now."

They gathered fruits to eat to appease their hunger. Sonallal kept asking questions to which Kissan could answer only with questions, and Sonallal understood that there was no response. Only action could put an end to all their questions. They began the descent.

'You see, Sona, it is sometimes more difficult to come down than to come up..."

Kissan took the clothes he'd brought for his friend out of his bag and helped him dress. A question was burning on his lips. Had Sonallal climbed so high in his state of exhaustion after he'd left that punishment? If he'd had enough power to climb, then the fight for freedom was possible. They might be physically exhausted, but their determination would remain intact. At the next meeting, Kissan would make this argument.

In late afternoon, he accompanied Sonallal to the river. Kissan was well aware his friend was still within the scope of terror. The shadows of the trees that demarcated the path made them jump. They had left behind the cane fields, already cut, and before them lay the cornfields they would soon reap. They passed through an ebony wood, the gigantic trees obscuring the light. The air was heavy, Sonallal was sweating, and his forehead was dotted with beads of sweat.

Kissan tried to reassure him, pretending nothing was wrong, trying to help the mischievous spark return to his friend's eyes. But Sonallal remained dazed, haggard and the depths of his eyes read only horror. Kissan no longer recognised the playful and vibrant young man who had been his friend. Any expression on his face was gone, and Kissan wanted to ask him to leave behind this strange lethargy that had gripped him.

The murmur of river water refreshed the atmosphere even before they entered the river. Heat dissipated on its banks. The two boys sat on a large rock and Kissan plunged into the water. "It's great, it's fresh," he said to his friend.

Sonallal clapped his feet to the water with a mechanical gesture. He looked away, staring into the waves, his body motionless, tense. Kissan took a little water in the palm of his hand and threw it in his friend's face. Sonallal jumped out of his torpor. He wiped the water from his face with the back of his hand and turned towards the bushes. "Did you hear that?"

Kissan didn't hear anything, but suddenly someone burst out of the bushes and advanced towards them. Kissan had never seen him, but Sonallal knew him. It was a resident of the nearby village where he'd gone on his mission. The boys jumped to their feet.

"How did you get here?" cried Sonallal.

The man sat on the riverbank washing his face, passing his

tongue over his lips so as to swallow the droplets of water. "The village chief sent me."

Sonallal looked at Kissan. The fear in his eyes had given way to intrigue. He was curious again.

"He wanted to tell you that our village is in agreement with the cause. We have sent an emissary from our village to the next village over. You have our support; that is certain. Our chief wants to speak to the man you told us about," he said to Sonallal.

Sonallal turned to Kissan, his eyes brilliant. He touched his friend's shoulder, "He is here, you can speak to him."

"Perfect. You asked us to make a decision as soon as possible: well, here it is. I was going to search for him in the village, but here he is."

"Rest a moment with us."

"I have to get back to the field tonight to guard it. The monkeys otherwise destroy the corn."

"Did anyone see you come here?"

"No, I came through the forest."

Kissan and Sonallal accompanied him as far as the margosa tree and took his leave. "You tell your village chief that I am going to visit him very soon," said Kissan.

The two young men sat down under the low branches of the margosa tree. This tree had a story. The head of the village, when he was still alive, used to say that Buddhists had been the first to tread on the island. It was they who had planted the margosa tree that had flourished ever since. He himself was famous for his Buddhist and altruistic advice. Work tirelessly for the good of others, he kept repeating. The old man was also a great artist; he had painted several images of the Buddha on the wall of his house and written some of his favourite maxims. One day, the foremen had come and daubed over the frescoes with cowdung.

Kissan had been young, but he had been shocked. At home, the 'Hari Om' that was painted above the door was covered over. All the inscriptions in Hindi were systematically erased. Anyone caught writing this language was immediately punished. Gautam knew someone who had received a dozen lashes on his back. Dawood's embroidered cap was confiscated. Kissan, to channel his rage, often wrote Hindi sentences on the rocks along the river. On the big rock where he would sit every night, he had written, 'A little respect for our work, please.' The eddies of the river broke against the inscription.

The two friends took the path back to the village. They walked side by side, holding one another by the shoulder and, for the first time, feeling there was real purpose to carrying on. Moonlight flooded the road and Kissan felt hope swell in his chest. A mongoose crossed the path precipitously. The croaking of frogs could be heard by the well by the banyan tree. The noises continued to grow as the boys approached the village. It was going to rain.

Usually Kissan rejoiced at the thought of rain, but that night, everything was changing and he could hardly stop the crazy machine that occupied his brain. 'Rain benefits crops,' he said to himself, 'and harvests only benefit the bosses: we do not get double the grain... When there is no rain, we get less grain. Everything to account, and never in our favour. Against us. Any drought, and our pay is cut right in half. Enough of rain. We cannot continue like this. Not with the beautiful shiny leaves that taunt us.' He tore one off furiously. 'We should pull out all the plants.' And he laughed at the thought. The vegetal scent that came from the crumpled leaf reminded him suddenly of the smell of trodden grass which had accompanied his antics of the night before. The rain would come, and it would cease, but the memory of this night would never leave him.

21

The old tamarind tree saw the seasons pass, saw its own leaves turn yellow and fall and then the next season of young shoots appear. The cycle repeated, imperturbably, year after year. Kundan admired the tree's ability to stay forever young, each new spring, even though around it, things had aged decades. The old tamarind tree had managed again to cover itself in shoots that would tomorrow yield fruit. This tree had lived entangled in human history, with memories of the past held close.

Today Sonit was hanging from one of its branches, dead. A crowd pressed around the tree, containing their anger in rumbles. Someone came running with an axe in hand.

"Cut down the tree."

"No," said Kissan. "Don't kill the memories." They listened to Kissan now. The noise diminished. 'This tree will survive us. It holds the memory of our suffering far beyond our death." A part of the crowd dispersed; people went home. Others stayed with the tree until the last moment. Sonit's body hung stiffly now, as the guards watched it.

"Please leave the body. We must cremate him."

This was more than the guards had expected at this hour. They had received orders and they would not cede.

Kissan and Kundan were able to keep the peace. They knew that nothing would tear apart the rope from Sonit's neck. The dozen guards were armed, unattackable. They had no position; to fight would be to risk too many men... Kissan tried to restore calm. He took a few steps back, looking at the rope hanging around Sonit's neck, and he seemed to feel the rope around his own neck. He swallowed more and more often, putting his hand to his neck, feeling a kind of nausea.

A little further away, a pyre had been erected and a fire already lit. Kundan, standing by the fire, felt neither the cold of the night nor the heat of the flames, through which he saw Sonit's naked body swaying at the end of the rope. It seemed alive, despite the odd angle at which his head met his shoulder. He dreamt, despite everything, of detaching Sonit and very slowly making him swallow a last mouthful of water.

The flames, rising high now, lit up like orange flares. Sonit's inert body was in a halo of golden light. Poor people came here to seek their fortunes and left as naked as infants. The tension had eased a little since Sonit had been found. A guard pushed the body with the tip of his rifle and the corpse swayed.

"At least he no longer suffers."

"Have you ever seen such an abject hanging?" murmured Kissan. But Kundan did not respond. Images were surging in his mind, unburied memories that brought tears to his eyes. The earth had swallowed up so many corpses... one day or another she would tell their story. All he could think of now was that the young needed to change things. The older generation had already served as a model and did its best to help them, but they were so ignorant themselves.

"Each generation will degrade with age. However, before sinking into a rehashing of its lost values, it should have the sense to discern what the aspirations of future generations will be. Otherwise, it is only reactionary, unable to understand or to communicate." This is what Kundan told the youngsters when they asked what should be done, although it was not quite the answer they were seeking. Basically, there was only one thing Kundan wanted to convey. "You should never rely on what the oppressers say," he insisted, "not one word."

In the past three weeks, the bosses had promised and then broken their word at least twenty times. Despite the intervention of the authorities, the situation had not changed. From time to time, the Special Commission and the League to Protect Labourers could intervene and protect them, but the changes they wrought did not last long and the fate of the Indians got worse again. Sonit had paid with his life for his visit to the authorities. He had been telling them of the terrible conditions on the plantation. Now he was hanging by a rope from a tamarind tree.

Everything seemed unlikely, meaningless. They had been ordered to leave the body in place for seven days. The guards who watched over the body kept a handkerchief to their nose because of the strong odour, fighting against hundreds of flies who buzzed around the body; emaciated dogs who tried to approach. Some said that the aim was to encourage the spread of disease. During the last epidemic, the village population had been severely affected. Only the medicinal plants that they had gone to fetch from a nearby village had saved some of those who were ill.

Kundan was summoned the next day to the boss.

"Do you know what he wants?" he asked the foreman. Probably he didn't know... anyway, he never replied. This foreman was one of the cruelest of the foremen. At the inauguration of the railway, he had been seen tying the hands of two labourers to the railroad tracks before giving the train the signal to depart. His own father had killed the youngest child in the village, who was buried in the field where he'd planned to lay the foundations of his own home.

Kundan went to the boss, his head buzzing. The boss began to speak immediately. "I want to make you a proposal. Your young friend, what is he called? Kissan, right? Jitwa tells me he is a very good worker. I intend to make him a foreman: he'd be the youngest foreman in the establishment."

"He has the skills for the position."

"What do you mean?"

"Kissan is a labourer. He knows most of the work in the fields and he does very well, too."

"Do I understand, then, that you agree?"

"Do not take this the wrong way... but it would be better if you ask him directly."

"So, I made a mistake by calling you here?"

"I did not say that. But it is not for me to answer in his place."

"Understood. Send him to me next Tuesday. The same time." And the Lame Man left the room without waiting for Kundan's response.

"You can go now." Jitwa stood in the doorway and beckoned for Kundan to leave.

22

A new *baithka* had been built between the ebony wood and the large field where the village children played *gulidanda*. A stream crossed the field before flowing into the river. Beyond lay a windswept plateau. Those winds came from the summits of which, from the plateau, there was a magnificent view.

From their last visitor, they'd been left some brochures and newspapers. Kissan concluded, after reading them, that the outside world was very different from his. It was impossible to measure by a simple glance at the horizon the vastness of the difference. He felt trapped in a measured space, like a dark box. Closing his eyes, he tried to imagine the world in its diversity.

He saw immensity and light, in that world that was not his, that would never be his. Even his own children would never have it – nor, perhaps, his own grandchildren.

Would that day come at last where the chasm between their world and the world of the whites would be filled, and would they finally get to the other side? Or was their only success at the end of each exhausting workday, as if that was all there was? Kissan was no longer alone in asking such questions. His friend Kundan also reflected on them and tried to provide answers to the many problems that made their lives unbearable every day. If young people could not find another strategy, Kundan knew, they would not get anything done and they would remain stuck in the same impasse. Fortunately, some of them had in them the acrimonious spirit that led them to face each moment head on. They often paid too much for it. But at least they were able to manoeuvre amongst the endless questions and illusions. What misery was theirs... what shame to be unable to raise themselves above the yoke. It was overwhelming for a man to feel this way and humiliating for him not to be able to react.

He never wanted to impose on Kissan. He had little to prove... he could not set an example. His only asset was his experience, and it was a rusty weapon with a dull blade. But he wanted with all his heart to help Kissan commit to the fight for a solution. He fashioned, in his own way, an escape for his brothers from their miserable condition.

Kundan was confounded by the carelessness of the labourers, especially of the youth, who routinely ignored the dangers. When he remembered his own youth, he did not remember himself to be so careless.

Kundan looked at the darker clouds arriving on the edge of the plateau. "Yesterday I was called to the boss," he said, when Kissan arrived. The young man realised immediately that it was serious. He had travelled the road in a hurry, and now he waited impatiently. Kissan was all ears. "I'm not going to sit here. The boss wants to name you foreman."

"Me?"

"Yes."

Two martins came quite chose, flying down and then turning sharply towards the sky. Kissan watched them a moment and then he turned to Kundan.

"Why me? Others might do just as well."

"Perhaps he'd already asked them."

"And you think they all refused?"

"Apparently."

"No, there's something not clear here. Employers make decisions and impose their will. They don't ask our opinion. So why did he waste his time proposing all of this to you?"

"To impose conditions." The two martins made another circle around them. 'How did you respond?"

"What would you have wanted me to say?"

"You refused, I suppose?"

"I said I'd prefer for you to give your own response."

"When?"

"Tomorrow."

"What should I do?"

"Decide for yourself. You're your own judge."

"Me?"

"Yes, you. It's an important post."

"No. Not you, too, Kundan... I never thought you put stock in such things.'

"And you? What do you think of them?' They sat side by side in silence for nearly an hour. Then they took the path home. Kissan shuffled his feet, concerned. The twilight had spread its sails on the field. The path grew dark and it seemed cramped. Outside the village, they heard a baby crying from hunger. "When they want to silence a dog, they stick a bone in its mouth," said Kundan as they entered the village.

Kissan lowered his head to pass the threshold in front of him and his friend followed, head held high. You never saw Kundan bend his back when crossing a gate, even a low one. This attitude was his futile resistance, a small clear act of defiance.

23

Pushpa had just gone to fetch water. As she headed towards the well, her mother looked away. The view of the trail filled Phool with sadness.

Later that day, she met Kundan on his way home. She tapped him on the shoulder to stop him. "Devnanan, I want to ask you a question."

Kundan did not reply, but sat down near Phoolvanti on the platform. His face betrayed his fatigue. He looked up at her, and with his fingertips he scratched the earth embedded in the palm of his left hand. She finally decided to speak. She had wanted to for several days now. "My brother, did you two meet?"

"What?"

Phoolvanti hadn't expected this reaction. She hesitated for a moment. "Pushpa's father."

Kundan saw emotion take over Phoolvanti's face and alter her features. He feigned incomprehension. "Pushpa's father?"

"The cloth that you gave my daughter..."

She was so agitated that she was unable to finish her sentence. Kundan looked in his heart. The images of his time in prison rose to the surface; he saw his friend Mangru and their conversations rose from the depths almost intact. He had fled, but prison was still present in him, lurking in a dark corner of his memory. He would never have conceived of such a coincidence. He wanted to wipe the slate clean, change his identity, his appearance, and even his memories. He had left Kundan in prison, dead like so many of his friends. Devnanan had replaced him. But suddenly, as if propelled by a thunderbolt, Kundan felt Devnanan to be a virus within him. Phoolvanti's voice interrupted his thoughts, "Please tell me, my friend."

Kundan was afraid that Phoolvanti would not be able to guard his secret. "How is he? How is Mangru doing over there?" she pressed. And suddenly pity took away all his apprehension. He felt his heart break, or rather liquify like wax. But how could he tell this woman the reality of the prison? How could he tell her about the humiliation and misery lived day after day in that awful place? If a lie would soften Phoolvanti's anguish, he would lie.

Telling her the truth would only increase her share of suffering. And she had plenty.

He lied and did not regret it for a moment. Kundan told Phoolvanti her husband was doing quite well, and in this he was not quite lying. Anyone who left the prison was doing better than he was when suffering the horrors of that hell. Mangru finally rested in peace.

Kundan stayed up all night. He was tense, anxious and unable to get rid of his feeling of discomfort. He was hardened with purpose, had driven from his hearth every personal feeling: he had forged an armour against the pain. But now the feelings he had buried deep within came back in full force. Compassion for Phool and her daughter filled his heart. He nourished his desire to see Pushpa throw herself in his arms. He had endured the worst of ordeals with Mangru and he considered Pushpa to be his own daughter. It made him more vulnerable than ever.

The night wore on slowly. A light rain began to fall. Usually, the sound of rain on the roof soothed Kundan like a lullaby. But that night, sleep had deserted him and the song reminded him of other drops of rain from far away in his early childhood. He was about five-years old and someone was singing to him nearby in a soft voice to lull him to bed. Kundan heard the melodious voice of the woman he called Bhawji.

It was all so far away... the rain was still falling in fine drops, but Kundan did not see the remaining ripples. The only thoughts that came to him were those of Mangru and Harbassia. The latter attenuated his malaise. Harbassia was the water carrier who slept with the boss. Kundan had never dared to ask her how she could be his mistress. The villagers did not like this, even though it was often in their interest. On many occasions, Harbassia had pleaded their cause in sensitive cases and obtained a reduction in punishment.

The rain had stopped and the insects had ceased their buzzing. It was the most oppressive hour of the night, dark and long. It reminded him of prison. Kundan closed his eyes and remained motionless until the tension he had accumulated decreased and then disappeared completely.

He woke up late. The sun was almost up. Kissan shook him with all his might.

"We will not escape tomorrow's lashings."

Kundan jumped out of bed, rinsed his mouth with a sip of water and grabbed his pick. He quickly rushed out and was on his way to the fields, where the work had started long ago. Kissan walked in front of him.

"Who woke us up this morning?"

"Mathura."

"He was just whispering, instead of shouting at the door."

"And you were sleeping like a horse.' They arrived at the entrance to the field where the labourers were working.

Ramjee saw them immediately. "And what time have you arrived, then?" They had already begun their work when he called them loudly. "Do you think you're all-powerful, or what?"

Two Creoles came forward and one of them grabbed the rod that Ramjee threw at them. Kissan cried, "If that rod touches either one of us, you had better watch out."

The three foremen froze in amazement. The labourers who had been stooped, working, stood up to better see what was happening. The two Creoles exchanged taken-aback looks, knowing that the matter was beyond them. One of them advanced towards Kissan, 'What did you say?'

"You heard me fine,' said Kissan in the same tone. "But I can tell you again, if you want. I know we're late. So what? This doesn't happen often. We'll stay later tonight to finish the job, nothing more."

The one who had the cane in his hand advanced, but all the labourers took a step towards him. He stopped short and looked around him. All eyes were on him. He had intended to continue, but it was better to stop there.

Ramjee and his friend did not try anything. There was silence, and then Kissan returned to his work place, followed by Kundan. The foreman stood motionless and watched their silhouettes advancing in the oblique light of the rising sun. The other labourers made no gesture as the two men returned. When everyone returned to work, they withdrew. The voices of men singing rose up:

The night has ended, our
nightmare finally over;
the day has broken,
we walk together...
still walk together, hand in hand...

This was the first song of the labourers that rose freely. It was heard on the neighbouring fields and rumours filled the atmosphere. The feeling of freedom raised their torsos, even though it was limited, as in their hearts remained fear and apprehension. They all knew that before long, the boss would come. Only Kissan did not care about the consequences. A few days earlier he had refused the foreman's post.

The sun had reached the woods where the foliage shone on Raymond's carriage. The sun shone on the edge of the trees and the light diffracted into a thousand shiny pieces that spread out over the fields. The foremen were agitated at the sight of the carriage and began to speak up. No sooner had he set his foot on the ground was Raymond assailed by their cries. They all told him about the incident at once. To everyone's surprise, the boss kept calm. He whispered a few words in Ramjee's ear and immediately the three men made their way to the tree and hung several bags from its branches. The labourers kept working. Even before they had time to understand, the foremen cut down the bags and the boss's dogs rummaged through them for food. Kissan was climbing on a rock to speak to the workers, but Raymond's voice stopped him. "Not a word," he thundered.

Kissan hesitated a second too long. Kundan was already close behind him. "Shut up," he whispered to Kissan. "You're courting disaster.'

Raymond continued to yell at them. 'Return to work immediately; otherwise, your ration of rice and lentils will be thrown to the dogs." The labourers stood still, waiting for Kissan's signal. When everything seemed in order, Raymond led Kissan and Kundan to the tamarind tree by the river.

"Congratulations," he growled. And he slapped each one of them. Kundan did not flinch; Kissan boiled with rage. "Another incident like this and all the labourers will be without food for a week. What are you trying to cook up?"

"We want to be treated like humans," answered Kissan in Bhojpuri.

"Speak French. I can't understand your savage language."

"We do not understand you either," said Kissan in Hindi. "What are you saying, idiot?"

Kundan interrupted. He knew a few words of French and used them to explain, "Patron, what have we done wrong? Since we have worked for you, it's the first time we're late. It's normal for it to happen once."

"It is not you who can come and tell me what is normal. I want to know what is on your mind."

"We told you."

Raymond screamed, straining his vocal chords, "I want to hear it from you."

"Until now we were used to bearing it in silence," responded Kissan in Bhojpuri.

"Speak French,' roared Raymond.

"But still we suffer. We have only one idea in our heads and you must understand us. We are human beings who deserve respect."

"Are you saying this to me?"

"Yes, to you, who takes men and treats them like dogs – worse than dogs." Kundan interrupted. 'Kissan, stop, I'm praying you will."

Raymond's already aghast face took on a red tint like that of a crayfish.

"Do you understand the consequences of what you're saying?"

"Go ahead, tell me."

"You will be thrown into prison for the rest of your days."

"Is that it? And then what will become of your green fields without anyone to work on them? Will they become cemeteries?"

Kundan put his hand over Kissan's mouth, "You're not helping matters, you know, Kissan."

Raymond wiped his face; he was sweating. "You must take your excuses to the foremen."

This time, Kundan responded first, "Excuses? Why?"

"Then you prefer the whip?" Raymond's voice had a lower tone, pouty, with the effect that it sounded louder.

Kissan responded in almost a cry, "There is no chance that we will apologise."

Raymond forced a smile on his face to hide his surprise. He felt fear suddenly. He raised his whip, but the lash never arrived. He stood immobile, indecisive. The sun had risen far to the west; it had not much further to go. Raymond had never thought a labourer would be this audacious. At the moment he was due to strike, something prevented him. It was the first time he had not followed through with the whip.

Raymond wiped his forehead and moved towards his carriage. The driver had not left his place, and the two Creoles stood there as well. "Bring me the two thieves," he ordered, before getting into the carriage. When he was gone, the foremen came. "Well. Do what you're told."

The labourers had already regrouped around Kissan and Kundan. The foremen turned around towards the carriage, but it had taken off. "Let's get back to work," Kissan told his comrades.

"We will not let you go it alone," cried Sonallal.

Kissan put his hand on Sonallal's shoulder, "Come on, get back to work.'

"Listen, it's the first time we've stood united. Do you think it's a good idea to stop your friends in their tracks?"

Kundan responded to that, "What matters is to move forward together, regardless of speed. One thing at a time... when opportunity strikes. When one rushes, it can ruin everything. I speak from experience."

"I think now is the opportune time."

"You'll understand when you're not in the heat of action."

"We took a long time getting angry... so we had better benefit."

"Sonallal is right: now is the right time to act."

"No. Enthusiasm and passion are not enough."

"Wait, and get back to work. We are headed to the boss's house."

"Kissan, this is your chance to get rid of this powerlessness which you have blamed for so much."

"Yes, Kissan. If you prevent us from acting today, you'll regret it."

Kundan raised his hands in a bid to get everyone's attention. "Give us two hours. If we haven't returned, then you can start the assault. Until then, get back to work." There were murmurs, but everyone took his advice.

One voice said, 'Devnanan is right.'

The two men went then to the boss's house. Neither of them seemed outwardly anxious, but they felt a gnawing within. Two guards received them and took them to Raymond, whose eyes were red and swollen. But his face was calm again, and hard. In a slow voice, he called a guard, "Make them shirtless and give them each twenty lashes."

Kissan and Kundan were returned to the fields before the agreed time. They were both smiling broadly, and this was the first time anyone had been seen leaving that house with a smile.

That evening, when they got back to Kundan's house, they massaged one another's back with soothing ointment. Despite the whip burn, they fell asleep immediately. The night was short and tomorrow would be a new day, in which some incredible surprises were still to come.

24

The air was stifling and at night they could barely distinguish the line of the road. Kissan was so tired that his eyes were closing on their own. It was mechanical. Fear and anxiety gripped him. If Sonallal had not been with him, he would have turned back. His friend looked up to try and see some stars in the cloudy sky. They had already reached the junction, after having crossed the river. At first Sonallal did not want to face facts, but now he knew without a doubt that they had gone astray.

"What's the matter?" Kissan asked.

"I think we've gone the wrong way."

"... what should we do?"

Sonallal made no reply but, feeling his way, he spotted a tree with a smooth trunk and climbed it. Once at the summit, he looked around him and what he saw was reassuring. To the west, a few twinkling lights. Approaching the hill, the path that skirted the village. The ebony trees were so thick in the woods they had not even noticed the lights. He came down from his perch.

"We have left the village behind us."

"How? What now?"

"We must turn back and return to the south." They began to run silently. Sonallal regained confidence and, as they approached the village, their fear diminished. Nothing was ruined by entering the village from the wrong end. The last time they tried to enter, they had very nearly ended up in the firing line of the guard who was monitoring the main access point with a good rifle. They'd had to go home.

But tonight, they crossed a wooden bridge and arrived safely on the outskirts of the village. A raffia braid served as a fence; they slipped below and went inside.

"But beware of dogs," Sonallal whispered. Followed by his friend, he went towards a light he had seen from afar. Sonallal had no doubt they were still awaited. As they approached a hut from which came the sounds of soft speech, Sonallal pressed himself against the door and called softly, "Hey, friends, open up."

"Who is it?"

"It's me. I'm with Kissan. Open up, quickly."

The young men entered to a room lit with a dim oil lamp. About twenty people were gathered there, their faces drawn with fatigue. The two young men sat in the circle and discussions resumed.

As head of the village, it was Luchmansing who spoke first. He asked Kissan several questions posed by the villagers. Kissan tried to answer each one and also to explain what had already begun in their village. But not everyone understood and he'd had to explain again, using arguments he'd brought up constantly when discussing matters with the labourers in his own village. Roosters could be heard crowing when Luchmansing called the meeting to a close. "Kissan, if you could come back tomorrow evening after your day's work, we could discuss this a bit more," he said.

"It will be more difficult to avoid the guards in broad

daylight..."

"Don't worry about that; we'll deal with them."

"I'll be waiting near the banyan tree," said someone else.

"Okay, then, I'll be here as soon as possible."

The man who had spoken was a very young man. He accompanied the two friends to the other side of the enclosure. "Everyone does not agree with our village chief," he explained. "But the young people do, and we are fully committed."

"That should be enough."

"This matter is sparking arguments in all our families."

"Don't worry, it will get better."

"One of us left the village yesterday to visit the village on the other side of the mountain."

"We would like to meet them upon their return."

"Yes, I'll see to that."

As soon as they arrived back in their own village, they could see the lights and hear the clatter of dishes as the women prepared the rice. They separated and Sonallal went to his home. Kissan, on the path to his house, stopped by Munia's house. He called her outside. She emerged on the door with a pan in one hand and a lamp in the other.

"Ah, Kissan, it's you. Come in."

"No, I'll be late for the fields. How is your father?" Munia did not respond and Kissan understood that her father was not feeling better. The old man had been bedridden for more than three months and a doctor had not been sent to his bedside, despite multiple requests from the villagers. Recently, Kissan had been harassing the foremen to send someone. They always responded the same way: "For minor illnesses, medicinal herbs should suffice." But the *panditji* had tried every remedy he knew and had found nothing to heal the old man. Discouraged, he had confessed his powerlessness.

Kissan glanced around the room. Munia's father was lying in a corner and in the dark, he looked as thin and dry as a skeleton. His skin had turned a leathery brown. Eyes wide open, he stared at a point in space. Sunuwa, his son, should have been at his bedside and should have been in charge of his father's care, but since he lived with Marceline on the other end of the village, he only gave his sister half of his salary, keeping the other half for his mistress.

Kissan look leave of Munia. He got home to find his father had a fever, as well. The young man approached and put a hand on his forehand. Raghusing looked pale, and asked his son, "So, where did you spend the night?"

Kissan was silent.

"It'll all come crashing down one day."

Kissan motioned to his father to keep quiet, that he was too ill to make a speech. He took his bag, his pick and his lunch, and headed out. "I'll be late again tonight," he said to his mother.

On the way, Kundan told him that Phoola was bedridden too. Fifteen people were already suffering from the same fever.

"Let's hope it's not a new epidemic," sighed Kissan. He thought of three years ago, when almost sixty people had died. One after another, they had fallen ill. In a week, twenty people had passed away. They could not even cremate the bodies and there was no religious service. The bodies had been piled in a cart before burial in a mass grave dug in the forest. Kissan remembered the atmosphere of those days.

The boss came into the fields in the morning. Kissan came up to him, his pick on his shoulder.

"You're coming like that?' shouted Raymond.

Two foremen were immediately next to him. Kissan put his pick on the ground and went up again. "I have something important to say.'

"I do not have time; go away."

"An epidemic is developing."

"So what? What would you have me to do?"

"We need doctors and medicine."

"It is we who decide whether to send them to you."

"Once everyone is dead..." The two foreman restrained Kissan with their arms and kept him immobile until Raymond descended from his carriage. All the labourers were on the other side of the hill and could not see anything of the scene. They could see only when Kissan resumed his place, pick in hand.

He had seen his people die like cattle. Throughout the island, hundreds of people had been killed during the last epidemic.

Carts carried fifty corpses each. The mass graves contained many more. Kissan remembered the day they buried one of the dogs in the same pit as its master. At the thought that his brothers would suffer the same fate, he felt his heart jump and his mind become indignant. 'Impossible," he said. "This is one of those diseases caused by the change in the season. The *panditji* will find some remedy..." With each stroke of his pick-axe, Kissan repeated these words as if they had the power to ward off the danger.

It was almost dark when he arrived at the first building. Kissan could see that the houses of Luchmansing's village were arranged in circles, which offered a much larger central space. It seemed much friendlier than the narrow band separating the two long rows of houses in his own. To the east, the mountain ridges formed a bulwark and brought a security that one did not feel in the plains. He felt protected by the peaks. In the middle, stood a peepal tree whose shadow housed the well.

Kissan was led immediately to the village chief. To enter his house, Kissan went through a fence and arrived at a typical house, where the roof was of bamboo and the interior walls were of vacoa leaves. On one side, though, there was a picture representing the battle of Rama and Ravana. Luchmansing took a seat and motioned for Kissan to do the same.

Luchmansing told him what had happened that day. "This morning, Nandu was released from prison. He had been there for two days. He wasn't wearing a shirt, and you could clearly see the whip-marks on his back. He carried a blue skirt and a white blouse, and no one asked him what he intended to do with them. Well, we know what is associated with women's clothing... Many of our girls have clothed themselves with such products before going to the boss's house. Every time I try to intervene, but to no avail. One day in September, he had been sought for the same thing. He cried, but I could not do anything. Two young women, Bhagwati and Tangechi, have already committed suicide: hung themselves. Two others drowned themselves in the river's fast currents. Nandu may become another suicide. Tonight, his own daughter has been called to the boss. He came begging to me. 'Luchmansing,' he said, 'I am holding my daughter's shroud.'But, despite his prayers, Nandu knows that there is nothing we can do. His daughter, Rekha, will go. Even dead, she would be taken...

"Nandu lost his wife six months ago. When he heard the news, he fainted in the fields. The foremen said they enjoyed the comedy; they seized him and threw him off a mound. He injured his left leg and his ability to do the job. For days, he refused to eat, for he couldn't bear to be a burden on the community. Then one day, the foreman saw him refuse food. If he'd had full use of his leg, he would have been able to get away, but he couldn't. The first lash of the bamboo stick didn't hurt: he screamed with rage rather than pain. He went crazy. I can still remember his screams... like an injured beast. 'It's my choice,' he cried. They whipped him until he was silent.

"The boss and the foremen have taken to calling him 'the black cat.' They say he has nine lives, because he's resisted their blows and their punishment. They've done everything... he never lowers his head. One day, they took him out to sea, tied him to a boat and then left him. His life was saved in a storm... the winds reversed the currents and the waves brought the boat crashing back to the reef. He escaped unharmed... Another time he was shot, but the bullet went through his shoulder and he survived. In the field, supervisors made him lift huge rocks that four men could not carry. His legs bear the traces of the dogs sent to chase him and scars from the lashes he's received. But he's never submitted.

"His daughter is the most beautiful girl in the village. The boss has had his designs on her. But she's not only beautiful; she is also brave. She's always put him in his place when he was inappropriate. Rekha has inherited the beauty of her mother, but her mother was not so courageous."

Kissan went with Luchmansing to Nandu's. When they arrived, the man was holding his daughter in his arms and both were sobbing. Kissan saw a young girl with tearful eyes, and understood why the whole village was ready to sacrifice for her. Her beauty took his breath away. Breaking away from her father, Rekha fell at Luchmansing's feet. Nandu's sobs gradually ceased. "They will come looking," he said.

Nandu looked like an old man, tested, branded. They could see his bones through his skin when he leaned. In his eyes, everything was gone; they had the radiance of two dull pools. He had a beard and white hair, and an ascetic look. Everything had been conspiring to crush the man, destroy him, but he remained alive and Kissan could see the audacity in his drawn features. Although Kissan knew nothing of him, he understood that he had a personality out of the ordinary. He only wished he'd met him sooner.

Today, he seemed to have lost his head. Nandu cast lost, distraught looks around himself, his expression that of a trapped wolf, his mouth a bitter and cruel shape. Rekha kept a straight face, as if all emotion had deserted her. She looked first at her father, then Luchmansing, and read the prayer in his eyes. She seemed unable to utter a word. From time to time, sobs shook her.

The clothes had been thrown on the ground. They lay crumpled in the dust, but even so it was obvious they were beautiful clothes compared to those Rekha was wearing, which had been mended and patched a hundred times. 'Like those of the women in my village,' Kissan thought. He would have done anything to bring a smile back to the girl's lips. Nandu seized the hands of the village chief and implored him, 'Take Rekha to your house. They will be here soon.'

"Nandu, you know that they will find her there, as well."

"But if we interrupt them... we are five hundred in the village."

"Nandu, we all love Rekha like our own daughter, but..."

"I will not send her there. They should all die, those dogs, drown in their own manure, impaled..." He tore into his hair. Kissan stepped forward and took Rekha's hands.

Others were coming to the house. Some had even come inside. Suddenly, someone shouted, 'The carriage has arrived."

"No, no," Nandu yelled, stamping. He flung his arms widely, hitting the walls.

Luchmansing approached Rekha and put his hand on her shoulder, "Come, my daughter, come to my house."

Nandu suddenly stopped waving his hands about. Luchmansing has started to walk away with his daughter. He turned to look back at Nandu, "Nandu, I'll take care of her. You save youself.'

"Truly? You'll hide her?"

"Yes, but please, save yourself. Hurry up and run away, otherwise..."

"Otherwise the dogs will cut me to pieces. Don't worry."

Rekha rushed out to meet her father for a last hug but Luchmansing held her back, "We have no time to lose." The crowd that had gathered let them pass.

Luchmansing ordered them to disperse quickly. Then he strode away, followed by Kissan and Rekha. At the threshold of his house, Nandu looked away. He could hear the wheels of the carriage on the way. Those who were still about advised him to flee, but he remained on his one good leg, motionless at the door. Outside, the night was quite dark.

When they arrived home, Luchmansing fetched a bundle and handed it to Rekha. Then he turned to Kissan, "Here begins your first mission. I will entrust Rekha to you. We'll go together to the enclosure, but then you must take her away from here alone. In the future, our two villages will be linked in action. But you must protect the honour of our daughter; in return, you can always count on us. Do you think yourself capable?'

"Absolutely."

"Come then, we'll leave from behind."

For once, Nature was in their favour. Heavy clouds darkened the sky, and the night was inky. They crept in the dark until the enclosure and then Luchmansing stopped, "Well. Farewell and good luck, my children.'

Rekha fell to his side, shaken by sobs. Kissan heard her voice for the first time, a voice broken by grief, "Take care of my father.'

'Pay attention to your way, and do not tarry."

Kissan helped Rekha over the fence. He felt Luchmansing's eyes on his back, following them. The old man did not leave until he saw the two silhouettes disappear into the depths of the wood. They walked as fast as the opaque darkness allowed. Often they stumbled, but they fell quickly back into their stride. Each insect noise, each snapped branch, each birdcall or bestial cry worried them. They would stop, listen, look without exchanging a word, regain their breath and then carry on. Soon, they heard the barking of village dogs.

They stopped running and Kissan became aware of the responsibility he had been given. Rekha, because of her beauty, symbolised the wealth and honour of the villagers. They had placed in his hands a treasure, a supreme good that usually would not consent to depart. His responsibility represented the confidence afforded by the village and Kissan felt his courage grow, as if the villagers were walking beside him. He was the only one who could guarantee the safety of this precious young woman and this pride helped him master his fear. He turned to Rekha, "You're not afraid?"

She did not answer. Kissan did not know where to go. His only idea was to put as much distance as possible between them and the village they had left. They were already out of range, but the young man did not want to take any chances. They heard a rubbing noise nearby.

"A herd of deer," he said. He could not see anything in the dark night, but he recognised the sounds of the animals running through the woods, their sides brushing against the low branches. They were not boars: too bright, too fast. Kissan had one day chased a fawn he had seen near the river. He had not been able to keep up with it, very fast even though it was very young. If only he could run at the same speed... 'Would I run away?' he said to himself. Deer were always in motion, flying from one shelter to the other, but they died in the forest in which they were born. 'And us? Will we, too, get caught in this forest?'

He kept going as fast as his feet could carry him. Suddenly, he realised that Rekha was no longer with him. He stopped and went back into the night. Even before he saw her, he heard her crying a few feet away. "What happened?"

She stopped crying and Kissan approached her. She was sitting on the ground and the young man lowered himself beside her. "Have you hurt yourself?" he asked softly.

Rekha was silent. They did not hear the sound of insects, nor a breath of air, nor the rustling of the leaves. The sky was starless and, above their heads, motionless. The air was heavy and full of sweetness. They sat a few minutes without speaking, until the clouds thinned in the west and let the stars appear. The heavy perfume of the vines and creepers exhausted them, with their physical fatigue doing the rest. They could fall asleep, but they needed to continue. The guards could still find them...

'Are we far from home?' Kissan asked the silent night. Kundan often said that the night had no ears and today Kissan understood what he meant. Gradually, the rest of the stars appeared, peppering the sky with a faint light. Kissan continued his inner monologue. 'How far are we from the stars? Infinitely far, certainly... but that may be shorter than the distance between labourers and their employers. Kundan said the other day that even if we reduce the distance between the earth and the stars, we cannot fill the gap between us and Raymond.'

What a night! The locusts had resumed their squeaky chorus and they had become even more tired. They walked in the dark, their legs heavy and had to sit down again. A few drops fell. "You'll catch cold," said Kissan.

They took shelter under a tree. When the rain had ceased, they continued to walk. Kissan still did not know where they were, but it seemed they would soon reach the village. They should no longer be too far. He looked again into the night for clues, but he saw nothing, not even the light of one lamp. He thought about what Kundan had said about blindness preventing man from recognising what he wants. 'Sometimes,' he'd said, 'When you reach a destination, but it fails to meet your expectations, you can spend several hours turning around. You might even arrive in broad daylight."

"And then what do you do?"

"Get sent to prison, where you exercise in the dark." Rekha had gotten left behind again. Kissan felt she was struggling behind him. The darkness had lost its density gradually, as the clouds dissipated. The young man turned around and called behind him, "Are you there?"

She started to move again, as if the mere act of being spoken to was enough to try again. Kissan had not heard her voice since the night before. The dawn was coming, but the hours before that seemed endless. And the day would bring new dangers. They could be found more easily. When dawn did rise, Kissan saw two whites coming towards them on horseback. He pulled Rekha into a ditch and they fell flat. They spent the day tiptoeing from one hiding place to another, often in thickets. The day was much more dangerous than the night.

25

Finally, they found their way to the fields. Rekha had no energy; her feet were leaden. She was breathing heavily and yet she did not stop. They reached the outskirts of the Pieter Both mountain, which Rekha had heard of so many times. She had dreamed of seeing the landscape and now she was going through it as if on a race, pursued by dogs, harassed by fear and fatigue. They attacked the foothills at full breath, sweating enormously, and the sweat evaporated leaving them with a strange sensation of almost absurd freshness. Kissan seemed at times to be at a loss. "How will we be saved?" he asked, stopping suddenly, then changing his mind and resuming his course, thinking of the dogs at their heels, the punishments if they were found. 'We must save ourselves and flee,' said his inner voice. 'To hell with these ideas we hold on to even at a loss to ourselves...'

When they reached a hillside, Kissan turned. The valley had disappeared under the fog, like a milk-filled bowl. They saw no one and nothing, but the sound of voices reached them. The sun continued its course towards the horizon, towards the sunset. Like the birds, they could see the sea stretched before them, reddened by the sun. The mountaintops were purple and dominant. Gradually, the colour of the sun on the sea faded to orange. Then they regained the blackness of night. They walked, groping, as small animals grazed their feet and ankles and ran away. The moonless sky was desperately short of stars, but for them the darkness was a blessing.

News of their flight had spread and they had dogs loose behind them. They could hear them barking in the distance. Torchlight tore holes in the ink of the night. Kissan would have preferred to continue through the bush, but because of the dogs, he chose to stick to the thickets. He entered one now and Rekha followed. Coming out of the thicket, they found a slippery slope of rocks. It seemed too dangerous to venture forward. Kissan stopped. Around them, bats flew within inches of their hair.

Kissan had hoped to make camp when they crossed the river, just before nightfall. But the guards and their dogs followed them and now he no longer knew where to go. The only sound he was able to perceive was his own breathing and he was so tired, he could not think. He imagined being torn apart by dogs, caught by the guards and sent before a boss who would whip him to death before throwing him in jail. He tried to calm down and listen, but he heard nothing now but the sound of rain. Feeling his hair wet with water, he opened his mouth, raised his face to the sky and collected a few drops on his lips. He had not had anything to drink since the night before...

He had almost forgotten Rekha, who followed him like a shadow, pressing forward when he pressed forward, pausing when he paused. He drew her to him and hugged her in a gesture that betrayed his distress. Kissan saw a dim light, later, and guided their steps in that direction, hoping with all his might that it might be a village... his village. But, as he approached, he realised that his fears were accurate: they had gone in the wrong direction. 'If Devnanan were doing this, he would have gone the opposite way.' They turned around and Kissan assured Rekha that he knew where to go. He said that their march in the opposite direction would not be for long.

They soon reached the outskirts of a large plain and before taking the path upon it conclusively, Kissan wanted to take a break. He pitied Rekha, who never once complained. She refused to stop, terrified at the thought of being caught. She had only one thing on her mind: to finally enter Kissan's village, where Luchmansing assured her she would be safe. She could hardly stop walking.

Despite her discretion, Rekha's presence did not help Kissan. He was so disturbed by the responsibility that had been placed upon him, he was unable to think. He was in uncharted territory and to move around when he did not know the area was terribly difficult. He was scared, but Rekha was scared also, and he was then more worried than if he had been alone.

The night withdrew gradually and the first light of day seeped into the darkness. When they had advanced upon the plain, the sun was rising and they could finally see where they were. They perceived a kind of roaring and shouting in the distance. Only when they reached the plateau, did they understand. They were directly overlooking the sea and a view opened up before them of which Kissan had dreamt dozens of times. He contemplated it: the beach where his father had arrived on the island. On the beach they saw a building. On one wall there was a small platform. Just behind it stood a guard, a rifle on his shoulder.

Seagulls circled, screaming. Rekha finally spoke, "Where are we?" she asked in a voice distorted by fear.

"Now that the day has broken, we will find the path." Kissan did not voice his fear of being seen in daylight.

A boat was moored on the beach. A board acted as a gangplank for the passengers. Those who had disembarked were lined up in a row, their baggage at their feet. Guards circled around them. Before them was a scene Kissan had only heard of: behind a large parasol, a small group of whites, whips in hand, hotly debated the price they would offer to buy the new labourers. The passengers were numerous; the majority were men, but there were also women in long skirts and saris, and children. As the labourers unloaded the ship's hold, blacks held the reins of the boss's horses.

Kissan had heard a lot about the sea and he knew it had never been far away. Yet he had never seen it, and he discovered it was not like what he had imagined. He saw only infinite expanse, without waves or swells. From his observation post, he could not hear the song of the ocean; only the rumble of the surf, which nonetheless gave his heart a huge thrill.

But he saw, too, the miserable state in which the passengers had just arrived. He could read in their bodies, in their faces, in their helpless attitudes, the cruel disillusionment they were undergoing as the shadows extended around them. They had left their country for what they believed to be paradise, but now they had set foot in hell. Two guards brutally pushed a woman from the top of the gangplank. As far back as he stood, Kissan could hear her sobs. He could not restrain the tears that came to his eyes.

They had to leave. A guard could look up and see them, and it would be very difficult, then, to escape. And the spectacle upset him, burning his eyes like a hot bar of iron. They resumed their journey. Fatigue marked Rekha's face; she looked drawn and her eyes betrayed her exhaustion. They went through a wood of casuarinas and ended up on a hill. To the east, the sun had already passed the treetops. They found some fruit to satisfy their hunger. Kissan's confidence returned. By the end of the day, they would find his village.

From time to time, he would ask Rekha a question, but she was not very talkative and he did not insist. They reached a waterfall and avidly drank the fresh water that ran past the rocks. The perfume of the flowers made the air delicate. Yes, they were in paradise... they carried on.

Suddenly, they heard a noise, a rattling of chains and strikes. Not far away, prisoners were working on the rails. They turned around to skirt the site. They also avoided the fields where the labourers were busy. The sun started its descent. Kissan wanted to climb a coconut tree, but Rekha objected: "This is not the right time to climb a tree."

"Why? The devil decides the time," Kissan said, laughing.

She nodded, with all the naiveté of the superstitious, "You go on then. One day, my uncle climbed a tree at this time of day and fell off."

"The devil pushed him," Kissan said. Kissan leapt onto the tree. At the top, he threw down a coconut and then jumped down. His eyes shone, "We are almost there. I just saw the hill at the back of my village."

Rekha's eyes brightened for the first time. Kissan opened the coconut and handed it to Rekha. They both drank the milk. By the time they had eaten its creamy innards, they were headed towards the hill. Kissan preferred to bypass the ridge, as they would be most visible at the top. They had regained strength, but they were not any safer.

When they arrived at the village, Rekha gave a sudden cry, "And if the guards get us here?"

"Don't worry. They have to circulate in the entire village." But she continued to whimper and Kissan, too, felt his apprehension rise.

"What will happen to my father?" she asked.

"Nothing, that is what I have been told," said Kissan, without any conviction. What would she have him say? They washed their hands and faces in the river. Some of Rekha's freshness and beauty reappeared, despite her fatigue. Her bright eyes were vivid, intense. For the first time, as he dipped his hands in the water, Kissan thought about his two friends, Pushpa and Satya.

As darkness fell, they saw few people at the entrance to the village. They crossed Hamza's mother at the well. Kissan did not know what to do. Should he take Rekha to his home or to Devnanan's? What would his parents say? Although he had spent one night away from home, he felt he had been missing for an eternity. It was better to go straightaway home.

He brought Rekha to the courtyard of his home, where they were greeted by his mother and sister.

"Who is it?" called Raghusing to his wife.

From the tone of his voice, authoritative and annoying, Kissan knew Raghusing was feeling better.

26

Most of the others who'd been afflicted were feeling better, too. There was less reason to fear a new outbreak, now. The *panditji's* tisanes had been effective.

The young man was feeling more upbeat after getting home from a visit to Kundan's that afternoon. Then several of his friends came back from the field. Their knapsacks were flat, desperately empty. The rice and lentils for the week had not been distributed. Kundan asked why, but no one could tell him.

The committee met that evening. Sonallal and Kundan made their reports on their contacts in the neighbouring villages. Kissan spoke of his mission, and of Rekha. Everyone agreed that she must be protected. Kundan summed up, finally, the villagers' situation: many families were starving. Hunger was not new, but the magnitude of the situation was unprecedented. Kundan also spoke of a granary near the mill, full of provisions. "Why do they let us starve when the granaries are full?" Some saw a golden opportunity to take their long-awaited revenge. Kissan heard them present their point of view and then spoke, advocating immediate action, as firmly as possible.

Kundan alone objected, "I had time to observe what is happening in the two villages with which I made contact," he said. "Similar things are happening everywhere. So I suggest that we wait until we are able to rally with four or five villages together, and only then act."

Kundan spoke at length and explained his project in detail, explaining patiently every time someone raised an objection. Kissan knew that the first action had to be infallible; it was the only way to succeed. Without having prepared a sufficient response, they risked derailing the whole project. Before separating, they all recited the verses of the *Hanuman Chalisa*. Everyone then thronged the door, but Kundan held Kissan back, "Stay a little longer," he said softly.

He waited until the room was empty and remained silent for a moment, sitting next to Kissan. "What did you think of this meeting?"

"It was by far the most interesting of all those we've had. We're finally organised."

They commented on the points raised during the meeting, discussed a bit. Then Kundan came to the point, "Have you seen Pushpa?"

"No."

"She is very sad ..."

"Why?"

"Because of Rekha."

"What do you mean?"

"You could have prevented this."

"Prevented what?"

"She is jealous and suspicious. You could spare her that."

"But what is she jealous of?"

"Be kind to her. I'll see you tomorrow morning before work."

When Kissan returned home, he found his mother lying on the single mat. Beside him, his sister and Rekha were not sleeping, and were chatting quietly. They were silent when he entered the room, and Kissan thought of Pushpa. So, she was jealous...

The next morning he found her busy grinding rice in a mortar. Kissan spoke with her and and did not find any reproach in her voice. Kundan was mistaken... They talked long enough and not once did Pushpa allude to Rekha's presence. Kissan was careful not to bring up the subject.

On the road leading to the fields, he met Dawood. "We live in rainy days," he said, putting his pick on his shoulder.

"I feel that today we can cope," replied Kissan. "We've had worse; the present is bearable."

"How much longer will we suffer this treatment?"

"Until we can do more. How old is your little brother?"

"Two and a half."

"Soon he'll be older, and he'll look around at what we have left him. Do you want him to suffer the same humiliation?"

Dawood did not answer. They reached the field, but were turned away. It was announced that they would not sow today because the rain was not due to stop for at least a week. The foreman directed the labourers to a field in the middle of which they were ordered to put a pile of large stones. The rocks were enormous and it took almost the strength of three men to lift one. Some of the labourers could not even roll them and their cries of pain could be heard when the whips of the foremen fell on their backs. Those whose hands were bleeding pressed against the largest stones and pretended to push them to take a moment and wipe their skinned palms. Kissan looked at Dawood and murmured, out of breath, "This isn't the kind of life you want for your little brother."

Half-dead with fatigue, he fell, then he received an initial boost, then a second wave and a third ... The sun was setting. The horizon was tinged with purple, the colour of the flowers just before cane-cutting. The lyrics of a song came into his head:

The fire that burns on the mountain
everybody can see, my brother.
The fire that burns in my heart
no one can see, my brother –
nobody sees it.
Broken rice, one house from another,
they are divided, my brother,
but human suffering:
how do we share it, my brother?

Rekha stood before him, silent, while Sandhya gently applied a balm to his wounds. The hair on his back, gluey with blood, looked like tiny rows of cane. In his feverish eyes could be read an infinite obsession with the fields.

Rekha slowly approached him. "Does it burn?" she asked in a timid voice. Kissan motioned that it was better. Rekha did not move; she was now near his shoulder. "No news from my village?"

Kissan made no reply, but stood up and sat on the bed. He grabbed the bowl of water Rekha handed to him and swallowed in one gulp. "Are you worried about your father?"

She grabbed the empty bowl and turned before leaving the room. Kissan glanced at his sister. Sandhya smiled. "She is really nice, eh?"

"Is that a remark or a question?"

"A question.'

"What do you think?"

Sandhya did not have time to answer, for her mother called out, "You have not lit the lamp, my girl? First check whether there is any oil left."

Kissan closed his eyes and imagined standing on the top of the mountain that was shaped like a man. He looked down and was dizzy, wanted to raise his head, but could not. Kissan kept his eyes closed. Kundan's voice aroused him from his drowsiness; he'd come in and was shaking him violently. "Everyone is ready. We're waiting for you outside." Kissan jumped out of bed. Outside Sugan Bhagat was singing:

More flour, more salt
What will I put on my plate, my dear?

Your home is too humid
My meal is all wet.
What will I put in my oven, my dear?

27

Kissan was trying to overcome the despair that overwhelmed him periodically, when he felt the situation was so cruel that he could not imagine any solution to his problems. Sometimes, he felt so tired that he aspired to stop thinking, stop feeling. The *Vedas* often said that true existence is the one that has encountered many obstacles, and faced the worst. The sacred text could be read to say that man did not gain his status as a human being until after having triumphed over his last obstacle. But what was the last obstacle? Kissan had no idea, and, to date, no one had ever given him any clues. He was preparing to undergo the worst punishment he could imagine, without abandoning his repeated attempts to break the yoke that held him so firmly.

"Do you think it will change one day?" Rekha asked him.

"Yes, I think so." But his voice was a little hesitant that evening. When he thought about the future he had the impression that their destiny would play out on the flip of a coin. But to think about the end result, whether defeat or victory, was to do wrong: this was also one of the lessons of the *Vedas.*

"It's too dangerous," said Rekha.

"All games are dangerous..."

"We must have a little patience."

"You see that mountain? It is she who can teach us patience. Because she has been waiting for centuries, still and heavy. But tell me, Rekha, what's she got after all this time? Nothing."

"So why engage in a losing battle?"

"The goal is not to win but to fight."

"Is that all?"

"Yes, that's all."

"Even if we know we're going to lose?"

"When did you learn to speak, Rekha?" The girl was silent. She was naturally quiet; she listened very carefully to people and did not interrupt.

Kissan launched into a long monologue, "We do not want a palace, nor do we want to feed our dogs with what would be enough to quell the hunger of scores of workers. As long as our feet will carry us, we will not need carriages. We do not wish to accumulate a lot of unnecessary clothing. But that does not mean that we are ready to be crushed, our breath suppressed and our land taken. We do not ask for butter and cream with every meal, but at least we demand rice, and not accompanied by lashes. We want to work hard in the fields, shed our sweat and give the best of ourselves, but not in exchange for kicks and bamboo strikes."

Kissan liked to talk that way to Rekha. He knew she understood and approved of it. He had never forgotten the day with her when he saw the sea for the first time. Since then, he often thought of the ocean. 'When the fight ends, will we be free at last to contemplate the beauty of the vast sea?'

He had been captivated by this spectacle and when he told Kundan of his fascination, his friend had described other landscapes that he had seen on the island. Kissan wanted to see the sea and return to the visions of paradise he never tired of admiring. The night before, he had been so tense that he had a hard time falling asleep. Tonight, he sank more easily into his dreams. He saw himself in a dream with Rekha, visiting all the island's beaches. Sometimes the sea was calm, sometimes it was boiling, a wave of destruction in a storm-like whirl. Always, it rolled to their feet in a resounding splash. The ocean was a changing colour, ultramarine blue to pale green. And these colours took on infinite shades, ever-changing hues. A rainbow in the sky appeared before them and they ran to meet it.

The next day, Kissan told Rekha of his dream. She listened attentively. "Don't you feel sometimes like running behind a rainbow in the sky?" she said at last.

"Why do you ask?"

"It's just a question; you can't ever catch it."

"The true dream is to achieve the impossible, don't you think? After all, you were there with me in the dream..."

Rekha did not answer. The mill siren buzzed in their ears. The early morning breeze blew timidly. In the soft light, Rekha looked to Kissan exactly as he had seen her in his dream, except she lacked a nose ring. In his dream, she also wore earrings, bracelets on the wrists and anklets. But it was the same girl, no doubt.

In the evening, returning from the fields, Kissan learned that some labourers had decided to leave the village. They wanted to abandon this miserable life and move further into the interior, where it is said that the earth was of seven colours. A labourer from a nearby village had told them they could make charcoal to ensure a comfortable income.

"You are all cowards," Kissan reproached them.

There was a meeting that evening, not in the *baithka* but on the central platform, under the banyan tree. Rekha, for the first time, participated in the discussions. Her voice, soft and deep, left an impression on Kissan. 'Suppose we manage to run away from here... there is no guarantee that we can stay in another place and that we should not have to run away again. We can spend our lives running constantly and never find peace. It took us twenty or thirty years of this dog's life before thinking we could improve our situation. Why not, for once, fight this fight to which we have committed ourselves?"

It was a way of seeing things that had never been put forth. A great silence followed, then the discussions resumed. They did not hear any musical instruments that evening, only more discussions in which everyone took part. Finally, those who were to flee the village abandoned their project.

Kissan went home around midnight. Lying on his bed, he looked through the little window at the starry sky and he seemed to see a star brighter than the others, one he had never observed. His excitement and joy, caused by Rekha's speech, kept him from sleep. From now on, nothing could stop him. Devnanan was not alone at his side; there was also Rekha. Her presence strengthened his conviction and courage. He felt invincible.

In the next room, Sandhya and Rekha did not sleep either.

While he tossed and turned, Kissan tried to find the dream of the previous night. But his thoughts were so agitated that he managed to find only fragments of dreams. Not one of these pieces belonged to that dream. Kundan's words came back to him just when he was waking. "Kissan," he said, "this is our first battle. We must not let our forces fall apart at the crucial moment."

But why did he say that? What did he mean? Kissan felt that it could have been Rekha. And he'd immediately exclaimed, as if to defend himself, "But Devnanan, what makes you think we can be divided?"

"I am saying that we must remain united on the same front, without being dispersed. We need all our concentration directed toward a single goal."

Kissan could not understand what Kundan was driving at. At the time he sat on a pile of dry leaves between the rows of cane, his head in his hands. 'And if we lose this battle? But why would we lose? For a thousand reasons... No, there is no good reason.'

These were his thoughts in the field in the morning when he heard Raymond's booming voice. The servant who supported the palanquin in the front tripped, causing its collapse. Raymond came out of the palanquin and already had his whip in hand. The whistling of the whip cracked in the hot wind. Not a sound came from the mouth of the bearer. He whipped the man with a vengeance and then Raymond and Ramjee approached the man, who was lying face down. With one foot, Ramjee turned him on his back. He remained unconscious... Another foreman turned him on his stomach.

"He is finally dead," he said, looking at Raymond. "It's true, sir, he is dead." That night, it was this scene which haunted Kissan's sleep. The beaches of paradise were far away.

28

Seven villages acted in concert. An uneasy silence invaded the fields. Sitting under a peepal tree, Luchmansing harangued his men, "Do not let anyone run away."

Ramotar Mahton, of the coastal village, had gathered all his labourers on the beach. In a voice filled with emotion, he declared, "One hundred days for the jeweller, one day for the worker."

Mukhram Sav gave the same speech to the people of his village, "We will cut off once and for all the bitter cane."

The inhabitants of Kissan's village gathered along the river. Kundan spoke, "It's time to show what we are truly worth. Just as when Hanuman revealed his true strength, we face a challenge united today."

The sun had not even risen when the foremen came to the field. The labourers turned a deaf ear. No one left the rocks on which they were sitting. They sang the quatrains of the *Ramayana*. Moreover, in seven places, the labourers of the villages were singing the same verses with the same determination. This lasted all day.

At dawn, the boss appeared at the edge of the river in his palanquin. He was surrounded by four guards and began to threaten them all, then relented and exhorted them, "You are ruining your future by following a few agitators."

Kissan laughed. "What future? Have we not already established the stakes?"

The palanquin left; then the sun went down. The labourers continued their struggle. Emissaries crossed in the night, ensuring that all were prepared to continue. None of the seven villages had received food and men were dispatched to the woods in search of fruits and tubers.

The next day, the same scenario was repeated. The fields were empty. At gathering points, the labourers sang. The foremen and guards watched them, helpless. In the evening, the leaders of each village met in a secret meeting.

The fields were again deserted the next day. It rained heavily and the labourers sat in the shelter of the trees. The bosses of the seven plantations met. They had waited until the threat had continued for several days, until the ideal time for planting was about to pass.

That night, the employers agreed on a meeting with the representatives of the seven villages. It would take place in the coastal village. For the first time, carts were sent to fetch those who lived far away. And for the first time, the labourers came up on the verandah of a big house with their heads held high. The bosses spoke, one after another. Of the labourers, only Kissan opened his mouth. When the bosses understood that neither their threats not their cries would intimidate the seven men, they got up, went into the house and came out later with glasses in hand. There was a long silence. Raymond finally took the floor.

"Well, tell us a little more about what exactly your complaints are."

Kissan could stand no longer. "Can we sit down?" he asked in a weak voice.

The bosses looked at one another in their chairs and Raymond nodded. The seven representatives sat on the floor. Kissan spoke a bit with the others in Bhojpuri and then he spoke in Kreol. "Our first demand is the right to respect. Stop treating us like animals; we want to be seen as human beings. We do not ask for affection, but at least spare us your strikes and blows. We were already given that promise, but it has not been kept... I speak on behalf of the labourers of the seven institutions represented here. We are ready to starve, but we have our demands."

"Well, what is the next demand?"

"First accept the first one."

"We first want to know all your requirements," said a big, broad-shouldered white boss sitting next to Raymond.

"Our second demand concerns the freedom of movement. The villages are virtual prisons. We want to be able to move beyond the enclosures."

"Is that all?"

"We are seven, and say each village has different requirements."

"Continue."

"We demand the right to form village committees and hold meetings, and also religious services."

"But that you do already. Otherwise, how would we be here?"

"Yes, but we are forced to do so in secret. Our fourth demand: we do not want to be deprived of food or medicine."

"In my property, no one is deprived of food or medical care,' cried the big boss.

"We are not talking about a specific property. If our demands are not generally accepted, tomorrow it will not be seven villages, but seventy which cease to work."

"But you threaten us."

"No, I only hold you to account. It's not over: our fifth request is for women and girls in our villages. You must respect them. In this last month alone, four girls have committed suicide. And finally, we want our children to be able to learn to read and write.'

"So these are your requests."

"And if they are not granted?" asked another boss.

"I already spoke of the consequences."

There was silence. Then the owner of the coastal village got up and looked closely at the seven men sitting on the floor. Finally he turned to friends and broke the silence, "You will have our answer in three days," he said in French.

"The answer lies in a word, yes or no, and we want it now."

"I tell you that you will have it in three days."

"Then we will resume work at that time."

"Bastard," roared the boss.

Kissan rose and his comrades did the same, "We have not come here to be insulted."

The boss lashed out. 'Get out,' he cried, pointing the way with his finger.

"Very well, we will leave. Let us know your answer in three days."

Kissan and his friends were heading out when the big boss stopped them. "Begin your work tomorrow. We do have the right to reflect for three days."

Outside it was night and a storm rumbled in the distance. As the lightning came closer, they heard the first drops crashing.

Kissan protected his head with a hemp bag folded in four and walked away in the rain. We will resume work in three days,' he said back.

"Tomorrow we will send you your rations of rice."

"Do it in three days." The seven men left in the rain. The others returned to the house, where dinner was waiting.

They marched to the coastal village, whose representative led them to the village chief. They were ready but tired. On the threshold, they took off their hats. There was a stove and what cooked on the embers filled the room with an appetising smell. In the light of the flames, the village head's hair took on the colour of cane creepers. With respectful gestures, he asked his guests to sit down and served them himself before starting the conversation, "So they have accepted our proposals?"

Kissan turned to the head of the village. He chewed on beans. "We have to convince him," he said, his mouth full.

"You mean they did not agree?"

"They require a period of three days to think it over," Kissan responded.

"Why?" Receiving no response, the village chief left that line of questioning. "What do we do now?"

"There will be no sowing."

"Okay, but if after three days, they refuse?" They waited for the rain to calm down a bit and took their leave, each on his path home. The storm roared no more, but lightning crossed the sky from time to time. Kissan paid attention to the direction he took; this time he'd decided not to make mistakes along the way. Devnanan awaited him halfway.

29

The labourers stayed at home for a fourth consecutive day. The sun was hiding behind the clouds. It had stopped raining, but the weather remained overcast. The river was almost at flood level. In the fields, the cane had recovered and had a new sheen of green. But the farmers themselves did not look better and the smile of Nature, refreshed, was not reflected in the faces of the bosses forced to cancel their hunting party. They had agreed to meet the next morning.

They decided to agree with what Kissan had proposed the night before.

Although Kundan was absent that day, with only a few who knew the reason, the labourers did not want to wait. By this time, with the weather heavy and wet, it was better than sitting around on the rocks doing nothing. They would not have to look far for wood. They cut down some trees in the forest, they took up large rocks here and there and began to clear land on the banks of the river. It would be the location of the first *baithka*. Everyone thought that, by devoting two hours daily, the house would be built within the week.

Some expressed reservations: because the land did not belong to them, building a *baithka* there could attract trouble. Kissan replied that the land belonged not to the bosses, but was property of the state. It was resolved once the house was built, they would notify the government by post. The *panditji* had some knowledge of law and confidence enough to remove their last doubts. What they needed was to build the *baithka*. As for the consequences, they would see. The *panditji* had said that the labourers had never shown such courage.The town bore witness.

The villagers were sweating profusely in the hot and humid air. They had sent the women into the fields to pick the straw that would form the roof. The straw was soaked and could easily be tied in bundles. Work had been the currency of all four groups who took over part of the construction. While working, Sugan Bhagat sang:

What pleasure do you feel, my prince
when you oppress the poor and make them cry?
This field is yours, the sweat is ours,
and yet, my prince, you do not want to hear us.
What pleasure do you feel, my prince
in exploiting us?

The sun was hidden and it was hard to get a sense of the view. The birds had gone with the last rays of the sun among the treetops, to the west. The mill was not working, otherwise they would have heard the siren at night. Kissan was concerned about Kundan's absence. He should have been back by this hour. What was his mission, anyway? He stopped Sonallal. "You said Devnanan left?"

His friend looked at him in wonder. Finally, he answered, "He's gone in search of Ramjee."

"Why?"

"Satya told him that you have Rekha hiding at home."

"And so?"

"Then he rushed to Luchmansing's village to tell the foreman there. When Devnanan found this out, he ran off behind him. He went saying,'I wish I knew how this traitor was going to meet his earthly end."

"Why is it that I didn't know?"

"I thought he would have told you at home."

Kissan calmed down a bit, "You didn't try to stop him?'

Sonallal did not answer. Kissan was scared now. But impatience took over. He knew that the owners would find them the next day. He had found out from Gaston, a Creole who worked at the plant.

Kissan was beginning to understand that he had been overconfident. He'd imagined the victory already... but the whites were far from being as flexible as the bamboo sticks with which they had the habit of striking. He had made the mistake of believing he could convince them quickly. Now, it was more evident than ever that bosses did negotiate with the workers, but what else would happen?

It had been four days and they had eaten nothing. Provisions that they had been sent from the neighbouring villages had lasted two days. And now Kundan had disappeared suddenly. Kissan was so eager to know the answers that he felt overwhelmed by a kind of torpor that only the presence of his friend could dissipate.

It began to rain.

The night before, when he was in heated discussion with Gautam and Dawood, Gopal had mentioned Ramjee, "Can you explain how, in the blink of an eye, Ramjee was able to acquire so much land?"

"No need to widen the head to figure out," replied Dawood. "Everyone will agree that was by betraying them that he got all this. "Why talk about what everyone knows?"

After a pause, Gopal continued, "My friends, since it is through us that he has achieved his harvest, we should have a share of whatever is grown in his fields."

"Right."

"And it is also true that right now we do not have many dining choices..."

"I see where you're going with this..."

"Why should we die hungry?" Gautam said. "So we should take a share of Ramjee's harvest. It's a perfectly valid argument."

"Then you're ready?"

"Why not? My father always taught me that we should not hesitate to steal what belongs to the devil."

That night, the three boys made their way towards Ramjee's field, two large jute bags in hand. They came back with loads of corn and sweet potatoes.

The wind rose up, but the rain would soon stop. Pushpa took advantage of the weather to go with her friends to the banks of the river. They brought filled flatbreads and boiled potatos. Pushpa left the company of the two young labourers and headed for Kissan, who was busy digging holes around the enclosure posts. The young man stood up on seeing her.

"It's raining again. Go and take shelter under a tree."

"Did you hear what Harbassia is saying?"

"No. What is she saying?"

"She claims that there will be a cyclone."

"Just because she said so doesn't mean that it will happen."

"The sky was red yesterday afternoon."

"Forget it. And take shelter."

"It's nice to get wet."

Kissan took refuge under the tree canopy and Pushpa followed. "Kissan, cyclones destroy houses... and they dash hopes."

"Devnanan hasn'tcome back yet?"

Pushpa removed a piece of bread from her bag and handed it to Kissan. Before taking it, he stepped forward and held out her hands to the water of the dripping leaves. Then he wiped them with a corner of his *dhoti.* Then he came closer to Pushpa, but took the bread and sweet potato and began to eat. The others devoured their meal in silence.

"You're not sad, Pushpa?" Kissan asked between bites.

"Why? Because we have nothing to eat?"

"No, not because of that."

"Why should I be sad?"

"I wanted to be sure."

"No. I'm not sad at all."

"I'm glad then, Pushpa." The rain stopped, but still, drops pierced the canopy of branches. Kissan noticed in Pushpa's eyes tears that glistened, but he took them for raindrops.

30

"We have taken the first step. We cannot go back." Kissan repeated these words as much for himself as to convince others. He had found it hard not to sink into despair and his friends noticed. Others preferred to say, "We dared to brave the dragon, now we must expect it to break loose."

But anyway, all were eager to know the outcome. More than ever, Kissan was worried about Kundan's absence. He sat like a caged animal, depleted by worry and anxiety. No doubt his friend would have known how to calm him. Rekha was worried for him and his mother too.

"Your eyes are so sunken these past two days that you could put a handful of rice in them," said Rekha.

Kissan buried his head in his hands and sat down opposite the picture of Hanuman. He had no strength to pray, but he needed to temper the internal fever that had upset him. He felt responsible for the fate of too many people. His father had warned him, "Kissan, you're going to put the responsibility of a thousand people on your back. If you win, everyone will be happy. But if you lose, they will fall all over."

This was no time to think. He remembered a remark Rekha had made and his dismay, and it made him smile. "How is it, now that you have played a decisive role, that you are in such a state of lamentation?" she asked.

Kissan looked up and saw his mother in prayer. She invoked the Sun God, Surajnarain, to attract favour for her son. "We prefer to die of hunger if it will stop these atrocities."

The truth is that Kissan had always shown a lot of hesitation, and reflection. He would never have imagined that the resistance would be so great. He doubted everything and kept questioning. 'Why do they not react faster?'

He had always, from his childhood, lacked patience.

Nothing contained him, ever. Kissan considered impatience and dissatisfaction to be qualities that enabled him to move forward. He looked at the picture of Hanuman. The hero had a mountain in his palm. Kissan did not know why, but staring at the picture he had just discovered something else. Despite its burden, the face of Hanuman had no trace of suffering or effort. He thought he heard voices blowing in his ears: 'Lift the mountain ... lift it. Who says you have not got the strength? The mountain ... the mountain... the mountain, Hanuman! The force...' This was the god of strength that he worshipped. It was in his name that Rekha was mixing earth and cowdung in a small mound on which she planted a red flag. This flag, fluttering in the wind, was supposed to take away all the villagers' fears. So why did Kissan tremble so much? Why had fear seized him now?

He stood up abruptly, as if to get rid of these thoughts harassing his mind. In the courtyard, he saw Rekha forming circles with sticks of incense around the altar. The red flag seemed immense. Rekha had said that it was the same flag that adorned Arjuna's chariot, which Krishna had driven in the *Mahabharata.*

Rekha caught his eye. "What is her name? Harbassia or Gharbassia?"

"You can say it either way."

"She came to see you."

"What did she want with me?"

"I told her you were not here."

"She told you nothing?"

"She just wanted to see you."

"It was definitely to bring me the boss's threats."

"You know what she told the women she saw in the fields?"

"No."

"That if they continued, the boss would undress the whole village."

"I would like to see that. Let me first go and see if Devnanan's returned."

"Do not go there alone, Kissan,' Rekha advised, "while he is away."

The sun had not risen, but birds sang loudly and there was

hardly anyone out, because no one went to the fields. He heard no noise from dishes or pans. Kissan felt the cold wind blowing from the mountains onto his skin. He breathed deeply the smell of wet earth that reminded him of frangipani. A long time ago, the wind in the morning had brought its freshness and that sweet fragrance.

As he walked down the road, mud stuck to his feet. He found Sonallal in front of Dawood's. The *panditji* sang songs before the holy *tulsi* plant.

Gopal's sister swept the courtyard. Gautam appeared from behind the house; he was washing his teeth with a piece of guava stem.The *panditji's* prayers had ended and he approached Kissan. "The body leads us to hell, but the soul leads to heaven."

Kissan did not understand everything the *panditji* said. He went to the well along with Sonallal and Gautam. The prayers of the *panditji* hadn't yet reached their ears. The night before, Kissan had prayed, too, at the insistence of his mother. He said the words hastily, but then he felt an inner peace that had surprised him.

The rainwater had accumulated in large puddles. Gautam and Kissan dried their *dhotis* on their knees. Sonallal wore pants. Kissan's *dhoti* was all torn: it was his father's, which Rekha had washed. In spite of washing, it retained its brown colour, as if the fabric was impregnated with earth.

They met Harbassia, leaving Sougwa's house. Even before she opened her mouth, Kissan asked, "You came to see me, Harbassia?'

"I wanted to give you the boss's news."

"I'm listening."

"You have to go there, he wants to see you."

"But I already saw him yesterday."

"He is very angry with you. If you do not obey, he will go after you all."

Sonallal interuppted, "Is he going to also go after you?' he said mockingly.

"I said what I had to say. Do what you want."

"Can you do us a favour, please?" Kissan asked as gently as possible. "What?"

"Convey my answer to the boss. Tell him we will not go to the property. If he really wants to meet, let him come here in the fields..."

"Urchins! You are all peeing fire. You do not see that you put the whole village in danger?"

Sonallal quipped back: "You have nothing to fear. Your place is in the castle, not the village."

"In blindly listening to Devnanan, you've gotten worse than ever."

The boys did not answer and walked away, cursing Harbassia.

Kundan's door was still closed. They sat on the threshold. Kissan needed him; he was the only one who could restore his courage. Suddenly, Pushpa appeared, "He's not yet returned?"

She shook her head. Sonallal had grabbed a piece of wood and was using it to remove the mud stuck to his heel.

"You still believe they will give in?" she asked Kissan.

"Yes." His voice lacked conviction.

"And if they do not?" Sonallal asked.

"They will," Pushpa said in a firm voice.

Kissan looked at her and then turned to Sonallal. "If they refuse, it will be even worse than before. Is that what you are worrying about?" Sonallal did not answer. "Think, Sona, can there be worse than this, here, today?"

"Then why do you look so discouraged?"

Gautam intervened. 'I did not lose courage, my friend. But I think about Devnanan and it worries me. Well, whatever. Let us get up; we can go to the river before sunrise."

Pushpa looked away. The clouds still littered the sky. It was to rain again soon.

31

The second watch of the night was about to end. Kundan followed the foreman Ramjee, without even bothering to hide. He would certainly have lost sight of him if the path had not been so slippery.The recent rains had made the roads impassable and Ramjee had injured his foot in falling. And then he did not know the road to get to the other village. Finally, the darkness did not help. But what helped Kundan keep track most was the smell of marijuana. At one point, he called out, "Hey, Sirdar, stop a bit."

Ramjee was afraid and, despite his injured foot, he ran, panicked in every sense, not knowing where to go. Kundan followed him, climbing the slopes of the mountain, back down the other side. Several times he shouted at the other to stop, but the foreman panicked, fell several times, sat. Kundan also fell and his knee was bleeding. Slowly the dawn came and the daylight finally lit up the landscape. It had stopped raining. Kundan saw Ramjee before him, still running. The distance between them, although it was rather short, remained constant. Not that Kundan was not faster, but Ramjee ran for his life, while Kundan wanted to stop and talk to him to avoid a catastrophe.

Kundan had vowed never to let Rekha go while the boss had rights over her. Rights! Another word that made him laugh and also cry... in this country, the same word does not mean the same thing for everyone. Violated rights, rights abused, rights buried forever, the right to crush others, the right to die of hunger!

He had done what he could to protect Rekha, even if he had only seen the girl twice. And he knew that it was mostly because of Kissan. Kundan loved Pushpa specially... but he knew she was courageous, and she could handle a painful sitaution. Kissan had followed through in each of his initiatives, he had observed; he was the villager who he knew better than himself. And so anyone who would seek to bring Rekha back to the boss would find him, Kundan, across the road, standing strong like a wall.

The rain had stopped completely. Day broke on a forest still simmering after the night. Above the green hills, the clouds were scattered. The sun was darting forth his first rays when Kundan caught up to Ramjee. He lay wounded, near a small creek. In his eyes Kundan could read his fear and his mouth was wide open. The smell of marijuana in his clothes saturated the air and obscured the subtle fragrance of the morning. Blood was coming from his ankle and he had injured his hand and forehead. Kundan came near him. They stood, silent, for a long time. Each recovered their breath; nothing was heard but the murmur of the nearby river. Before them stood a grove of mango trees and three paths, each leading to a different village. It was there that the labourers rested in the evening when returning home after a day of work. Kundan washed his hands and face in the cool water of the creek. Then he looked eastward.

The landscape that opened before him was familiar. He was surprised, because he had never been here. Yet this river, the banyan tree, this remarkable mountain in the shape of a man ... the soldier who was returning to camp, the inviting banks of the river, the naked woman who bathed the horse, the guard, the high walls of the prison ...all these images rose up, hot. But Kundan stood, impassive. The river was still flowing; it did not change, the mountain always presents the same soft colours, but Kundan's black hair had turned white and his face had lost its freshness. Despite the cold morning, he felt the warmth of these images rising in him. He saw the whole scene in its most precise details. He came out of his reverie to find that Ramjee had risen and had already crossed the creek.

"Stop!" he cried.

His voice rang out, but the foreman continued to run, surrounded by echoes of the cry bouncing from one hill to another. He was running zigzag through the bushes. Kundan called out again. The echo answered his words again. Ramjee did not stop; he stumbled and fell and started all over again. He was so out of breath that the sound of his breathing covered the murmur of the water. Before long Kundan was by his side. They stared at each other, panting. "You shall go no further," Kundan shouted without taking a breath.

"You're going to stop me?"

"Sit down."

"I do not have time."

"Sit down, I tell you."

"Why do you want me?"

"You've exploited the labourers your whole life."

"I'll make a complaint against you."

"Ah. Yes. And to whom?"

"The boss."

"Before you have had time to sigh, you will be before the big boss from above."

"Let me go."

"To go where?"

"I will go home."

"You have a house nearby?"

"Well, tell me what you want."

"You have betrayed the labourers for your whole life. Now it is finished."

"Okay, I will no longer betray anyone."

"All your life you've beaten poor people who do nothing against you."

"I'll not do it again."

"All your life you have sold the girls and women of the village. And you take all that is to return to the villagers."

"I'll stop, I promise."

"You sold your people as slaves."

"Now that's over."

"You put your business above all else. You sell the work of labourers and you draw the profit."

"Well, you delay me."

"Do not worry, you will not be late, you will arrive just in time."

"Where?"

"Your destination."

"But I have no destination."

"Then sit down."

"No."

"Sit down, I tell you."

Ramjee fell to the ground as if Kundan had pushed him. Kundan took his own place in the wet grass. "Admit it, you were off to the boss to prevent Rekha from hiding with us... but you have to understand one thing: if you take Rekha, you cross the line. And even death can't take you back."

"I... I will not give up any such information."

"You lie."

"You'll have everything you want."

"I want your life, Ramjee."

"I will speak to the boss to give you land."

"It is you who are going to need land. To be buried in."

The foreman rose with a start and resumed his course. But he had barely taken a few steps when he stumbled and fell. Kundan walked towards him slowly. Ramjee clasped his hands and begged him, "Forgive me, please."

"History will see this as the turning point."

They heard barks. Ramjee sat up, ears alert. "The guards are coming near," he exclaimed. "Speak, then, speak. Tell me what you want."

Kundan still froze, silent. His eyes were more brilliant than usual. He did not hesitate for a second.

The barking of the dogs grew closer.

32

It did not stop raining for three days. Ordinarily, Kissan would welcome the change, but today he did not like the damp wind and cold. Inaction weighed on him and even his impatience evaporated. They would soon be in the fourth day of the strike. The bosses had not given their answer.

From the top of the hill where he stood, Kissan was looking at the path leading to the village. It remained empty and not a sound was heard. Everything seemed to have stopped. Labourers tinkered without enthusiasm, busying themselves with a little housework, but they felt discouraged. And then the bad weather did not help. The sunflowers, usually affectionate, seemed to be sulking. Raindrops falling from the leaves of the trees gave off the air of crying.

Kissan was bitingly on edge. He feared an inglorious end; his hopes were dwindling by the hour. If only he could take upon himself all the surrounding inertia, sadness, defeatism and helplessness that paralysed all the villagers. If he could make a friend smile, the atmosphere would take on a carefree gaiety. But that was wishful thinking and in the battle he offered, he would lead them to their end without being able to escape the blows that pounded his conscience.

Pushpa was just leaving. What he had told her had only increased her sadness. After his departure, Kissan's thoughts slipped to Rekha: Rekha and her innocent smile. His heart was a whip and he was so beaten that he thought he was going to faint.

Concerns and problems presented themselves suddenly disproportionately large. He saw himself facing a real demon, a dragon, alone, naked and unarmed. But he had not yet given up the thin protection, that is hope. He had to stand, stand firm in the storm. And he would do.

Further away, the villagers cut down trees. He heard the sound of crashing trunks on the floor and the noise of the fall reminded him of that crazy night during which, with Rekha, he'd sought the path home. The sounds penetrated the windows and banged against his eardrums, striking a chord in him that connected him to life, to reality. He felt that he had plunged a knife into his brain and the blood had spread inside his skull. Submerged in anguish, he saw his end and that of the whole world.

Kundan had not returned; that would have at least been able to restore his confidence. But the human being who slept inside him rose sharply. Kissan laid down his hoe on the ground and stood up. Then he began running. This morning as he left home, Sandhya and Rekha had accompanied him to the threshold.

"And if the employers refuse?" Rekha said.

"They will be obliged to accept, and they will do so," replied Kissan, full of confidence.

With what confidence he had spoken to Rekha! When he came in tonight, she would come to meet him, eyes full of questions. What answer, then? Kissan could not imagine for a moment presenting himself as a loser before her.

He remained full of contradictions. Seeing the rain continuing to fall, he deplored the mess involved in their prolonged strike. In the fields, they had already dug the grooves and the cane was in place. They had only to spread fertiliser and cover them with soil. He did not believe that the owners were ready to lose all this.'Finally, is it them or us who lose the most?' he wondered. 'We all live off this same land... after all, there is not much difference between us, so why can we not compromise? But what compromise, and in what way?'

And his mind kept going over the same questions, relentlessly. He walked more quickly, harassed by all the questions left unanswered. He had not owned up to Rekha when she had asked why he cared so much about her, nor had he been able to explain to Pushpa why the atmosphere was so heavy when it rained. He remembered that night: Rekha's father, dying, his body covered in blood after she was beaten, asked him, before old Luchmansing: "Can I give you my daughter, and will you keep her future in your hands?" Kissan had known what to say; his heart had already said yes. 'Can I leave my daughter in your hands?' How could he not answer such a question?

Sonallal put down the bundle he was carrying and sat on it. He was still holding a piece of flatbread wrapped around a sweet potato. He wiped his face with a corner of his scarf and munched a piece of potato. Then he turned to Kissan. His friend was silent. Sonallal glanced at the path, desperately empty. He finished eating and was about to leave.

"You know how many days have passed?" asked Kissan, holding him back.

Sonallal hesitated for a moment. "Half a day or so."

Suddenly they saw a figure appear on the trail. Kissan's heart began to beat louder. They soon recognised Dawood, who was running towards them.

"What's going on?" Kissan cried even before he'd reached them.

"The boss is on his way. He wants you to bring everyone together and end up at the mill."

Kissan did not lose a minute. He began to call as loudly as he could all who were in the area and spread the message. Spurred by curiosity, he ran, followed by a few who rushed behind him. As he reached the mill, he ceased to run, but he could not quite slow down and still walked with long strides. About forty people had gathered around him. The Lame Man was sitting in his carriage and was soon surrounded by a crowd of villagers. Two other bosses were with him and they awaited the arrival of the others before giving their verdict. Finally, Raymond came down from the carriage and said, loud and solemn, "We accept your grievances."

He could not say another word, because as soon as his words were heard, there was an explosion of shouts of joy. Kissan, his voice broken with emotion, advanced and he said, "Many thanks, boss."

"You must get back to work tomorrow."

"Right now, if you want."

"No, you can rest today."

They could not believe their ears. When the carriages left, Kissan was carried in triumph by the cheering crowd. He advanced to the front of the procession and the labourers followed, singing and dancing. Kissan did not even think to worry about Kundan, his joy was so great. If Devnanan had been among them, he would dance with him. To him he would dedicate this victory. But when he had time to ask if anyone had any news of him, no one knew or had passed his friend.

Approaching the village, he was joined by a small group of women who mingled with the crowd. The children were soon caught up in things, too, without really understanding the reason for this unexpected festivity. It was still raining, but no one cared. They sang a song of joy, then another. In the blink of the soul, it was night.

Kissan suddenly looked up and saw Rekha. A smile lit up her face and expressed deep joy. Kissan smiled back. For a moment, he thought of her father. Rekha did not know he was dead; Kissan had not dared to tell her, and was awaiting the right moment. He rushed toward her, grabbed her hands and led her into a frenzied dance. Tears gleamed in their eyes.

Night had fallen. They lit torches and the singing continued. Gopal was the last to return to the village. On hearing the news, he began to jump and shout. He forgot to tell his friends that Kundan had been arrested and had been imprisoned for the murder of the foreman Ramjee. Raising his hands in chains, Kundan had given Gopal this message: "Tell Kissan I'm going home."

Gopal did not understand what he meant.

33

The villagers became seriously concerned after the sudden death of eight villagers. The week before, a strange disease had wreaked havoc in two villages to the south. The man who had brought the news was still in hiding in one of the village houses. He had been arrested while he was cutting wood to cremate the remains of his wife and son. The man had strangled the white man after getting a hold of his whip. When he arrived in the village, he suffered from a high fever. The *panditji's* remedies reduced his fever, but the same day, eight people fell ill. They complained of headaches and their bodies became covered with brown patches. The road leading to Rekha's village was closed. Even the *panditji* had succumbed. They could no longer make use of his preparations of medicinal herbs.

Kissan had gone to the boss three times and each time he had been promised that the drugs would soon arrive. But the number of sick grew.Those suffering from fever had been dragged to the fields by the foremen; they, picked by hand.

It had not been a week since the agreement had been reached, with the assurances given by the whites. And now everything was again as before. When Mitwa had died, two foremen went into his house, each pulling an arm. Taleb was dead also, dead on the fields. The two foremen had slung his body into the well from which the village drew its water. In the evening, two villagers were lowered into the well to remove the body, but dawn was breaking already and they could not bring up the entire body. For three days, they abstained from drinking well water, but this could not last. The path that led to the river was closed. Kissan was agitated and warned the foremen and the boss, "If you do not act, I will find the Protector of Labourers."

He was much talked about these days. In appealing to him, Kissan hoped the labourers might perhaps be heard. The new government, they said, was more favourable to farmers. But the boss simply replied: "And how will you do so?"

Kissan could only repeat himself. Most roads were closed, and, even if he found one passable, he would not have had the opportunity to go. As it was, the instant he tried to leave, they fell upon him. They threw him in the plantation cellar, bound hand and foot. He was let out after three days with measles, and when he returned to the village, he found three bodies burning on the same pyre. Twenty others had succumbed to the epidemic. To be freed, Kissan had to swear he would not encourage the labourers to revolt and not come to complain to the boss. Otherwise, they would take him back to the cellar.

The young man saw his ideals go up in smoke, bright as the cinders that projected their sparks into the night. What could he do now? Not that he was afraid of the dark prison, but how could they regain strength while the epidemic continued to spread? And when he came back home, he still had no news. Rekha was his first thought and he rushed towards the house. But his legs refused to run. This was the first time he felt so weak, and he held on to a branch to get back up. He could barely support the weight of his body; his head was spinning and he pressed a hand against his forehead, while the other hand was holding the branch. Even his wrist had less force than he needed... With great difficulty he resumed his march. The village houses appeared to depart as he advanced on his way, the ground slipping under his feet, the horizon flickering.

The first person he saw was the only one who he had not thought of yet. Pushpa came towards him, her arms full of fresh grass. Seeing Kissan hardly able to stand, she put her herbs down and approached him, "What happened to you, Kissan?"

Kissan put a hand on her shoulder and she helped him sit on the edge of the road.

"How is my family?"

"Do not worry, they are all doing well."

Kissan was silent.

"And you, how do you feel?"

"The best I can feel." It was a late afternoon without sun. Not a breath of air stirred the leaves on the trees. Kissan's eyes were rivetted to the barricade that marked the entrance of the village. From the exterior, it seemed that it was so fragile that it would have been enough to push it to make it collapse. Always the same stories about broken down walls...

"You want me to bring you some water?" asked Pushpa.

Kissan started. "No, I'm going," he said, quickly. They took the road to the village. "What's this grass?"

"That's for my little deer."

"Your little deer?"

"Ah, yes, you don't know. But we see you so little these days...

Dawood captured it in the woods and it is keeping me busy. It has already grown up. Come, I'll show you."

"Not right now, Pushpa. Another day.'

Thick, heavy clouds obscured the sun and sky. It was as if the sun deliberately chose not to attend these long days of misery. Holed up somewhere, thought Kissan, disappeared into the void. 'I'm like some dog howling at the moon, trying to devour a piece of this pale cake. But he has to bark until death: the dog never gets the moon.'

Kissan left Pushpa in front of her house and continued on his way. The village was empty; all who were not sick were attending funerals. You could see the flames of pyres rising from the direction of the river.

When he got home, Kissan pulled himself together. He found his father in bed in the same condition he had left him. His mother was on her feet. Sandhya and Rekha were mending old clothes. Kissan was relieved and happy to see them all together and they all smiled when he entered the room.Their eyes spoke their relief.

"Kissan," said his father.

His mother pressed against him, and Sandhya got up hastily. Rekha had tears in her eyes.

Kissan knew that there was no food at home. It was at least three days since there had been anything. He turned to Rekha and said softly: "Can I have some water?"

34

They used the mill's cart to transport the bodies to the other side of the river. They burned three or four corpses on the same pyre. The village population was halved. They couldn't go out without the unbearable smell of cremation in their noses. Many labourers died in the fields and others caught the epidemic there. More and more people were coughing... It was a boat from Spain that had brought the germs causing the disease. Nobody had done anything to prevent its spread amongst the Indian labourers.

While everyone had one thing in mind – keeping death at a distance – Raymond's son, riding his horse near Dawood's house, called out in French. 'What's your name?"

"Dawood."

"Ah. So it's you." Two days earlier, Dawood had told a foreman he did not care for orders from the boss's son. When he saw the barrel of a gun in the hands of the young master, Dawood thought about his brother. This rifle had killed him. Dawood said not a word; he stood motionless on the side of the road, ready to receive the punishment reserved for him.

"Come forward a little," said Raymond's son. Dawood took two steps forward. "So, Dawood. You know your wife is very beautiful," said the young French boss.

"Excuse me, I do not understand, sir."

"Your wife," he replied in Hindi. Dawood felt the hair on his back stand up. "She is very pretty..."

"Sir, my mother and sister died yesterday ...both of them."

"You do not have any children?"

"Not yet, sir."

"Send me your wife, and you'll have a beautiful white baby. Gaston will look for her in the afternoon. He will bring her to my home."

Dawood was petrified. The horse walked away. Nearby, the fires were still burning. You could hear the cries of women, heart-breaking sobs.

Dawood had not moved. He heard the sound of hooves get softer, and every crack of iron on the stony ground drove a nail into his flesh. He heard in his mind the sound of his wife Zinat crying at the funeral of his stepmother and stepsister.

The mill no longer turned, the fields remained desperately empty. The children were starving, parents wept in silence, not having the strength to cry out their pain. Everywhere, there was nothing but sadness and desolation. Hovering over the whole village, death, claws out, picked up his booty.

Dawood did not move. The wind that had howled for three days left his ears, but he heard the grin of death, hungry for life. He felt a hand on his shoulder. It was Kissan. "What did he say to you?" Dawood did not respond. "He is not just; he is a monster. You should have punched him in the face and tore out his eyes."

But Kissan knew he would not have dared, either.

Dawood spoke at last. 'Gaston will come this afternoon.'

"I'll take care of it."

"But..."

"What can be worse? They deprive us of food, drugs... what else can they take from us?" They returned to the village. Every day, the evil grew worse. From the houses, you could hear people coughing, moaning, crying, others groaning in agony. Kissan's parents were ill. He visited four villages in three days. They found no cure, and not a single *panditji*. Corpses, however, they did not lack.

The previous evening, a meeting had been held. Some had returned to the proposal to storm the boss's house. Kissan was adamant, though, "Not now, it's too early."

"Kissan has aged," someone remarked.

Kissan laughed. He remembered his father saying, "He who rushes for rice ends up with an empty plate."

They had deferred the decision. But impotence paralysed the survivors and everyone felt trapped.

Dawood felt the same. He felt the futility of any action and their resignation to a fate that was bent on reducing them. Standing in the middle of the street in the heart of the village, he began to howl like a terrified beast. The villagers came out of their houses quickly. Dawood fell on his knees and remained prostrate for a long time. His cry had released accumulated tension and now he caught his breath.

"What did he say?" asked those who had rushed outside.

Kissan asked them to go back inside, helped his friend up and took him home. The he called Zinat. She appeared thin, but her face was always beautiful. Her eyes were sunken, but this gave her face a new intensity. Kissan noticed that pain gave certain faces a strange beauty.

"Zinat, look after him well."

"What has happened to him, Kissan?" she asked, her voice low.

"It's nothing. A weakness... and you, how do you feel? Do you have a fever?"

"No, it's going, I am well."

When Kissan had left their home, Dawood opened his eyes. He looked at his wife at length.

"Why are you looking at me like that?"

"Just looking at you, that's all."

"What is it?"

"I did not realise you were so beautiful."

"But what are you talking about?"

"Who do you belong to, Zinat?"

"I suppose I belong to you."

"No, Zinat, no."

"Those others who I belong to are dead."

"You're not mine." There was a long silence, then the sentence fell like lightning. "Zinat, this afternoon, you should go to the home of the boss's son."

Zinat felt the panic rise in her and she began to cry. Dawood soon followed. He clasped his wife's wrist. "Zinat, it is not the first time it has happened... our brothers and our parents are dying for lack of food and care. And this epidemic that continues to spread... cannot we try something? Perhaps the two of us can get there. And if we succeed, would it not be a wonderful contribution to the revival of the village? Do you understand me?"

Zinat heard the voice of a man on the brink of madness. She could not say a word.

"We could save our whole community. It's not expensive to pay for something to eat again, and for medicine. Are you listening?"

She nodded.

"It's an opportune time; you should take advantage. What do you think? Why aren't you saying anything? Answer me."

"What should I say?"

"Are you ready?"

"Ready for what?"

"For food and medicine to finally return to the village."

"How could I oppose it?"

"Good. So, it's almost two o'clock. Go and dress, please."

"To go where?"

"To the home of Raymond's son."

"Have you lost your head, Dawood?"

"No, I speak knowingly and I have my conscience. It's now or never. It will not be the end of the world; go. All you have to do is ignore a few minutes and tell yourself that you act for a great cause. You are a woman, Zinat and the body of a woman is not a piece of flesh. It does not get dirty because it is touched by an insensitive hand. You will not be tarnished in any way, but remember, before you give him anything, dictate your conditions and make sure that he accepts them."

Nearby, they heard someone burst into tears. Another villager must have passed away.

35

The trail led into a large meadow. Kissan ran with all his force and stood in front of Dawood and Zinat. He felt so weak, he could barely stand and he stumbled on the cut grass that covered the ground in long sheaves. Dawood and Zinat had to stop. They were standing near him, as he stood panting and puffing like an animal, trying to catch his breath. The couple said nothing.

Kissan looked and looked at them, "Where are you going?'

"We have nothing here," Dawood replied after a long silence.

"You're escaping?"

"We do not have much choice."

"And how far will you run?"

"You prefer that I entrust Zinat to that pig?"

"What do you take me for?"

"So what do you want?"

"We can stand up to him,' said Kissan, with effort. "That's what we did when they started. They took any woman, they took off her clothes in front of everyone, and they..."

Zinat interrupted, "Kissan, we can still go and try our luck elsewhere.'

"There is not anywhere else on this island, Zinat. The territory is vast and it seems that there are empty spaces. But this is a prison from one end to another. You will find nothing but the bosses' dogs ready to jump on you and devour you.

"Then we will find a place to die."

"Dawood, you can even speak like this?" The sun had just gone down, scattering its last golden brown light. "It is dark," said Kissan.

"Now you realise?' Dawood replied, his smile sardonic.

"Come on, let's go."

"Where?"

"Back."

"Are you inviting us back?"

"Have not you a house?"

"Must it be me alone who is brave?"

"It's now or never to be brave. Today, the whole village needs you, Dawood."

"Running out of corpses?"

"No, we are short of hands to bury our brothers.' The first star was kindled in the sky. Kissan put his arm around Dawood's shoulders and continued to argue. His friend was unresponsive. Kissan repeated, "Think carefully, Dawood. Who else do I have? If you really have to go, find me someone to replace you. Someone to assist me in this final battle and who will support me when I take my last breath." Zinat had tears in her eyes. But neither of them realised it. "Turn around, Dawood. There is no better place to die than your own house, I assure you."

Dawood was silent. A phrase that his father often repeated had returned to him in memory: "A man should never discover the animal within." He suddenly understood the sense of the words and they made him shudder.

"Let's go back to the village," said Zinat, a lump in her throat.

Dawood did not reply, but he began to walk like a robot to the village. Kissan heaved a huge sigh. He turned to Zinat and together they followed suit. The night was dark, the sky full of bright stars. An east wind blew from the mountain. Dawood was walking like a sleepwalker. In his ears, rang the latest words of Islam Miyan: 'To keep things balanced, the world's rhythm has three stages: first, the desires of the men are layered over the years. Then, the accumulation of those bloated aspirations encourages combat. And finally, confidence on the part of the warriors, of those who would destroy evil.'

Dawood walked faster and faster. If he were to die, he would want to die as indeed Islam Miyan had, killed trying to stop a black foreman who was pissing in the village well. "How did I think of running away?" he asked in disbelief.

For several days, it was rumoured that the Protector of Labourers would come to the village. Hopes revived. 'Everything will work out; it will pass.' Others said he was going to send their grievances to the government. The days passed. They constantly spoke of the imminent visit of the Protector of Labourers, but he never came. Or rather he came, but he stopped at the owner's house. They soon learned that he had turned away, all very satisfied. He did not take the trouble to go into the field; he did not cross the boundaries of the great houses. Raymond and his foremen portrayed the life, oh so sweet, of their expensive labourers.

'I miss the presence of Devnanan,' Kissan thought on such occasions. The disappearance of his friend had shaken his confidence considerably. The action plan proposed by Kundan was still locked in the *baithka*. Kissan thought that the time had come to carry it out. But how? Without him, it seemed insurmountable. Kissan had long studied its pages, and his friends pored over the plan in detail. He had read and reread it. They had to take the plunge now.

One after the other, villagers succumbed to the epidemic. Twenty men were killed, besides women and children. If death continued at this rate, within a month, the town would be a cemetery. Kissan was obsessed with the question of time. A split second was enough to derail everything.

In their homes, fear reigned. Their eyes no longer reflected suffering, hunger and anxiety – only emptiness. There was not a sound; doors and windows were closed, as if people were afraid to be on the threshold of death itself. Occasionally, someone sang a verse of *Hanuman Chalisa.* But nothing happened and death roamed, omnipresent. The survivors were waiting for the end. Some were still attached to a talisman supposed to protect them, or implored the mother goddess. But mostly they felt that all was lost.

Kissan's father was dying. His skin grew paler by the hour. His eyes were drying up, sunken. His wife hugged her eldest son. "Nobody will be spared, Kissan," she moaned.

"But, Mama, there is still time."

His father had hardly any more. He died in the afternoon. Standing in a corner of the room, Kissan looked at the haggard women crying. Finally, he pulled himself together. He pulled his mother, Sandhya, and Rekha off the remains. But his mother threw herself again on the chest of the deceased.

"No," Kissan screamed, 'do not touch him."

His father's death had forced a passage in the house. His father had given way, he who claimed that one should never despair of life. Was it really a resignation, or did he simply reach the limits of resistance? Kissan could not take his eyes from his father's face and his thoughts were jostled, stirring questions and doubts in a breathtaking dance.

His mother was a shell and she only came to herself much later. She had not said a word since the death of her husband. She spent the night awake, lying in the dark. Kissan was sad, of course, but above all frightened. He felt welling up in him a vague anxiety that gave him chills. He might fight against this growing fear, but he could not overcome it. He finally understood that the death of his father was not just the physical removal of a body, but that through the death of this man, an epoch had ended. He felt the fear of an insurmountable present. Kissan felt his integrity was cracking, but remained determined not to lose ground. He had to overcome fear, to return intact.

His legs were shaking, his lips dry and he heard his own voice whisper edifying maxims. His brain refused to function; everything was going wrong, he was dizzy, his body failed and his spirit had no companion...

He left his home. Outside were even more dogs, howling of death.

At one point, the labourers had wondered why the boss left all his workers to die. After all, he had lost much of his workforce. Without it, the plantation would return to the wild and their mansions would soon be lost in the woods. But they understood the day they heard a foreman explain that within two or three days, a shipload of workers would arrive. They came from Bihar, like the villagers already here. They waited for some three hundred and fifty people: Satya's uncle had already found them for the boss. He would receive fifteen annas per month per person upon delivery. So why worry about the sick?

36

That evening, Kissan gathered his courage to go and find the boss again. He found at the door seven dogs working on three large bowls filled with cooked rice. That would have been enough to feed the whole village for three days. Kissan was mesmerised by those big tubs of rice. His hunger was gnawing at him, and he had to make an effort not to throw himself down and mingle with dogs to devour their pittance. No one stopped him and the boss himself had not the slightest frown when he arrived. Such silence sounded strange. Kissan turned around.

But there remained no one. He had already suffered from his despondency. And the terrible misery of the villagers was such that he could not stop people from reacting. His own mother was bedridden. They had to make a decision, whatever it was. They had organised a meeting in haste and fifteen people made their way from their homes to the granary. The food was locked and dogs roamed freely. Seeing Kissan arrive at the head of the group, the guards had readied their guns. But the villagers were determined and before the guards had taken stock of the situation, they fell on their backs. The dogs jumped but soon took flight because the guns had changed hands. They tied the four guards together, they opened the granary door and eight men rushed inside. The guards could only watch the looting. They broke their guns and threw them to the bottom of the river.

Everything happened in record time. In the days that followed, there was no guard in the village. Kissan was not summoned, did not receive a punishment, did not hear the rattling of chains. Now the boss continued smoking his pipe and did not even leave the chair in which he rested.

After three days, they had almost forgotten what could have been. Kissan's mother had died the night before. The next day, a ship landed with her cargo of workers, all young and industrious, full of hope and enthusiasm.

□

PART-II

If tears could turn stones into diamonds, they would have seized the tears of the poor.

The day sweat and tears turn into pearls, they will seize the labourers' skin and confiscate their tears.

1

This land was so rich in memories... with its aromatic soil, its green fields and undulating leaves caressed by the wind.

The wait.

It had lasted seven years. The pile of stones at the back of the cabin was almost as tall as he was. For seven years, he'd added one to the top every day. But the strength and the patience that had animated him in those years had decreased. There was no need for that pile of rocks; the trees growing on the mountainside sheltered him from view. But he'd continued to build. A seven-year work sentence...

It was what they had inflicted on his son. And that interminable period had ended. He had to stay a few more days, raise a few extra stones. He was told that prisoners were often released early for good behaviour. Apparently, his son had not had the privilege. He did not need to recount the huge piles of stones to know that Madan had not received a pardon.

Often, he would stand in the middle of the cabin and look at the plain below. A path ran zigzag towards the village. That day, he'd travelled the steep path to the first houses. The villagers did not conceal their surprise when they saw him coming. He had become so frail; it was hard to imagine him doing this type of exercise. But he'd left that evening by the same perilous path. Dhanlal insisted he come again, but he would not listen. It had been a long time since he had been seen in the village. Really, he was going down to ask Dhanlal how many days remained until the release of his son.

According to the villagers' calculations, the seven years had elapsed.

Kissan had lived every day in anticipation of that last day in prison. He looked twice his age... the weight of countless lashes of canes, whips and the mill's yoke, but also of Rekha's sudden death and Madan's arrest. He must have been only fifty years old, but he was burnt out. They had taken everything from him and he was wrung.

The villagers thought first that after his release, Madan had strayed, had wandered to another part of the island; he would eventually return. The idea reassured Kissan, who returned to his cabin on the mountainside. In the evening, the villagers saw a small light flickering at the top, and they knew that the old man had reached home safe and sound. Every night, the glow gave them assurance that he was still alive. After a few nights without light, they were alarmed. They rushed up to the cabin. Kissan was there, exhausted, burning with fever. The villagers made every attempt to bring him relief. The light always came back after several days without news of his son. Sometimes as he returned to his cabin, he was blinded by the sun, its light reflecting off the stones of the path, and Kissan would be plunged into darkness. His eyes would stop responding, his hopes diminished to some degree. 'But no, this has nothing to do with it,' he said to himself. And then, 'Why not? I have been disappointed in my expectations at every turn of life; why should I not think of my vision as part of that?'

Many other small parts of him had stopped working and he no longer retained any illusions.

In the valley, the villagers regarded him with more respect than was usually paid to the elderly, but Kissan knew they paid homage to a man who was no more. He knew that he was not more than the clothes of an aborted revolution that villagers hung from a tree so as to preserve its memory. To him, they were only skin and bones. It seemed that his diluted blood carried nothing of yesteryears. He understood that his son's blood was also diluted. Because they were both made from the same cloth, while his life unravelled, he knew that his son's strength of mind existed somewhere. It was inconceivable that he had been killed... they both swam against the tide, and Madan had the strength to swim. He might get carried away, but he would not sink. Madan had to be better than his father; otherwise, he would sink in the currents and eddies.

In Kissan's eyes, his son's imprisonment was a source of both sadness and pride. He experienced through Madan what he wanted to endure himself, completing his journey, adding an episode that he had not been able to live directly. Madan had not been born when his father had first longed to be locked up in one of those cells where Devnanan had spent the greater part of his life. It was an offence to swim against the current, but contrary to his expectations, he had never been condemned for it. He felt contempt for the real force of his movement and he considered that the revolution had lacked depth, intensity. Otherwise, how could he explain why the situation had never changed after all his attempts to make a difference?

A few weeks later, Kissan was busy planting dandelions in front of his cabin when a man appeared. He wore only a *dhoti*. His back showed signs of lashes. His ribs jutted out and his face was so thin that his eye sockets were sunken. Stubble was scattered on his sunken cheeks. The man was from prison, carrying a message from Madan. "Do not worry about him. He is doing well."

Kissan drew some fresh water and offered it to the visitor. The man told him anecdotes from prison, his words contradicting his good news.

"How much longer?" Kissan asked.

"He should be back before the next full moon." Since then, four moons had come and gone. He felt that he would not last to see the next one. Dark, moonless nights were the most terrible. Then, dreadful thoughts haunted him.

This time last year, a cyclone had been on the horizon. When the winds had begun to rage, the villagers had come looking for him. But he would not follow them and had holed up in his cabin. When the storm became imminent, the villagers returned down the path to their homes. Inside his frail hut, Kissan passed the terrible hours, winds howling around him, sky rumbling and clouds breaking over his head, shaking the mountain. His cabin had been under attack, trembling again and again. At the third trembling, the roof got carried away. It was an old tamarind tree that proved to be Kissan's salvation. He clung to its trunk with all his force as the surging battalions of lightning put the sky in turmoil. Trees were falling around him, torn leaves and branches spinning through the air at full speed. After a few long hours, dawn broke. The wind had abated, but the rain continued to pound down in whirlwinds. Dhanlal had braced himself for the rainy paths and slopes of the mountain to climb to the cabin with two other men. Despite the destruction of the cabin, Kissan had refused to go back with them to the village. The villagers decided to rebuild his cabin instead. But for Kissan, it was not the loss of his small cabin that mattered, but the destruction of the fields on the eve of the harvest.

If a cyclone came this year, there would be a shortage of vegetables again. Kissan thought back to those years in which there had been a dearth of greens. Rekha had had the ability to predict hurricanes. When she was still alive, she had dried vegetables in advance and kept them in anticipation of the days that followed the destruction of the fields.

Rekha had not died in the village, but in the cabin. It was she who had insisted on building this shelter at the top of the mountain. They had left the village together to come here. One day, she had said to her husband, "We were born in the whites', territory, in houses they built, working on their land, but I will not die in their space, believe me. I want to reach the end of my life outdoors, in a place that does not belong to anyone."

A few days after that, they had left the village for the mountain. She had not lived another full week... but Kissan had done it so his wife would not die a slave. He had installed large slabs of black rock on the mountainside and he had scattered her ashes on land in the valley that did not belong to the white men. Only two places lay beyond their overwhelming instinct of ownership: the sea and the arid mountain summits, where there were no stones.

When he had still lived in the village, Kissan was the village elder. He gave advice and often said to those younger than he was that beyond this earthly life, there was another. But in his solitude, he found that his life as a man was the sum of several lives. He had been a labourer, back bent all day in the cane fields, and he had been the instigator of a revolution. Now he was a free man, far from home, far from the dreams of his youth.

He had lived this new life, this changed life, for seven years. But he had been kept waiting. He waited for his son. And if at the time it seemed it was not his moment, from now on every hour seemed to belong to him fully, though he did not benefit.

From the beginning, the weather had played against him. The wind had come – a strong wind that had made flight futile. The cries of martins, sparrows and nightingales filled the sky in cacophony. Gusts of wind from the west were warm and humid, overcoming those from the east. The wind blew to fight being mute. So it was better to gather one's forces and accumulate enough energy to really fight. But he had been a poor fool. He had been defeated and had accepted defeat, and, ever since, had kept going over it all in self-pity. The wind whistled into his ears Devnanan's words – words that haunted him: 'to heal, there are several fronts. To lose on one does not mean that the battle is over...'

Was the battle still on? Did Madan continue to fight?

All these questions lay suspended, without response. Kissan's expectations, as far as the seven years in prison went – these were of their own making. And only death would bring him the peace to which he aspired.

2

It was terribly cold. Kissan was standing on the threshold. To stave off the chills, he kept his hands clasped under his armpits. His teeth chattered and his blood curdled. He curled into himself. He tried to keep his hands on his scalp to protect it from frostbite, but they did not want to leave the shelter of the armpits where they had taken refuge.

The weather had turned wet and cold, with gusts of wind that slapped Kissan with rain. Kissan, obsessed now with heat, watched the lamps twinkle in the distance in the valley. His lamp was suspended from the cabin without flame. Outside, Nature was frozen. The cold had been here for two or three weeks, but suddenly Kissan found it more pungent, more incisive.

Kissan tried to warm himself by breathing into his arms, but this presented more difficulties. Around him, there was not a croaking toad, not a barking dog: just the silence of winter. The animals were hiding. He had goosebumps. Successive waves of chills made his body numb. The stars in the sky did not move, frozen in their tracks. His teeth resumed their infernal waltz and Kissan clenched his jaws with all his might. His hands left his armpits to go up towards his shoulders, whose skin was as cold as inert tambourines hanging from a beam. Memories came back: he'd been the same age as his son was now when he'd received his first tambourine. Dawood had taken ten days to make it; God knows how he'd made its black skin, as in the new village, there was still no goat. He'd spent three days curing it in the fire and when Madan was born, he was ready with his tambourine. A crying baby accompanied by Dawood's instrument. Dawood's wife, Zinat, had sung the first song after Madan's birth. Kissan was still, watching the lights of the village. Twenty-six years had passed since the bard had come to the east of the island for the first time. Then, the tambourines had been constantly ringing.

The enthusiasm that had marked the construction of the new village did not last long. The day they assembled the bamboo to make the roof of the last house, Mr Maurel arrived in his carriage and advanced toward Kissan, saying, "These houses are on my land."

He had to hand a number of documents that proved that the land belonged to him. Kissan replied that the land belonged to the government, but the boss began to scream that he had purchased it and that they only had two alternatives: leave the village or work for him. So in order to inhabit the new village, all of its families were employed by Mr Maurel.

Kissan understood that this would breed the same slavery, in another form, that they believed they'd escaped. But they had put so much energy and hope into the construction of the village; they had already worked so hard that no one wanted to leave. It would have also meant that they were abandoning the tracts of land on which they had begun to farm. Kissan soon realised that the small green fields operated by Maurel encouraged villagers to work the land around it. He protested in vain. All that was left was to suffer the consequences, even if they were harsh...

They were assured that after three years of work on Mr. Maurel's lands, they would become owners of their homes and the land on which they were built. This promise was never kept. While the labourers were free to cultivate their personal plots or the rocky slopes of the mountain, they only had an hour or two every night and usually, when returning home after work in the fields, it was already dark. They managed, however, to maintain small vegetable gardens, and the vegetables they harvested improved the standard of their life.

Kissan felt his eyesight blur and his eyes take cover under a dark veil. He felt at times like they were dead. His eyelids would close of their own volition, unable to open, in a blink trapping him in the interior of his head. His legs were no better. The night wore on, dragging her heavy coat, casting a dark shadow. One after the other, the lights went out in the village. The few bright points Kissan distinguished disappeared into the darkness. All that remained was silence and his body was paralysed.

When he was completely frozen, he returned to the cabin, shivering, weak to the extreme and desperate. In the inside, the dark was full of whispers and they recalled Rekha's last breaths, before death had won. She had been panting so hard that the sound of her breathing filled the room, covering his, and since then her panting was still in the walls of the cabin, so he never felt alone. The invisible presence of his wife was with him night and day. He thought the panting he heard in the cabin would be without end.

Indistinct whispers marched against his ears like an army of bugs. He seemed to hear snippets of the songs he once hummed in the fields. But now the melody was punctuated by groans of agony from Rekha. A month earlier, he had left the hut brusquely to rush to the top, through the bushes that covered the sides of the mountain. Out of breath, he'd sat on a rock overlooking the sea where a boat was moored to the beach. He thought a moment, in a kind of hallucination, that it was the ship that had brought his father to the island along with hundreds of other labourers.

Although he had not sung for many years, he had felt the need to sing softly a new song that came, suddenly, at the sight of the boat. In it, he expressed his anger at the ignominy of a trade that apparently would never stop. India, Bihar, Arrah, Calcutta, boats, confident passengers, dreams of gold to be found under stones, then Mauritius, caning, whipping, hunger, disease...

The night wore on, entering its darkest hours. Kissan, his stomach in knots, breathed with difficulty. He took a deep breath and air pushed its way down to his lungs. In the dark, he sat down on the wooden bed, ran his tongue over his dry lips and cleared his throat. He wiped his watery eyes on the back of his hand and lay on the narrow bunk. Through the interstices of the roof, he could see no stars. He grabbed the bag of hemp in folds at his feet and covered them. The fabric warmed them a little. Not a sound came from outside. The silence was thick and black as night.

He closed his eyes. Some faces appeared, vague and imprecise, but none were Madan's. And like every night, when sleep finally came down on his breaking body, he heard the same words, "Tomorrow morning, Madan will be back."

But every morning, the sun that would bring his son would be hiding behind the mountains.

The rain that had begun to fall again cooled the air. Kissan was curled up in bed. He stuck one end of the hemp bag over his feet and covered his head too. He used more coal, lit more embers over fire. During the last rain, the wood was completely soaked, so that he could not make charcoal. Usually, when the villagers climbed up the cabin with sweets and other little things to eat, he filled their haversacks with charcoal in return.

But waiting for his son had so reduced him that he had not the strength to go to collect firewood. He seemed to have become useless. He cursed this miserable life. Every day he resolved to resume his activity the next day, but the next morning it came to nothing. Idleness held him tight; he had even lost his appetite. The boiled potatoes he had prepared two days earlier remained in the pan. For two days, he had not seen Dawood's son, so he couldn't give the potatoes to Farid's dog either.

Kissan fidgeted on the board that was his bed and on the

kinks in the burlap bag. He did not sleep; sleep had moved away permanently. But he still refused to be dominated by doubt. Madan would return. Seven long years had passed and the separation was about to end. His confidence, however, felt tested and he cried with impatience. He could not wait much longer.

3

They were shrimp fishing at the edge of the waterfall; Kissan watched Dhanlal and Dawood from a few feet away. They jumped when he struck a twig. Fishing was prohibited at that location. Swimming, too. Dhanlal had been caught one day.

At the time Kissan and his friends had settled there, the land was free; no one was in charge of what was prohibited or not. When they arrived, it was a barren land, rocky; nothing grew but a few trees. But they had worked with zeal, removing the stones from the ground one by one. A group of a dozen labourers planted corn. Dawood had given them two ears to start with, recovered in a field on the other side of the mountain. Then they'd also grown sweet potatoes and vegetables. The tomato plants already gave beautiful yields when Mr Maurel claimed the field. From that day, they lost their independence. Every drop of their sweat belonged to someone else. Mr Maurel built two sugar plants. Seven hundred labourers, in three villages, worked for him. He had witnessed the accidental death of twenty people without blinking when a millstone about the size of an ebony tree collapsed, killing eight men on the spot and crushing twelve under its weight. It was said that Mr Maurel did not flinch at the horrible spectacle. He did not even take out his whip.

"He has not yet returned?" Kissan asked abruptly, coming up to the two fishermen.

He received no other answer than the murmur of the river singing softly. They stood there listening to the freshness of the morning. Drops of bright dew showed themselves on the new leaves like a young man's thoughts. But his thoughts now remained dull and wavering in the darkness of his bereaved soul.

A cardinal perched on a tree on the other side of the river

held his attention for a moment. But soon he looked away. In the dense foliage of the mango trees, the unseen birds twittered. Their trills resembled the sobs that burst inside him as impatience gnawed. Dawood took a few tobacco leaves from the knotted end of his *dhoti* and crushed them to pieces in his hand. Then he rolled up the tobacco in a small piece of paper and threw a glance at Dhanlal, who brought out a lighter he had made. Dawood offered a cigarette to Kissan, who refused. Dhanlal refused accordingly: it was impossible to smoke in the presence of Kissan, in the same way it would have been impossible to smoke in front of his father.

"Dhanu, you think he won't come back?" Kissan asked in a low voice.

There was a long silence, then Dawood decided to speak, "Perhaps because of this nasty business..."

"What business?"

Dhanlal took over, "There were mass arrests recently. Of the one thousand labourers who gathered in the courtyard of a temple, seven hundred were arrested."

"When did this happen?"

"'The day before yesterday."

"Were you there?"

"Thirty labourers from here were there."

"What for?"

"To speak out against the abuses and excesses."

"Why didn't you tell me?"

"Next time we will take you; just let us know." For a few moments nothing was heard but the murmur of the river flowing behind them.

"How does this relate to Madan's release?" Kissan finally asked.

"Kissan, it was Madan who organised the first meeting of labourers in the temple that we built. It was the first building of its kind and it is possible that they arrested him, right? I see two possibilities: either they decided to postpone his release as a result of this incident, or Madan joined the protesters once he was out of prison."

"You mean he was arrested again?"

"Maybe."

"Even before he came back?" No, that he refused to believe. Moreover, Dhanlal was speaking nonsense. Had he not predicted the return of Madan the next day for days? So why say it wasn't true this time? No, it was ridiculous.

They heard a noise coming from the undergrowth. A mongoose? They had focussed their attention when they saw a figure approaching from the trail. Although he was still far off, they recognised his hat as that of the foreman Anthony. In one bound, they disappeared and fled down a path that led to the village. Kissan did not utter a word. The two men wanted him to accompany them to the village.

"Zinat would love to see you," pleaded Dawood.

"It will be a distraction for you," insisted Dhanlal.

Kissan did not reply; he was already on the path sloping down to his cabin. In the distance, they could hear the boss's dogs barking. The boss was deer-hunting with his pack, the very same howling dogs who had shred the poor Sunuwa. He had been gathering wood in the forest when Mr Constant's son, hearing the warning sound of broken branches, had fired. His dogs, maddened by the smell of blood, fell upon Sunuwa and devoured his flesh. Mr Constant's daughter, touched by the plight of the widow and Sunuwa's five children, had sent them seven rupees. She had also given the police officer in writing the report on her oath that Sunuwa was solely responsible for the accident he had suffered.

Sunuwa was the man who succeeded Gautam in teaching the children the *Ramayana.* When Mr Maurel, with his battalion of guards, had appropriated the village land, Sunuwa told his students, smiling, "This country belongs to you. It is the land where you were born and where you will die. This gentleman's papers perhaps prove that this land belongs to him, but tomorrow it will carry the mark of your feet and your labour. And that, no one can take away. It's a dream that you must cherish, awake as much as asleep."

He did not know to what extent the children understood his message, but he told them what he thought was important. On the day of his death, Kissan tirelessly repeated these words. But even the older ones did not understand his speech, and as for the younger ones, it was an illusion to think that they were listening. Sunuwa had also said that it was necessary to abolish the old law and replace it with a new, fairer law... But who would draft the new law? What would the new text be? And who would cancel the old one? Kissan was never able to answer these questions; they remained outstanding, like so many others.

A stream flowed over a bed of well-polished black stones. A wild almond tree's roots dipped in the cold water, halfway between the village and the cabin. Often Kissan would sit there, perched in the place where he felt truly at home. He had bathed in the creek and put his clothes out to dry during the day. He would snatch a handful of tiny flowers and sitting on the ground, sing softly. But for several days, he had not bathed and he had not washed his clothes. He'd stopped singing and did not touch the lovely, multicoloured flowers.

The day had tiny flowers. And also thorns. He saw his body bloody, studded with drops of blood. After Sunuwa's death, he went to Mr Constant with the seven rupees to be forwarded to the widow.

"Excuse us, sir, but this money, we cannot accept it."

The man turned red; he looked at Kissan like his eyes were out of his head. Then he held his fist over his shoulder and roared an order. A black guard rushed in, a whip in his hand. The whip lashed the air. But just as his wife had pity on Sunuwa's wife, he had compassion for Kissan. He began to laugh a laugh of denial. And he called his three dogs. He stroked them, and, still laughing, he said, "Tell me, Kissan."

"Yes?"

"I hear you ran very fast." Kissan bowed his head. "I am counting to three. And you're leaving." Kissan did not respond to the boss's threat. Then he nodded, and the other laughed again. "As soon as you are gone I will count to a hundred. Then I'll let out my dogs. One... two... three..."

Kissan ran out. Moments later, he had the dogs after him. He was running like crazy. He ran as fast as he could, even more quickly, breathlessly. A little later, the dogs brought their master back a piece of cloth torn from his *dhoti*.

4

From the top of his slope, he looked at the labourers cutting cane in the fields. Down there, the world was busy – a world from which he had long been excluded. But he had his own tasks and he had under his care the pruning of the canes, purple and bright. The fruit of his work was secure; this was white gold, whose value increased daily. But he would never taste the sweetness of pure sugar. He would only reap the pressed rods from which he could still extract a few drops of juice.

He felt bitter contemplating the landscape below. The martins, in their graceful flight, flew over the fields in strips where the cane had just been cut. Their cries annoyed him. He looked on as they flew at the stems, nibbled on the flowers of the cane and enjoyed the hunt.

He remembered Sita and Ramba fighting in the fields when they picked up the cane leaves after cutting, filling their bags. Their quarrels always started the same way: "You're as aggressive as a martin, Sita!" Ramba would say. And her friend picked up all the leaves before her and ran away laughing.

Kissan loved Sita deeply. He had long cherished the dream of having her for a daughter-in-law. One day, on the strip of wetland that separated the two fields, a band of martins fought, hovering over each other. Sita threw them the piece of cane she had to suck. They made up around it and rested a little further, before resuming their parade. Kissan said to the girl, "Tell me, Sita, would you marry Madan?" Sita ran away to the martins. That same evening, Kissan composed a song to the accompaniment of the tambourine:

For their young, sparrows peck
but here's the martin dispersing squeals,
The sparrows' nest on small trees;
the martin has his nest atop the coconut palm.

Later, Sita heard Madan singing this song and she questioned, "Madan, why did the martin perch so high?" She had re-posed it again, in another form, "Madan, why don't the other birds build like the martins?"

Madan came to find his father to ask him the question in turn.

He looked serious and Kissan always worried when he saw him wear that severe expression. Several scenes came back to him, precise down to the smallest details. One evening, Madan returned home after a hard day's work in which he had filled twelve cane-carts. Kissan called him. "Madan, you really like Sita, don't you?"

"You know, Dad."

"No, I do not know."

"Wouldn't it please you, to have her as your daughter-in-law?"

"This is not what I'm asking."

"With your permission, I'd like to marry her."

"That's not an answer to my question, either."

"Without her, I..."

"Come on, stop talking nonsense. And answer me frankly."

"I like her enormously. More than I like myself."

The second memory brought up Vivek, Pushpa's son. He returned from the mill where he had ground three cartloads of cane. Kissan stopped him on the way.

"Vivek, wait, I have to talk to you." The boy stared nervously. "Madan and you, you are good friends, yes?"

"I have no better friend than him."

"And Sita?"

"..."

"Answer me, Vivek."

"You know."

"What?"

"How much I like Sita."

"I do not claim to know."

"Without her, I..."

"I just want to know if you love her really."

"Yes, I love her like a madness."

"You love her more than you like Madan?"

"Let me love her as much as I like Madan."

The third memory, finally. Women washed clothes in the river. Sita stood on the sidelines and the water lilies were a veritable floating mat. Kissan was alone. "Sita, can I ask you a question? Who has the closest friendship in the village?"

"Everyone knows it."

"Who?"

"Vivek and Madan."

"Would you like their friendship to last forever?"

"All the world wants that."

"But you, what do you think?"

"I think like everyone else."

"That is to say?"

"They will remain friends."

In the last memory, the *panditji* stood at the door of the *baithka*, reciting the marriage verses. It was evening. Vivek had between his fingers a pinch of pigment and he applied it to the line that parted Sita's hair. The same evening, they had celebrated the Janmasthami, the birth of Krishna and the day before Kissan had had a strange dream. Sita was there, motionless, in her bridal veil. Vivek and Madan stood ready and when the horn of the *panditji* sounded, they began to run. The whole village had gathered around the margosa tree and expected them to be back before sunset. They had left the trail and attacked the slopes of the mountain; they had to cross it to go to Mr Maurel's house. There, they had to find his whip, and bring it back. Whoever did so would have Sita as his wife. In his dream, it was Vivek who was returning with the whip. He awoke with a start. But he did not regret his decision.

These old memories, long forgotten, had come back suddenly. They now haunted his mind, sharp as blades. 'Who would come back?' he asked himself bitterly. And for the first time in his life, he doubted Madan's intentions. Why had he led this revolution with such ferocity? Was it not escapist? At the time, Kissan had thought that his son had enough audacity to engage in this fight. He who had such experience of life and men, how could he commit such a miscalculation?

Seven hundred people arrested within the precincts of the temple...

And even if Madan did return, how would he be welcomed? With kisses, sighs of relief? Would the battle end then?

But how did a man fight alone against a force capable of stopping seven hundred people in the courtyard of a temple? The confidence and determination Kissan had shown in his life were gone.

Down in the green fields, the cutting was going well. The plants were dense, great canes and bumper crops. There would be a lot of sugar this year. This would bring more money than usual.

He recalled a scene, so often repeated in his mind. Seven labourers stood before the boss, speaking with one voice, "We demand a wage increase. Our children's clothes are in tatters. We never have enough to feed them, and nothing to put on their backs..."

The boss did not even respond. And as always, they had cut the canes, despite the growing bitterness.

Kissan awaited Madan's return.

5

It was rumoured that a government appeal had been launched to improve the labourers' conditions. A new committee was put together to investigate the situation. The rumours led everyone on the field to believe that the labourers would be reimbursed for every drop of sweat. But when the officials came to visit the fields, they saw that the inspectors' skin did not shine with sweat. They had been blotted. The guards were on alert. The sugar trade had a bright future; the owners could rest easy.

"Wait for the sea water to become soft," sneered Mr Constant. "That's right, wait! Enjoy the fruit of patience... Later, there will be days where you can drink the water from the sea..."

There were a few optimistic rumours. Things would change, definitely. They should not give up hope. Compared to the time when people did not even have the right to open their mouths, the current situation was not so terrible. At least they had the right to complain.

For some, it was all talk; for others, they were words of comfort.

Amongst the bosses, the labourers' patience was always a subject of praise and admiration. A government-wide policy had prevailed, sustaining indecision and inaction. Meanwhile, the labourers continued to toil in the fields. They had paid their contingent of sweat to the furrows. The crops continued to be produced and the owners met the envoys of the government, asking, 'Do you see any rebellion? Who is complaining here?"

After the investigator came to take the measure of the situation, they had never heard from him. He had simply disappeared into the wild.

The oldest man in the village, after Kissan, was Dhanlal's father. He was only two or three months younger. Sugan Bhagat walked bent, broken in two by a life of labour. His face was furrowed in countless wrinkles; he had sunken cheeks and eyes. He had arrived by boat in the middle of the plague and of his fellow passengers, many had died scarcely landed. Sugan Bhagat had tried many times to leave the island, but he had never succeeded. He was not allowed to return to India until after his contract of labour was over. Accused of violating the rules of the plantation, he had been ordered to pay a heavy fine that ate up his monthly salary. Remove a third of his debt, and at this rate, he would have had to work thirty years to pay the entire fine and fulfil his contract.

"After my death, you cut my body into pieces, and you'll pay my debt with that," he would often say to his son. The village people had nicknamed him Uncle Idiot. He used to comfort the desperate always in the same way: "It was much worse in my time,' he told them. 'You do not know the tags that we wore around our neck. Losing them meant three months in jail."

Everyone knew that if there was anyone who had lived those dark days in the flesh, even more than the old idiot, it was Kissan. Yet he refused to talk about them, even when the villagers asked him questions. His silence had given him the kind of desolation that the passage of a cyclone gives the landscape.

Whenever Uncle Idiot went to gather *ganja* plants in the mountains, he stopped at Kissan's. "You spend your days asking yourself if you succeeded in your life or if you failed. But it is a vain debate, my brother, and the short time you have left to live, you better enjoy it without getting worried. Come on, it's time you left the game."

Kissan was never able to understand Sugan Bhagat. He had been away from the game for a long time. But, even apart, he could not escape the consequences of playing all his life.

To understand the consequences fully, the game had to end. It had now lasted a good time, since his father had set foot on this island. Soon, his life would end. The third generation had taken up the torch. How long would it carry on now?

Sugan Bhagat never understood why Kissan was so closely linked to the fight, why he could never quite become detached. Basically, it would still be part of him, even after his death. In the village, Kissan taught children to play the Indian village games of *gulidanda* and *kabaddi*. He explained to them that one should not leave the game until the game is over. It is a sign of weakness and cowardice. Even if he is losing, the player must carry on.

The sun was at its zenith when, while cleaning his pipe, Sugan Bhagat began to make his way home. He had spent two hours with Kissan and was the only one talking. Kissan had sat silent as the grave and when Sugan Bhagat could no longer abide his silence, the visitor had left earlier than usual. Kissan accompanied him to the door and sat on a large rock under the shade of a tree. The strong smell of *ganja* floated around him. As he did not smoke himself, the acrid and penetrating smell irritated his nose.

He was quite surprised to see Sita advancing between the trees, branches in her arms. When she was near, Kissan asked her what she was up to. This was the first sentence he uttered since the beginning of the day. Sita put her burden down and sat on a dead tree trunk.

"I hear that you raise a little heifer?" he asked. She nodded. Kissan contemplated Sita's face, prematurely wrinkled. He remembered it a few years earlier, when he still lived in the village. She had been a beautiful girl, singing merrily, but working hard. Kissan saw himself sitting with his son, reading to him the verses of Ramcharitamanas. Soukhdeva sat next to them, munching on coconut. Kissan had been so charmed by the melodious Sita that he forgot the verses he was reciting.

"*Chacha,* you do not come down any more?" asked Sita.

"Oh, my daughter, my old body no longer functions."

"Zinat said that it was not that."

"Really?"

"It is because of Madan that you're so sad, isn't it?"

"How's your mother-in-law?"

"Madan makes you so sad!"

"If Madan does not care for me, why is it that I would worry about him?"

"My heart tells me that he will return."

"He will not return," Kissan yelled like one possessed.

Sita did not expect this reaction; she recoiled.

"No, my daughter, he will not return. But no more of this... how are you?"

"I'm fine, *chacha,* otherwise I would not come up to see you." They were silent. In the distance they could see Banshi and Sohna advancing towards the rocks, in the bushes. They went up to the hives. Kissan knew that if they found the honey they would leave him one or two days' worth. Banshi was a natural with the hives; bees could land on him without stinging.

"Sita," Kissan said, "How can you be sure he will come back?"

"He will return, *chacha,* I promise." To the west, the sun passed over the ebony trees. A couple of hares ran to the bushes. A breath of fresh wind gave Kissan goosebumps.

"Sita, I have not even had the opportunity to ask you the name of your youngest son."

"Parkash."

"It means" light", no?"

"Yes, that's what the *panditji* said."

"The light does not like to remain trapped..."

"What do you mean, *chacha*?"

"Until the darkness has hidden, how can the light hide? Parkash... will he have the same life we did?'

"Fate will decide."

"No, my daughter is not a matter of fate or destiny."

"So, what is it?"

"I do not know; let it be. How can you be so confident about Madan?"

"Because there is no reason to despair."

"Until yesterday I believed so myself."

"*Chacha,* I came to ask you to come down to the village with me. Here you will despair. And after all, Madan will stop at the village first.'

Kissan gave a long sigh, one that betrayed all his weariness. "But when?" A breeze carried the smell of dandelions. Kissan remained seated. Sita was waiting for him to rise.

6

Kissan took his book and sat down. He dipped the bamboo in the ink made of plum extract and told the story of Soma and Santu. He wasn't yet halfway through; he'd left off with Soma, alongside her new mother-in-law, grinding, humming. Kissan did not invent anything; he just wanted to transcribe the facts as they took place, to save their history. He wrote in dialogues. He remembered the tune Soma hummed that day and began by transcribing the words of the song:

Even if the West is blossoming
I do not offer thee my hand;
Along the river, stop the chants
and the immolation of young widows,
Roudwa's mother sobbed, 'Oh! my daughter
How can you suffer that burning fire?'

"Put the flour in my bag, my daughter. I'll see if I can borrow something to grind with from Karim."

"Do you think we can get him released, mother?"

"We cannot live without hope, my daughter. Even in Lanka, as a prisoner of Ravan, Sita never gave up hope."

"I am starting to lose confidence. And this house seems gloomy."

"And your brother who could not do anything..."

"I cannot speak of him, *Mataji;* he has not been on our side since he took the job."

"People change so suddenly, sometimes."

"Do not say anything. Just thinking about it hurts. If we could buy him, then..."

"You tell me to keep quiet and then you talk about it. Poor Santu! Who knows what will become of me?"

"What does your heart say, *Mataji?*"

"He will be released, of course."

"But who will get him out?"

"No one is greater than God, Soma."

"Do you believe yet, after all that has happened to us?"

"We cannot face life if we stop believing in God, my daughter. Come on. You have to eat something; you had nothing to swallow all day yesterday."

"At times, I am convinced he will be released. But just as soon my hope shatters. I do not know why."

"Do not let your hope break so easily, Soma. The men your father went to find may be able to do something."

"But *Pitaji* has been gone two days."

"Patience, patience..."

"I have a huge ache in my stomach. I feel discouraged and *Pitaji* was too."

"It's not so easy to meet people in high places."

"You mean it is normal that it takes time? But *Mataji,* how can I live when this impatience is draining me?"

"You have no choice, Soma. This is not the first time that you've suffered. Everyone suffers here. And others more than us. We still have a little flour, so let's make two *rotis.* Your father might come in and he would probably be hungry. Ah! Jhouni, here you are. I must go out to take this flour. Stay with Soma in the meantime, please."

"Okay, auntie, but hurry, we are reciting the *Ramayana* this afternoon and I still have many things to prepare."

"But Jhouni, I thought they were arrested yesterday when Harinanan Bhagat sang the *Ramayana.*"

"That is not a reason to sit and do nothing. We will not burn our books and wait."

"Very well, my daughter, but be careful."

"I wish I knew how they can confiscate copies of the *Ramayana.* And how many people they can throw in jail ... Come on, hurry up, we wait your return.'

"Jhouni, why do I feel so discouraged?"

"A little patience, Soma."

"I've always had it, but this time..."

"Come on, think no more of it. I brought some rice."

"Jhouni, stop giving us rice."

"Why?"

"Don't you understand how indebted we'll feel?'

'Do not consider it a debt, period. Can I ask you something, Soma? Could you, at least, consider us not to be strangers?"

"Jhouni, I have always thought of you as a sister."

"To hear you, you would not know."

"I never thought that on the seventh day of my marriage, I would have to face such a catastrophe. My heart beats so hard that I'm afraid. This morning, my mother came to see me. When she left, she wept. If my father learns anything, his condition will get worse. All our neighbours are complaining and feeling sorry for us, and I cannot cry. Don't you think it's odd?"

"You're crying inside, where it's most painful. You're destroying your interior. I do not know what possessed us to leave our country to come here... but here, all the misfortunes of the earth are gathered. What you saw, we all lived at one time or another. But we are afraid of adversity, to confront it. We came looking for gold... We knew there would be a price to pay! Soma, not only is there no gold when you lift the stones, but now our hands are trapped under the stones. And we will not work them out alone."

"We have not even had time to really look at ourselves."

"Well! You will need to wait a little longer."

"Three days ago, I left him to go to the kitchen. I never thought that this meant I would leave him for good. Tell me, Jhouni, what do you think? Answer me frankly."

"About what? I have already said that I trust in God. Everything will work out. All you need is a little patience."

"That is what I lack most right now. Believe me, Jhouni, I begin to lose hope and every second seems like an eternity. I cannot breathe and I'm afraid all the time. Jhouni, was he really capable of murder? No, do not say anything... I refuse to believe that he killed someone. You were not there that day, Jhouni, otherwise, you would have seen the innocence in his eyes."

"I do not think he is capable, Soma, only..."

"What?"

"A farmer labouring under a blazing sun receiving a whipping... it is understandable if he lost his temper. In any event, if he did, it was only to defend himself. Or he lifted his pickaxe to protect himself and it fell in the wrong place."

"Right now, he rots in a dark dungeon, with nothing to eat or drink and they beat him, whip him. Jhouni, our men give themselves body and soul to live in this country, why in exchange do they reap injustice and infamy?"

"It is awful, Soma. Those who have worked to clear the forests and turn them into large green fields live in awful conditions. It is they who produce everything and they do not even have enough food or clothing. That's the most ironic thing: work and one is crushed; do nothing and one is enriched. How a handful of men can crush thousands remains a mystery to me. It is we who work and someone else enjoys the fruits of our efforts."

"You think it will be like this for a long time?"

"Who knows? We are not asking to live in luxury and yet we are denied the minimum. As for respect and human rights..."

"How long are they going to oppress us?"

"You reason in reverse, Soma. Nobody is oppressing us unless we let them crush us. Look at your brother, for example."

"Jhouni, for heaven's sake, do not talk about him."

"Everything has an end. Fortune favours one day those it crushes underfoot another. Soma, you read the *Ramayana,* so you should know that those who believe should not be afraid of the danger. You are the daughter of the *Ramayana* chanter, three months in prison for having read a few verses. I still remember it. That's why I cannot believe that Vinay has negotiated with the whites..."

"Jhouni, you should go talk to the foreman Harkoo."

"Shut up, do not remind me... It was he who was behind this absurd idea to replace animals by men to pull the cane carts. It seems that the bosses were so pleased with his good services they offered him acres of land along the river. God grant that his land becomes a cemetery!"

"And that *Pitaji* comes back soon!"

"Soma, deep down you curse your bad luck. But you know, your fate is no worse than any other Indian labourer."

"No, Jhouni, I'm not complaining. One day, someone will kill these men. Believe me, I am proud that my father is on the side of rebellion."

"It's good. I see that time has taught you to speak up. But I know what to do to see your sadness disappear. Soma, I have to go, otherwise my mother will start to make a fuss. Don't despair, eh?"

"You can go, Jhouni, it's fine... This solitude, why does it weigh so much? But, oh! Who are you?"

"Well! My daughter, why are you so afraid of seeing me?"

"But I'm not afraid ..."

"You did not even say hello to me. I am Harkoo, the foreman. I want to talk to your father-in-law."

"He went out. But I think he came to see you earlier."

"I do not see your mother-in-law either."

"She went out with the flour."

"What a pity you are in such a nasty home alone! It hurts my heart to think a pretty girl like you lives in such a dump. Ohh! My poor legs..."

"Sit down a moment."

"Ah! Thank you, thank you, my darling. You know, tomorrow the boss will lend me a carriage. The life of a Mogul shall I live! I do get tired more after a walk. And I have a beautiful white horse. Really, I pity you. Have you heard of Jasoda's daughter? She is beautiful, like you, very nice. She lives like a queen since she went to see Marcel."

"Chacha, I'm glad you're here. Everyone claims that the life of my husband is in your hands."

"Ah! that's true ... But it also depends a little on you."

"What can I do?"

"Santu has committed a crime. He killed a white man. A man who killed God could be saved, but killing a white man..."

"He is innocent, you know. Save him."

"It will be very expensive..."

"You know our situation. We do not even have food. And not a penny either. We will not be able to give you any money."

"It's not just money ..."

"What else?"

"It's just that Mr Roland... only he can make the decision."

"You can convince him?"

"I see that you do not know Mr Roland. He will ask me who I am daring to plead for and why the person does not show herself."

"You mean someone in the family should go?"

"He will not listen to anyone. And then there is another problem. Tomorrow he'll go to his other plantation and will not return for three months."

"Three months? Meanwhile, anything could happen!"

"I see only one solution. You have to go and find him right away."

"Now? But *Pitaji* is not at home."

"Oh! No, only you can convince Mr Roland. Just by seeing you he will feel sorry."

"I cannot leave. My mother-in-law has not returned either."

"Well! In that case, I'm going. You just have to await the return of your mother-in-law. If Roland is already gone, you will have lost a good opportunity.'

"Wait, *Mataji* will not be long."

"She will have been delayed by rain."

"What can I do?"

"Would you have an objection if I take you with me?"

"No, but..."

"Well, listen! I'm going."

"It's raining..."

"I am not made of salt. I will not melt."

"Wait for me, I will accompany you to Mr Roland."

"Hurry; take your cloak and come with me."

Kissan gave a long sigh. Today, he wrote for longer than usual.

7

When Sita must have been twelve-years old, her father took her and left the coastal village of Alette. The village where they settled next was nothing like the one in which she spent her childhood. Like other girls of her age, she had spent her life on the beach, in the sparkling sand. The sea swelled and became troublesome. Huge waves, high as mountains, came crashing against the black rocks and spread their foam on the shore, destroying the castles, rushing on to the beach as storms subsided, in search of collapsed buildings. They remained on the sand as long fringes of foam.

Sita loved being sprayed by the surf and then she would swim to the other side of the reef to reach the pits dug by the sea in the black rock. The other girls began to scream, but she did not listen and she came back much later, clothes stuck to her skin with seawater. She took the end of her friend's wrap to wipe her streaming face.

Sita found it very difficult to leave Alette. After what had happened, however, they truly had no choice. Her mother worked in the boss's garden. She had obtained this position after her husband's accident and she had done a lot of begging for it: she had three mouths to feed. The village chief had interceded on her behalf. Then the boss's son had taken a liking to her. He liked girls with dark complexions and brown hair. Often he was heard saying, "I love that brownie," speaking about Sita's mother. Rumours soon spread. It was claimed she was pregnant and she carried a white child in her womb. Sita's father was the last to know. The next day, Sita's mother disappeared and was never seen again. After seven days of searching, her husband heard someone say behind his back: "The sea is like the Ganges, only its depths can house fish...' Others responded, 'It's just gossip; she was the victim of a false rumour."

Sita and her father left the village and after three days of wandering, they met Kissan. It was through Kissan that she met Vivek and Madan. And because she valued Kissan's perspective, when the time came, she accepted his choice. She married Vivek. Yet at the time, she would have been unable to say which one she liked the most. It was only after she married Vivek did she realise that she preferred Madan. In moments of solitude, she wondered whether Madan's absence had not strengthened her feelings, or if they were rooted in Vivek's inability to make her happy. Sita looked in the past for indications of the love she had always felt for Madan, and she found all kinds of evidence, however small.

At the entrance of the village, under the banyan tree, there were large rocks marked by *sindoor* from a past ritual. Mr Constant had been injured kicking these stones. Slow to heal, he was superstitious enough to fear another incident under the same tree after the next ritual. As Sita took the opportunity of the coming ceremony to make a garland of flowers, Vivek and Madan came running towards her. It was already late and they stretched two hands out towards the garland. "Sita, give it to me," they cried in chorus. Sita approached them delicately and laid the wreath in Madan's hand, and he went off with a laugh. The same day, at the end of the ceremony, they all visited the well to wash their hands and feet. "Give me the first bucket of water," she had told the two boys at once.

Scenes like this: she had dozens in her memory. One evening, they returned from the fields, reaching the stable while cutting sheets of cane to suck on. The two boys had each got a stalk; she had only been reprimanded. She said nothing. Along the river, with Vivek's splashing, she cried and got angry with him. But when Madan sprinkled water on her, she stood, closed her eyes, and waited for the droplets.

Kissan was most unhappy to see Sita without Madan. His prison sentence was over, now. She, too, was dying of impatience to see him. She had asked Vivek several times, "Why hasn't Madan come back yet? What could delay him?"

"Why don't you try to find out?"

"But how?" Sita did not know.

When he came back from Sugan Bhagat's, after smoking ganja, Vivek saw things differently, "You only care about him, don't you!" he said angrily. And when he came back from working under the foreman Philip, he went back regularly to see Philip's wife, Andrea. Vivek would accuse Sita on his return, "Do you care about Madan more than about me?'

Seven years earlier, when Madan had been put in chains and taken away by the guards, Sita was crying, like all the other villagers. But she felt something that belonged only to her, a sense of pride for her hero, who had just been arrested for a just and worthy cause. The whip marks on his back left large red furrows, but his expression did not reflect fear or resignation. Sita could not help admiring him. The bond between them strengthened her pride.

As time passed, the memories she had of Madan had become more blurred. But they returned to the surface, suddenly, the day Vivek slapped her for the first time. That day, her heart wept. She bore the insults and kicks without a tear. When he struck her, Sita thought of her father and mother. But if there were two other people who also comforted her when she thought of them, it was Kissan and his son. And in difficult times, she missed Madan the most.

When Vivek did not return home from Andrea's that evening, Pushpa said in a voice full of anger: "By taking you as my daughter-in-law, I have destroyed your youth, Sita. You should have married Madan, not Vivek.'

She repeated it in the presence of her son, the next day. "If what you really wanted was that damn white woman, why did you marry Sita? To ruin her life?"

"I did not ruin her life... she receives her share of food every day, right?"

"Look at her a little. She is as thin as a stalk of cane. Here is the full effect of what you give her to eat! And do you think that food is enough for a wife? If her father were still alive, I would tell him all of this."

From the first three months of her marriage, she would never have foreseen this. She had been treated like a queen. After he finished work, Vivek came home and spent time with her. He would return laden with fruits from the woods. "You're going to stain your shirt with plum juice," she would say, laughing. But he didn't care.

Then, when he started sleeping with Andrea, he came home drunk and his breath smelled of wine. He vomited in the house and it all went horribly wrong. Sita cleaned and Pushpa cursed fate. Sita tried hard to make him see reason, but Vivek would just become aggressive, "You'll never understand what a real woman is."

"She's no more woman than I am."

"She's made for pleasure."

"She is perhaps a little more beautiful, that's all."

"She is all that you are not."

"Oh, I get it."

"You don't get it. You're as cold as a winter evening, while she smoulders. I like fire, not ice. You know why I smoke weed and why I drink? Because it makes me hot and I love the heat. What kind of a woman is unable to warm up a man?

Sita remembered one day Madan had told her, "You will make a man so happy." Today, she wondered which of them she believed. She kept fretting. 'What kind of a woman am I? What is a real woman? Why am I a woman? Is there something I lack that I need to become a complete woman?' And she remained devoured by doubt.

8

There were a dozen men. Seeing them attack the climb, Kissan thought right away that Madan had been released. They were still too far for him to recognise them. He sought his son in the group. He must have come down to the village and the others led him here. Kissan felt his heart leap into his chest; it was nailed there, unable to do anything. Should he go to meet them or let them come up to him? If he moved, the wait would be shorter. But he was unable to decide.

The sun was slowly descending towards the horizon. It seemed to Kissan that they spent a lot of time coming up. Then dawn came and they arrived in the dark. He did not recognise Madan amongst them. He wanted to shout, 'Why not move faster?'

His eyes scanned the group, in search of his son. He remembered the way his son walked and thought he could recognise his walk. His impatience made the distance longer and blurred his vision. They walked in single file on narrow trails and the silhouettes became more and more distinct. And when they were at his level, Kissan felt his hopes dissolve, his eyelids unblinking, he remained standing, unresponsive. Inside him, he felt a definitive darkness.

"A terrible thing has happened, Kissan," said Dawood, "You're the only one who can help us." Kissan was silent, gnawing concern in his eyes, always the same.

"They are trying to break our backs," said Dhanlal.

Kissan then realised this had nothing to do with Madan. "What's going on?" he asked softly.

"The boss has given orders," began Dhanlal. Nearby, a group of martins flew off and over them, chirping.

"What orders?"

"The land behind the village, where we have our gardens, from now on..." Dhanlal could not even finish his sentence as anger strangled him. He looked at Dawood, who continued, "We no longer have the right to grow anything.'

"Why?"

"The boss has forbidden it."

"But he has no right."

"He's put fences around the plots, and says we have no right to set foot there."

"Wait, I do not understand..."

"He is going to build a new mill on the land."

Kissan remained silent in thought for a moment, then he said, "He can't do it!"

"It's already done. The fields are surrounded by barbed wire, guarded by armed men. We have not even had time to harvest the vegetables."

"The ownership of this land has been decided. The owner agreed that it was ours."

"Yes, he said he agreed because at the time he needed us to work his fields."

"He has made a promise to the entire village."

"Do we have evidence?"

Kissan did not know what to say.

"I do not think they will construct a mill," Devraj intervened.

"Really?"

"They have brought two hundred pigs to the edge of the field. They will build a pigpen." The setting sun sprinkled the earth with rose tones.

"Kissan, you're the only one who can guide us," said Dawood. A pair of martins flew by.

Kissan waited until they disappeared, "Do you have any ideas?"

"No, we got up here right away."

Kissan was thinking fast, 'Am I still part of the village? Can he who has lost a battle return to the fight? I, who doubted the boss's good faith from the beginning and warned us never to believe their promises?'He thought for a long time. "Do not allow them to take the field."

"Kissan, it's not so easy."

"Easy, difficult... those three acres belong to us; there is no reason why the boss should be there."

"What should we do?"

"Nobody is going to work tomorrow. I'll come with you."

"Do you know what is behind all this scheming, Kissan?"

"Nothing at all, it's just a whim. The whites are used to doing what they want."

"This time it is not just a whim. They realised that with our small fields, we have much improved the ordinary conditions of our lives. Fresh vegetables are good for us and we are healthier. How can they support that? They believe they are masters of every cell in our body, so how could they accept that we work on our own behalf?"

Sugaṅ Bhagat, who had remained silent until then, still under the effect of *ganja,* finally spoke. "And what will we do once we're back in the village tonight?"

"Regroup first, then we'll see."

"If you ask me, we will not accomplish anything."

"You suggest that we sit idly by?"

"We are one hundred and fifty labourers. We only have to go and complain to the boss."

"And ask him frankly to give us our land..." a young man continued.

"And if he refuses?" said another.

"We will send a petition to the government."

"You have already forgotten the national petition that was just signed by thousands of labourers?" interjected Dawood's son, who was the youngest of the group. It did not help. Dawood motioned him to be quiet. He did not want Farid to disrespect his elders.

But the pessimism of his message was carried forward by Dhanlal. "Kissan, we have to face facts. First, rain or shine, the bosses are white. Next, they know the government will let them do as they please, will never put its nose in their business. You know the village of Juvence? Two labourers there were whipped in the presence of two policemen for a whole half an hour, and then they were the ones arrested, under the pretext of inciting rebellion! When the wife of one of the men threw himself at the policemen's feet, they arrested her, too."

"I understand what you are saying."

"You understand nothing at all! Otherwise, these injustices would have come to an end long ago. If we continue to play the moderation card, we will remain in the same situation and it could last for years, decades. If you want my opinion, we must drop the tools of the jeweller and take up those of the blacksmith."

"You said just two minutes ago that the whites were supported by the government. Under these political conditions, how can we act otherwise than with moderation?"

Farid replied promptly to his father, "But we've tried that from the start! As a result, we suffer, heads down and submission has become our second nature. I've had enough and if it were up to me, I'd go after injustice with a sickle in my hand."

"If you want to die young, go for it," replied Dawood.

The first star had appeared in the sky. Kissan recommended that the small group return to the village immediately. "See you tomorrow morning in our gardens.'

When everyone had gone, he returned to the cabin and lay down on his bed. He breathed, felt life in his muscles. He felt much the same as he had felt long ago, a young man of Farid's age. In the darkness of his room, he seemed to rest in a cave... he lived handicapped by old age, supported by crutches of memories, yet as determined as the first day he had fought back.

He heard the chirp of a cricket and other little noises in the night. Farid had encouraged him to construct the wall with a window so that the starlight could enter and the breeze finds its way to his lungs.

Suddenly panicked, he closed his eyes and refused to reopen them. A vast plain lay before him, intoxicating and swept by a wind of freedom. A sound came to distract him – the song of the crickets in the desert who came to the depths of his solitude to carry him back to reality.

9

On one side of the fence, the green fields; on the other, the labourers dressed in their earth-coloured shirts and dirty *dhotis*. On the grassy path shone the morning dew. The labourers had arrived at dawn, armed with sickles and hoes. The two guards who were watching their field stood back, so that they had a view of the gathering. The smell of tobacco came from the green fields. Some men sat on their heels, others were standing. Kissan was expected.

When he appeared, three hundred eyes turned towards him, asking the same question: 'What now?'

Kissan spoke first with Dawood, then with Sonallal. The others had gathered around him and soon they cleared a path for him to get to the big rock. He climbed to the top and looked around about him. "I must first ask you," he said. There was a silence, and Kissan said in a feeble voice: "Will you keep your fields, or not?"

Several answers shot forward, "We want to keep them, of course."

"No question."

"We will not leave them. No way!"

Kissan spoke again. He spoke slowly, often pausing to catch his breath. "All the surrounding land belongs to us. We cleared the forest for our fields. We nourished them. The law was not on our side, so we kept quiet. We only know that these three acres of land, at the cost of our own great efforts, have been built up with crops, our *baithka*, and our Kali temple. Here, while I live, no one here will build an enclosure for raising pigs. We have never offered a pig to Kali, and we never will!"

Some were surprised to hear Kissan talk about religion because it was the first time he had done so. But they knew enough to know he was serious. On three acres of land there were fifty plots, each operated by two families from the village. They were not uniform plots and they were not cultivated in the same way. Sonallal was responsible for managing them: if a family inherited a plot away from the river, he made sure that by the next season, it was irrigated enough to be fertile. All afternoon, once they were home from work on the plantation, the labourers cultivated their plots. They planted eggplant, tomatoes, beans, even sweet potatoes. With the exception of Sugan Bhagat, who cultivated only corn year-round, others grew everything from pumpkin to spices. The harvests of all the fields were first distributed in the village and the surplus was sold elsewhere. The money that was raised was the responsibility of the *baithka* committee, who used it for community purchases. They had already built a new hall and paid for the marriage of several girls in it. They planned to improve the temple.

Women helped in the gardens until sunset. The children waved pieces of metal to keep the birds away. Girls watered the garden and weeded. Gautam's son did nothing agricultural: he sang all day for the villagers and afterwards, tried to attract the village girls. Most of them refused because they claimed that the boy never washed.

It was in these small gardens that the labourers forgot the bosses and their cane fields. As an antidote to the gruelling work on the plantation, the work on these plots gave them a kind of intoxication, a feeling of freedom. Here there was no bamboo cane, no whip, no injuries and no foremen. These fields were theirs and they loved to work with dedication, pride and pleasure. Sometimes, the boss sent some of his men to pick some vegetables, but most of the harvest went to the villagers themselves, who worked the fields. It was undoubtedly their greatest satisfaction.

And it was going to be taken away.

After how many atrocities, how much punishments and abuses had the three acres become the labourers' property? History itself should have granted them the land, but it was not so easy. At the time of their arrival, there had been only a handful of men in this part of the island. Only after they had cut the trees and transformed the earth, taking away the stones one by one, cutting the brambles and vines, had whites come to this corner of beautiful fertile fields.

Kissan had spent the night thinking about all those who, like him, had poured blood and sweat into every inch of this prosperous land. They had done so only to fill the coffers of the bosses and when finally, they had managed to acquire a small portion of land, this small piece of land had become synonymous with their identity, their freedom. It gave them a guarantee that they were not here in vain, not only here to be reduced to virtual slavery; it told them they had the right to lay here the foundations of a new life. Only these few acres allowed them to reject the terrible feeling of inferiority that marked their current condition. It was a first step towards the liberation of future generations and if they took this away, then on what grounds would their children be raised?

All these reflections had prevented him from sleeping, but they had also distracted him from thoughts of Madan.

Some labourers proposed to break the new barbed wire barrier and return to the cane fields. Kissan dissuaded them. The vegetation that this field contained held their souls, tied against their will to the tender shoots of tomato plants, into the bright undressed leaves of the eggplants, to the twisted vines of the pumpkins, to the young zucchini flowers and and strong corn. Gautam's son walked into the crowd singing. The sun was already high in the sky. Everyone sat on the road and some sang along with the verses of the *Ramayana.*

Some in the crowd knew that a scene would begin to play out, one which everyone knew by heart: first the lashes, then the gunfire, arrests, and voila, a return to normality... The owner would arrive home looking happy and successful. But no! This time, they were determined. It would not happen like that. The beginning might be the same, but the end would be different. They would not leave head down and spine bent.

The first scene played as usual. First, they heard the barking of dogs arriving from the west. Then they saw the distant silhouettes of additional guards. Seven of them arrived in uniform. Foremen dragged behind and finally the boss's carriage. The seven guards took up their positions, guns in hand, a short distance from each other. The foremen were holding sticks, surrounding the boss, standing in front of his carriage.

No one got up at their approach; all remained firmly seated on the ground. Only Kissan advanced to the carriage and stood before the boss.

"What is this, then, Kissan?" he said in a voice that betrayed his anger.

Kissan answered in the same tone, "I do not have anything to say, sir. We did not start this, in any case."

"What are all these people doing? They should be at work... do you know how much their absence makes me lose a day?"

"How much, sir?" Dhanlal asked, standing up in the background.

"Fifteen thousand rupees!"

"Fifteen thousand rupees! A hundred rupees per labourer? That's really what we are worth? When I think that you give us eight annas a day, hardly a fractional amount..."

Kissan motioned to Dhanlal to be quiet. "We are not here to talk about money."

"This land is in the middle of my property."

Behind them, Farid cried, "Kissan, tell him that we do not intend to discuss it. He has only to tell us if he agrees the field is ours or not. We have no time to examine his forged documents."

The boss laughed. "This land does not belong to you anymore."

"We will not move from here."

"Then feel the consequences of your obstinacy and your lack of respect: ten guards are coming from Mr Constant in a minute. I advise you, when they come, to get up and go back to work."

Kissan, his hands clasped, declared with great modesty, in

Creole, 'Boss, my entire life, I –"

"Kissan," Farid cried, "do not ask for charity!"

"I have sacrificed my life for men like you. I implore you, for the first and last time, let us keep our three acres of land. Here stand our crops, our *baithka* and our temple. Leave them to us and I agree to spend my days at your service."

He had not gone two steps forward when he was shoved by a foreman; it made him fall. Dhanlal and Farid rushed to help him up and immediately a shower of blows fell on their backs. The villagers rose up in a single movement and rushed forward. Guns pointed towards them. Kissan straightened his back and cried, "Stop, all of you, stop!' He ran in front of the labourers and spread his arms as if to contain the crowd, but the men had already been caught throwing stones at the foremen. The boss had stood back, close to his carriage. He gave the order to fire. The ball went right to Kissan's chest and brought forth blood. He collapsed.

Far from the sacrificial altar.

10

They had killed Kissan. His blood flowed on the earth's path and coagulated. It formed a *tika* on the ground and Kissan's mark was seen on the surface of the earth like *sindoor*. The villagers were without cries or tears. All remained stunned, frozen.

Kissan's death heralded the death of history. It meant the end of an era, but also the end of any illusion. They knew which side fired first. No sooner was the shot out and approaching Kissan, did the rumbling sound of the crowd rise up, threatening. This had not yet reached the boss's ears, but all the guards and foremen wheeled about and prepared for flight. The labourers continued to throw stones. Farid repeated Kissan's last words. "Stop!" he roared.

All the men stopped. Kissan's heart ceased its beating. From the east, there appeared a young man, very tall, with a long beard, wearing a blue shirt. They first recognised the striped shirt: more than seven years earlier had been the day of his arrest. They recognised Madan.

To the west, the sun hid his face behind dark clouds.

Madan was sweating, but his eyes were dry. He advanced and the crowd parted to let him pass. Like a sleepwalker, he came up to his father. His face betrayed no emotion, not the slightest reaction. The others sighed, wiping away their tears. Madan remained standing, motionless, silent.

A group of women arrived, alerted and already in tears. Some knelt beside Kissan's body. Others touched Madan to comfort him, but he remained unmoved. Pushpa, who had rushed to the body, stood up and wrapped her arms around Madan. And suddenly it started to rain, fine drops that nobody noticed. Raindrops slid on to their hair and faces. Madan closed his eyes; everything was silent. The women were crying softly. When Madan opened them, he saw Vivek and Dhanlal. Then he saw Farid, who bit his lips.

He gave a long sigh that made them shiver. He covered his face and hands and began to move his head frantically until Vivek came to lay his hand on his forehead to stop it. The *panditji* advised them to take the body to the *baithka*.

Madan was sitting near the body, his head leaning against the white wall of the room where they kept his father. Thoughts jostled in his head. If only he had arrived a few minutes earlier... Did this show that he was powerless to thwart fate? He heard someone say the word 'coincidence'. But what was a coincidence? And for whom? He heard another talking about 'the inevitable'. But what was inevitable? And then patience... moderation... what patience? For what? But patience led to despair. How far could he escape?

His father was silent and that silence weighed on him. He held his breath to hear the silence better. He certainly had something to say. The need to persevere, to survive the fight...

In prison, Madan had a dream, had already formed plans, to continue to live, to fight. He had sworn to lose the naivete that had helped him believe in the merits of a losing battle. Now there was nothing left. No battle: the uprising had just been lost in his mind. On his way home this morning, he had taken the wrong path. Then he found two or three landmarks in the mountains and the fields. He'd been breathing hard, contemplating these familiar sights as they called him home. But that call had been an illusion. Back home, he still had the sense he was wandering like a lost traveller.

The next day, when Kissan's remains were taken out of the *baithka*, they finally saw the tears gush from Madan's eyes. In the funeral procession, Madan noticed with surprise the presence of many people from neighbouring villages. This was the first time he had seen one village feel sorry for the misfortunes of another. He was told that the labourers in neighbouring plantations went on strike upon hearing of Kissan's death. Madan remembered the day when, after the arrest of five labourers from a nearby village, his father had demanded all the nearby villages join in protest and be compassionate. He claimed it was useless to declare war if all the villages would not unite in the same spirit. At that time, the villagers had failed to agree and two of the five prisoners were killed in jail after their arrest. Furious, Kissan then called a meeting. "Within seven days," he declared, "I wish to see all the villages united, ready to speak with one voice."

Around Kissan's funeral pyre, they discussed these historic moments.

But the day Kissan had wished for came after his death. Madan then understood that his father had not given his life for nothing. That evening, when everyone had gathered for the reading of verses from the *Ramayana,* the *panditji* read the story of the death of Rama's father, Dasharatha, and he added, "The death of Kissan should not be considered an end." No one knew what he meant exactly, but most of the villagers saw a new phase, full of confidence and strength, when each, supported by others, would have the courage to hold his head high.

Madan's feelings were different. He felt as helpless as a tree shorn of its leaves by a cyclone. The freedom he had felt on his release from prison had frozen, pressed tight in his fist. He watched the people around him and read on their faces pain and exhaustion, despair, fear. Even more than sadness, apprehension prevailed.

The prayer ended. Dhanlal spoke. He was responding to Sugan Bhagat, who had proposed sending a petition to the government. "No one will support us outside," he said in a voice fraught with emotion, "We must act alone. No one will fight for us. It is our job to lead the fight, sustain it."

When he opened the door, the prison-keeper told Madan, "Do not start fooling around! If you again encourage labourers to riot, they'll lock you up again. And this time, you will not come out!"

Madan felt deprived of everything and not without cause. What remained in him that could inspire a fight? How could a man coming out of prison, weak, discouraged, still find the energy to start the fight?

A few stars scattered in the night gave the sky an ashen beauty. Madan could still hear the crackling fire of his father's funeral pyre. But beyond the body of Kissan gone up in smoke, was there anything else that had disappeared that day in the ashes? Madan was overwhelemed with questions. He remembered his mother, who laughed at him, saying, "You're just like your father; you still have questions. But instead of endless questioning, you'd better act." Rekha: his mother. Her death, too, he had not expected. Madan gave a long sigh that shook him from head to toe. He closed his eyes and felt tears beading under his closed eyelids, like the last drops wrung from a lemon.

The first time he had returned from the fields, he'd had tears in his eyes. Madan had started working at twelve. He was already tall and well-built, and the owner had hired him without question. His father told him, tapping him lightly on the shoulder: "The first day, it's hard for everyone." Then he turned to Rekha, "You'll see, Madan will accomplish what no one has ever done. But he must know all the difficulties of working to be able to one day make a difference. Remember what I tell you, Rekha. Madan is our only hope to put an end to this era of the whip and the bamboo cane."

Why had these old memories come back to haunt him now? Near him, Dhanlal had fallen asleep. Madan lay down on the mat, hands folded under his head, eyes toward the ceiling. The lamp was still smouldering, as did the remains of his father. The rain had stopped, but drops continued to fall from the trees like inexhaustible tears. The lamp would burn down soon; its pale light was beginning to flicker. He got up and reached for the bowl containing oil, pouring it on the small piece of wick. The light came back and held until dawn. Madan took up his position on the mat, his head resting on hands and remained awake until the flame took its last breath.

11

Three days after Kissan's death, the government-appointed Protector of Labourers made his appearance in the village. Mira saw his carriage in the distance, then lost sight of it when it was hidden in the margosa groves. She thought at first it was the boss, but soon she saw that it was just a regular carriage that stopped at the entrance of the village. Two men accompanied the Protector, books and documents in hand. One was very small, the other as well-built as the man they were escorting.

Mira, the first to see them coming, was afraid: would they arrest Madan again? Recurring arrests had happened before: the day after Mithwa's release, five plain-clothes officers came to the village, arrested him again and took him away. No one had seen him since.

But when the man approached, Mira recognised him. This was the second time he had come to the village. The first time, he'd looked like any boss and he had kept his distance. After his first visit, the most fantastic rumours had spread. "The situation will change," they said, "this is our Protector."

He had promised the moon. But something important happened when he came... what exactly? Mira could not remember. It was the time of her mother's death and the memory of that pain eclipsed all else. Mira remembered that when he arrived, thankful villagers had covered the Protector with garlands of flowers. He had given a long speech. Mira had learned nothing, but it had seemed to appeal to the others. The village was joyful; songs and dances had followed each other throughout the evening, until she learned about the death of her mother. Brutally.

At the other end of the field, two goats were grazing quietly; a dog was sleeping under the canopy of the first house in the row of houses at that edge of the village. The man and his two assistants went to the centre where a small crowd had already formed. No one bowed. The last time, not only had everyone come to meet him, but when he left, they had filled his carriage with presents. Everyone nourished hopes, but his visit was followed by arrests, even deaths. What would happen today? Mira's concern was growing. She was especially worried about Madan. She ran to Zinat, whom she found grinding corn. Sapura, Zinat's daughter, was mending Farid's *dhoti.* "Auntie, the man has came back."

Zinat stopped and looked at Mira. 'What man?'

"The one that was here when my mother died. Didn't you say then he was not a Protector, but a curse?"

Sapura looked up at Mira. 'I'm afraid,' Mira said to Zinat.

"Afraid of what?"

"Of what might happen after his departure."

"The trouble came before this time! What could be worse than Kissan's death?"

"I fear for Madan. I'm afraid they'll arrest him again, like they did with Mithwa."

"Why would he be arrested?' For Zinat, this didn't seem to be a possibility. Mira sat down with her and helped her turn the wheel. She had been eleven years old when Madan was arrested: how old her mother was when she had married. This was common practice in the village and neighbouring villages. Someone had proposed to marry her, and the opportunity had been discussed at the town hall. Dawood had spoken for his wife Zinat. "Mira is an orphan, certainly, but there is no pressure. If she does not feel ready for marriage, why force it?"

Later, some felt that they had waited too long and that she must find a husband soon. But Kissan and the *panditji* had then said, "Leave her alone."

Today she was eighteen years old, and she was the only unmarried eighteen-year-old girl in the village. This did not affect anyone, and most of the villagers remained indulgent, considering that she wasn't a burden.

"Auntie, you're sure about Madan," said Mira.

"Yes! Nothing will happen to him. And Madan is not even in the village; he is in his father's cabin. They will still not climb up there..."

Mira gave a long sigh of relief and began to sing, while continuing to operate the wheel:

Her scarf is soaked by the rain
in the biting cold and the blustery night,
During the night she turns the mill
and the ground flour weeps.
Her scarf is soaked by the rain
in the biting cold and the blustery night,
In a distant land, another holds her beloved
And her beloved does not remember her...

"Sapura" said Zinat, "go scatter the birds from the drying rice." Sapura rose. When she had gone, Zinat turned away from the mill. "Mira, you are trying to do exactly what I..."

"Go on, what are you going to say?"

"What I did myself twenty years ago."

"What?"

"I was in love with Dawood long before he noticed it. If Raghusing had not been there, our marriage would never have happened. I should play this role and serve as intermediary between you and Madan."

Mira continued to turn the crank. Zinat laughed, "What are you doing? Your mill is empty!"

Mira was eager to catch a handful of beans in the basket but they fell at her feet. She poured them into the mill and began to grind.

"Little lunatic! Before I get involved in this story, try to learn more about Madan. What kind of boy he is." Zinat took the ground flour and poured it into a canvas bag. "I can inquire as to whether Madan loves you or not."

"Can I ask you a question, Zinat?"

"About Madan?"

"No, I would like to know if it's you who chose Sapura for Farid. Or did he?..."

"Can you see Farid asking a girl anything? No, he saw Sapura on the wedding day."

"Sapura was not from here..."

"My aunt lived in her village. But why all these questions?"

"Farid and Sapura make a harmonious couple."

"You want to know if Madan and you will make a harmonious couple..."

Mira slowed her movement and added a few grains to the rim. "I shall never marry, so the question does not arise."

"Oh! Can you tell me then why you lower your eyelids like a frightened doe? Look into my eyes when you talk to me, please and I will see if you're telling me the truth. I've seen others, you know."

But Sapura had just entered and the discussion was cut short.

Back home, Mira found her aunt sitting still. She approached her and, seizing her head with both hands, knocked her forehead against the skull of the old lady. "Break my skull, why don't you, if it's any relief," squeaked the aunt in a high-pitched voice.

"Oh! Even the stones of the mountain couldn't break your skull, it is so hard."

"Where were you?"

"I was on a walk."

"Always on the loose! Are not you ashamed, all day long, you, a girl? At your age, I already had five children..." Mira became serious. It was enough that her aunt spoke these words; it felt suddenly silent and dark at once. She plunged into a deep sadness. She had been a mother of five, yes, but before the disaster, where Mira's uncle had also died. The cyclone had torn the banyan tree that had fallen on the roof of the hut, crushing everything and everyone in its path.

12

Madan finally managed to relax. He took the big book that his father had written in and went to the river. There, he settled next to a wild almond tree and opened the book. It was the story of Soma and Santu that Kissan had written in dialogue. It was a large book and Madan decided to read from beginning to end. His father's writing was articulate, readable.

"Tomorrow I am going back to work."

"How can you? Your leg is still not healed."

"Luchya, what do you want from me?"

"I never asked you to return to work immediately."

"But you said that what Santu brought home was not enough..."

"That's true."

"That's why I intend to go back to work tomorrow. It will be something gained, rather than me sitting here all day. Ah! I wonder where God is sometimes. He deprives me of a leg just when we have a new mouth to feed. Us two, we can still go to bed hungry, but Santu, who works all day and our new daughter: we cannot leave them like that."

"God is watching over us. Why do you worry?"

"You repeat that every day.'

"You're not even able to stand. How could you work?"

"All you have to do is make me a new saffron ointment tonight and tomorrow morning, the injury will be better."

"You had better be careful. If you ever get another wound there, you will remain crippled for the rest of your days. Soma, did you cook for Santu?"

"Yes, mother."

"So, come sit with me."

"I still have things to do in the kitchen."

"You have a whole life to be cooking in this house, so come and sit, please, we want to talk to you. For a long time, we have not seen a wedding here."

"What do you mean?"

"Well, my daughter, since we arrived here, yours was the first."

"Is that possible? There probably were others..."

"It's just that if we had the right to marry, we would feel we were considered human beings."

"It's still the case today, Luchya, that we are not allowed."

"Yes, but it was impossible to enact, then. When we got off the boat, the women had their heads covered with a veil. And men were asked to choose their partners among the women present. No one had the right to raise the veil. The men looked at the feet of girls and their jewels to decide. Your father-in-law, he had not even seen my feet. I was there before him, and when he heard the white man shouting, he reached out, pointing to me completely at random."

"And all marriages were like that?"

"If you call that a marriage..."

"Luchya, forget such hardship, it's in the past.'

"Soma, you cannot imagine how lucky you are, and you, Santu. You had no music, no singing or dancing, no sumptuous feast for your wedding, but at least Santu did anoint *sindoor* in the parting of your hair. In fact, you are the first true bride of Mauritius."

"Luchya, look at the mending you've done on my *dhoti*, it is already fraying.'

"I mended that *dhoti* two days ago!"

"I had nothing to do with it."

"Oh, so it's my fault!"

"Luchya, it is neither your fault nor mine. It's the brambles of the forest. Yet I have not stepped outside for several days... No, it's your thread that's not strong enough."

"Soma, there's a needle and thread in the small trunk. Bring them to me, please."

"I cannot separate myself from this *dhoti*. I've worn it every day that God made for twenty years. I came to Mauritius in it and it accompanies me in the sun and rain. I do not know how much longer it can last, for it really is in tatters. When I think that it's the one I wore during the crossing, I still remember my mother at the time of our farewell. 'Lakhan,' 'she said, 'in the *Ramayana,* Ram is exiled far from home. My Ram, my youngest, you have not even had time to enjoy my milk, as the epidemic has washed over us. It's you, Lakhan, who goes into exile today. May the goddess protect you, my son. And do not forget us when you have made a fortune in Mareech...' I have always remembered her. But I have not found a fortune in Mauritius. The only thing I harvest here are tears and blows."

"You are always rehashing the same old memories."

"How can I face the future in a hell like this?"

"Others do."

"They have tried dozens of times, but they can not change the situation."

"Who told you so? Soma, tell him everything your brother is doing right now."

"I know what he is doing. But it is useless. You cannot intimidate bosses. What her brother tries today, I myself hoped to do in my time. But the whip put right my ambitions."

"And if everyone is united, if all the labourers stand as one, that will not help anything?"

"What are you talking about? Do you see the labourers uniting as one force?"

"Father, this is what my brother is trying to do. He wants to unite all Indian workers before the fight. Two days before our wedding, he went to find the boss at the head of a procession of five hundred labourers. And he warned that if their demands were not taken into account, they would go on strike."

"The bosses do not care. It is we who have the most to lose by going on strike."

"Better to die than to accept these conditions. Young people should follow your brother's example. Only then will things change...

We heard that in Mauritius
we would find something to get rich
but we gathered only bamboo smacks
on the back of the head and even the neck,
like beasts from mill to mill, field to field;
from India now we are orphans...

"Stop humming this song."

"But why? Because it makes you sad, Luchya? That's why I sing. My mother said that we should not be dazzled by this country of which we boast. "Who knows if it's not all a trap,' she said."

"Well! My mother told me, 'There is no need to regret the seeds that the bird was plundering in the field'."

"You see this plate tin, Soma. This is my identity card! In India, my name was Lakhan Thakoor. Here I am only the number 45. And all this for two bowls of food a week. The island takes its revenge on us, who have planted the arrow of the God Rama."

"Soma, will we have something to eat tomorrow?"

"We have enough rice."

"And what shall we do after tomorrow? Santu's not received his salary for four days. What shall we eat in the meantime?"

"I know, Luchya. When I'm sick for two days and they withhold four days' wages... No money, no rice and that the debts we have incurred for the wedding."

"Why worry about debt? Santu will pay them."

"As long as I live, these debts will be mine, and not those of my son's. Soma, bring us some water."

"Do you want some yoghurt drink? Jhounia has brought some."

"Certainly."

"The foreman Harkoo said that a new governor has been appointed and it seems that, when he assumes office, the conditions of labourers will improve."

"And you believe what that liar says? It was he who, in India, promised us paradise. Ah, his honeyed words! I can still hear them: 'Here in Bihar, you are ten who have to share a grain of rice, while in Mareech, fruit, silver and gold await men to take them. Under every stone, there is a treasure, and, in every grain of sand, gold.' Why does this bastard swear, hand on his head, to make us rich in one night, eh, Luchya?"

"Please listen to me. Stop rehashing those awful memories."

"You're right, my daughter."

"There is still a little food. You want it, *Mataji?*"

"No. Keep it for Santu. He will arrive hungry and thirsty. This morning, he was eating a *roti* with stale old eggplant."

"Tell me, Luchya, which song will you hear?"

"You and your songs! No, I do not want to hear any, I have quite a headache."

"Then how about the *Ramayana?* It's great for migraines. And it is the only book that can make us want to survive in this hell."

"It's true. But for now, I prefer silence."

"If you do not want to listen, you just have to read it.'

"I told you at the moment I do not feel well."

"Come here, girl."

'Soma is busy, leave her alone.'

"She will have all her time without us soon. Santu said that you sang the Ramayana very well. Have you ever read it?"

"I do not read very well."

"Try it."

"I'll sing it tonight instead."

"Okay. No reading for tonight. But, then, could you sing a song now?"

In your own palace he conquered you,
You must leave your kingdom
In combat you look like a young God
so capable; you fight like a lion
yet they leave without a scratch.

"It's true that you have a beautiful voice. Listening to you, I feel rejuvenated."

"Thank you... you must go to the fields with your injured leg, otherwise, they will withhold another four days' wages."

"Don't be upset."

"Oh! But I'm not upset with you in particular. To me, all the labourers are in the same boat. How can you bear such a miserable life? And you push your children in the same way, and your grandchildren inherit the same submission."

"What else can we do?"

"You just have to do as the black slaves did: refuse to work like animals."

"Luchya, you're crazy. Our people, the people of Bihar, we are not afraid to work. Work has value and you yourself say that work is everything in the life of a man."

"But not so much! Even an ox would not do as much."

"And yet we're getting there."

"For what reward? Insults and kicks."

"When food is scarce, Luchya, work is something to fill the belly."

"Maybe you men, you still have enough energy, but us women, we can do no more. You think it's easy for us to see you die out there? Yesterday Danwa was beaten and this morning, his wounds were still bleeding. And they harnessed Rookmeen's two sons to the mill day and night for I do not know how long."

"All in good time, Luchya. One day, everything will work out. We have been trapped, for sure, but now we will not give in so easily."

"Instead of waiting and suffering, it is better to face them all at once, once and for all. For how long can we endure this nightmare?"

"Luchya, the fruit of patience is sweet, you know."

"Long overdue, fruit will rot."

"You women! From what you say, everything is simple. But between saying and doing, there is a big difference. We spend our days wielding the pick and shovel, mouth shut and feet shackled. Talk about suffering when we cannot even straighten ourselves; talk about human rights when we have no right to wipe our foreheads. What can we do?"

"We women, we should go to the boss screaming and demanding justice. How long will this torture last? O Surajnarayan, the Sun God, when will your lightning fall on those cursed murderers capable of so much wrongdoing?"

"You'd better pray for your situation to improve, rather than wishing evil upon others. Luchya, what happens to us is only the fruit of our bad deeds in previous lives."

"In that case, should we close our eyes and accept our fate, whatever it is?"

"I can endure anything."

"It is said that slaves in chains do not survive, but that is what we're doing."

"Suffering is not doing anything. Man must first face his own demons, before facing those around him."

Madan heard a noise behind him. It was Devraj. He closed the book. "Madan, someone has come to the village."

13

The man went to the gardens, where the labourers had gathered. He looked them in the eye, but they did not move. They were one hundred and fifty villagers sitting cross-legged on the floor. When he was near them, those who had been reading the *Ramayana* grew silent. His two friends stood beside the Protector. The man took the bag that was with one of them, lifted it and asked, "Who is your leader?"

"We are all leaders," replied Dhanlal without rising.

"I want to talk to a trustworthy person."

"We all are."

"I am the Protector of Labourers."

"We know."

"I am sent by the government."

"Last time you were too."

"You see this paper? The owner of this property wants this property checked."

"Are you here to represent the interests of the owner or...?"

"This letter comes from the court."

"Three months ago, we filed a complaint and no one came to see us. The boss wrote and three days later you appear."

"I came to stop the riot."

"What riot?" Farid rose. "You are not on our side."

"A traitor." Several men stood up in turn.

"Go away," said Dhanlal. "What you have to say does not interest us."

The man tried to remain calm. "I'm here to protect your interests," he replied, "you're wrong about me. But they are very strong and we cannot fight against these people. Elsewhere, work has resumed. You have no other way, either. We cannot live in water and be the enemy of the crocodile."

"You mean, even in the jaws of the crocodile, we should stand still?" Farid replied.

The Protector made one of his cronies wave the paper he had. "Do not make things even more difficult. Under the law, this land belongs to the houseowner. Give it to him. It will be better."

"That is not under discussion."

"This land has belonged to us for many years. And not a piece of paper can prove otherwise."

"When it was covered with brush, it belonged to nobody. So how come he wants it now?"

"The harvest is ours; we will not let anyone else take it."

Everyone was talking at the same time, in French, Kreol, Hindi and Bhojpuri. The labourers rose one after the other. Soon, everyone was standing.

"And how long can you live without working?" the man said softly.

"If you were someone who cares about our interests, you would have an answer."

"I am your Protector."

"No, you're wrong."

"Within a week, you will not have a grain of rice to put in your mouths."

"We are already starving."

They could see an expression of surprise on the man's face. He did not expect such a determination. "You should listen to me, otherwise you will regret it."

"We regret having done so once."

"Enough! I want to talk to your leader."

"We do not have one."

"The village chief, then."

"No one is in charge of the village, either."

The Protector turned to Dhanlal, who had spoken the most, "What's your name?"

"You do not need to know," replied Dhanlal in turn.

"I want to talk to you privately."

"If you want to tell me something, you can talk to everyone." Dhanlal knew, as did all the other villagers, that the man was a traitor and instead of seeking to improve the situation of labourers, he played them all for personal gain. No one believed a word of what he said this time. Everyone was still in discussion when Madan arrived, sweating, crushed by the sun. All eyes turned to him and when he was close enough, he asked, "Who are these three?"

Even before the labourers had time to open their mouths, the man answered, "I am the Protector of Labourers officially appointed by the government to defend workers'rights."

"In truth, the lackey of the bosses," corrected Farid. "He just advised us to give up our land."

Madan was silent a moment. Then he approached the man and said, "You arrived at the right time."

Then he turned around and walked through the crowd

towards the fenced-in fields. He grabbed one of the wires, shook it violently and tore it. Labourers rushed on other parts of the wire and, in no time, the fence was down. The access to the field was clear. All the villagers ran to their plots. Madan returned to the man. He wiped his brow with the back of the hand. "This is our answer. You can go now. And do not forget to mention in your report that it was I who tore the first stake."

"Are you really looking for trouble? Think about the consequences."

"We do not care much about the consequences."

The man returned to his carriage, empty-handed. The thirsty vegetation began to come to life again. Madan stood where his father was killed. The ground bore marks of browned blood. He lingered a while and then headed for the banyan tree. What had happened was not due to a fit of anger, but was the result of three days of reflection. But standing under the tree, he asked further questions. "Slavery is abolished. So why should we remain bound by this contract? For if we are not slaves, we are not obliged to work for a particular owner. We were born on this soil; we have rights. If the forest is owned by the State, this means that we can clear it and live our lives as we wish. Whether or not we have it for all eternity, how important is that? We come empty-handed, and we will return likewise.'

It would have remained a monologue if Farid, Vivek and Dhanlal had not come to find him. "I was told that a great lawyer has come from India," said Dhanlal, "a man who fights for our cause. We want to go and find him."

"What for?" asked Madan weakly.

"To share our problems with him."

"What can we gain from this?"

The friends looked at one another in silence.

Madan said, finally, "All right, find the lawyer."

"You should come with us."

"When will you leave?"

"Tomorrow."

"How many will we be?"

"Dawood, accompany us."

"Of course." They all headed back to the village.

"One more thing, Madan," Farid said suddenly. Madan gave him a sideways glance. "We'd like it if you lived down here, among us."

"And the cabin?"

"Dhanlal lives alone. You could share his home."

Madan did not answer. In the afternoon, when he'd descended, his book in hand, he met Sita at the well. He would have passed without stopping if she had not stopped. He recognised her voice. She was changed. Madan felt pain bruise his heart, but he did not show it. "How are you, Sita?"

"All right, you?"

"Okay." He did not know what else to say. "This morning," he managed to add, "I met Vivek. I asked him about you."

"Your father thought about you constantly, you know."

No sooner had she uttered these words than she knew it was a subject not to be addressed. Madan's lips were trembling; he forced himself to smile. But it was a smile that in truth did not resemble his. The evening wind hung on the words.

14

The sun had not risen when they took the path towards the city. There were only four of them: Vivek was missing. He did not spend the night with them and when Madan went to get him, Sita was outside. In response to his questions, she merely turned her head to hide her tears. Along the way, Dhanlal told Madan the whole story.

Early in the morning, the villagers went to work in their small plots with as much fervour as before. Sitting on a branch, Gautam's son sang out loud to encourage those who worked. The ground was saturated with the smell of the dew at night and a thin fog floated atop the gardens. The sun played hide and seek behind the clouds, and, still half asleep in the mango tree, the birds stood still. The flocks flew away as they woke little by little, in pairs or in groups of four. The labourers' fear dissipated as the mist and the heat rose. It was four days since anything had been picked. It was four days since they had tended to the fruit and the pumpkins had become enormous. The martins had attacked the corn cobs, partridges had pecked at the roots of pistachios and had made a feast of the cucumbers and melons. But no one worried. The pleasure of being in the gardens with family and friends prevailed over all the rest.

The sun was at its zenith and the work was well underway when old Sugan Bhagat looked up the road from the mill. A cloud of dust approached, but gradually he could distinguish a herd of pigs, followed by a dozen armed guards with their dogs on a leash. There were over a hundred pigs and by the time the villagers understood what was going on, the guards had taken up positions around the field. They let loose the dogs first and pigs came after them, causing a huge stampede, trampling everything in their path. In no time, the entire field was devastated. Sugan very nearly fell into the well, Hanif tripped and was trampled on by several pigs, Bharatlall Ramsewak fell and broke his leg. As for those who started throwing their spades on the animals, they gave up after seeing guns pointed at them. Sumangal and Danpatwa were arrested and taken away. They were attacking two guards, trying to take away their weapons.

When the pigs were gone, there was only an embattled field, where a few minutes earlier small gardens had stood. Several months of labour had just been wiped out: jagged fragments of plants and smashed vegetables mixed with the soil. The rest had been devoured by pigs.

Among the injured, Sonallal was the worst affected. The dogs had bitten him hard, all over his body and his wounds were bleeding. Everyone was appalled; people were standing on the ruined ground, looking empty and helpless. They discovered later that they were missing five men, including Sumangal's sons. One villager said he heard a guard shout that they needed their labour to crush the canes stored for four days at the mill. Usually, they employed eighty people. With five, the work would be... everyone chilled, thinking of the torture that was to take place there.

Some were silent, too stricken to say a word; others sobbed softly, but all remained stunned by the violence that had reached their flesh and struck them deep within themselves. Amidst this leaden atmosphere sprung a frightful cry. Sugan Bhagat was bent in half, grinding his teeth, his eyes rolled back in their sockets. He screamed again, as a man possessed. They thought he was having a seizure, and several people came forward to help, but he stood up and leaned against a rock.

This was the second episode he'd had, the first dating back many years, when he had just arrived from India. He was one of three brothers who had promised their mother never to separate. But upon their arrival in Mauritius, each was bought by a different owner. Sugan was the youngest and, when he understood that he would be separated from his brothers, he fell back and howled like this. He would never see his brothers again.

He heard a buzzing bee. But it was only the sound of his own voice coming back to him after its echo swirled in the air and weakened gradually.

He covered his ears with both hands. When he'd visited Kissan, he always carried something to smoke. He drew a breath first, then began to talk, "You see that mountain, Kissan. Imagine us fighting against it... in such a battle, win or lose, it's the same thing. For if we lose, we will have our heads crushed by a rock, but if we win, it means that the mountain is ready to give. And then what will happen there? It will crush us if it collapses." It was not the *ganja* that made him speak thus. But those who heard him did not recognise his voice.

Before him lay a field of devastated ruins and desperate people. Tears came to his eyes, but he would not let them fall. As a diversion, he reached into the folds of his *dhoti* and heaved a profound sigh. What he sought was not there. Next he sought Vivek, but did not see him. He put up his pipe on the ground.

The sun's rays pierced their skin like daggers. Everyone was sweating. "What will happen to our friends?" asked someone out of his torpor. They all remembered what had happened the last time they had arrested eight labourers. It had rained then, seven years ago, and Sugan Bhagat had been one of the victims. He had the scars from that episode: his neck hung all wrong and his head leaned to one side. For twenty-four hours, he drew a wagon by his neck, affixed to the wheel. At the time, it was indentured labour. At the end of his contract, he had indicated his desire to return to India, but they had confiscated his papers and he had been told that the boat that could take him home had been shipwrecked. It was that day that Sugan had started smoking *ganja.* They say that grass makes men merry, that those who smoke, laugh, but Sugan... he began to cry like a child.

On the other side of the hill, opposite the village, in a house with walls of raffia, Vivek burst out laughing. Andrea liked to see him in this state of euphoria. But Vivek only laughed like that when he smoked. At first, Andrea could not stand the acrid smell of grass. She put in front of him a bottle of French wine to try to drink for the intoxication that comes from *ganja,* but it did not work. She preferred the wine. Vivek was persuaded to try, but alcohol put him in such a state that Andrea was frightened. Vivek didn't laugh; he'd shattered the mirror against the wall. The *ganja* thus had returned. Vivek lit his pipe. On the pillow, Andrea whispered in his ear, "Vivek, I have never known a man as perfect as you." It was a compliment she gave him often. "It's true; you are the most accomplished man I know."

They stayed up until the rooster crowed. That morning, Vivek remained on the sheets, Andrea's room smelled of perfume; her pink silk clothes hung at the foot of the bed. In a pleading voice, she whispered, 'I'll be alone now. Stay with me."

"I'll see you tonight."

"No, if you go, you will not come back."

"What! You doubt my word?"

"No, but I beg you, stay."

"Let me go, Andrea, I'll be back tonight."

"No..." She entwined him in her arms, laid him against her. At the mill, they untied the hands of the five labourers. They were tied together by the ankle. Then they put on their shoulders the yoke used by oxen. The whip whistled over their heads. Drops of sweat stained the ground, like drops of sugar flowing into the river, like beaded lace on their backs. Amidst the whistles: the groans of men, sighs.

Vivek was sweating, too, in the greenhouse against Andrea.

Her words were sweet to him, tickling his ear. "Vivek, mon *cheri,*" she sighed. She nibbled on his earlobe and whispered, 'You are wonderful." Vivek did not speak; he did not attempt to answer. 'You have so much experience, and you can last so long. Oh! My dear!" In the devastated fields, desolation reigned. Faces reflected their fear, as they looked upon the destroyed crops. No one found the courage to return to the village. The sun disappeared behind large clouds and the breeze, which had once whispered happily, sent them bitter reproaches.

When he reached orgasm, Vivek heard a pleasing moan, coming as if from a long way away, interspersed with sighs that were still excited. As Andrea's passion rose, Vivek also wanted to talk, to pour into Andrea's ear a few words of love, but he could not find the words.

"Oh! You are a magician," Andrea purred in a tiny voice, as if anyone could hear them.

Moving his fingers up and down more quickly, he had her writhing in his grip, "Vivek... Vivek oh, yes! yes!'

Her cry broke, the world outside no longer existed, they came to one another, bestowed all their forces to this enclosed universe, contained between the walls of the chamber. The silence weighed upon them like a drape covering their naked bodies.

In the field, the labourers rose out of their torpor, "We must get them."

"It may take some time."

"We can not abandon them."

"But we cannot release them."

"We are one hundred and fifty strong."

"There is nothing to do here, anyway. To the mill!"

Sugan was still sitting on the rock, paying attention to what others said. He got up very slowly and raised his arm to attract attention. "We will go to the mill, and we will enter it, I tell you that."

"So we go," shouted someone, "and pick up stones along the way." Sugan shouted, "Wait a minute! Let's wait until Dawood's return.'

Hesitation rippled through the crowd.

15

The room was empty, the bed unmade. They had left it and walked to the sea. The sun had reached the horizon and the waves were swelling, seeking to engulf them. Sea foam, the colour of milk, splashed on the black coral and sea spray fell on the white sand, iridescent, gradually melting away.

They left their footsteps behind them and one could follow the long ribbon of their steps walking away. Vivek had dark skin, almost as black as the rocks, while Andrea was as white as the foam of the waves coming ashore to die. It was dangerous for her to lead him this far. Vivek was always afraid and this was the first time he'd taken such a risk.

"Nobody can do anything to you as long as I am with you," Andrea reassured her friend.

Andrea was not French, not fully. Her mother was a Creole and her father, although she had never known him, was white. She had inherited his fair complexion. Vivek was aware that the mere act of walking with her was enough to be shot in the back. He knew the fate of those who looked at a white woman.

They reached the top of a high reef and sat facing the sea. "Vivek, I have something important to tell you."

"That's why you made me come here?"

"You regret having come this far with me? You told me the other day you could go to the end of the world to collect *ganja.* Am I not more important?"

"What do you want to tell me that is so important?"

"What do you think of Mr Constant?"

"Why do you ask?"

'It doesn't matter... you can tell me later. What do you know about your people?"

"My people?"

"Yes, your race."

"What's going on in your head today? You know very well what I think of my race."

"I just mean what you know of your race."

"Well! I know as much as you do. We were born to be slaves and slave away like cattle."

"This is not what I meant... I feel that you are not proud of your race."

'Because I come to you without worrying about what they think? Andrea, understand this: whatever our situation here, I am proud to be Indian. If I started to tell you the glories of my country, you wouldn't believe it."

"The fact that you're Indian has nothing to do with my question."

Vivek looked at Andrea with a look of astonishment. 'You asked a question about my race..."

"Yes, well, your caste. The foreman said that those of India's priestly caste, such as Kissan, barely consider you human beings. They even prevent you from entering temples."

"Who told you this nonsense?"

"Bisnis, the foreman, told me. The day before yesterday there was a dinner at Mr Constant's and Bisnis stated that among Hindus, there were more than ten castes.'

"Your foreman is a liar. An impostor."

"Leave him where he is. I am only interested in your happiness."

They were silent, listening to the sound of waves rising up to them. Vivek did not understand what Andrea was trying to say. "My happiness?"

"Yes. I was told that people in your village are set to elect Madan as village chief."

"You astonish me! How do you know?"

"As Madan belongs to a higher caste, the highest position goes to him."

"You are completely wrong, Andrea. There is no caste in the village. We never make any distinctions between us, not even between Hindus and Muslims."

"It seems that there are sixty-five of your castemen in the village."

"No, there are a hundred and fifty men, all alike."

"I'm talking about your caste. It is that which is best represented. The leader should be from the majority caste."

"Andrea, I can ask you something?"

"Of course."

"You've gone and invented all these stories... for what?"

"I asked you just now what you thought of Mr Constant."

"Ah! So he is behind it."

"Constant thinks you should be..."

"He must have a very good opinion of me, right? Look, Andrea, there must be lots of things you want to tell me. Let's find another topic of conversation, please. He pulled some grass from a corner of his *dhoti* and began to crush the nuggets in his palm. Andrea stopped. "What else?"

"I want you to have a clear mind and answer me clearly."

"What can I say?"

"What would you say to becoming village chief in Madan's place?"

"Please, let it go."

"No, Vivek, I cannot. This is what Mr Constant asked."

"Aren't there enough of us to beat him with bamboo?"

The waves continued to surge, two or three small swells followed by a large one which came to smash against the rocks, breaking into exploding droplets of water as it reached the sand. To the west, the scarlet disc of the sun disappeared into the sea, the horizon red along its entire length, and colour flooded the eye in shades of purple and orange.

Vivek asked Andrea to come closer, but she did not move. "Wait a minute. Listen to what I still have to say." Vivek had already stood to leave, but he waited. "You will be surprised to learn that my husband did not leave the house."

"What?"

"The last two days he was hiding in the back room."

Vivek could not believe his ears. 'What?'

"Look over there, towards the big rock." Vivek turned his eyes and a shiver ran through his spine. He remained silent for a moment, then asked, "So all this time he was watching us..." Andrea did not answer. Vivek trembled from head to toe. His whole being refused to believe it and he wondered what kind of man he could be, before understanding finally. "Oh, I know now," he murmured. "Mr Constant and your husband... they both await my answer.'

In response, he saw Philip advancing. The white man looked

at his wife. As she did not speak, he stood in front of Vivek. He carried no weapons and it was the first time that Vivek had seen him without a gun.

One day he'd asked Andrea, "Why is your husband so distant with you?"

"You're not very close to your wife yourself."

"He also has a mistress hidden somewhere?"

"No."

"Then what?"

"Women do not interest him."

Vivek was reminded of Soumna of the village, whom everyone called Shikhandi, who acted as both man and woman. Faced with Philip, Vivek was silent. 'When I think of you in the next room while...' he thought. He could not get the measure, precisely, of this man. Andrea had stood up between them and he felt a sense of disgust.

The sun had set, the sky was just a red immensity and the sea, tired of having roared all day, seemed to be finally calm.

He looked to both spouses. They both waited for his reply, his eyes fixed on him. They formed a triangle and stood motionless, until it was quite dark. Then they walked along the beach, before returning to the trail. Andrea went first and her husband behind her. No one spoke. When they arrived at the point at which their paths diverged, Vivek asked, very low, "You want my response?"

"Yes," replied Philip." Tomorrow after lunch." And Vivek went rapidly to the right, leaving them to take the left path.

16

A voice screamed in his heart, 'this land is ours!' But, invariably, Madan was invaded by the same doubts. 'If this land is ours, why has someone else made a fence?'

A third voice, calm and determined, was heard in turn, 'Our land cannot remain a prisoner; we must liberate it. Our identity depends on it, our future as well, and our honour.' The echo of his inner voice seemed to come back from the mountains, amplified. 'Freedom: freedom for our land! How can they take away the land we have wrested from the void with our hands, land we have grown, that we have given life? How can we accept that they are confiscating the fruit of a life of work and sacrifice?'

Madan left the cabin, went round the big rock and then to the base of the slope to stare down the trail. He could see the field below, in the darkness. It was a piece of land they had created entirely on their own. It was necessary at all costs to prevent the whites from taking it over. They must protect it. He would see people from the village and tell them, 'The land belonged to nobody. How, once we turned it green, can it become the property of others?'

Madan remembered the day he had gone home, his back streaked with the marks of lashes he'd received in turning the mill. The next day, when he refused to go to work, his mother comforted him, "If our people had remained at home for fear of the whip, we would have long ago been destroyed."

"You mean it's the unbearable suffering that has preserved our people? Well! I know that soft cork forests do not suffer in silence. Tomorrow, after tomorrow, my hand shall rise, and..."

"I think it would be better if you go to your plot until your anger subsides, my son."

"I will not work, I'm tired of this slavery."

"I'm talking about your field you have on your own. You call that slavery?" Madan felt his ears buzzing. His own field... his own land... had they been naive enough to believe it belonged to them? His body was suffering from a tingling that travelled across his back. In prison, locked up between the high walls, he often thought of his village. But the colours he'd missed were subdued... even the sun seemed to swim in murky water. Ah! If he could make it disappear, this time. This impotence was a deep black. But if he lived in the dark, it was a profound space, empty, not darkness filled with invisible eyes that could run through him at night with their sharp points.

He climbed, climbed further, until he could no longer feel his muscles and tendons. Finally, he stopped and looked down: the village was tiny, surrounded on both sides by green fields and woods. In the distance, he could distinguish between two villages, and beyond, the blue of the sea, motionless. Madan also saw a river that ran between the hills and a mill whose smoke obscured some of the surrounding area. Before him, out of sight, the cane fields stretched on. Over the fields, flocks of birds buzzed, silent as the souls of labourers, their tears and the resignation of the women left in the village.

Madan could climb higher, but he turned back. The sight of the fields had crushed him and he felt in his breast a throbbing, the questions coming back again in bursts: 'Who owns these fields? Those who work it or those who own a piece of paper? Land, cane, sweet syrup... what are they?' He heard the revolt rising in him like a surging wave. What terrible irony, what injustice! Some sweat, others enjoy fruits of work; some receive the sour taste of suffering while others, the sweet taste of sugar. On one side, the hovels of the labourers, made of mud and straw. On the other, the blue stone palaces of the boss on his three acres. This was the difference between those who accomplished the task and those who sat comfortably, reaping the benefits. It was for asking just such questions of ownership that Tamby, a coastal village boy, had been convicted. In prison he'd been in the same cell as Madan. One day he asked Madan, "You know what cane sugar tastes like?"

"Everyone knows it's sweet."

"Don't you know that sugar has two tastes?"

"You mean that there are two types of sugar?"

"Sugar is sweet, but it can also be bitter."

"How?"

"You're one of the farmers who produce sugar cane, aren't you?"

"My whole region produces it."

"And you never asked why sugar makes some kings and others miserable? The bitterness of the poverty of your life: you've never asked where it comes from?"

Tamby came from the psychiatric hospital from which, for lack of space, he was moved to the prison. The guards had warned all the prisoners that the man was crazy, but his comments did not give off that impression at all. "The doctor also assures me that I am crazy," he explained to Madan, "because, instead of worshipping the Son of God, I pray to my gods and my black goddess. He claims that all those who pray to statuettes are fools."

Tamby's father must be of sound mind, for he had converted to pray from now on to the Son of God. His mother was not crazy either, any more than her three sisters were: all had become Christians. Madan had never heard anyone else with Tamby's way of expressing himself.

'The harvest, this wealth that you produce: who gets it?' Madan was thinking about him while he was reviewing the uncultivated fields. "If this is not for us, let us set it on fire.' He imagined the cane fields on fire. He stopped and laughed. Below, a plantation was in his sight. In his mind, he saw it burn, illuminating the dark night in a huge bonfire.

He could always dream... Many memories had fled from his mind, but not this one: the field had been on fire and the flames had devoured the canes, engulfing the countryside under their hot tongues. Clouds of smoke rose, the violet hue of cane juice. Madan, with all the other labourers, had risked his life to extinguish the fire.

"The fire will destroy everything; the whole field is going to be ruined," cried the villagers, terrified.

But whose field? Nobody, apparently, had posed the question. That day, Madan had burnt his hand trying to put out the fire. His face had been black, covered with soot and ash. His hand still bore the scar of its roasting and his eyes had taken weeks to recover.

That year, harvest-time brought the labourers misery and famine.

What did they have? Even the homes that housed them were not theirs. And now the boss would take ownership of what they considered to be their land. It was done; the wire already lined the field.

Far below, at the foot of the mountain, Madan saw Zinat holding a bundle of dry wood. When he joined her, he took over the bundle and placed it on his shoulders. 'What will happen to the field, Madan?'

"We will keep it, Zinat."

"This is what we have always believed, but can we?"

They saw Mira's aunt approaching, a bundle of grass atop

her head. When she caught up, Zinat took the bundle from the old lady. The village was close by. Madan looked at the horizon. He saw a day without sunshine, which would end slowly.

17

The lawyer listened to the statements of the villagers with the greatest attention. The four who met him were pleasantly surprised to see that he wore a turban. He was one of theirs and that fact alone encouraged them to tell him everything, without omitting the slightest detail. After listening, he asked, "Have you written evidence?"

"No, nothing on paper," replied Dawood.

"Before we issue you a title, the court will ask for evidence."

"We have been working this land for over twenty years, Lawyerji. Can we provide better evidence?"

They had brought all the money saved by the head of *baithka*. The lawyer would not agree to take a penny. He sent them home and said he would return in three days to complete his investigation. They left confident and it was dark when they arrived in the village.

When they learned that the field had been devastated and five people arrested, Madan froze. For the space of a moment, he felt as if his heart had stopped beating. His first reaction was to rush to the mill, but it was too dark. He ran to the field and fell near the shed, unable to stand. As a child, he had worked in this field with his father, often at dusk, and even moonlight. Twice he had seen the fields devastated by a cyclone. But that which had survived a fire had gone up in smoke. Madan remembered that terrible day; the images were stuck in his memory. Once they were out of danger, off the burning fields, Kissan had said to his son, "We must commit ourselves to work harder tomorrow and even harder the next few days, so that one day the future will finally shine for us."

The villagers had taken turns spending the night in the field to protect it from wild boar, hares and deer. Sitting in front of a small campfire, Sugan Bhagat would tell them about India. Madan relived every moment related to this field. How many times had he chatted with Sita, for hours, sitting side by side on the edge of the well? And the harvest! What happy days. They sang and danced on the site late into the night. And when it rained at last, after a long drought... the joy of those moments, when the first drops fell, wide and warm! Oh, all that was present in him, alive, exciting.

The next morning, Madan went to the mill with a company of a dozen people. Some in the village wanted to stop them, but he calmly replied that they would not pick fights. They were too few to declare war.

"How, though?" Madan questioned what they could do instead. "We're certainly not going to beg..."

Neither Madan nor any of his companions knew exactly what they would see when they got there. Reaching the edge of the river, Madan came to a halt. The others followed his example. They all stared into his eyes with the same question, 'Why have we stopped here?'

Madan wiped the sweat on his forehead and gave his instructions. "To rest. We must be masters of our reactions; they should not be able to control us."

"Why are we not waiting until lawyer comes back?" Sohun asked. "With him, it might been easier to have them released."

"Too late to turn back. Once there, we'll see if we can get them out or not."

"We will meet the guards..."

"They will not shoot us if we are just looking." They set off again. But as they approached the mill, their courage was sinking. When he heard the dogs barking, even Madan was frightened. Even so, they were determined and no one slowed down. As soon as he saw them, the guard posted at the entrance shouted to warn the guard who was a little further inside. By the time Madan arrived at the door, a dozen guards were already assembled there. Madan asked his friends to stop. He advanced alone. "We want to see Mr Constant."

The Creole guard, the most sturdy of them all, replied by shouting, "Mr Constant does not live here. If you want to see him, go to his house."

"Where are our friends?"

"They are at work indoors," replied the giant in the same tone.

"We want to see them."

"And me, you want to see me?" Madan did not answer. The others were moving towards him. "You're not allowed to enter here. Stand back."

Madan complied. "Give us back the prisoners," he said quietly.

"You decide when the sun should rise and set, is that it?"

"We never hide the sun from others."

"Clear off! Get out of here immediately."

Madan had often had the same thought, 'But where? Very far from here. Because we've had enough. But if our fathers and grandfathers did not leave, despite the terrible living conditions, even worse than ours, why should we? Every cell in our body has grown on this land. We could find no other land where we feel more at home, even in paradise. We bought this land with our blood and tears. And we will continue to water it with our sweat, until it is a paradise. Thus, nobody can act against us.'

Yet those who held the whip were not about to let go. How could it be otherwise? If the powerful began to sympathise with the poor, if the rich were interested in the miserable, then the situation would improve. But who wanted such a change? When despair took over, Madan abandoned himself to the darkest thoughts. But the discouragement never lasted: if someone else took control, why would it not change? Madan had heard that even the shape of the mountains changed over centuries. They could find a solution, but it would take time.

The difficulty was that they lacked time. They had already waited too long.

Dhanlal and Farid placed themselves at his side. The foreman yelled, "Get out."

"To go where?" Farid asked.

"We're not here to talk to them," Madan murmured in his ear. Madan kept his calm. Inside the mill, the millstone stopped rolling for a moment and at once, the cracking of whips could be heard. But no human sounds came to them, no crying or complaint as the blows rained down. Madan shuddered. Why was there no reaction?

The scars on his back grew hot, as if alive. In some places, the leather strap had torn the flesh to the bone. He groaned inside himself, clenched his fists as hard as he could. He was filled with shame.

18

Madan felt exactly the same thing today. He felt paralysed, unable to make any movement, numb. He sat down and began to read the next section of the story of Soma and Santu in the notebook his father had left behind.

"I waited for you yesterday, Vinay. You promised to come to see me... Mama was to come too, but I have not seen her, either."

"Dad was not very well, that's why Mama could not come."

"It's only for three days I have not seen them, but I feel it's been years.'

"Satwa's mother was just wondering how you felt in your new home. And how your in-laws were. And my friend Santu."

"Well! Your dear friend is already back to work the day after his wedding. We have not even had time to get acquainted. I'm beginning to think you were right."

"About what?"

"When you said that men here are as in prison, although it seems they come and go freely."

"I told you that myself?"

"How is the movement? Everyone here speaks only of you. When they started singing your praises, it made me so happy."

"What do they say?"

"People are confident that you will fight the injustices they suffer."

"Really?"

"Just yesterday, a dozen women wove crowns for you right here. My mother-in-law went on to say that we will soon see the end of our suffering and that the labourers would gain all their rights."

"Let's talk about something else. Tell me about you."

"No, tell me first where you are in your fight for the cause."

"The battle is over, Soma."

"Really? The agreement was concluded? Our situation is going to finally change?"

"Yes, we signed an agreement... I cannot speak for others, but my situation, will probably improve."

"What do you mean, Vinay?"

"I have been a nice idiot the whole time and I thought more of others than myself. Soma, I am pleased to tell you that starting tomorrow, your brother will become the main foreman of the plantation. No black man on the island has ever had a salary like that they'll give me."

"Will the wages of the labourers increase?"

"I don't know."

"But isn't that what you fought for?"

"Yes, it was the goal of our campaign, but when I saw the chance that I was being given, I realized I was an idiot and needed first of all to think about myself."

"Vinay, this is not like you to joke that way."

"But I'm not kidding."

"So, it's true? You have abandoned the cause and prefer your own pockets? You leave your friends out at sea and you run away to the shore."

"I knew how to swim and I'm out. Would it be better if I stayed and sank with everyone?"

"No, I do not believe you. You could not do such a thing."

"You talk as if I had committed the worst crime."

"What could be worse, really? What did the labourers do that one of their own has become the cause of their loss?"

"How about the brokers that led our ancestors here by promising them the moon and the stars?"

"My brother, do you really want to sell yourself?"

"You spoke of an agreement. That's what I signed, that is all. I would have had to be stupid to turn down the proposal they made to me."

"All our hopes are lost."

"Not mine, anyway, nor yours, for that matter. I can now offer Santu a very good position."

"And the other labourers? You will sit on cushions, while they walk on beds of coal?"

"They only have to be careful where they put their feet."

"I do not understand you. It is you who's always claimed that the Indians on the island live in darkness... How can you speak today? Have you forgotten that you had that injury to your ankle a few months ago, when you got a pile of stones on your foot? And you were docked six days' pay, while you were gone only two."

"Well! Precisely. It is this kind of situation I have changed."

"But you had to make things change for everyone."

"Why should I sacrifice myself for all those unable to take care of themselves? There is nothing to learn from the lazy."

"Oh, my brother, how sad! How can you treat labourers as lazy? We transformed a wasteland into green fields. Miserable, lean and hungry, we go naked because we do not have clothes, we are afraid because we lack rights, we die by the hundreds of fatigue and fever. No doctor, no remedy..."

"It's all in the past, Soma. I do not want to hear about it."

"But nothing has changed, and how long it will last? And don't you dare say that the argument is over. The day before your wedding, sitting under the mango tree in the company of friends, you shouted that our children were deprived of education, we were not allowed to pray to Goddess Kali, that our goods were confiscated. Now you say, *'It's all in the past.'*"

"I suppose I need your excessive sentimentality. After all, you are my sister, I can make this effort to listen."

"But I'm not the only one who will say this. Yesterday, you said we should cut down those who come here as brokers."

"Listen, I came with a proposal for Santu. If he accepts, he will live like a prince."

"And what is this proposal?... Oh, Santu, here you are.'

'You look anguished, brother.'

"Vinay, what will I do? Vinay, what will become of me?"

"What happened?"

"Find me a place where I can hide, quick."

"Why do you need to hide?"

"They are coming, they are all after me!"

"But who?"

"Hide me, Vinay. They will kill me!"

"Who?"

"Harkoo, and the boss too. Where is my mother? Vinay, Vinay, my brother, my friend, please, do not abandon me."

"But, will you tell me what you did?"

"There are the police, they are almost here."

"Why do you want the police to come here?"

"To arrest me. Soma, they're coming to take me and kill me."

"Sit down and tell me what happened."

"I killed him, Soma."

"Who?"

"I cannot stay here. You hear the galloping of horses, the rattling of chains, the sound of boots? Listen."

"Santu, asnwer me. Tell me who you killed."

"Mr Lapierre. He died, I saw his blood flow, rivers, rivers of blood. He died instantly. They will take me and kill me in the same way."

"Santu, can you tell me from the beginning? Why did you kill Mr Lapierre?"

"I did not mean to."

"How did you then?"

"I was all alone. I do not know how it happened so fast. I was digging trenches in the field and I was sweating. The heat was terrible. My back was broken, I could no longer remain bent, and this time the..."

"And you found the opportunity to go sit on the pile of stones."

"No, I just kept going. I didn't realise that Mr Lapierre had arrived, his big bamboo cane in hand, and before I had time to say a word, wham! He begins to beat me. Look, here, look, Soma, do you see blood on my back?"

"Then what?"

"I do not know. Everything happened in a flash."

"You killed him."

"Yes, exactly. On the spot."

"With what?"

"With my pick. How could I have guessed that after one thrust he would fall down dead? Soma, bring me some water or I will die of thirst."

"My brother, what shall we do?"

"Water, Soma."

"Good. Santu, I have to go."

"Vinay. Wait. If you go, that will help me?"

"What can I do now?"

"You are my best friend, my brother-in-law... you are everything to me, for us all."

"Santu, I have to work and..."

"No, you cannot go away like that. They will kill me."

"And you want me to make me kill myself?"

"Vinay, you're the only one who can save me. The only one!"

"Who saw you hit him?"

"Nobody."

"Why did you run?"

"Everyone told me to flee. Is that you, Mama?"

"How are you, my son?"

"The police are after me, they'll come for me, Mama, I do not want to die. I did not mean to do it. Truly, Vinay, if he had not continued to beat me, the iron would not have reached his temple, I would not have killed him."

"Vinay, what is he saying? Has he lost his head, does he have heatstroke? Karim, my brother, try to reason with him."

"Santu! What the hell are you doing here? For the love of God, save yourself as soon as possible. They are already at the river. Luchya, my sister, do not sit down. Tell your son to flee quickly."

"Karim, what's going on? Explain to me."

"But, uncle, shall I run away?"

"Karim, I want to know what happened."

"This is not the time! If you want to save his life, find your son a safe hiding place, otherwise you will regret it all your life."

"But, what's happened?"

"Nobody move."

"The house is surrounded. That's our man; pass the chains."

"Harkoo, will you tell me what he did? What have you against him?"

"Go! Advance!"

"Please, I am begging on my knees. Forgiveness. Excuse him. Let my son go, leave us our best storyteller, he who knows all the *Ramayana*."

"Tie him tight."

"Tell them, Harkoo, that if they show mercy, we will spend the rest of our lives in the service of the bosses. Have mercy, please and release Santu. Forgive him, we are your servants, your slaves, you can ask us for anything. Give him one more chance, one more..."

"Courage, Santu!" Madan felt his eyelids fall. He closed the book.

19

Mira found Zinat near the stable, a bundle of clothes in her hands. Mira took the bundle and they walked together to the river. For herself and her aunt, Mira would not have needed to go do laundry more than once a week. But when she came down to the river, to wash Soudhiya's linen, or Lavangiya's, she crossed Zinat's path, and so every day Mira went to the river.

Pushpa never called her by name. She nicknamed her Belrani and other women followed suit gradually, so that soon became Mira, the *belle-rani*. Sugan Bhagat told her the story of Princess Belrani: 'The youngest of seven sons of a king discovered one night Princess Belrani hidden behind the vines. The girl, invisible by day, stupefied him. He had never seen such a beautiful stranger. Pushpa's allusion was obvious. But when she told the girl not to take on as much housework, Mira Belrani answered, laughing, that only activity kept her healthy.

The mountainside had its own panoply of colours, green at the bottom, then yellow and brown in equal measure climbing up, and finally grey and black at the top. The valleys extended one after another, and the gentle foothills soon became steep terrain illuminated by the sun. The sun slid into the shadows behind the clouds, then turned sentinel on a lifeless pile of rocks. It looked like an artist had sculpted the expessive forms: roaring waterfalls, ravines, peaks at the top, sinister in their solitude. Zinat noticed that Mira kept her eyes fixed on the top.

"If Kissan saw you, you know what he would say?"

"Fear not, the mountain will not crumble."

"You're the one who would say that."

"So what would he say, then?"

"He would say, 'Beware, it's just a witness, silent and motionless. It will not come forward to protect you'."

At times, you could hear the wind in the mountains, but usually only a great silence came from the sleepy summits. Mira had nightmares, returning periodically to haunt her. She would wake up screaming.

In her view, the mountains, in their silent immobility, represented the intransigence against which Madan fought in vain. Mira wanted to know why, since his return from prison, he gave himself so thoroughly to an unreachable goal. She had not had the opportunity to approach him to ask. Madan, perhaps, was unaware of her existence.

They had known one another before his arrest, but after so many years, how could he remember her, who had then been a child? Moreover, he had not come to seek her out, as he had done with Sita and others. She had seen him several times, sad, immersed in his thoughts. Mira tried to remember his smile, without success. Madan had been all smiles before his time in prison.

Beyond the mountains, the sky was deep blue, bright. Wispy white clouds drifted westward. That day, they did not hear any echo in the wind as it blew through the ravines; just a slight hiss as it grazed the stems of wild bamboo, rustling the leaves in a soft murmur. The red earth of the path was still wet with the rain of the night. Mira rubbed her feet against a stone to take off the layer of mud caked on her heels. Then she went on her way.

Where she was washing her clothes, there were a few flat rocks. The banyan tree uprooted during the last hurricane had overturned across the river and was now used as a drying spot. Mira deposited her bundle near the trunk and got her soap ready.

She joined Sita, who was picking guavas. Sita threw a few in Mira's direction and jumped down from the rock where she stood. She picked up the guavas she'd dropped on the ground and returned with Mira to the laundry. The first time Mira had come to the river, she'd enjoyed using the scrubbing soap on fruits to create foam and bubbles. In doing so, she forgot to wash the clothes. She kept up this childlike mischief a very long time. Instead of rubbing the clothes with the soapy fruit, she would keep the fruit in her hands and play with the soapy lather. She had gradually abandoned the hobby and became the fastest and most effective laundress in the village.

Mira's thoughts whirled in her head like the swirls of the river against the rocks. The vows that she formed with the flow of the river were frail, but she remade them every day, offering her promises to the water, hoping she would be able to keep them. Her dreams, however, sank every time, and she plunged into the water to catch her breath.

The sea was not far, but Mira had only been there twice. She had told her story to the waves, convinced that the mother would keep her secret. She had heard the long lament of the swells, her incessant complaints and Mira took her in confidence. Then she'd wanted the waves to give her something in return, but they did not. Mira complained to Zinat.

"The sea always claims the land that belongs to it," replied Zinat.

Mira had found the sea beautiful; she could not see any trace of despair. The waves changed shape, but they never disintegrated. It was the same with the river's waters. No obstacle could overcome them. The currents never ceased their movement. Neither rocks nor reefs could hold them back. Mira had learned to have energy from the river, though she was not able to maintain its pace. She felt in her movements a momentum that carried her forward.

She often felt alone, even in company. Sadness came often, but when she recalled the sea and the river, the solitude of their waters seemed so familiar that she confided her melancholy there and left it to drift with the currents. When her uncle had been a cook at Mr Constant's, Mira was able to observe closely how bosses and their families lived. It was a life of opulence, entirely different from her own. A lavish house, expensive clothes, food, books. Mira had been small at the time, but not small enough not to notice the glaring difference between the two lifestyles. And she felt that those around her were silent; that no one deigned to answer the questions of a child.

When she watched the long line of workers on the paths, snaking their way to the factory or the fields, it seemed that rather than walking, they were crawling in search of a piece of bread. She heard talk about the future and it seemed a future of a row of corpses without souls. Nobody in the village was going forward.

Sitting on a rock, Mira watched the horizon in the hope of catching the sun rising or finishing its daily travels. If something as wonderful as the sun's trajectory could happen – if the course of the world could be traversed in one day – then the gap could surely close between white and black, pink and brown. But Mira was concerned that the gap between them was too deep. Could Madan fill the space? She had once posed the question to Zinat.

"Why always reduce everything to Madan?" she'd replied with a laugh. "When you wash clothes, do you tear the water? Can you crack the knife? No. Well. The equality of which you speak is just as impossible.'

Mira went to hang the clean clothes on the trunk of the banyan tree and came back to Zinat. She gathered her courage in both hands before asking the question that burned on her lips. She ventured, in a timid voice, "You could not have prevented Madan from going to the mill?"

Zinat twisted her wrap energetically for emphasis. "Fool! I only found out his destination after he'd already left."

"Who knows what he may attempt under the heat of anger..."

'What will happen will happen. Why worry about it?'

Sita grabbed the bundle that Mira had suspended from a branch and sat down beside her. She started to undo the knot and stopped abruptly. "Can you tell me what he has in there?" she asked, smiling at Mira.

Mira did not answer.

"You could imagine; try smelling it," ventured Zinat.

"Certainly not!"

"Is it *kheer?*" Mira looked at Sita. The rice pudding in the bundle was absolutely divine, but that did not surprise her. She felt sad suddenly that Sita had prepared the pudding for Madan.

Sita radiated joy that day. The certainty of Vivek's return made her so happy; she could still hear his words: "Sita, it took me a while to realise what was going on behind this game of seduction, but I've left it now..." Sita had just found her husband, and, even better, Vivek knew the answer that he would give to Philip.

20

The lawyer had sent someone to the village in his place. The five men were still being held. Madan did not understand why they had not been freed yet. What wrongs had they committed during the negotiations?

The lawyer's emissary brought a message, including a letter in which the lawyer detailed the reasons for his absence. He spoke of a meeting scheduled with the government in front of whom he intended to plead their case. Madan reread the last part of the letter aloud to all the villagers assembled:

Do not take action in the heat of anger, for you risk bringing the whole project to an end. The problem will be better resolved when the tension has eased. Tomorrow, I will visit you. I am sure that all your difficulties will find resolution, and I know we will see improvements in the lives of Indian labourers in this country. Have hope!

He gave no details as to how things would be settled, but his promises restored the villagers' confidence. Dhanlal claimed that in every neighbouring village, they swore by the lawyer. It was said that he had solemnly pledged not to return to India before they regained their full and fair rights as farmers. At his request, the government had appointed a new commission whose members evidently had integrity. They worked honestly and without fail to address all the problems faced by Indian workers.

Dawood did not want to discourage the villagers. He knew by experience not to trust people. Commissions and emissaries... he had seen them come and go without ever seeing the situation change.

The next day, at dawn, the villagers sat on the road, waiting for the lawyer. The weather was cloudy but not raining. The night before, Madan had climbed to his father's cabin. He could not stand the feelings of failure and disappointment that oppressed him. He had spent the night in the mountains, with only Farid's dogs for company. In a corner of the cabin, an old wooden chest contained some books and notebooks. Madan had found his father's journal. Kissan had set new words to old songs and written a few personal notes. Madan came across a passage where his father wrote about one of the happiest moments of his life:

I'm going home, my back numb again from a beating. The sun has just gone down, there is still a bit of light. Rekha takes my pick, takes my bag off my shoulder and asks, 'Do you know what's for dinner?' I offer a few names of the dishes she usually prepares. Rekha laughs and she leads me into the kitchen. For the first time, I see steam rising from all four pots that we have. She takes the lid off of the first one, and I see dholl-puri. In the second, eggplant and potato, in the third a pumpkin dish, and in the fourth, tomatoes and peas. I must be dreaming! Rekha tells me that all the village pots contain the same delights tonight. This is the first harvest of the community field. And this is the first time in my life I am eating these sumptuous dishes. The first! And it was from our field that these treasures have come...

Kissan had written the last sentence in large letters. It was the same field that was in the process of being taken from them. Kissan had given his life to try to protect it. 'If they get their way,' Madan thought, 'what will I have? The deflated hopes of all my friends?'

On the same page, Kissan had scribbled a song, the words almost illegible. Madan strived to decipher it. The song went something like this:

No need to plow with your copper bowl
An empty trinket on the empty bench.
There is nothing left to put in it,
Nothing to eat in the copper bowl.

Only by reading the notes on the following pages, did Madan realise that the song dated from a period where there had been a famine. The food shortage had lasted over a month and there had been absolutely nothing to eat. Madan thought of his friends, unresolved, exhausted, discouraged. In their eyes, he did not read any determination. Most had weary, emaciated figures, sad, stooped shoulders ... and these days, especially, the look of despair. A sea of despair. A jungle of sadness in which Madan was alone. He shivered.

The day before, when he descended from the mountain, just before sunrise, he had run into Sita. Her eyes glittered now, happy and he could not detect the painful shadow he had seen not long ago. She drew water from the well and handed the bucket to Madan. He tossed away the wooden rod that he was chewing and rinsed his mouth with fresh water.

"You look very happy. Good news?"

A glimmer. Luckily, as he rarely saw in Sita's eyes, dancing. But she did not reply to Madan. Pushpa, a little later, told her about Vivek's return. Madan listened and then asked, "Where is he?"

Pushpa hesitated for a second. "He must be taking a bath."

The sun had begun to set, but it still hid a bit behind the trees when Vivek appeared. Madan watched him come. A memory came back to him, of a day when Vivek had abandoned their game of *gulidanda* for fear of losing the game. Madan had gone to get him and convinced him to return. Vivek had returned to the game and finally ended up as the winner.

Today, Madan felt doubly happy for his friend – because of Sita, but also because Vivek had returned to the camp of struggling labourers. Nevertheless, he was a little apprehensive because he knew Andrea, and she was a witch, despite her beauty. Her mother was an expert in black magic and considered to have all kinds of evil powers. She could bewitch anyone. Madan knew that Philip would never hurt a friend. But in the case of Andrea, he was less sure. She was not going to quietly accept his rejection. It was said that her mother was able to kill a man at a distance of a dagger. This was the reason no one dared to intervene when Vivek had been infatuated with Andrea.

Madan was left playing with Sita and Vivek's son until Vivek came out of his bath. He had really changed... A little later, they went to the field, where all the villagers had gathered to await the arrival of the lawyer. "Your time in prison has made you seriously emaciated," said Vivek.

"Have you ever seen someone leave that place fatter?" Madan replied, laughing. Two pairs of partridges flew past. The sun remained hidden, now behind the clouds. In the leaves, small beaks stuck out of the nests clinging to the branches.

"You have shown courage," said Madan.

"By refusing their proposal?"

"No, by leaving Andrea."

For a moment, Vivek did not answer. "I saw her the other day. She is still beautiful, incredible. I can't believe I was able to leave such a gorgeous woman." Vivek fell silent.

"You do not regret it, at least?" Farid's dog ran alongside them.

"Why should I regret it?"

"You look a bit shot. The consequences of leaving..."

"I'm not worrying about leaving Andrea. I'm worrying about something else."

"Yeah?"

"Whether the lawyer will come."

"Oh, don't worry, he'll come."

"Well... I get the impression that he was visited by the boss."

"You mean he was bribed?"

"Who knows?"

"No, Vivek, it's impossible. If you'd seen this man, you'd never think so."

"I think there's hardly a man yet who dares to confront the whites' government."

"He doesn't have to confront anyone, only assert our rights."

"No one will get hurt?"

"Accepting the truth does not mean defeat... this time we will use the law."

"I remember something you had said one day..."

"Yes?"

"The law of the city is not the law of woods and fields." They were silent. Madan and Vivek looked at the field. "You think they will obey the law?"

"We'll see."

Everyone was there. Vivek and Madan walked through the crowd and joined Dawood. Farid's dog, which had run ahead, jumped on them, wagging his tail. The sun was now high in the cloud-covered sky. The air was heavy and the heat rose.

"He's here!"

All heads turned towards a movement on the path. Then the people rose.

21

The lawyer's voice was as serious as his words were significant. He seemed to weigh each word before saying it. As he spoke, his face flushed and the veins in his neck bulged under his skin. The man exuded gravitas, and everyone was listening with bated breath. Before leaving, he told them, "The law has protected you today. Tomorrow it will be your unity that will save you."

When the lawyer was gone, the villagers were slow to come out of their reverie. A little later, the lawyer and his assistants returned with the five prisoners; this was a surprise for the villagers, who greeted them with shouts of joy. It was an explosion when the lawyer spoke, "I regret that your crops are destroyed. But one thing pleases me: now no one can take this land from you. It is imperative, however, that two or three of you come to my office next Monday. I will complete the necessary paperwork so that your property is registered. We will also take care of the land on which you have built your homes. For all these formalities, you will need to bring a little money."

A long sigh of relief rose from the crowd. In no time, a garland of flowers was braided and Dawood, hands trembling with emotion, placed it around the lawyer's neck. Madan accompanied the lawyer and his men to the river and asked the lawyer, "People do not want to work on the plantation any longer. From a legal standpoint, can the boss force them?"

"He has no such right. You can set your own terms and if he accepts, you'll have no reason to refuse to work for him. But you must present your conditions. The situation is much improved on plantations now and workers tend to get twelve annas a day instead of eight. If you ask me, while looking after your own plots, you can also continue to work on the plantation. And the money you earn can be saved to buy more land currently held by the State. The day will come when you will not need to work for others. As for your current conditions, an investigation is open and your boss will soon receive a warning from the government."

They crossed the river and Madan took leave of the lawyer. He returned to the village and found Farid, Dhanlal and Vivek. Songs and dances were well underway; the sound of cymbals and drums surrounded them. It was not until dawn that they became aware that they had been partying all night. It was daylight now and no one had closed their eyes. Madan was still dancing, wearing a turban like the lawyer's. He also unearthed an old umbrella and took it, holding it open on his shoulder while continuing to dance. He never looked at Mira. Occasionally, Madan let his eyes fall on Sita.

By torchlight, Mira sat watching the crowd, trying to measure the intensity of her joy. It presented itself gradually, rising and then sinking into a kind of blurred unconsciousness. A yellow leaf fell from the wild almond tree into the heavy dew. Mira thought it looked like a shooting star; her aunt had said that they granted wishes. She made one: that Madan would keep that smile forever, that the joy he had at this moment would never leave him. The leaf hit the ground near her foot, but she did not notice. Earlier, her aunt had left the party, grumbling, "They have nothing to eat at home and all they think about is fun."

Mira wanted her to understand that the pleasure of victory was better than a full stomach. Food could sustain life, while the success of an entire village was the spice of life, the soul of a people. But try to explain that to an old aunt... her aunt could only repeat, "Your father was delirious all the time. You are like him."

The women began to yawn and most of them went to bed. Mira did not move. The air smelled of tobacco and *ganja.* Finally, they felt the spicy freshness of the morning. The light of the torches was weakening, the sparks exhausted, out of breath. The singers grew silent and the sound of the tambourine weakened, gradually losing its rhythm.

Mira remained in her seat until Madan left, Dhanlal at his side. She walked slowly towards her home and when she arrived, threw herself on the bed without turning on the lamp. Her aunt was snoring. Mira closed her eyes. Everything revolved. She was drawn out, half-dead with fatigue. She opened her eyes to stop the vertigo. Dawn was not far off; already the cocks crowed. Mira was taken by a waking dream: the sea rose up on the cliffs, huge waves gushed atop the rocks, kingfishers with long beaks perched on the wall of the whitish reef in the distance, and above them, the sky, deep blue, reflected the ocean. There were sandcastles on the beach. Someone called. She turned and saw it was Madan. He bent down to take her hand and they both ran down the beach, along the waves, hand in hand, the wind carrying Mira's wrap over the waves. She started to shake, to breathe harder, her beauty suddenly flushed and Madan reached towards her, his hands on her hair, her face, her breasts. "Mira..."

She cast her eyes towards him behind lowered eyelids. The sea roared behind her. Mira was troubled. "Your beauty irritates the waves."

She withdrew her hand, and ran away, but he ran after her, his voice transcending the roar of the sea.

Her dream was shattered suddenly. She could hear her aunt moaning in her sleep. The girl jumped up and, in the dark, quickly went to the old woman's bed, rocking her. The screams stopped and Mira returned to her bed. Outside, the night was playing its last card; the first rays of the sun had already begun to appear. Mira fell asleep with difficulty. But she had just enough time to dive into sleep so that her aunt had to shake her, "Hey, princess, it is daytime. Wake up."

"Let me sleep, please."

"You would not last two days in the hands of a mother-in-law."

Mira turned to the wall and pulled the sheet over her head. Her aunt went away, grumbling. If she had the habit of always hassling her niece, Mira's aunt also recognized her good qualities, especially in front of others. When Parmouti began praising her daughter-in-law, her aunt let Parmouti speak, and when she had finished, responded, "I feel that you haven't gotten a good look at my Mira."

Mira was due, that day, to pick up some acacia for fodder. Getting up, she saw an armful of branches of acacia in the corner. "Auntie, you've already picked up the fodder for goats? Oh... I'll hear about it all day."

"You sleep up until noon... and can you imagine the young people plan to sing the *Ramayana* late tonight?'

Mira could not believe it. How had her aunt spoken such a long sentence without including a single swear word? While brushing her teeth, Mira climbed on to the pile of rocks behind the house, where, once the fields ended, you could see the sea, far off and silent. For her, it symbolised the future, although it took confused and imprecise forms in her mind. She began to dream and the ocean embraced her, or, rather, she embraced thinking of being in its arms! The dream: waves stopped at the threshold of the house, where they died unclaimed and turned to spray, exploding into a thousand invisible bubbles, like dreams that leave nothing in their wake. The heavy breathing of the waves could lull a man to sleep.

Mira tore the stem from a guava and rubbed her teeth with it. Then she threw the stem away and went to the well. Sapura was there drawing water; Mira took a little in her bucket and rinsed her mouth. Then she washed her feet and hands. "How late did you stay out last night?"

"Until Madan..."

Too late! Mira fell silent and Sapura laughed. The birds perched on the banyan had nothing to equal the chatter of the women clustered around the well. Parmouti's daughter-in-law was at the centre of the conversation. Although she had been the last to arrive, she claimed her turn under the pretext that her bucket was the first in line. Parmouti always boasted of her tricks...

Under the eyes of such a girl, Mira filled her bucket and went running. She emptied the contents into her basket and prepared to return to the well when she saw Madan approach. She was startled, and the joyful expression on her face instantly disappeared. She adjusted her shawl and remained motionless, waiting. She felt that it would fly away and leave her naked. The bracelets around her wrists jingled.

In the distance, Gautum's son could be heard. He was

humming a song while tapping his fingertips on a copper bowl to keep tempo:

Has dawn appeared? Is the night over?

Mira was unable to look up. The weight of the world was crushing her shoulders and her eyelids were heavy burdens.

22

With the assistance of the lawyer, the villagers were granted land titles and, the next day, the parcels of land were divided afresh. This time, there were one hundred and twenty plots, one per family. Each family was entitled to a field of thirty feet by twenty. Mira's aunt's field was right next to Madan's. Under the terms of the contract, the families became owners of their field after seven months of cultivation. All the money saved by the head of *baithka* was used for the legal formalities, but everyone was happy. It had been decided, in the presence of the lawyer, that each family could keep the money that they made off their field.

It was rumoured that Mr. Maurel had labourers brought in from another village. It was said also that Mr Constant was preparing to leave for abroad, where he intended to buy slaves. On the other side of the river, a wall had been erected on which hung a sign: 'Access Forbidden'. Two worlds clashed now and if, inadvertently, a villager ventured on to the other side, he was welcomed with gunfire.

Two days after the finalisation of the new plots, Mr Maurel walked to the village. He drank water at the well and spoke in Bhojpuri to ask the villagers to return to work in his plantations.

"Tell me your conditions," he told Madan.

"We do not want to work for you."

Mr Maurel turned to the others, "Do not listen to him. If you are not working, how will you raise your children?"

"You believe that there is only one place where we can offer our services? You're not the only boss."

"They will not give you work elsewhere."

"There is always work for a man worthy of the name."

"All of my foremen are new. And I promise you that henceforth you will not have any reason to complain. Do not believe what the lawyer said and instead think about your future. He acts in his own interest in pushing you towards conflicts because he earns his living by resolving them. But it is never free."

Madan laughed, "Mr Maurel, we will no longer work for you."

"Well, I'll give you until tomorrow to decide. Otherwise, I will hire other labourers. I will return.'

"No need to bother. You will receive the same answer.'

The same afternoon, Mr. Maurel sent two foremen after Vivek. But Vivek did not appear and it was Pushpa who received the two men. "Go back to your boss saying that my son will not come, even if you cover him with gold."

The foremen were trying to intimidate labourers, but such a time was over and the villagers were not intimidated by their threats. Everyone had endorsed Dawood's motto, 'Here on earth or in the beyond, we will not give up.'

The next day, everyone was in their garden. Families whose parcels were in the forest began to clear them. Everyone came to give them a hand and, after three days, that work was done. All vegetables and fruits that had been recovered after the devastation had been stored in the *baithka*. Potatoes, onions and cassava had not suffered too much damage. Everything else had been eaten by pigs.

The seventh day, they began sowing. Fields buzzing with activity, the atmosphere was as clear and pure as after a violent storm. Gautum's son was walking from one parcel to another, singing. This gave their time on the cultivated land a special beauty. It was probably the first time that the people were working on their own land with perfect legality. But there was something else special: all the women were there, farming alongside the men.

Sugan Bhagat had no trouble convincing Mira's aunt to plant her plot with corn and pistachios. She knew nothing of agriculture, but Dawood had offered his advice and ensured her that those two plants required little care.

Mira, once the work was done for the day in their own field, went to help the neighbours, to give them a hand. She was dying of impatience to see the first seedlings. Every other day, she came to scan the earth at the place where they had put the seeds. It rained. The next day, the first shoots pointed out of the surface of the wet land. She walked around the gardens and stopped at every tiny plant. Even her aunt could not contain her excitement, "They all come out at the same time!"

Mira had heard that plants did not grow quickly. But she refused to believe it, instead imagining that they would reach her height in a day... three days later, small weeds appeared around the young plants. Mira began to tear them out and with the same energy, she attacked the weeds that were already invading the area around the pile of stones, when she saw the shadow of Madan looming on the ground and stop in front of her. Mira wiped her sweaty brow and looked up. Without his smile, Mira would have had difficulty recognising him, as he had shaved his beard. "Well, well. I think you win."

Mira did not understand. She got up, fumbling with her sickle. Madan laughed, "Your plants are sprouting before ours. Bravo!"

Mira felt a great pride, but had nothing to say. Madan stood a moment looking at her. Small patches of earth spattered her face and Madan noticed for the first time that she had very bright skin. He could not determine if the earth brought out the milkiness of her skin or if the earth itself added to her natural beauty. "What happened to your aunt?"

Madan left her with a laugh. It was not the first time he'd left Mira speechless, but he did not pursue the conversation. He dug holes on his plot for planting tomatoes, with seeds from his friends. The martins were beginning to scratch the earth to peck at the seeds. To make them flee, he also installed white flags here and there.

They decided to dig three new wells, one at the edge of the ancient forest, the other in Madan's plot and a third as yet to be determined. The well in Madan's plot was almost finished, for they had hit water sooner than expected. According to Sugan Bhagat, water from this well would irrigate twenty surrounding fields. To determine the location of the last well, Dawood had proposed, to avoid any dispute, to draw lots. Mira pulled the short straw but refused to enjoy the benefits of having the community centred around her plot. Yet in time, she would have to accept the few privileges in exchange for seeing her field trampled by all those who came in search of water.

"In fact, do not expect to be able to grow anything in the vicinity of the well."

Madan shook his head, settling the arrangement with a smile. In his field, there was a big margosa tree under which villagers sat down to talk about community problems. Around the trunk, there were flat stones that served as benches. Madan sat on the slab on the side of the *baithka*. He tried to remove a thorn stuck in his heel with the help of another thorn, and while searching for the thorn, he began to reflect on the proposals received at the latest meeting. Two labourers from a plantation nearby had brought a message from their boss. They stated upfront the improvement in living conditions enjoyed by workers in their establishment. Then they spoke of their village chief, thanks to whom these changes were in place. Inspired by Kissan, he had led his fight to the end.

The working conditions seemed really favourable. They worked every day from 8 o'clock in the morning for four hours. Leaving every day and returning home at night brought an element of freedom, which many found attractive. But in return, there would be a daily 16 kilometres round trip walk, for the plantation was 8 kilometres from the village.

A meeting was held that evening at the *baithka*, and it was decided that those whose families were large enough to support their field in their absence could go to work at the Mon Repos plantation. The harvest was not for six months. Meanwhile, all the money they could earn by working in decent conditions would return to the village. Madan joined the company and led the group of ten labourers who would go to work there. Dhanlal would take care of his field during this time.

The next morning on his way to his plot, Madan ran across Sita. She stopped him, "Why did you propose to work for another boss?"

"Vivek will not get hurt."

"But you will!"

"Our fields are not going to bring us food right away."

"And if it's a trap?"

Madan laughed. Two martins were fighting nearby so aggressively that they fell from the branch of the margosa tree on which they were perched. Before they hit the ground, they flew off, screeching.

Madan saw Deolall approaching, bucket in hand. "Looking for a drink or did you just get water for someone else?"

"No, I was distributing the curds."

"Ah, I had completely forgotten that the cow was calving. How's the little heifer?"

"She jumps and plays with her mother."

"You see Mira, in that plot over there? Give her my share of curds, would you?"

Deolall was the son of a man who had a reputation as the most laborious man of the village. He worked every day, longer than anyone else. He was also responsible for fetching fodder for the two cows in the village. And he had no equal in roof thatching. When discussing the cultivation of the fields, Deolall's father surprised them all by declaring that he would continue to plant sugarcane.

When asked why, he replied, "It is cane that made this country. It is through it and for it we have suffered. I will not abandon it now."

"But Soukna," said the head of the *baithka*, "what will you do with your sugarcane? The mill will not buy it."

"Do not worry. I will extract the juice myself and I will make candy canes to take to the market."

No one could find fault with that. Once Deolall left, Madan approached the well. But he could not sit long under the banyan tree. The smell of the coal that was being burned in the oven was unbearable. He went to the cabin with a mind to continue reading his father's book.

He took the road by the beach, impatient to resume his reading. Sitting on a rock, he raised his eyes for a moment and whispered to the sea, "Soma would not follow Harkoo..."

"It does no good to lament, Luchya. We cannot sit here, arms dangling. Let's go search for Soma.'

"I do not know what got into me... If only I had not left, it would never have happened.'

"Luchya, just be quiet. I have already explained that everything is written and that no one can change his destiny. Now, let's search for Soma."

"We have not yet recovered from Santu's arrest and now..."

"Shut up, now. That's an order. Here, look. It's Vinay. We will not stand by and wait."

"What do you want me to do after all that happened? I forgot myself to gain from these people and now look what's happened..."

"Vinay, you've already said so, that's enough."

"Now all we can do is hit our heads against the wall until we die."

"Come on, get up before we're all reduced to this."

"I dare not show myself."

"All your friends are waiting for you outside."

"To spit in my face, I suppose."

"Get up, my son, and help us in our search."

"To find what?"

"Soma, of course! She's gone."

"The whole village can help us with that: we need to find Harkoo."

"Come with us, my son, we can still find her."

"I do not know if it is too late, anyway; Harkoo will not escape us this time."

"Vinay, forget about revenge. Come, help us look."

"I cannot promise Soma anything. But I shall find that foreman, even if he is hiding in a crowd of whites."

"Vinay, where are you going?"

"Does he run fast, Karim? What will happen if he actually attacks the foreman?"

"If he does, it will not be a great sin. One day or another, one of us should, anyway. Our daughters are powerless to stop the bastard. He will have put an end to the existence of a creature too vile to speak of."

"Karim, you also think we should fight evil with evil?"

"Goodness corresponds to goodness and evil echoes evil. We

could never fight poison with holy water, even if we added milk."

"You worry us with these formulas. Santu's in prison, you're acting up. Vinay, do you want the same fate? Come on, stop while there is still time."

"You think you can stop me, Luchya? No one can block the waves of the sea when they are angry. You can hold them with dikes, levees, stones, but they will all eventually yield. The waves are made to advance... This is certainly the only lesson our chains have taught us. Vinay's reaction comes right on time. He has redeemed himself. We all want more rights and freedom. But you cannot get them by worshipping at the feet of our oppressors. We must move forward unabated. We must."

"Go and stop him, Karim, please."

"I can't."

"If everyone works together..."

"I'll see what I can do."

"Oh, my God. What will become of us? A guard. Guards are here."

"Where is the number 710?"

"What number are you talking about?"

"Where is he hiding, that little bastard Santu?"

"You probably know better than me."

"Get out. Or tell us. Where's Santu?"

"He is in prison."

"He is no longer in prison."

"Then he must be at the Sultan's palace!"

"Listen, my darling, do not joke with us. Tell us where to find Santu or else I'll arrest you all."

"Why look for someone you have already thrown in jail?"

"He escaped. Last night! And we believe he is hiding here."

"What? He has escaped? Is that true?"

"Do not act innocent. And give us this man now."

"Not so fast. Show us your search warrant."

"Santu has really escaped?"

"How do I know?"

"He cannot escape us this time."

"If he is really out, what will he do now?"

"I cannot believe it, Jhouni."

"How on earth did he run away?"

"Aren't you already more worried for your daughter-in-law?"

"I wonder where he is hiding."

"Luchya, you have already forgotten Soma."

'I need a drink."

"Santu, you're here! So it's true. And you just missed the guards."

"My son, you've become so thin."

"You cannot stay here, it's too dangerous."

"Did anyone see you coming here?"

"You look tired, Santu. You who looked so fresh and so young just three days ago..."

"Mama ..."

"Jhouni, bring him something to drink quickly."

"I'll get him some milk."

"No, water, please."

"Guards are at your heels, Santu. It is not wise to linger here."

"I will not let anyone take me again."

"They can come back at any moment."

"Give him the drink, Jhouni, I want to give him a drink myself, too."

"We will sit under the margosa tree. Do not make too much noise. At my signal, you run away behind us."

"Mama," said Soma, "please."

"You must go, Santu, and quickly."

"But where is Soma?"

"My son, keep quiet!"

"They will keep coming back. In my opinion, they will not be long."

"No, do not say that!"

"Go get Soma, please, Mama, I want to see her before I go."

"Where are you going, son?"

"I do not know. But I cannot stay here. Jhouni, call her."

"Take time to rest a little."

"I escaped yesterday. A whole army of guards has been after me for hours. So how can I breathe easy when even those who are free have hardly the right to breathe? I wanted to rest for a moment, but I am now a hunted man."

"Sit down a little."

"Give me some water. Mother, have you been crying? Your eyes are all swollen."

"Oh, my, it's nothing. You have not seen your face; it is so pale."

"I cannot return to that hell."

"Well, Jhouni will bring you water."

"But, is Soma sick? I managed to jump the wall of the prison to visit her and she is not even here when I arrive. Will I have to go to find her myself?"

"Wait, my son."

"I have the right to see my wife."

"It is not that, Santu."

"What? Is she not at home? But why did she leave? She could not bear to suffer a second? Why do you not answer? Why did you let her go? And I thought she loved me. How was she able to be so selfish?"

"Soma is not selfish, Santu."

"She's not here, but where is she? I want to know."

"I hear dogs barking. Guards!"

"Let them come. Tell me first where she is. Father, tell me."

"Come on, lying is no use."

"Tell me the truth."

"Ah, Santu what can we tell you?"

"Where is your daughter-in-law?"

"She is gone."

"So I noticed."

"Last night, she..."

"Do not tell me. She understood that there was no profit in this family..."

"You do not understand. It's true that she's left the house. But not for the reasons you think. And it is better that you do not know why."

"What are you talking about, Jhouni?"

'Just know that women do not leave their homes easily. There must be a good reason why she did.'

"I want to know."

"Nobody knows."

"We do not know. The whole village is looking for her."

"The whole village? But what are you talking about? What could have happened? Mama, why don't you say anything?"

"What do you want me to say, my son?"

"Why did Soma go?"

"I'll see if the guards have left."

"Jhouni speaks nonsense, but you know. Where is Soma?"

"We do not even know if she is still alive, Santu."

"But what are you talking about? Why don't we find her? What was going on?"

"After your arrest, we were all running to and fro to find a way to make you free. And..."

"Go on..."

"Harkoo took this opportunity..."

"Yes?"

"Harkoo likely took Soma to the boss's house."

"And then?"

"The poor girl could not defend herself against him, I guess."

"Wait, explain yourself better, I do not understand."

"I'm afraid she has undergone the same treatment as Raghuvir's daughter."

"No... no! Mama, it is not possible! How does something like that did happen? How? And you, you could not stop it? Soma, where are you?"

"We have looked for her for hours."

"Here is Vinay."

"Even Vinay could not do anything for her? I should have stayed in my cell to rot. How did this happen, Mama, how?"

"Vinay, do not just stand there. Have you found her?"

"My son, speak, please. Karim, you were with him? Or have you found the body?"

"On the banks of the river. But this is not the time to take care of the body. Care instead for those who are alive."

"Why do you say that?"

"We must hide Santu and Vinay as soon as possible."

"Both of them? But why?"

"Vinay just killed Harkoo."

"As if the killing could restore Soma to us."

"I see the guards on the hill; there is no time to lose. Vinay, take Santu with you."

"Why should Vinay go with me?"

"But Santu, he committed a murder."

"Where are you going?"

"To the foot of the mountain."

"And no one has seen you?"

"No, no."

"Good. This land knows the taste of our sweat, it's time she learns the taste of blood. Vinay, here you are once more the brave man you were. The fear has left you and also our servility, which forced you to react without any support. Now, you're the one who will maintain the fires of the struggle. Out of the embers, a huge fire will be born that will destroy this unjust world."

"They come! Get away!"

"Let them come."

"No. Vinay, listen to me. You are the head of the workers, not I, but listen to me, anyway. The fight begins today. You have always supported the truth. Well, if today you strangled evil, then that is a triumph. Let those who have poured their sweat on earth become the real agents of their prosperity."

"They are here! Save yourselves!"

"Karim, uncle, the life of an Indian does not have much value. If found, it is absolutely necessary that we be found guilty, but they need one. Not two. Vinay has proven himself by serving his people as best he can. Uncle, you have to look at everyone in the village. Vinay's place is at the head of the oppressed. All I want is for Soma to be offered a beautiful funeral."

"Santu, we have you! You can not escape us!"

"Do not worry, I'm not going to run. Come on, do your work, bind me. The first time you arrested me for killing a boss; this time it's for the murder of a foreman. It is I who killed Harkoo. You will find his body at the foot of the mountain."

"Santu, what are you talking about?"

"I said what I had to say."

"No, you can not go alone!"

"But I can, Vinay. Replace me in this house. Be Santu here, Vinay at home, and for all the villagers. I kneel at the feet of my parents and ask for their blessing."

"You'll also throw yourself at the feet of the boss..."

Madan closed the book and sighed deeply. Before his eyes, waves sobbed softly, relentlessly.

23

He came from afar. He was not wearing a beard, nor did he have long hair. But everybody instinctively called him the *swami*. Nobody knew who he was and they thought he must have amnesia. He never spoke of his native village. He claimed not to remember his name; at his age, nobody would know how to give him one. But they had confidence in him. Madan approached him several times. His face reflected a rare innocence and a strange light shone in his eyes. Madan often listened to his deep voice rising like an echo from the depths, sometimes hesitant or trembling, but driven by a power that would have moved a rock.

He held his first speech in the *baithka* before seven people. "We must take care of the night around us. God gives us such a beautiful land... we must break the yoke that the powerful impose on us."

He was able to talk non-stop for hours. They finally got tired of listening; some yawned and some even fell asleep. He always returned to the same idea: one day or another, this country should belong to those who work the land. "Our future government," he predicted.

They said he was crazy. He heard them laugh and it made him laugh. It was a strange and mysterious laughter, with an indecipherable accent. The children teased him about his odd attire, but he never scolded them. When asked about his past, he smiled and invariably replied, "My past and my present are the same thing. What I am today is what matters."

"And your future?"

"You are my future." Very few understood him, but everyone gave him their confidence.

They had therefore come to accept what he said. "The only thing we need," he would repeat, "is a future. It is why we must work with courage and determination."

Sometimes, he would plow a neighbour's field or help with some community work. Sometimes, he comforted the sick; sometimes, he had a kind word for the lonely. His arrival brought new life, a kind of renaissance of the link between the villagers.

He spoke of what were truly hungry and miserable days, and they appreciated even more the relative prosperity that they enjoyed. They all were surprised to see him so dynamic and wondered from where he drew such energy.

His hair was thick and matted. He applied a *tika* on his forehead with the earth's dirt, claiming it was more pure than sandalwood. This did not please the *panditji* at the temple, who began to criticise him. He listened to him and then laughed. But the man would smile when he was reprimanding them and he laughed when they thanked him for services rendered.

"Why thank me?" he asked. "Thank rather the feeling that has just hatched in you. Because if it remains dormant, it will be useless. Only deployed does it makes sense and then it is worth more than propriety. It is for me to thank you. You do more than me... and the little that I do, you feed me, you give me clothes. You do not work just for yourself but for all humanity."

Madan could not discuss matters with him. The man did not often respond. What Madan wanted was someone to come talk to him, help him, contradict his analysis, draw out the truth.

One day, Madan was with the *swami* on Kissanwa's plot. Kissanwa had been ill for a month and could not work his land. His family was on the brink of hunger. The *swami* stopped those people who were going to bring him food. "He needs your support, not your charity. His field is abandoned: you should all get started and work on it. His wife and children will then grow and produce their own food."

They were ten friends who did half the job. They paused. The *swami* wiped his forehead and dripping with sweat, said, pointing his wet fingers up, "Look at that water. It is purer than the sacred water of the Ganges."

After this, he placed on Madan's forehead some dirt he had gathered in his hand. The hand formed a *tika* on his forehead. Madan felt a coolness seep through him. He understood what the *swami* meant when he claimed that the earth was the purest and freshest matter. He felt rested, regenerated.

About twenty young people from the neighbouring village came to see the *swami*. "We have serious concerns,' they said."

"Young and strong as you are!" replied the man, laughing.

"We have no future here."

"There is no lack of work here. Look at all these fields, all the bush around you. There is work everywhere, and work well... that's the future!"

"We would like to work at the height of our ambitions."

"Work is lofty, too. Of what are you capable?" No one could have any argument against his conviction. Soon, they were behind him. Never had work seemed so pleasant and so valuable. He passed through the ranks, distributing pats on their shoulders. He brought each of them water in his bucket and when one of them felt tired, he took his place. Everyone was showing signs of fatigue, but not him. His face kept his strange light and his eyes shone bright and alert in the blinding light of the sun.

"Organise yourselves," he said to Madan. "Get up and see for yourselves what all there is to do. Do not ask others to submit their strength to foreign hands, as you then weaken it. You are my future, but yours is your labour, your unity and your solidarity. Do not haggle your future. Oh, no! Have confidence in your happy tomorrow."

"But this future you speak of... the bosses hold it tight in their closed fist."

"No! You are the only reason for your helplessness. The future of a man is in his hands. It can shine when rubbed and if it is polished carefully. Go! Break down the walls that separate us from each other. We must co-operate, we must unite and agree that all walls are barriers!"

His words penetrated Madan's consciousness, bringing a new

energy. They seemed to be renewing his blood, regenerating his passion. Then the *swami* left and went to another village. They panicked a little, as if only in his presence could they implement the new resolutions. Their motivation was gone and their example was gone. They flapped their wings, pinned down like wounded birds.

When, after three days, someone announced that he was back, the villagers forsook everything to go to the river where he was to arrive. They welcomed him with wreaths and garlands of flowers. But he, instead of thanking them, began to reprimand them. "You would have done better to stay at work. I see that you did not understand my message... why welcome me? Welcome instead the work with gratitude; it alone will build the foundation for a society and allow it to develop."

"Of course."

"In the future, we will do what you say." All the villagers departed and they each went about their own tasks. For the first time, however, a slight hint of bitterness had pierced his words. Or rather, a hint of exasperation, like a mother who gives her child a light slap.

The night was cold. They were all sitting around the fire. The *swami* spoke, "With the living conditions they have imposed on us, we have lost confidence in ourselves. In the village where I have been, people have even lost faith in the land they work. Their confidence is buried under thick layers of dust. It must be extracted and they must break the cycle of despair."

The speech continued and sounds fell out of his mouth like glowing embers. Madan thought that they would disperse like flying ash. There was a barely audible, sharp pain in his voice and it seemed at times that he was letting out a long wail, like that of the waves of the sea. Later, the villagers learned that where he had gone, he had been welcomed with stones. The owner had been a charlatan. He had spent three nights in a brothel, the only one not partaking.

Some young villagers learned this from the mouth of an outsider and they were so furious they were ready to run to the village where the *swami* had been abused in this way. But the *swami* heard about their expedition and he stopped the heroes on the way.

"*Swami*, we'll make them pay dearly for this humiliation."

"It's a childish reaction."

'"Do not try to dissuade us."

"Why do you want revenge?"

"Because we love you and we will not accept..."

"Good. Listen to me for a moment. You want revenge because you love me, you say. But affection sometimes leads to impotence. We should love one another. But, one day, I will separate myself from you. What will happen then? You will be disappointed and you will forget all moderation."

Everyone looked at him, eyes wide, trying to understand him.

The next day, after lunch, he went up on the big rock and announced in the most natural way, "Tomorrow, I will leave you. My goal has always been to keep moving. I leave with the conviction that you will have a bright future. You will stand in the rain and the sun as in the storm. These days will pass, no matter what. And one day, you will see a rising sun, whose rays congratulate you and all those who cheat you will be crushed, will be on their knees to ask for your forgiveness. I am leaving tomorrow. But keep this in mind and do not be sad: even in my absence, work must not stop. Do not be overcome by inertia and passivity."

Madan tried hard to dissuade him; the villagers begged him and wept. But nothing and nobody could make him change his mind.

The next day, they all looked at him go and he disappeared on the horizon, while the sun set. Thus he left, leaving the whole village in tears.

Three days later, they found his body near the river. The plantation owner's dogs had torn his clothes to pieces. On his chest, next to the point where the bullet had passed through, they discovered, printed with a hot iron, his prisoner number.

24

Mira was whitewashing the walls of the *baithka*. She chatted with Ramba. 'You think black magic is real?"

"All I know is that my brother did not die a natural death."

"You think that someone cast a spell?"

"It's obvious. We did several sessions to reverse the bewitchment, but the village *panditji* said we could not save him. The fate that Andrea's mother set for him was too strongly entrenched."

"And you believe that?"

"You do not, perhaps?"

"No."

"Well, well. You'll see what happens to Vivek."

"You mean he's is also bewitched?"

"You remember the doll that was found on the doorstep of his house..."

"Yes, I was with you that day."

"It had seven needles in its chest!"

"Frankly, I do not understand the fuss around this ridiculous incident. Everyone is terrorised. My aunt is trembling from head to toe, locked in her house. This is the first time I've seen Zinat afraid. Only Vivek is unaffected and continues to laugh."

"That's just a facade, in my opinion."

"I heard from Zinat that he fears nothing."

That evening, all the villagers assembled in the *baithka*. Dhanlal had fashioned with his hands a little altar of wet earth on which he placed a statue of Hanuman surrounded by flowers. Pushpa and Vivek sat side by side. The *panditji* applied a *tika* of white powder on the idol's forehead and bestowed upon him a few petals while reciting prayers, looking towards the doll and its needles. Then he asked Vivek to close his eyes and throw a handful of rice grains on the fire, while the *panditji* continued his prayers.

Outside, Deolall had prepared a small bonfire of dried twigs. The *panditji* stopped his incantations and spoke in a clear voice, "No one is greater than God. Everyone is free to do as he pleases! But that does not mean that one can go against the will of God by using magic and witchcraft. Is there a better remedy than to believe in God and leave our fate in his hands? Simply by invoking the name of Hanuman, our worries vanish. Today we will pray together. We will chant the *Hanuman Chalisa.* But first, we'll burn the doll at the stake. By the grace of God, this figure will be reduced to ashes and the evil designs of the enemy who cast a spell on Vivek will be annihilated."

Sugan Bhagat rose, took the doll and placed it on the small logs Dhanlal had prepared and set it on fire. Whispers of fear could be heard in the crowd. The *panditji* sang louder verses about Hanuman. Everyone sang with him. Dawood and Hanif, who sat side by side, recited verses from the Koran.

The doll was soon completely scorched. The *panditji* placed a few mango twigs at the altar and said again, "God willing, no one can do anything against Vivek." Still, their fear remained intact.

The sun was already floating towards the sea by sliding towards the horizon. The clouds from the east invaded the sky in the west. A warm wind blew, giving off a dry heat. Vivek went home, holding his mother's hand in his own. In his other hand, he carried a prayer book that the *panditji* had given him.

Instead of going home, Mira went to the fields. This was the hour when partridges and martins returned to the nest after having one last peck at the peanut plants. The night before, she had stayed late at Zinat's and in the morning when she arrived at the field, she saw twenty or thirty plants, their roots laid bare by voracious partridges that had eaten all the seeds. The traps that Gautam's son had prepared for the birds had not deterred them.

Mira ran from one small field to another, singing to chase away the birds. A couple of martins flew off. She sang loudly:

Fly away, fly away, martin with your big wings,
go away along the river; your chicks are hungry.
Fly away, go away now, come back on harvest day
in lieu of one grain, thou shalt have a hundred: fly away!

Two partridges hovered a moment at low altitude, then went away. They landed in Madan's field. Mira threw rocks without achieving anything. She made one or two more laps around the plots and went home.

Night was falling to the rhythm of her steps. The slowly

descending darkness spread like the torment inside her. The first time she had felt this burning, she had almost choked. She usually told Zinat everything, but she hid this longing. She had neither the words nor the courage to tell her of the secret sting which reached into her flesh. It was her fight and she had to fight alone. But she could not help but wonder: 'Is this really a burden I have to wear?'

She lacked dynamism, energy and was easily irritated. The heat of desire rendered her soft and brought tears to her eyes and even hunger and thirst could not hide a painful gnawing envy in the hollow of her belly.

"There are ways to meet this kind of desire," said Sandhya. "I can tell you, if you want..." Sandhya spoke of solitary pleasure, ecstatic intoxication... Mira pretended not to understand. Sandhya insisted, 'When you reach orgasm, then you moan very hard."

This made Mira very sad. She was working harder and her miserable body revolted, giving her sweats and palpitations. Sandhya made fun of her, "You should drink."

"Really?"

"It will help you feel in control." A few days earlier, in the shadow of the trees, Sandhya had told her in detail of her amorous adventures with Devraj. For an hour, Mira had listened and the story's intimate scenes had so excited her that she had a twinge of regret, of pain mixed with diffuse pleasure. "You know why your chemise is so tight and so short?" Mira looked at Sandhya, taken aback, but when she opened her mouth to explain, Mira covered her mouth with one hand. Back home, she took the mirror down from the shelf and held it to her at eye level. Then she bent slightly down to contemplate her bust and rested her eyes on the edge of her chemise where it met the skin of her belly.

Her aunt did not like to see her suck cane juice. "Ah," the old woman said to her, "still always with sugar in your mouth."

"I am no longer a child. It is safe for my teeth."

"It is not appropriate for girls."

"Why?"

"Oh, you and your questions. You do not know that sugar gives hot flashes?"

Mira fled to the river where she plunged into the cold water.

It cooled her body and also soothed her mind. At Zinat's, she'd found an old book that had belonged to Madan's father in which Kissan had laid out the lyrics of his songs. In the light of the clay lamp, she deciphered the handwritten pages. She had come across this book by chance one day while Zinat had been looking for lice in Sapura's hair. She'd always liked Kissan's songs, but what attracted her even more now is that they were written by Madan's father.

She walked in, humming the last song in the book:

Life is like sunset
on a quiet trail
the wind stopped
in the evening light.

Mira had learned that song quickly and she turned it over in her head. That evening, she sang it along the river. One day, she was working in her plot, singing it in a melodious voice, when Madan came up quietly behind her. Mira stopped singing.

"Where did you learn this song?" asked Madan.

Mira stiffened and could not answer. Once alone, she felt exasperation dawning. She wanted badly to respond, for it was the eleventh time Madan had struck her dumb: she kept count. And, as she had promised herself on previous occasions, she vowed to speak at the next opportunity.

When she returned home, her aunt was trying to feed the neighbour's kids. She began to reprimand Mira, "I have forbidden you from going to the field. But you do not stop..."

"My aunt, at dawn, the birds peck at seeds."

"Don't you think maybe it's unsuitable for a girl to go out alone at this time and walk through the fields?"

"There are no wild pigs in the area, as far as I know."

"One day they will come."

"Aunt, we can not even see the shadow of a pig."

"Zinat was looking for you just now."

And her aunt went into the house. Mira grabbed the bucket and began to wash her hands and feet vigorously. When she was finally home alone, Mira drew the bolt on the door and locked herself inside. She took off the necklace she had received from her mother. She longed so much to get rid of the obsessive thoughts that troubled her; she wanted to erase from her mind all that connected it to the past, present and even the future. But the past clung to her, as sticky as the worst adhesives, the present boiling in her like a storm, and the future was a tangled web of dreams. In seeking a way out of the spider's web, Mira dove in further.

She took care not to show her friends such a state of sadness; when her aunt caught her in the process of brooding, she told her, "don't be so broody, or you will never be married." She searched in vain for the link between the two states... Mira forced a smile and walked away. "You look like a witch,' grumbled her aunt to her back.

Once her old aunt left the house, Mira closed the door and barricaded herself in search of a moment of peace and solitude. But memories of the past and dreams of the future came back to torment her, chasing each other relentlessly. She was sandwiched between oppressive periods of time. The pain grew in her, until her teeth were on edge.

The pain was unlike any other. It caused a hunger in her naked body and she shivered with cold, crushed by misery and deprivation, aware, also, of the plight of others. And then there was another pain, more intense, above cries and tears. Altogether, these formed a huge volcano from which burning lava threatened to escape at any moment.

"You are so beautiful, Mira," her friends told her and these words made her mad with rage. All her bad luck, and all she had was her alleged beauty.

"If she had not been so arrogant, she would already be married," Ramba's mother had told her daughter. "All this happens because she knows she is beautiful." Ramba's mother had wanted her for her son, Sumangal, but her aunt had refused to make arrangements. She had sustained her refusal and what was most troublesome was that from that day Ramba spoke to her no more. She claimed that her brother had been driven mad by Mira's cruelty and that he had hanged himself out of love for her.

Mira never imagined that her childhood friend could become a rabid enemy. Few people knew the actual reason for Dadhiball's suicide, but they were aware that Mira was not at fault. The young man had been violated by a Creole foreman. And if Sandhya had not been there to explain how such a thing was possible, Mira herself would not have known how a man could take advantage of another man. Dadhiball, mad with shame, had hanged himself in the pine forest.

Zinat knew everything about Mira and what she did not know, Mira did not know herself. But from somewhere, there was a memory, almost a dream, which came back to haunt her periodically. She must have been five or six-years old. It was not so old and yet it seemed to belong to a very distant past. Something had happened, something vague and incomprehensible. A man had come from a remote location. But someone had caught up, or surprised, and Madan was involved, with a sickle. And Mira recalled that just before, a girl from the village had disappeared. After three days of fruitless search, people had begun to whisper that she had been sacrificed at the site of the new mill of the neighbouring institution.

Mira then remembered another dream she'd had, a few years earlier, after attending a ceremony in honour of Kali. The goat that was to be the sacrifice had broken the rope that held him back and rushed into her arms. On this scene she had superimposed the image of Madan, but she did not know why, as he had been in prison.

There was not a breath of air. The night was warm, humid. The sky seemed to freeze, the dark clouds stopped on the spot. Mira was sitting under the night's canopy in search of a little fresh air. Her aunt cried for the second time, "It is no good to sit out at night. And then the dew will fall."

Mira lost her temper, "Stop with your nonsense. You're an idiot." A little later, she saw Farid's dog. "Auntie," she called inside the house. Her aunt, who had fallen asleep, was startled by her whining.

"But what are you doing?"

"Can I go for a walk to Zinat's?"

"Don't you know the time?"

"I'll be right back." Mira called the dog and went with him

towards Zinat's home. The walk, she thought, brought her a little calm and rid her of the tension that kept her from sleep.

Madan was there. They spoke of Vivek. "I think it's fear that makes him sick," said Farid.

"No," replied Madan softly.

"What then?"

"I do not know."

Zinat spoke, "I also think it's fear that gives him a fever."

"Ah, but Vivek is not the sort to be intimidated by stories of witchcraft."

"By hearing about it all the time, he'll perhaps be affected."

"You've also fallen sick. You won't blame that on black magic?" No one spoke for a while.

"Vivek is sick?" Mira asked Sapura. She nodded and Mira shivered unpleasantly. Zinat pulled gently on the wick of the lamp that had been growing weaker. "You will see; tomorrow, he will be fine."

Mira's eyes were fixed on Madan, but when he turned to look towards her, she lowered her eyelids. She wanted to affirm, to note that she, too, did not believe in witchcraft. But she could not make a sound. "If it were so easy to eliminate one's neighbour," she said to herself, "then what justifies the existence of God?"

During the discussion she had with Sandhya, she was adamant: there was no such thing as black magic. But a memory came back to her, a few years old, before Madan's arrest. In the forest, a tree had fallen, probably an old tamarind tree, its roots rotted by rain. All around the stump, mud had collected, very red, which they used in masonry. One day, Kunti returned to the village, panting, as if possessed. Seeing her coming out of the forest pale with fear, the villagers gathered near the wells and assailed her with questions.

"What happened to you there, Kunti?"

"Near the stump in the hollow earth, I heard voices coming from the roots."

Everyone was amazed.

"You've gathered some *ganja* for your father and now you've come home drugged," Mira had said, laughing.

Kunti could not be dissuaded. "I heard them speak of a ring of silver coins... a voice said, The treasure is in the roots. I am the guardian. If you dig, you will find gold, but if someone else digs, they will find coal.'

"Oh. If you were not drunk, you dreamed it."

"If you do not believe me, come with me and unearth it." The whole village went after her. Once there, they heard nothing more. Kunti insisted they dig around the root from which the voices had come. At an arm's depth, they fell on a coal seam that looked like scorched earth. But no treasure. Some dug a little, then gave up.

The following days, the villagers spoke only of this. Sugan Bhagat explained that before being inhabited, the island was frequented by vessels from pirates. The treasure may have been hidden by pirates and the voice was that of a slave prisoner who had been left on-site to monitor the loot. Mira, even then, denied the occult. But something was amiss and she had some doubts. Before her marriage, Kunti had seizures during which she screamed and jumped until she was unconscious. They had to use purification rituals and various exorcisms to calm her. The *panditji* had finally admitted that it was the wandering soul of the slave prisoner who made her mad. But after her marriage, Kunti was back to normal, which indicated to Mira that all this was not serious. Even the ugly face of Andrea's mother did not alarm her. But the doll did upset her and she was anxious.

"Madan, you can walk Mira home," said Zinat.

"No, I can go alone."

"It is on his way. There's a bad wind tonight."

"Zinat, you know that I do not believe these things."

"Some do not believe until they are victims."

"Come on, Mira," said Madan.

She stood up. Outside, a light rain fell. They could hear dogs in the distance. Arriving in front of Mira's home, Madan said, "I think you are much more afraid of me than the devil." She ran to her door without a word.

25

Madan reflected on the decisions that had been made by the community. He did not know what was right. Another meeting was scheduled for today that Madan did not intend to attend. But he suspected that many would look for him at Dhanlal's, where he was staying. It was pointless, therefore, to avoid confrontation. He had the responsibility to say clearly, 'from tomorrow, we are going to work in the Mon Repos plantation.'

In reality, the decision was already final, but Madan no longer approved. He was in a bind. Should he give his consent? The work would not be hard; the pay was decent. There was a different issue, as well. The villagers wanted to stop drinking water from Ramessur's, Soudron's, or Nalletamby's homes. But these three were just the only ones from the village, not the only ones involved: overall a hundred or more labourers were converting to Christianity. The missionaries claimed to have converted more than three hundred. They boasted that they were getting them on the right track, that of belief in the Son of God. Sivenas was now called Simon and once a simple farmer, he had became a foreman. Pounousamy, after he adorned his neck with a cross, had obtained a position as the head cook on his plantation.The list was endless.

"I do not see how not drinking their water will solve the problem," declared Madan.

The head of the *baithka* had not responded. It was necessary, in one way or another, to prevent the villagers from dropping out of their community. Soudron and Ramessur had refused to come to the meeting; they had told the messenger who came to fetch them that they were too busy with their new fields, which were much larger than the plots that they had been assigned here.

"We already sell our sweat to feed ourselves," Madan had declared, "will we also lose our friends?"

He knew that the only way out was never to send anyone to work in another plantation or to interact with the missionaries. But he doubted that this could put an end to the bargaining, to the dishonest propositions, to the benefits offered to the Indians to give up their names and their religion.

"If everything went well here, no one would think of changing their religion," said Dawood. "If the situation does not improve, this kind of question will arise even more. Those who engage in this practice dare not approach us."

Madan did not share this view. What was the relationship between a man's position and his temptations? One who accepted the softness of a stranger's hand could not help but extend his other hand to grab a bigger piece.

When he arrived at the *baithka*, Madan learned that Soudron had left the village at night. Nalletamby and his wife were preparing to do the same. Sugan Bhagat told the latter he should not leave like thief on the run, but Nalletamby said his wife was expecting a child and he did not want to see the child grow up in poverty. In a nearby village, they had been offered a house, a good job and a better future.'What is the future?' wondered Madan. 'Nothing but foreign... how can we give up everything that makes up our lives to follow a stranger?'

He ran to Nalletamby's, "Do you know what you are doing, brother?"

"My father came here from Madras. And you know why? So his two sons could know better days. He died in a cane field, spitting blood. As for my brother, he was slaughtered after insulting a white man."

"You're not the only one to have lived this kind of tragedy."

"This is like all of our stories, I agree. And that's precisely why I am about to start another life."

"By giving up your culture, your religion?"

"Our ancestors had already given it up on the way here."

"They had sold their bodies, Nalle, not their soul." Nalletamby had tears in his eyes.

His wife joined them. She was crying, too, "Madan, my brother, try to make him see reason."

Madan has faced Nalletamby and took him by the shoulders. "Can I ask you a question, Nalle? You have your beliefs; you've turned to the Christian faith. You are free to do is what that makes you happy. But how can you sell what rightfully belongs to your child without asking his opinion?"

"I do it for his own good."

"Are you sure?"

"Do you really believe that his future is here, in this life of misery that we have known?"

"Here at least we do not betray ourselves. I see that you have not abandoned our religion completely: you wear a red *tika* on your forehead... Please, think before you decide to convert."

"Which religion is better than that which allows man to live happily?"

"How do you know that this life is for you? You have not even started to live it!"

"I can see how other people live."

"Their truth is not yours. The grass is always greener elsewhere, Nalle."

"Let me do what I want, Madan."

Madan was silent, then said softly, "All right, do as you like.'

Madan was about to leave when Nalletamby's wife splayed herself across the door. Madan wanted to leave, but she barred his way.

"Tanguechi!" cried her husband. She did not move. Nalletamby came towards her, seized her by the arm and pulled her inwards. Her ankle bracelet was cut, and it fell to the ground. Madan picked it up, and slowly put it on the threshold of the house before disappearing.

He took the path that ran along the edge of the village and stopped on the outskirts of an old banyan tree. He always took pleasure in contemplating the young leaves that moved in the wind along the river. Every time he sat a few moments under the banyan tree, he fell asleep. The villagers did not like to venture there because it was the tree from which Nalletamby's brother had hanged himself, and it was said that his soul was hanging around here. It was also said that it was a place of rendezvous for fairies and angels.

Madan sat on a round stone, staring into the cluster of banana leaves. They fell in rhythm with his thoughts. He sat under the tree for a long time and the issues he had in mind always returned to the same haunting questions. 'Why doesn't the white man work the land himself? Are we doomed to this work by birth? Will the whites ever cut the canes? Why do they never dirty their hands? Is it God who made this decision? Or is it a conspiracy spun by those with the right colour and enough money? Yet none of those leaving here had money. So was it just a matter of colour?'

The next day, Madan went to the temple in the town of Mathura. When he returned, time had passed, yet nothing had changed. The fields at the foot of the mountain remained the same. They lacked only Nalletamby, who one day said, "The white man who bought me was lame. And he was as big as he was wicked. I was in my seventh day of work when they locked me in a 'dead box' for helping another labourer. 'Dead box' was the name of that cell because five men had already died in it. And that's what would have happened to me if I had not been hard."

Nalletamby's story was certainly true, but today Madan was struggling to believe it. How could a man who had endured it draw a line under his past and sell it to the highest bidder? Madan had chills.

"I was enclosed in the box. If that had been that, a man could stand it long enough, several days, a month, maybe. But in this case, they closed it, but put it on a stove full of glowing embers on which they threw a handful of red chillies. Prisoners would cough and sneeze so that in less than an hour they were half-dead. Most did not last two hours."

When the stove grew cold, they opened the cell door. Nalletamby had still been breathing. How could a man of this calibre accept defeat? He who'd faced the worst torture could be fooled today... it felt like truth did not exist.

Madan got up and went back to the village. It was warmer than usual and his clothes were soaked with sweat. He took off his shirt and hung it on the hook on his door, then he folded his *dhoti* into shorts. Finally, he sat down under the margosa tree. It was as if the wind was sulking, hiding behind any mountain it could. Madan was hot and his brain was hot too, his thoughts moist. He wanted to go to the river. The day before, he'd seen Mira coming out of the water, her clothes dripping, married to her perfect form. Seeing him, she'd crossed her hands on her chest and had tried to escape. Madan had barred the road with his arms extended and while she stood motionless before him, he had said these words, which came out of his mouth without any deliberate act of speech: "I have never seen you look so beautiful." Mira was frightened, and in a split second, she was gone.

Madan was sweating on the way to the river. He hurried to the water to wash, to get rid of his sticky sweat. Suddenly, he heard a voice behind him. It was Nalletamby. Even before he spoke, Madan guessed what he would say. "I am not going!"

26

Madan and his friends stopped going to work on the other plantation. They cultivated their own fields. It had not yet been a month and families were already beginning to suffer from food shortages. A week earlier, they distributed goods bought at the market with the communal funds. It was decided that they would make a distribution every two weeks. As for the fields, they wouldn't produce anything for another two months. At the well, in the fields along the river, there was only one topic of conversation: What will the children eat in the meantime?

'Should we have abandoned work for the sake of ideas?' wondered Madan. But he relaxed a little and set his mind free of emotional constraints, and he found the answer. 'At least we will preserve the legacy of our ancestors.'

Madan had made a list; he read their names and counted twenty-five. He intended to meet them under the banyan tree rather than in the *baithka*. All were faithful friends, about the same age as him and he could count on them. He knew none of them would refuse his proposal. He had already spoken to Vivek and Farid, who considered the idea excellent. With Farid, Madan had toured the village homes for several days, seeing that there was a handful of rice to eat every day. The only way to make it last as long as possible was to use the provisions of the *baithka* pantry. But all the families who had adopted this form of rationing had children. Madan worried about them. How could they sleep on an empty stomach?

The twenty-five men arrived, one after the other and sat

under the big banyan tree. Madan went straight to the point. "I know a way to prevent the villagers from starvation. And we can enact it." He looked carefully but found that their faces waiting carefully. 'I propose that from today we eat no more rice and that we give our share to the children. We can survive on the fruits we find in the woods. The rations of twenty-five men should be enough to feed a hundred children."

"I agree with you, Madan."

"Me too."

"I agree also.' They all agreed.

"I am willing to organise the fruit-picking twice a week," said Farid.

Devraj was proposed to lead it for two more days a week. Hanif, Bharatlall and Ramsewak signed on as volunteers. Madan was convinced that they could overcome the shortage. He told them of the next part of his plan. He would cut down the casuarina trees that grew plentifully near the beach and make them into charcoal they could sell in the market. The idea, as soon as he put it forward, was accepted. Sumangal and Danpatwa took responsibility for getting it done. Danpatwa added that he knew many of the Creoles of coastal villages and could, eventually, accompany them fishing. It could well bring fish, or at least money from the sale of the fish. They applauded his initiative.

The next day, Sumangal and other young men cut down the casuarina trees. Danpatwa procured a little bait, and, accompanied by Joseph and Hanif, they went out to sea in the same afternoon. The field work was also moving fast: all the villagers redoubled their efforts. They moved the small festivals that were usually held in the *baithka* into the fields. In the evening, there was dancing and singing in the moonlight, and those who wanted to work could continue. Some sang while working, others worked while singing. The same theme recurred in the songs: the impatience of the farmers before the first harvest:

Oh! It is a long time coming
This first harvest
Like a young bride
Her feet adorned with red designs.

The first harvest comes very slowly
Like the cold rain.
The first harvest lingers too
Like the husband who has gone
to the charms of his mistress.
It takes so long to return, oh! oh!

They saw the first grain of the corn cobs. They saw some flowers open on the seed vegetables. Pellets, the colour of milk, appeared on the roots of the pistachio plants. It had not rained, but the field was irrigated with well water and the fields glowed green.

Madan was already imagining the harvest; he dreamed of big baskets of food, when he saw Farid accompanied by a Chinese man, who wore a long braid. "Madan, I present you Ah Choy. He wants to open a shop in our village."

Madan looked at the Chinese man, who smiled with his teeth. "What kind of shop?"

The man stammered in Bhojpuri, 'Well! I will sell a little of everything, rice, flour, lentils, clothes..."

"But we have no money to buy it all."

"You will. You will soon... Look at these fields, there is plenty of money there.'

"It's possible. But it will be two or three months before the first harvest."

"It does not matter, it does not matter. Meanwhile, I will build my shop. And I will give credit. I believe in the Buddha."

The man spoke a long time. Upon leaving, he bowed several times to Madan. He kept smiling and when he left, he turned back, a wide smile illuminating his face.

"It would be very good," said Farid, "if we had a shop in the village. We would not need to go to the next village to do our shopping."

Madan was thoughtful. He spoke at last, "I hope he will not be the one to reap the fruits of our labour."

"What do you mean?"

"We should build it ourselves, the shop."

"Where would we find the money to do it?"

"Where do you think that the Chinese man came up with the money?"

Farid did not know what to say. Madan had always said that working the land was sacred. Still, the idea bothered him, 'Is that why we are so attached to this land? Is this not perhaps a ruse to keep us eternally labourers? Where does this absurd idea come from? If it's in our sacred texts, who wrote it?'

The lawyer, during his visit, told them, "You will not get anywhere if you stay attached to the land. There is another world, very different from yours, where money is power." Madan wondered how this world was so different. And he repeated what the lawyer had told him, "We risk nothing in trying."

'If we do not build it right away,' thought Madan, 'we will lag behind.' He wanted to encourage trade, and yet today he'd let a foreigner take the first opportunity. 'We are the architects of our own loss,' he thought, full of doubt.

The sun was burning less directly on them than usual, but the heat was stifling enough to cause discomfort. Sugan Bhagat kept saying it had never been so hot in Mauritius. In the afternoon, they seemed to melt. They all feared a cyclone. Madan tried to reassure them, "It's normal that it is hot; it is summer." But he was also well aware that the heat was excessive. The last time they had experienced such a heat wave, he was in prison. It had ended in a violent cyclone.

The well was almost dry. Although the leaves were beginning to turn yellow, through labour and care the villagers were able to maintain the green of the fields. Mira looked at the ears of corn plants adorned with long slender leaves. Madan stood nearby and watched her. Mira had not seen him and she continued to sing cheerfully. Silhouetted in a play of shadows and light, she disappeared before his eyes. Madan smelled trouble rise up in him; he had felt a slight pinching already on seeing her. The day before, Mira had brought him grilled corn. Madan wanted to know where she had gotten it but, but she had run away, pretending not to have heard the question. The image that haunted him was that of the girl coming out of the water, her clothes clinging to her body and light to her skin.

Madan decided to talk to Zinat, "Don't you think that Mira should get married?"

"That is for her aunt to decide," Zinat replied, laughing. "And you've never thought about getting married?"

"Here it is girls who marry first..."

"Yes, when they marry a man from another village." Madan was silent. Zinat jumped into the water, "If you want, I can offer your hand to Mira's aunt."

"What?"

"We were talking about Mira's marriage, right?"

"Zinat! I do not know what you're playing at, but I... ."

"Do not bother. I know already. You love her, don't you? When you were still in prison, she had already put your name on her lips."

These words reached Madan like a flash of pure joy.

27

Is a dream an unfaithful representation of human thought or pure imagination? This was what Mira was inwardly debating. 'If it's a representation,' she went on in her interior monologue, 'why do dreams maintain the semblance of reality? Unless my thoughts themselves are distorted and then they become straightened?'

Mira had a large imagination and the comings and goings of her thoughts rarely left her in peace. But her thoughts and dreams were contrasted in colour and orientation. She was so tormented and to calm herself, she had come to the conclusion that dreams and thoughts formed the two sides of the same coin. Thoughts were the blurry side, dreams the shiny side. But why did her dreams, as soon as they were exposed to the light of day, lose their lustre? Mira questioned Zinat, who burst out laughing.

Zinat was probably right when she claimed that they acted only according to one's true nature. This is how some people manage to flee from reality. They were happy despite the gap between their desire and their reality.

Mira had every reason to be happy. All those who passed her field claimed that the crops would be ready within a fortnight.

She was happy each day in her work, thinking of the harvest. The sweet smell of bread would be the reward of all her efforts. The next day she would not lower her eyes to Madan. Instead, she would look into his eyes to contemplate the reflection of her joy.

Mira was so excited that the two weeks of waiting seemed endless. "It's lunch time," cried her aunt over the pile of stones.

Mira was not hungry. In her bag hanging on the mulberry tree, there was cassava cake and a vegetable compote. "I'm not hungry. Take mine, if you want."

"Crazy girl, you think your belly just wants a breath of fresh air?"

Mira knew very well that if she did not share her meal, her aunt would not even open the bag. She went to wash her hands and face with water from the watering can and sat under the mulberry tree. Her aunt was already there. Mira chose her lunch, taking a small piece of cooked cassava on which she spread the vegetables. Then she handed the rest to her aunt and went towards Zinat's field. "You cannot sit to eat? That's why what you eat does not benefit you. You're as lean as a cuckoo."

Mira found Zinat eating the same cassava cake with Sapura. She sat down beside her. "Oh, but it's hot! It looks like it will rain coals."

"And no hope of actual rain."

"Last night it was unbearable; you could hardly breathe. My aunt says we will not escape a storm."

"That's what I think, too."

"But in that case, all the fields will be destroyed."

"May God preserve us from such a catastrophe." Zinat got up and went on weeding between eggplants.

Mira and Sapura were alone. "Have you been giving Madan singing lessons or what?"

Mira did not understand what Sapura meant. She looked at her. Sapura laughed, "Every time I see him, he is humming those songs, the ones you hum all the time."

"Anyone can sing them. You too, there's nothing stopping you."

"You'll have to teach me them too, then."

"And you think that I have taught Madan?"

"How else can you explain why he knows them so well?"

"But you forget, Sapou, that his own father wrote the words."

"Yes, but it was you who invented the melodies. You will not believe me, but I ended up speaking to Madan."

"What did you ask him?"

"Where he had learned these songs."

"And he told you that I had taught him?"

"No. He gave me a very strange answer."

"What?"

"He told me that he was a crow."

"But you, of course, know that there is only one crow in the village and that's me. Is that it?' Mira snatched the wrap off Sapura's shoulders and threw it in the branches of a mulberry tree, where it hung out of reach. Mira slipped away laughing.

The next day, while she was drawing water from the well, she had heard Madan sing a song she herself had started singing a few days earlier. At first, she was surprised and then she understood. Madan was watching her and listening to her sing without her knowledge. The idea made her blush. She understood better now the meaning of his words.'You want to deprive me of the sound of your voice, but you never will.' She felt an intense joy.

Mira, alone again, resumed the thread of her thoughts. But still she did not know how the words embodied her dreams and ideas. Mira was unable to formulate her thoughts and dreams and they remained fuzzy images, indistinct, without colour or shape. Despite her efforts to express what gave her life, she was unable to give these abstractions enough consistency to articulate them. In recent days, she'd been taking Kissan's book to the field and two days before, Madan had seen her while she was reading a passage.

"You found it at Zinat's, right?" She took great care of it and enveloped it in her wrap before placing it against the trunk of the mulberry tree. When, back in her plot, she covered the roots of the pistachio plants with new earth, she wanted to sing a song. She undid the folds of fabric and had to extract the book, when she saw Sita approaching, making her way through the plots of friends.

Mira gasped to see Sita so changed. She had lost weight, the skin on her face was dry, wrinkled and she looked like she had been prey to a long illness.

"Have you seen Madan?" she asked Mira.

"He must be in his field," she said, after a moment of surprise.

"No, I did not find him there."

"So he may have gone to monitor the steamed coal."

"Do you know how he usually goes home?"

"He will return perhaps directly, without going through here."

Sita left, but after her departure, Mira felt her presence stay on, as if she stood still, waiting for Madan. She began to imagine a conversation between them. 'You must see him?'

'Yes.'

'Why?'

'It is very important...' What could be so important? Mira remembered that Zinat had told her not to be suspicious. She was jealous, and her jealousy formed a terrible trap that could not be undone. She was caught and was struggling in the net.

The rain did not come. The heat was still rising. The small flowers of the young pistachios had poor resistance to the water shortage. Their leaves remained motionless; not a breath of air was caressing them. Mira sat in sweat. To combat the crazy ideas that tormented her, she imagined reassuring things. But the indecision did not leave her, and arguments tore her apart, truth and falsehood by turns winning, making her unable to concentrate on her task.She went back to work only to give up a moment later and was lost in thought again.

At the well, the talk was of the stifling heat. 'Even during the last hurricane, it was not so hot.'

"Oh, surely it was. But we forget once it's over."

"The wells will soon be dry."

"And not the least sign of rain."

"If a cyclone hits us, it's all over for our beautiful gardens.'

"At night, the colour of the horizon is terrible."

"Just because the sky is red does not mean that there will necessarily be a cyclone."

"Let us pray that this does not bode anything serious."

"Let us finish the harvest first, or else..."

"It would be total disaster. But do not despair at this point."

"All of the signs point towards it, though."

"The same signs also announce the rain sometimes. It's true that at this time the rain should be coming." Nothing could ease the fears of the villagers. At worst, they could hope that the storm would not come, in which case the drought would continue and the fields would still suffer from lack of water. But at least they would not lose it all. At best, they hoped, in place of the cyclone, for a little wind and rain to cool the atmosphere. Water, at any rate.

Vivek sought information from the *panditji*, "For the drought to end, we should sing at night in the streets, calling on the name of Indra, but to prevent the arrival of a cyclone, how should we pray?"

28

You suck the juice from Ramjee's cane
you leave the fibre, give it a good throw.

Madan was humming the words of an old song by Kissan using the melody Mira had composed. With five bags of coal, he had obtained a bag of rice for the whole village.

When Madan came to Mira's aunt's house to offer her a portion, he was received by Mira herself, who told him to wait a moment while she raced inside and spoke to her aunt. Then she came back, a bowl in hand and accepted the rice Madan had brought. "But on one condition, that you come and dine with us tonight."

Madan could not have been happier. Since morning, he had this song in his head and waited for dinner time, more and more impatient. The afternoon drew out. Finally, there remained only half an hour. Then Sumangal appeared, "Madan, come quickly."

"Where?"

"Pushpa's... she is very ill." Madan hung his sickle on a pile of stones and ran to the village, accompanied by Sumangal. Sita had come to see him two days earlier with news of Pushpa's ill health. Medicinal plants would only relieve the pain, but the *panditji* did not think he could save Pushpa.

When he arrived at Vivek's at a run, many people were already there. The healer came to meet him, "Her condition is stable. We called you because she wanted to see you."

Madan went to Pushpa. She had aged terribly in a few days. Three weeks earlier, she had not had these sunken eyes, that white hair and those innumerable wrinkles on her face. Seeing Madan, she beckoned him to approach and he sat on the bed. "You work too much, Madan," she said in a broken voice. "You're just like your father..."

"How do you feel, Chachi?"

"It's always the same with you. You can never decide which aunt you want me to be."

"Mausi, Chachi... it's the same thing for me."

The *panditji* interrupted, "You must not talk too much, it's going to tire you."

"Oh, I've never been talkative. Let me at least talk today."

The conversation soon turned to Kissan. Dawood had already told Madan what had happened between them in the past. His greatest regret had been that Kissan and Pushpa were not married. After Kissan's marriage to Rekha, Pushpa had remained walled up in silence and had not spoken to anyone for weeks. There was probably not much he could do, but Kissan was careful not to seek to know the reason for her sudden silence. Only after the death of his father did Madan understand the ties that bound Pushpa to Kissan. It was she who had appeared most affected by his death. And a cry of suffering which was hidden deep in his heart was not slow to rise up. Madan looked around. "Vivek?" he asked.

"I sent him for medicine to a village I know, on the other side of the mountain," said the *panditji*.

"He went alone?"

"No, Farid is with him."

Pushpa asked the *panditji* to read from his *Ramayana.* He sang the verses until she fell asleep. Madan questioned the *panditji*, who reassured him that Pushpa was stable. He was about to leave, but the other man held him back, "Wait unil Vivek returns."

It was very hot in the house and in Madan's heart. The moon, early in its course around the sky, shone just above him, surrounded by stars. He looked towards the margosa tree. There were twenty-two houses in the row until Mira's. In his mind, he listed the names of their inhabitants. It seemed so far away... and it had been three weeks since he had eaten rice.

He could almost taste it. Mira was waiting for him. Sita approached him, "You have not eaten, I suppose."

"I'm not hungry."

"We did not even light the fire. If you want..."

"No, I do not want anything. Just bring me a glass of water." Sita went to fetch water and Madan began to think about Mira. 'And if I went now? She will have prepared the rice and must be waiting with her aunt.' The *panditji* reassured him as to Pushpa's state, but Madan did not want to take risks. He was afraid. 'If I leave and something happens, I would never forgive myself.' So he remained, without moving, and Sita returned with water. Madan took the bowl she offered him and emptied it in one gulp. "Vivek will soon get the medicine?"

"He said he would come back with it as quickly as possible," replied Sita.

"What time did he leave?"

"Around noon..." They were silent. Inside the house, the flame of the lamp oil had begun to weaken. The crickets began their night chorus. Suddenly, the silence felt oppressive.

"It's hot."

"Yes." The conversation did not take off. And there was not a breath of air. "You did not believe me, Sita."

"About what?"

"When I said that witchcraft did not exist. I told you nothing would happen to you and Vivek, and you did not believe me. Everyone was terrified at the sight of the doll pierced with needles; they all were confident that you would never survive. I told you: no one can touch one hair on your head. How can black magic exist?'

"It must be very powerful."

"Ah, you'll believe in it forever."

"One is forced to believe in it when it happens to them."

"You said that Vivek had a slight insensitivity in his fingers for a few days... that's nothing."

"Sometimes, the suffering of one person affects another."

"Sita, you are well, as far as I know. As for Pushpa, that is old age, that's all."

"We cannot share your convictions."

"Talk about superstitions."

"Call it what you want."

"To hear you, it looks like Andrea's mother's arrow hit the target."

"Exactly."

"What do you mean?"

"She has not missed her target, Madan. But let's change the subject. What do you think about Pushpa? Do you think she will get through this?"

"That's it, I see. She is the target to which you allude. You think that instead of attacking Vivek, she attacked his mother."

"I never said that."

"But what, then?"

"I do not want to talk about it. Do you really think she will recover?"

"Yes... Let me ask you a question. You do not look very well, recently."

"You find me changed?"

"What's wrong, Sita? You seem unhappy."

"It is the effect of this curse."

"That again..."

"It seems we will have a storm..."

"Is it Vivek again?"

"Madan, there is a problem with Vivek. And I would tell you if I could confide in you."

"Confide in me, and I will try to help as best as I can."

"That's why I do not want to tell you about it. But I want you to know, because I cannot stand to see you ridicule black magic. And perhaps, after all, telling someone – telling you – will do me good. You never know."

"What is it, Sita?"

"I am so ashamed... but since you insist... Vivek is still alive, of course, but the witch has killed the man in him. It has been three months now that he cannot... He has become impotent. It makes him crazy: the day before yesterday he screamed that he would rather die than remain in this state. His mother overheard one of our conversations, and now she knows. For three months we've lived, Vivek and I, as brother and sister. Nothing happens between us. If you tell the *panditji*, maybe he could..."

Sita fell into Madan's arms, almost falling at his feet. He gaped, stupefied.

29

Madan could not believe that Vivek was the victim of a spell. He spoke to the *panditji* and they concluded that his impotence stemmed from an excessive consumption of *ganja.* Vivek smoked enormously. Madan wanted take him to speak to the *panditji*, but his friend flew into a rage as soon as Madan even mentioned the problem. Vivek started yelling that he was as manly as Madan, and screamed further to ask how Madan knew information that was so intimate. Madan did not answer, but Vivek seized him by the front of his shirt and screamed like hell, "How can my wife tell you about something so personal? What has happened between you?"

Madan was silent; he gently freed himself from his friend's grip. That evening, when he tore from the eggplants leaves the insects had eaten, Zinat came to him. "What have you told Vivek?"

"Nothing. Why?"

"He hit Sita and left her half stunned."

"How is this my fault?"

"He cried and accused her of talking to you about something. I wonder what it could be, for it to put him in such a state. He beat her so that her face has swollen up. And he ripped out handfuls of her hair."

Madan closed his ears, his eyes fixed on Mira, who worked in her plot nearby.

There was a scorching heat. The fields were parched, as the well did not provide enough water to irrigate them anymore. The clouds would gather in the sky, threatening and then disperse. It was hard to breathe. They were expecting rain; hopes were formed and then melted at the last minute, but they did not admit defeat.

Villagers sweated like cattle, but that was not enough to irrigate the land. Nevertheless, they each hoped for an improvement. If it were to rain in the following days, the harvest would still be good. So they cheered in anticipation of the next day. And their faith in better days remained.

The next day, the atmosphere had thickened. Early in the afternoon, a hot wind rose. Those who prepared for a cyclone mounted stones atop their roof. They fixed poles against the walls so their houses wouldn't fall apart. Gradually, the wind increased in intensity and the sky appeared threatening. The night did not help matters. There were no stars and the heavens were jet black. Suddenly, the wind blew harder and soon began to roar. Cooped up in their houses, the villagers were trying to get an idea of the real strength of the wind.

"If it continues like this," said Farid to Dawood, "the wind may blow even harder at night."

Sugan gave his roof a look of pity – it had already been damaged in a previous cyclone – and shivered. The house was already beginning to creak. If the wind was to rage, this time the roof would not be able to resist.

Madan opened the window and looked outside. The wind was such that he braced himself to keep the door attached. Lightning streaked through the night and Madan saw the trees bending, spinning their tops, while their foliage whipped around itself. He felt fear hit his chest, when the roar of the storm rolled to a terrible crash. The rain blew against his face. A gust of wind had become more violent because of its grip on his walls and it slammed against the window in a masterful blow.

Mira, at the same time, wanted to bring the goat into the house. But the wind was already so strong that she could not even open the door. A gust of rain fell upon her and the girl panicked. She retreated inside.

The wind blew harder. The leaves fluttered, the trees creaked, branches and trunks were broken. Young trees were uprooted. The houses shook, roofs raised by the wind, then lowered. Some had begun to pray to Mahavir *swami*, invoking the son of the wind. Roofs flew away, uprooted by the storm; the children began to cry and adults took them in their arms. They remained there, trembling with fear. The wind continued to blow and the storm raged.

A cyclone, a real outburst of rain and wind, roared wildly, illuminating the livid sky through a night that seemed like it would never end...

Barricading her home, Mira thought about its scope. Nothing would be spared, she knew. Her aunt was trying to comfort her, "The great trees suffer the most damage in this kind of storm. Plants are damaged, but we can always hope to get them back."

Pushpa lay in Sita's loving arms. Vivek tried in vain to light the waning lamp. The room was plunged into darkness and nothing was heard but sobs.

The second part of the night was the hardest. Everyone was afraid. Nothing could happen if the storm did not subside. At dawn, there would be nothing left... Sumangal's roof was the first to collapse. His family fled, escaping its fall and rushed hastily into the house next door. But at the same time, a terrible noise stopped them. Something fell in the yard; they thought that the banyan tree had been hit hard. But then another noise, a deafening sound and they knew lightning had struck. The children screamed in terror, as though the end of the world was coming. The family members closed their eyes and stood pressed against each other, motionless in their solidarity. Left to die, but together.

The wind raged and the fear grew. When would the night retire to make room for the morning? It would not stop. In the darkness that prevailed, the storm seemed even more terrifying.

Vivek was sitting next to his dead mother. At one point he got up and went to straighten a section of the wall that had collapsed. It was so dark outside that he could not see his hands. The gusts were so violent that he stumbled twice, but he managed to reach the back of the house. At the next flash of lightning, he raised the pole lying on the ground and leaned against the wall. The rain whipped by so vigorously, the wind swept his face so violently, that he could not breathe. He was thrown to the ground by a violent gust, causing the pole in his hands to fall. He straightened up as best he could, put back the piece of wood in place and was preparing to return when he saw the roof fly off.

Farid had been knee-deep in water. He had two beds stacked one on another and had made Dawood, Zinat and Sapura sit atop them. Thus perched, they held as firmly as possible to the bed as their bamboo roof began to disappear. Their wall of lime and dung had already cracked, creating an opening into which the wind blew, knocking down the shelves and furniture. The noise was deafening. The rain burst the roof and the storm manhandled the house on all sides. Not a square inch was spared.

At dawn, the wind changed direction. The gusts that had come from the west were done. In a frantic voice, Sumangal's mother explained that though wind changed direction, they had not seen the end of the storm. The clouds resounded with explosions, huge streaks of lightning formed in shattering whistles and the squalls followed each other without interruption.

The darkness persisted and the day took a long time to win over. Morning finally came, but the sun did not appear. Finally, the celestial roar fell silent and the storm abated. But the wind kept blowing, just as violently, from west to east. However, the daylight brightened their spirits somewhat.

Madan was the first to leave his house. Struggling against the wind, he barely managed to stand up. Every step was an effort and he had great difficulty keeping balance. Dhanlal cried from inside, "The storm is still too high, the trees are falling, it's dangerous, come back!"

But Madan did not hear. A branch missed his head and hit the house. He rushed against the wind. The gusts pushed him back, but he resisted and pushed his way between the branches that littered the ground, pieces of roof and walls torn off. He almost fell several times. He felt the wind increase in violence, dogging him. Everywhere, the houses had suffered. Walls had been washed away, roofs ripped off. Devraj's house had collapsed, taking the walls down with it. Filled with anguish, he looked about him, but he was relieved to see nobody. He continued his advance and met Farid, who had a bloody forehead. "And your house?"

"If it continues like this, I don't give it three hours before it collapses."

"Everybody all right?"

"Yes, okay."

"But you're hurt."

"I got bashed on the head. But it's not serious." A broken branch came right over them; they narrowly avoided it and continued their journey. Arriving in front of Mira's house, Madan used his force against the door while shouting her name. She opened it and Farid and Madan come inside. "But the storm is still going on," growled her aunt. "What the hell are you doing outside?"

"How are you both?" Madan asked, before seeing Devraj and his family, who had taken refuge there.

"We almost got crushed by the rubble," said Deolall. 'We formed a chain by holding hands and by some miracle we arrived. If the west wind were worse, we would have perished under the banyan tree just behind the house. It is serious."

Madan put a hand on Devraj's shoulder, "Come on, there are people who will need help."

Mira's aunt intervened. "You never think. You will not get around with this storm... Wait until it calms down a bit."

"If we delay, there will be nothing left to save. It's now or never."

"If the wind changes again, it's going to step up."

"That's why we need to act now." Madan went out with Farid and Devraj. Once outside, he had to shout to be heard, "Let us first see whose homes were destroyed.'

A gust blew violently and Farid was thrown backwards. Luckily, he stayed upright. The trio rushed, full of determination and courage, supporting each other in the heart of a storm that roared with fury.

30

The wind continued to wreak havoc on the trees. They pulled three bodies from the rubble of two houses. Madan and his comrades then went to Vivek's. When Madan saw Pushpa's body, the image of his father's death struck him: he saw the scene in an instant, violent and bright as lightning. Vivek was sitting curled up in his wet clothes. Madan turned to Sita, who was sobbing, her head down. He said a few words to Vivek, who did not answer him. In the absence of any reaction, Madan, with his two comrades, lifted Pushpa's body and went to place it with the other three corpses. Then he returned. "Vivek, Retnon's house is still standing. Go there with Sita."

Vivek did not move. Madan insisted, "This house will not stand long. Get out of here, go."

Farid approached Vivek, took him by the shoulders and helped him to stand up. Sita got up in turn and followed him. Outside, the gusts raged, whirling in all directions. Sita could not even take a step. She grabbed the raffia partition flying in the wind and held on to it. Madan rushed and seized her by the shoulders. Holding her tight against him, he joined the small group and held on until they reached Retnon's house. When they came out, after leaving behind Vivek and Sita, they found several people in the streets taking advantage of the daylight.

Around midday, the wind resumed its usual course. But it had not lost its speed and perhaps it had even grown in intensity. The villagers were all terrified at the violence of the cyclone. Madan, approaching Sugan Bhagat, fell to his knees. The men helped those families whose homes had been destroyed to safety, everyone taking shelter with a neighbour.

The wind grew, continuing its destruction. The rain came, completely soaking everything, then the wind changed direction again, weakened a little and started up again. It was like an animal keening. Finally, it calmed down and took its usual course, exhausted.

Only in the afternoon could they at last open their doors. The few standing trees had lost their leaves. The paths were littered with broken branches, fallen trees and parts of roofs. They began to take stock of the destruction, in an atmosphere of sadness that could have graced a great funeral. Mira ran to her field. In the distance, she could hear the sea roaring, surging again. Mira was still running to her shattered dreams: a place where the day before, there had been a forest of trees. They were fallen, shredded. She closed her eyes.

She opened them again, feeling a hand on her shoulder. It was

Madan. Mira fell into his arms. He pressed hard against her. The sea, not far away, swallowed what was left of the storm. The waves rose up, exhaling huge sighs.

Madan's mouth touched Mira's ear. "My mother," he murmured, 'said that man is constantly being put to the test by life. This is our test. If we sit and allow ourselves to be discouraged, we will have to admit defeat."

Madan felt Mira's chest rise up against his, full of sighs and sobs. She had dreamt so much of creating a good crop, of inviting the whole village to her home for a feast... What a great feast it would have been, all the villagers gathered in her courtyard, as if for a wedding. They would have told stories, tales, sung, made music. They could have set aside the flour to make bread. The scent of grilled corn would have filled the air for miles. It would have made their breath hot...

"Come on. Let's go, Mira. There is nothing to see here."

In the village, they were holding the first funeral ceremonies. Madan went into the house where they had gathered the bodies. Pushpa was the old one, covered by a *dhoti* given to her by her mother, marked with banana sap. Madan stared at her. One would have thought she had plunged into a deep sleep.

He heard people complaining that they did not even have flowers to decorate her body. 'What an irony of fate, to have a name meaning 'flower' and not having any for her last journey...' Madan thought.

The fires began to burn and they sought to recover some food not ravaged by the disaster. The flour had gotten wet, but they picked a few handfuls of surviving rice. Mira, who had spent the day in wet clothes, felt a fever mount at the end of the day. In the evening, it was pronounced. The mat that served as her bed had not yet dried; she shook with cold and fever. There remained not even a dry blanket, not a piece of cloth not saturated with water. She huddled in a corner of the house, covered with her aunt's wrap.

Part of the roof was gone and she could see the starry sky through the opening. Mira was lying on the ground, engrossed in her fever. A partition hung, half torn off. Her aunt folded it on the ground. "Come and settle down here, Mira." But the girl did not move. "Do not stay lying on the ground; it is too cold." She grabbed her by the arm, lifted her somehow and pulled her on to the raffia. She could not light the lamp, as water had mixed with the oil. The aunt thought to ask for a lamp at the neighbour's, but all the nearby houses were plunged into darkness. She heard Mira moaning in the dark. Through the window, she saw in the distance some houses where there was light. Mira's complaints became more frequent and her aunt sat down beside her. She put Mira's head on her knees and began to massage it. Her forehead was burning; she had a terrible fever. "Tomorrow morning, it'll be over," repeated the old woman, who could find nothing else to say.

But the night was just beginning and the morning was still far away. The aunt, however, knew no soothing words to say to a patient. The fever went up, and Mira became delirious. "You know in my field? You saw how the ears of corn had become fat?"

"Shut up, my daughter, stay calm."

"My aunt, yesterday, a troop of monkeys came to the field."

"Do not talk, it's going to make the fever worse. Sleep."

"Madan had brought me fish but I did not want it. He got angry. Zinat should have told him that I do not eat fish."

It was the first night after the cyclone and everyone went to bed early. The night before, no one had been able to sleep at all. Despite the distress and injury inflicted by the excesses of Nature, they found sleep very quickly tonight and they all gave way to oblivion for a few hours. The villagers, after all, were happy to have survived and they went to bed anywhere they could. The night was calm and soft.

Madan had heard of the dawn following a cyclone. They said it was more beautiful than any other, radiant and pure. The morning was sublime, but its beauty lasted only until he went back to the village, still asleep, eyes half closed. There he became aware of the damage. Everything had been ransacked, demolished. The efforts of several months, of several years, had been destroyed, and the present lay in this pile of rubble. Was the future there too, amidst the rubble? No. Madan did not give up so fast. The bright future of his dreams had suddenly fallen away, but he had not gone with it.

"This time we tried, and our trying ended in failure," he had said the day before to Mira. "But life is not made of a single heartbeat, is it?"

Several birds had died and their small bodies were scattered under the jackfruit tree, beginning to decompose. They had not buried or burned the three goats who had perished in the storm and their bodies already gave off a foul odour. In the streets, branches, leaves, trees, sections of walls, all chaotically intermingled.

Villagers gathered slowly. They decided to meet altogether at the *baithka*. They sat under bare trees, over a stratum of leaves. The sun was back, shining shyly, as if to apologise and maintain his innocence... but it had been so dark they hadn't been able to see their hands, so their most reliable witness had been their ears, struck by the horrifying roar of the raging elements.

When everyone was there, Madan called Farid to speak. But there was such a brouhaha that Farid waited a bit. Madan cut in, "I want you to listen to what Farid has to say."

Conversations stopped and Farid spoke, "What has happened has happened. We will not get anywhere if we remain idle."

He turned to Madan, who whispered, "Go ahead. Say what you have to say."

"There are three important things to do. First, we must rebuild the houses, then find something to eat and finally revive the fields. We must address the construction of the houses today and for that we'll need twenty men. In terms of food, we should recover a bit of the corn and cassava fields. In less than a week, that work will be done and five people should be enough to carry it out. Those who can look after their land should re-plant. We begin today. Vivek will cover the repair of houses: he can choose the twenty men that will help. I'll take five people with me to the field to see what remains edible. Madan will gather the rest of us to care for the fields. What do you think?"

"We are half-dead!" Danpatwa exclaimed. "What can you do with an army of skeletons?"

Madan rose, "We are still alive, and we will set in motion an army of skeletons, as you say."

And he went in the direction of the field, without waiting for the response of villagers, still shocked by despair.

31

Mira's fever had not gone down. The *panditji* had seen her in the morning and had done everything to reassure her aunt that she would be standing before the end of the day. The poor woman had to spend hours rubbing the soles of Mira's feet with a copper bowl. In the early evening, Mira was taken with chest pains. She had a hard time breathing. They made the *panditji* return with some tablets. He recommended that she keep warm and not breathe in the cold air.

Only after returning from the fields did Madan learn that Mira was ill. Immediately he went to her home, without bothering to wash his hands. Seeing her so pitiful, lying on the mat, he was afraid. "Since when has she been like this?"

"Since yesterday afternoon."

"You did not call the *panditji*?"

"He's been here."

"And what did he say?"

"It's influenza, it seems."

Madan approached Mira and laid his hand on her forehead. "She is hot."

Mira had waited for this moment for ages. Madan was so close to her. When she felt his cool hand on her forehead, she heard his thoughtful voice, sighed deeply and closed her eyes. "Her whole body is shaking; don't you have something to cover her?"

The aunt did not answer.

"I'll get something from Zinat."

"No, my son, stay with her, I'll go myself."

Her aunt went out and Madan took Mira's hand in his own. Mira tried to smile. Madan spotted the bed nearby. "Can you get up a second?" he asked Mira.

She nodded. "Do not stay lying on the ground."

Madan spruced up the little bed, then he leaned over and raised Mira against himself. While helping her stand, he put the mattress on a piece of the straw wall and helped the girl lie down again. "We started with your field today. You're going to be happy: despite the damage, we were able to collect three bags of corn. They are still green, they will not dry, but we can still eat them in the coming days." Mira's eyes were smiling. "You will not believe me, but I waited in the field all day. I did not understand where you were. I never thought you might be sick." Mira's eyes never left him. Madan began to speak and he did not stop until her aunt returned.

She was accompanied by Zinat, who laid two bags of hemp sewn into a quilt on Mira's feet. She bent over and touched her neck. "She is very sick! How is it that no one told me?"

"This morning, the *panditji* said it happened yesterday during the day. I did not see it fit to disturb anyone..."

"She has a raging fever, the poor girl." Zinat arranged the blankets over her. 'Kusmi, you gave her a drink?"

"I did not have water at home."

"I'm going to fetch some," exclaimed Madan, and rushed out. Zinat took a stool and sat at the patient's bedside. Her aunt had taken a tin from under the bed and filled it with oil borrowed from neighbours. She raised the wick on the lamp, lit it and placed it on a shelf attached to the central pole of the house.

Zinat spoke softly to Mira, "Does it hurt?"

"It hurts when I cough and when I breathe deeply."

"I'll get a fire going just now. You'll warm up and you will feel better." Mira was trembling with fever under the blanket. Zinat covered her again, adding thickness with more hemp bags. "That'll teach you to do so much work in your field," said Zinat.

Zinat had managed to heat Mira up when Madan returned with milk. Mira drank two sips and gave him back the bowl. There were only two cows in the village. One had become dry, but the other gave a little milk that was shared amongst the families where there were young children. Madan had obtained a small bowl with difficulty, and it annoyed him when he saw that Mira hardly drank it. Zinat noticed. 'Mira, drink this milk. This will give you some strength. We must not allow ourselves to be weak."

"Tomorrow she will get better..."

"May God hear you."

Madan went, reluctantly, accompanied by Zinat. In the dark street, they heard the voice of Gautam's son, who sang:

All the flowers of the trees have fallen like all the ye's tears.

Zinat went home and Madan went on his way. 'Man is never content with his lot,' he thought. 'Otherwise, we could be happy even in poverty, despite the suffering and failures. Instead, he is always full of desire.'

Arriving at home, he could still hear the echoes of the song sung by Gautam's son. Dhanlal and Danpatwa were not sleeping, but waiting. They intended to leave the next morning to go and sell bundles of wood. Starting at four, they would reach the market at about 7 o'clock. It was worth trying, since there was no other way to get a little money to buy food. The only uncertainty was the price of wood: no one knew how much could be earned.

The three friends chatted a bit and then Danpatwa fell asleep, followed by Dhanlal. Madan spent a lot of time trying to sleep. Finally, he got up, took a sip of water from the jug and went to Mira. The first rays of sun were breaking through the bare branches. Along the way, he met Hanif, his bowl in hand, going to freshen up. Madan laughed when he saw him running. But his laugh broke quickly and he hurried on. He passed the houses and counted eleven before he reached Mira's. During the cyclone, a large tree branch had fallen against the roof, protecting the house, as it were; the roof remained in place. He was a few yards from Mira: he saw her standing in the yard. His heart leapt in his chest. He joined her in two strides. "How are you feeling today?"

Mira laughed a little, but he could see on her face the marks of a great weakness.

"You should not get up so early. You will get cold again..." He suddenly remembered his mother at the foot of his bed when he was a boy. He always had trouble waking up. One morning, she crept close to him and whispered in his ear, "He who rises early is never sick, for the wind that blows before sunrise contains a nectar of health." "No, never mind, the freshness of the morning can not hurt you."

"I was thinking of you," said Mira.

"Really?"

"I thought if you sold my two goats, then we could buy food for a week or two."

Madan did not answer immediately, gazing at Mira. "Why did you think of that?"

"Everyone needs to eat, right?"

"We are doing what is necessary. Don't worry."

"But why not sell those goats? Without food, they will not produce milk. So take advantage of the famine and sell now."

"Who will buy them?"

"Everything is bought at the market."

"Good idea. We will do it."

"Ah, what I wished for did not happen."

"What did you wish for, Mira?"

"That the whole village would come and eat at my home."

"But who says your wish won't come true? Don't you remember that we have recovered three bags of corn in your field?"

"Go arrange to sell the goats."

"Your aunt might oppose..."

"She won't."

"Well, I'll sell them for you on one condition."

"Which is?"

"You need to pay a little more attention to *yourself*."

Mira laughed.

32

The more he thought about the impasse they had reached, the more Madan had to admit there was no alternative. They had to sign a contract with the boss once again and accept what they had previously refused. Bharatlall and Hanif disagreed with him. But Ramsewak said they could hardly do otherwise. Madan did not make a decision immediately. When he returned from the city where he had sold the two goats and purchased provisions, Madan sought Mira's advice, "What do you think we should do?"

Mira did not speak right away. They walked side by side,

and they soon came to Kissan's cabin, which clung to the hillside. Apparently it had not suffered in the storm. Mira sat on the tree trunk near the cabin and finally replied, 'Working for the boss in these conditions means losing all dignity.'

"You're right, Mira, but if we are too proud, we may starve."

"You spoke of an alternative once, which Bharatlall had suggested..."

"His brother works in a property which is a three hour-walk away. Working conditions there are much better. But it's far away."

"Making the round trip would take you almost the whole day."

"The idea is to stay put and return to the village once a week."

"No way. I will not let you leave."

"You do not know the proverb?"

"Which one?"

"Distance strengthens bonds of affection." Mira threw herself into Madan's arms. Holding hands, they walked to the rear of the cabin. From there, they had a splendid view of a waterfall that fell from the top of the mountain, exploding in showers on the branches. Madan often came here, but he had never been so moved by the beauty of the scenery and the grandeur of the wilderness. A rainbow graced the sky over the valley, connecting two summits with its subtle curve. It was sumptuous. They walked a little more. In front of them, the valley opened into an abyss. It stretched before them, devastated by the cyclone.'What a disaster,' thought Madan. But soon he realised that the beauty about which he had just raved depended on the desolation at the bottom. The rainbowed sky would not form so perfect a picture over lush green fields.

Mira's thoughts were quite different; they remained fixed on the whites' plantations and the need for men to work there. "It's still unbelievable," she exclaimed, "that in such a vast land, we cannot find a way to escape the merciless rod of the plantation owners."

"We have tried to make our way alone."

"But maybe not for long enough..."

They had already made their way back when Madan turned to Mira. "I find you very talkative today." Mira stopped talking immediately, which irritated Madan. He sat down on a rock and pretended to sulk.

Mira knew he would not move without impetus. "If you do not want to come, I'll go down again by myself."

"I think we have forgotten something."

"What?"

"You did not visit the inside of my father's cabin."

"Yes, but we've already left it behind."

"We're only halfway."

"You want to turn back?"

"I want you to see it."

"It can be another time."

"Once I'm gone, who knows when we will be able to come back here?"

"Where do you plan to go?"

"I think I'll go work in that far-off plantation."

"You aren't going anywhere!"

"But... we have to find food."

Mira gave him a black look. "Fine. If that's what you want, go. I won't accompany you to the cabin."

Madan pointed to the cabin, "But I can carry you up."

"All you want is to hold on to me." And they went up.

Mira put her arm on his shoulder and he whispered into her ear, "Do you know that you are very beautiful, Mira?"

"Stop tickling me."

"But I am not tickling you."

"Your words make me laugh."

They reached the cabin. Madan looked to the village below and it made him miserable. 'Look what a mess our poor village is!"

"We've gone through a cyclone, after all. How have we managed to rebuild at all?"

"I asked myself the same question. How can we forget such a trauma so quickly?"

"We have not forgotten. We are digesting the shock."

The door of the cabin, swollen with water, was blocked. Madan put the strength of his weight against the door. The door opened suddenly and a musty smell jumped to his nostrils. Mira was standing outside. “You do not want to come in?” She entered timidly. “So how do you find my father’s cabin?” he asked.

“It’s quiet...”

“I could never live in such a remote corner as this.”

“Really? This is exactly where I dream of living.”

“Are you kidding?”

“Not at all. This place is lovely.”

“But there is nothing around. The forest, the forest, only the forest.”

“You can always cut the trees to let in more light.”

“If you agree, I’ll start working on it tomorrow.”

“There’s no pressure.”

“There’s no reason to wait, either. It is a worthy task.”

“By the time we came back here, you will have changed your mind.”

“I doubt it.” Madan left the hut and sat under the margosa tree. He pointed to the right.” You see that house over there? You know what it is?”

“It is Mr Constant’s home.”

“It is where our resources are locked. He has acquired the sweat of our brow... what we will never possess.” Madan told Mira the story of this house, just as his father had told him. “You know what I want to do?”

“Rob the house?”

“No.”

“What then?”

“Point a gun at the boss and make him share all his property with the destitute labourers of this country.”

“That’s robbery in another form.”

“It just takes back what we’ve been robbed of.”

“What would you call it then? Courageous? The true courage would have been to prevent him from exploiting us beforehand.”

“Ah, if only that had been possible.”

“Forget all this. Come, Madan, we will end up being late.” Madan rehashed his questions in the morning. It would take a mere three days to deplete what was left to eat. Nalletamby told him that food prices had doubled in the city overnight. In addition, sellers would not trade with those who could not show their credentials. They had to present a card signed by a plantation owner to have access to the shops. They would never succeed in obtaining such a card.

Mira pushed Madan out of her reverie. "What are our exact provisions for next week, Madan?"

Madan had the sense that she could read his thoughts. "We're going to find a solution; don't worry," he said, after a moment's hesitation.

His answer lacked the conviction to reassure Mira. But, speaking with reasonable assurance had strengthened his own pace, and Madan walked with more determination.

The village was not far.

33

Two weeks after the cyclone, famine took hold on a disastrous scale. Their crying children broke the villagers' hearts. Madan and Farid walked thirty miles on foot to buy a bag of potatoes. Mira did the cooking and all the village children gathered around her home. Madan had buried half the potatoes in order to save them. But when his back was turned, children who had seen him began to dig up the precious potatoes. They were so hungry that they ate them raw. Those, who did not get one, wept.

Following a meeting in the *baithka*, they sent eight men fishing. With the money from selling fish, they hoped to buy some food. One of the volunteers slipped on a rock and broke his leg. While it was not easy to feed nearly three hundred people with the only proceeds from fishing, there was no alternative and this was all they did for some time. Many people refused to eat what was bought with money from fishing. They were offered rice, but they could not bring themselves to eat it. The *panditji* himself said that their religion forbade nothing if the alternative was starvation. They had to stay alive to defend their values.

The work on the fields progressed more slowly than before. Working on empty stomachs made them motivated, but sluggish. At first, for three days, they drank the water that had been used for cooking rice and only on the fourth, did they eat the rice itself.

When Vivek learned that the granaries at the plantation were full of food, he went off into the night. He could not let that food grow moldy while they were starving... On several occasions, he'd sought the opportunity to make some grand gesture, just to get rid himself of the feeling of inferiority that had come over him since he had lost his virility. He had initially been planning to go and kill Andrea. It was because of her that he was today in such a state. But that would only serve to prove that he believed in witchcraft, even though that was not the case. If he had to show everyone that he was still a man, it must be through a different, extraordinary feat. Now he knew the property and the granary on it, and he knew that the gate to the granary had been destroyed during the cyclone. It had been replaced by a wooden fence that was easy to overcome. But Vivek had forgotten one thing, and it was this that caused his downfall. The high walls of stone and wood that formed the walls of the property itself were studded with nails. Vivek could have run away and escaped the guards if his heels had not been bleeding.

Three days had passed since his disappearance. Sprouts began to appear. After watering his plot, Madan was about to go to Mira's when Bharatlall came up to him, carrying a message from Sita. "Are you sure? He has not returned for three days?"

Once he got to her home, he asked Sita the same question, "Why didn't you tell me earlier?"

"I kept hoping he would come back."

"He said nothing before leaving?"

"No."

"Do you have any ideas as to where he went? Did you two have an argument?"

"No."

"He must have told somebody something..."

"Devraj said they had smoked that evening, and then Vivek went to the plantation granary. Before leaving, he evidently declared that while he lived, no one would starve in the village. Yesterday, I sent Ramnarain's son to the big house to ask around quietly. No one has seen him."

Madan was thoughtful. "He was caught stealing supplies."

"You know Vivek; you know he was not a thief."

"Oh, he's not a thief, of course; he probably had good reasons to justify his actions."

"You think so?"

"Who knows? Perhaps the guards caught him. I will check with the boss."

"Madan, it is not prudent for you, specifically, to go." Madan did not answer. "Do not go alone, at least."

Madan left Sita and took the path that led directly to the property. He had not yet crossed the river when he heard someone running behind him. It was Farid. "I'll go with you."

Madan stopped. "How do you know where am I going?"

"Sita told me."

Madan went on his way without a word. Farid walked beside him. He soon broke the silence, "My youngest sister's baby son is dead."

"When did he die?"

"Just an hour ago." A hare ran away in a rustle of grass and Farid's dog plunged into a bush. Farid took no notice. "Three children have died in one week.' Several trees had fallen during the storm, blocking the road. Both men made their way around them in the woods.

Passing through the cane fields, Madan noticed that they had not suffered too much in the cyclone. "Farid, do you see these fields? It seems that even the wind fears the power of the rich. Our fields are completely destroyed. Here, they're intact."

"There are two things that have protected these fields."

"You will tell me it's because the plants were small and that the mountains blocked the worst of the wind. Nature, it seems, is not always innocent."

Farid was surprised by Madan's tone of voice and how quickly he'd been discouraged. He insisted, "Don't believe me if you don't want to, but let me tell you, anyway. Madan, in this country only sugarcane plants are resistant to hurricanes. Otherwise, agriculture is risky here."

"The poor fellow may sow iron, but if fate is against him, he will never harvest... Sugan is right when he says a dog is pissing on our destiny."

"When he smokes too much, Sugan also claims that the new generation is unable to think and if this continues, generation after generation, we will remain oppressed."

"He is absolutely right."

"Looks like you're high, too."

"You are free to believe that. But let me ask you something."

"Go ahead."

"Have you ever had a high fever?"

"No."

"So you cannot understand."

Farid looked at Madan fixedly, "What can't I understand?"

"Have you ever been starving?"

"I'm starving right now."

"Doesn't it make you crazy? Doesn't it make you angry?"

"I'm so hungry I could eat hunger itself."

Maran stopped and looked his friend in the eye. He took him by the shoulders and shook him with a good laugh. Farid's dog scampered before them in and out of the bushes. He approached a tree, raised his leg and remained a moment, motionless. Then he continued.

The granary was very close. As soon as they got close enough, they were arrested by two Creole guards. One was holding a stick, the other a gun. Their faces shone with sweat. "Where are you going?" barked the beefier one in Kreol.

As Madan and Farid were silent, he repeated it to them in Bhojpuri, "We came to speak to you.'

"Looking for work? There is none. A new boat has arrived."

"We have not come for that."

"You are looking for food, then?"

"No."

"You are in the forbidden zone here. You are not allowed to enter or exit."

"One of our men came here and he never returned to the village."

"We are here to take care of the granary, not of visitors. Leave, now."

"We would like to see the boss."

"Leave, or else." Madan and Farid did not move.

34

Farid wanted to turn back. Madan turned to him and read the fear in his eyes. Farid was one of the bravest men of the village. He was not so easily frightened. But this time, it was evident that he feared something. Farid feared that they would arrest Madan again, but Madan completely ignored his concern. On the way to the granary, he had said he would not return without Vivek. Farid knew that it would not be an easy task, but he also knew his friend's fierce determination. Probably the guards on the plantation would not let Vivek go. Anything could happen, including Madan's arrest. And Farid wished to avoid this at all costs. There was no question that the village would lose its vitality.

The plantation house was located a short distance from the granary. It was reached by a series of linked paths. Madan tried to calm down by thinking about Mira. The joy he felt dissipated his dark thoughts and they melted into happiness. Sometimes, he would forget that his life could have a meaning other than to watch Mira tirelessly. And when he indulged in these feelings, he began to dream of a better way to live.

"You know, Mira, I would like to see the village where my father lived."

"You want to leave this village... you want to leave me?"

"No, you do not understand. I don't know all of what my father experienced in his remote village, but it was much worse than our own struggle. The blood and sweat took on a different colour on that earth. I want to see that land and I want you to come with me. We will both go and discover what is out there. Will you come?'

"We can set off tonight, if you want."

"Let's wait until everyone can manage here. Are you sure you want to come?"

"I will follow you, even if you change your mind and you decided to go alone. I will run behind you."

"Mira, did you ever wonder how our love would feel?"

"I never thought you would love me."

"I never thought that such love was possible."

"Oh?"

"To be so insane for a woman."

"What a sales pitch."

"But I mean it."

"So why does a man who loses himself for love behave like such a timid lily?"

"You mean me?"

"I only see you once every three days."

"Do you know what I was thinking while I prepared the charcoal on the beach? I thought of you nonstop; I turned my eyes from the sea and towards the land in the hope of seeing you come to me. One night, I even dreamt of you in the cabin where I slept. You came to bring me a sweet cane. But that never happened in reality. Oh Mira, I'm obsessed with a single thought."

He paused. The girl was not looking into his eyes. She was crying, and Madan had trouble reaching her. He blinked. In the sea, recently, he had seen a storm. The waves were exploding and unleashed, the ground swells were violent. He saw such swells today in Mira's eyes. 'I know I could not live without you. If you knew what I went through during those three days... I wonder what state I would be in if the ordeal had lasted more." Mira placed her long fingers on Madan's lips and gently placed her head on his shoulder.

Madan and Farid took the sunken road that skirted the granary and led to the rear of the property. On the other side of a cactus hedge, guards ordered them to stop. They obeyed and the hoarse voiçe shouting orders brought up painful memories for Madan of the times before his arrest. He would never forget what he had been subjected to and yet he had forgotten to appease his desire for revenge, submerging it instead. His father had told him many years before, it was better to forget the worst, for if not, a man would end up not feeling quite alive. At the time, Madan had not understood; today, he became conscious that these were the words of a man defeated.

The grand tree stood still, upright, dignified, mourning its doom. On that terrible day, the tree had been covered with clusters of small white flowers, more numerous than the leaves. Mounesh was attached to a branch and everyone looked at him, speechless with horror. Nobody had dared to say, "Forgive him, sir." The big leather belt fell on him time and again, and the blows were ruthless.

Madan had gathered all his courage and came forward, "Stop, boss."

The boss took the belt from the hands of his henchman and grabbed Madan by the wrist. Then he began to shout, "You're going to take his place!"

It took Madan three days to recover from the beating, during which he lay still, incapable of the slightest movement. Mounesh did not survive; he died three hours later. His only crime had been to accept a gift that the daughter of the boss had given to him via a foreman. Mounesh, in exchange, offered the foreman what he could. The foreman thought they had arranged a meeting in the garden; someone saw them. The foreman put all the blame on Mounesh.

Later, Madan had heard that the girl had committed suicide by swallowing poison. Nobody had confirmed the tale. But afterwards, Madan had quashed any desire for revenge.

Today, he saw this tree, this house, this garden.... He shivered with disgust and hatred.

"Where are you going?" shouted the guard.

"We want to see the boss."

"Is he expecting you?"

"No, we are the ones who wish to meet."

"He does not have time."

"It will not take long."

"I am telling you, he has no time to receive you."

The second guard, who stood a little behind, stood in front of the door that opened to the cactus hedge. 'Why do you want to see the boss?'

"We want to talk to him."

"It is not possible."

"Just two words!"

"Two words or not, clear out of here. Go!"

Suddenly, Farid saw the boss coming out through the front door on the left. He touched Madan and pointed to what he saw. Everything happened very quickly. The two men rushed and the boss started yelling, "What the hell are you doing? How did you get here?"

"Sir, we have walked here to see you."

"Looking for work."

"No, sir."

"Rice, then?"

"No."

"Then you came for your friend, perhaps?" he asked with a wicked smile.

"Yes."

"And who told you that we keep thieves here?"

"He must be imprisoned in your basement."

"You've come to release him? Then give me two hundred rupees."

"Two hundred rupees?"

"If not, I'll hand him over to the police tomorrow. He was found trying to steal provisions from the granary."

"Sir, we do not even have two annas. How can we find two hundred rupees?"

The white man looked at Madan. And suddenly he changed his tone. "But it's you!" The two realised one another immediately. 'Dirty bastard! It is you who stood up to my head foremen. And it was because of you that my harvest dried up. He signalled to the guards. Four men approached and before Madan and Farid were able to make the slightest gesture, they had been thrown on the ground and were covered with blows. They covered their faces to avoid the kicks. Madan writhed in pain under the impact of the heavy leather boots that were plowing him in the stomach. But his anger was stronger. One of the guards lifted one foot to take aim and Madan grabbed his leg and swung. Two other guards jumped on him. Farid wanted to help him, but he was pulled back. Madan crouched, trying to parry the blows. Suddenly, the man he had knocked down got up and planted himself in front of Madan, rolling his big eyes. Madan rose, but the other pushed him down with such violence that he was hurled against the cactus hedge. Madan screamed and put his hand to his eyes. He gave a second terrible cry and sank. The blows rained on him still, but the guards stopped when they saw the blood running down his face. By the time Farid reached him, darkness had been forever installed in Madan's bright eyes.

35

Farid dragged Madan back to the village. When they arrived in front of Sita's, he called out. Sita was at her neighbour Ramba's. From Farid's tone, everyone realised that something had happened. Ramba ran out of her home in Sita's footsteps, followed by her mother and her brother. They all looked at Madan, stunned. "What happened? Madan! Your eyes!'

There was blood coming from his gouged out eyes, but he wanted to reassure Sita that he recognised her voice. He did not know what to do, so he stood motionless. He wanted to apologise for not having gotten Vivek back, but no sound came from his mouth. In the darkness he was bathed in now, he heard familiar voices.

"How did this happen? Who did this? Can you see at all?"

Farid did not speak either. And when Zinat appeared, he threw himself into her arms and burst into tears, "They took his eyes, Mama," he sobbed.

The dream she'd had the night before had thus come true. She did not even pay attention to her son's injuries and went straight to Madan. "Madan!"

Despite the night that surrounded him, Madan could imagine Zinat's tears without difficulty. Everyone crowded around him.

Far from the bustle, Mira was looking forward to the new vegetation that was flourishing in her field. It had rained for three days and new seedlings had appeared, lining the soft green earth. She was dying of impatience to show Madan the beautiful colour and wanted him to join her as soon as possible. She did not feel completely happy without his presence. At every moment, her eyes looked back to the path leading to the village. An hour earlier, Zinat had been at her side, gazing at the scope of the verdure. She was telling Mira her dream, "Last night I had a strange dream. There were a lot of flowers in front of your house. You were playing hide and seek with Madan and he was blindfolded. You laughed, you laughed... they say that good dreams are a bad omen. I do not know what it means.'

"Well. Your dream is true, Zinat; here I am, laughing."

"And I, my eyes are stung in surprise..."

"It's a good sign. Look at these revived fields. We must celebrate."

"Everyone is starving and you want to party?"

"Oh... don't say the same thing every day. Why would we not celebrate when we see better days ahead?"

"May God hear you, my daughter, and may you be right." After Zinat left, Mira had walked around the field and allowed herself to enjoy the miracles performed by the rain. Everything was reborn and she felt that life was starting again.

In recent days, Mira had been humming all that came to mind. A long jangle of thoughts would come to her, in no particular order and she would give them a melody. These were not songs, but rather sung phrases. The message was always the same:

Come, let us walk together,
forget our miseries and walk towards the mountain.
Down below, we will see more clearly, and our pain will fade.
Come, stay with me and our breaths will mingle;
we will walk on carpets of roses without thorns.
Suffering will come again, but let us accept our fate.

From time to time she stopped, threw a glance at the trail and then headed to another plot. She was leaving Ramsewak's plot to enter Hanif's when she saw Sapura running towards her.

"Mira! I've found you at last. Something horrible has happened."

"What?"

'It's Madan... he's lost his sight."

"What are you talking about?"

"He was stabbed with cactus thorns. He is blind."

"No." She ran to the village without even draping her wrap across her shoulders. All the villagers had already gathered in front of Sita. She stopped, suddenly shaky. What she heard from the crowd was a mixture of laments and sighs. She was surrounded, then, and a precipice opened under her feet; she felt her heart panic, then pulled herself together, trying to calm down.

She saw Madan when the crowd parted to let the *panditji* through. Under his eyes, the blood had congealed and Mira saw only two large black spots in place of eyes. She suppressed a cry and made a superhuman effort not to fall.

The *panditji* placed a hand on Madan's head in a gesture of helplessness. Mira ran behind him and stood next to Zinat. "Does he have a chance?"

The man did not answer. "Tell me. Tell me that all is not lost."

He remained silent. Mira felt the tears well up and she was overwhelmed, her heart swollen with grief.

The *panditji* looked at her and said softly, "I was able to remove the thorns, but I cannot restore his sight. I'll make a balm with leaves to soothe the pain and help the wounds heal. But I cannot do anything more."

Mira had stopped crying. "But there must be a way."

"We cannot do anything."

"Another *panditji*, perhaps."

"Try to understand, Mira."

The girl pulled herself together. She remained motionless for a few moments and then walked at a brisk pace towards Zinat's house. She heard her aunt, who lamented, "My dear Mira, who did you look at on the night of the new moon? A dog is peeing on your destiny."

Mira did not cry or complain. What did they think, all the superstitious villagers? Was Madan's blindness not that of the whole village? That's exactly what Zinat said when she saw Mira alone. "Our village has lost its sight."

Zinat could not scold her countrymen. They had already dealt poorly with all sorts of tragedies. When Soukram's wife was raped, no one said anything. Deaf to Kissan's exhortations, no one had dared to start a strike. Finally, in broad daylight, a man had snatched the scythe of the disabled villager Sourek.

Today, the village had finally become blind.

The next day, five friends went to the police station in the next village. Danpatwa, with clasped hands, implored the inspector, "Sir, a friend of ours has been missing for several days. Yesterday, two of our men were beaten without pity. One of them lost his sight in the fight. Without your help, injustice will reign forever.'

The inspector listened attentively, then he laughed, "Make sure you search in the river. Your missing man drowned, surely. As for your blind man, for me, the case is clear.'

"You represent the law, sir. It is necessary that the guilty be punished, otherwise they will continue their wrongdoing."

"What guilt? There has been no crime."

"Is it not a crime to hit someone and make him lose his sight?"

"But I did not see anyone hit anyone."

"It's the truth, sir; we do not tell tales."

"Which of you five was present at the incident?"

"None of us. But another resident of the village was there and can testify."

"One of my officers was on hand at the time of the incident. And he told me exactly what happened."

"Oh, no. There was no policeman. There was only the property owner and his guards."

"And you? Were you there?"

"No."

"So how can you be so sure?' The inspector was screaming. Danpatwa drew back, frightened by the violence in his voice. The man noticed this and lowered his voice, "My colleague said that your two friends had gone to the boss demanding food. When he told them there was nothing, one of them jumped on him. He was trying to strangle him when two dogs rushed towards the abuser. Your friends got scared and fled. In fleeing, one of them fell into the cactus. He lost his sight, but it's nobody's fault."

'It's true that he had his eyes gouged out with cactus thorns. But it is wrong to suggest that he fell alone.'

"Are you insinuating that I lie?"

"No, sir, not at all."

"Then get out."

36

It was a winter morning. Martins flew by chirping in the early hours, stopping in a pool of sunlight, looking for a little heat. They folded their wings noisily, and then silence returned, a long silence that seemed to stretch out to the fields and beyond, caught by the cold.

In the heart of the dark corridor that now served as his decor, Madan was pulling weeds. He felt for the weeds with his fingers and stroked the small eggplants. He did well, putting new earth around all the plants on his plot. He found peace amongst the furrows, a reckoning.

On the other side of the millstone, Mira watched him, pausing in her own work. She still had a dozen transplants to finish in her plot, but she would continue only after his friends helped Madan find his way to the next groove.

When the villagers tried to dissuade him from working in his field, Madan smiled and said, "I do not want to live like a dead person. The field is one of the few places where I can forget that I am blind. If you take it away, I will have trouble convincing myself that I am still alive. Till the day I decide to stop working, no one here will be able to make me change my mind."

Dawood had the last word, "Let him take care of his field."

Madan experienced an intense pleasure in feeling the new seedlings in his fingertips, after three days of rain.

"I do not know why you're in such a hurry to get married," he told Mira. "But do not confuse love and pity. Give me some time; I must get used to the darkness. I want you to be my wife, I hold you dearest in all the world, not just as a crutch. I need a few days."

Zinat also made his case to Mira, "Madan says what he feels, you have to understand. He will never regain his sight, but he can ease the sense of loss. It takes time for that. And you must give him this time.'

Mira accepted it with tears in her eyes.

The sun had reached its zenith, but it was cold. Mira and Madan sat in the sun regardless. Mira opened her bundle and took out cassava *littis* and some stewed vegetables.

"What did you bring today?"

"The same thing as yesterday."

"The vegetables were delicious yesterday." Mira said nothing. She had prepared them without oil, this time. "I will drink some water first."

"You always fill your belly with water before eating."

"Water does not fill the belly, Mira. It is not food." He paused a moment, then said, "And that's our luck, after all. If man could drink fresh water, no doubt it would be gold."

Mira spread some chutney on the *litti* and put it in Madan's hand. He was again lost in thought. "Mira, I just cannot make myself a new life. And there is something else that continues to worry me. How long will this situation last?" They sat motionless, their food in hand. Mira did not want to speak first. He was still distant... "Without doubt, it is love that causes us the most pain, Mira. Pushpa once said that only love can counter adversity and support us until the end. I feel as close to you as I will when I walk seven times with you around the fire on our wedding day. You worry, but you're wrong. For what is marriage, exactly? Nothing more valuable than the love we each exercise. Marriage is a promise, and we will keep it in due course.'

At the end of his speech, the wind blew, and Madan could hear his father in his memory. "You see, Madan," said Kissan's voice, "since we arrived here, we have held no ceremonies. Your generation is no longer enslaved, you are not bound by any contract, you are born with no obligation. And yet you are in bondage still."

"What are you thinking, Madan?"

"I'm thinking that Holi is in a month."

"It comes back every year, and then leaves again without anyone paying attention."

"This time it will be different, Mira."

She was silent, for she understood what it meant to Madan.

The next day, a meeting was held at the *baithka*. Madan, thinking about his father, spoke, "It is said that Holi is the feast of joy and prosperity. It symbolises victory over evil. In a few days it will be Holi, and the committee has decided to celebrate it this year, no matter what."

"We do not have enough to eat. And where will we find the necessary coloured powder to celebrate properly?" objected a voice in the crowd.

"We will cope, despite the shortage," said Madan.

At a short distance, sitting under a tree, Mira listened to him. She trusted him and believed in his cause. He had reason to want to defend their identity and she supported him in this fight. The whole village, and even the neighbouring villages, were beginning to realise that by asserting their own identity, they could make their voices heard and fight for their rights. She had confidence in Madan's plans for Holi.

After the meeting, Mira heard Madan saying to Farid, "My friend, I wonder if losing my eyes does not help me see below the surface, sometimes."

Madan thought back to his own father more than ever; he heard his words echo in his own resolutions: "Our biggest mistake was to fight for small things. The struggle remained confined to our village, even though we know this fight should extend to the whole country. There are still institutions where the labourers are not allowed to leave. In the end, I failed. But that does not mean that we should not try again. Eliminating injustice everywhere on the island is the real goal of our fight."

Mira had joined him and he addressed her "Can you imagine? In this country, there could be no disease, no poverty. So why are we subjected to deprivation? There is a government and a police force, and yet no justice is done. Mira, I remember what my father said. One day, before everyone met at the *baithka*, he said, 'This is ours. We have cut the forests and turned them into green fields. But we have not eliminated the human jungle that crushes and devours men. If we carry on in this way, we will not right the errors of this country. We will become inarticulate skeletons of labourers'." Madan stopped and took Mira's hands in his own. "If you're by my side, I will carry on my father's crusade; I will win his unfinished fight."

"We tried, Madan."

"We did not try the right way. Give me another month."

"A month! But what for?"

"I want to go from village to village and encourage people to celebrate Holi. I want this festival to be an opportunity for us all to meet and come together."

"That's great, all of that, but..."

"Oh, I know what you're trying to say. But do not think I'm weak. I am blind, but anyway, I will not be alone. Farid and Devraj will come with me."

Mira did not answer. And she was silent also when the three friends left. Away from the crowds, who had followed them until the end of the village, she climbed the big rock and watched them disappear. From where she stood, she could see cane fields waving all the way to the horizon. A single tree, a victim of the storm, stood without a leaf. She could not even tell what kind of tree it was. It was the only one not to have found its leaves again after the rains. All the trees around it were green again, while it was as dead as a reproach.

Mira did not have tears in her eyes. The day before, she had feared being unable to attend Madan's departure without crying. But now she saw him disappear, reappear around the corner, and then disappear again, and her eyes remained dry. When she finally allowed herself to vent her emotion, not a tear came. She had cried so long in the past that her tears had dried up.

Before letting him go, she'd whispered to Madan, "I have only one regret and that is not being able to accompany you and offer you the support of my shoulder."

"I only need two shoulders," he replied, laughing. "It is our first try, but I have my whole life. And then I have my friends. Do you remember when I was lamenting about Vivek? You said that Farid was my most valuable friend. Today, it is he who supports me. I will rest my arm around his neck and my thoughts will rest on yours. See you on Holi.'

It was colder in the morning. As the afternoon wore on, despite the food shortage, preparations for the feast continued. Sugan Bhagat brought the young people together and prepared them for the Ramlila.

Everyone was surprised to see Holi come so fast, because preparations were not quite finished. As for Mira, she'd thought she'd never see that day arrive. The party had started; she could already hear the drums and flutes. Standing on the big rock, Mira looked out on the trail. Before her, cane fields waved in the wind, their purple flowers newly sprouted. Near the coastline, the dead tree stood, its branches more and more white.

Mira stared until her vision became fuzzy, all green and grey, dust and tiny fields. She stood, stretched, staring into the horizon and her heart was pounding in her chest.

She waited for hours to distinguish, at the end of the road, three silhouettes arriving at last.

Her heart made a leap and jumped off the rock.

□□□